Praise for the no...

"Toni Blake's romances are s...
and addictive, a good night's sleep isn't even an option....
No one does it like Toni Blake."
—*New York Times* bestselling author Robyn Carr

"The perfect small-town romance."
—Eloisa James, *New York Times* bestselling author of
Born To Be Wilde, on *One Reckless Summer*

"With sizzling sensuality and amazing depth, a book by
Toni Blake is truly special."
—Lori Foster, *New York Times* bestselling author of
Driven to Distraction

"Toni Blake's *One Reckless Summer* is one wild ride! This is
just the book you want in your beach bag."
—Susan Wiggs, *New York Times* bestselling author of
Between You and Me

"Sexy and emotional."
—Carly Phillips, *New York Times* bestselling author of
Dream, on *Letters to a Secret Lover*

"A wonderful story of friendship, love and a surprise that
will keep readers turning the pages of this well-written tale.
Blake is a master of small-town romances."
—*RT Book Reviews* on *Christmas in Destiny*

"*Whisper Falls* is the enemy of productivity. You start this
novel, and nothing will stop you until you finish."
—*USA TODAY*

"A sexy yet also sweet romance that beautifully celebrates
friendship, family, and the true spirit of the holiday season."
—*Booklist* on *Christmas in Destiny*

Also by Toni Blake

The Destiny Series

Coral Cove

The Rose Brothers

For a complete list of books by Toni Blake,
please visit www.toniblake.com.

TONI BLAKE

the one who stays

HQN™

HQN™

ISBN-13: 978-1-335-50498-2

Recycling programs for this product may not exist in your area.

The One Who Stays

Copyright © 2019 by Toni Herzog

To Blair,
for staying

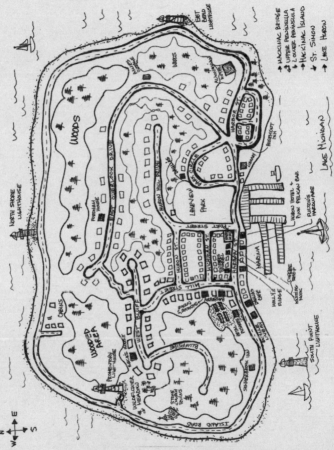

Part 1

"You people with hearts," he said once,
"have something to guide you, and need
never do wrong; but I have no heart, and
so I must be very careful."

—*L. Frank Baum,*
The Wonderful Wizard of Oz

CHAPTER ONE

HER GRANDMOTHER HAD always claimed the secret to living on Summer Island was owning a good sweater. "The kind that feels like an old friend when you put it on, warm and comfy. One that always feels a little like…coming home."

Meg Sloan had collected a few such sweaters over her fifteen years here and she wore one now—a thick cable-knit cardigan of cornflower blue. She wrapped it tight around her as she stood on the wide front porch of the Summerbrook Inn, looking out over Lake Michigan, watching as a fishing boat named the *Emily Ann* disappeared into the silvery morning fog like a ghost.

It was cold—but then, mornings here were almost always cold, the small island being situated off the northern tip of Michigan's mitten, near the spot where Lakes Michigan and Huron met. She told people she was used to the cold and didn't feel it anymore—but sometimes it snuck up on her, surprised her, and today the chill seeped right through the cable-knit and into her bones.

She watched the boat until no trace of it remained in sight, and even though it wasn't much farther away than it had been a moment before, the distance was palpable—and that seeped into her bones, as well. He was gone.

"It doesn't matter," she whispered to herself.

Of course, it did matter—when you have to talk yourself into something, obviously it matters. But she didn't *want* it to matter, and she knew that if you told yourself something enough times, it started to become true. "It doesn't matter."

It doesn't matter, even if you already thawed the steaks.

It doesn't matter, even if you need help with the shutters.

It doesn't matter, even if the bed feels colder now.

It always did on the first night Zack was gone, no matter how many blankets she added.

She took a deep breath, drawing the brisk morning air into her lungs, letting it wake her up a little more. A glance up Harbor Street revealed just how early it was— no one stirred, every business and home sitting quiet and still. A robin twittered somewhere behind the inn, reminding her spring had come and summer would soon follow. Life went on, with or without Zack, and as the island's name suggested, summer was *everything* here.

When a bit of movement drew her gaze to the flower shop up the street once run by her great-aunt Julia, she saw Suzanne Quinlan unlocking the front door. With her dark hair drawn up into a messy bun and wearing a thick sweater of her own, the current owner waved at Meg. "Someone's up and out early!" she called.

Regretting the reason for that, Meg forced a smile. *I could have stayed in bed,* should *have stayed there.* Watching him go didn't change anything—it was simply a compulsion, a silent goodbye. "I was thinking of making some pancakes," she called back impulsively. "You should come over—we'll have breakfast before you open."

Suzanne tilted her head, looking pleased by the suggestion. "Yum! Be down in five."

Meg was about to turn and head inside the inn—empty of patrons this early in the season—when she heard a familiar voice. "Is this pancake soiree a private party, or can anyone join?" She leaned forward past the wooden porch railing to see Dahlia Delaney pedaling her lavender bicycle up the street. The older woman owned a quaint lakeside café named after herself, which sat almost directly across the street from the flower shop—and she also happened to be Zack's aunt, the person who had introduced them five years ago.

Dahlia was a woman of her own, one who'd perfected the fine art of being both pragmatic and flamboyant at the same time, and Meg never minded spending time with her. "I think we can squeeze a third plate on the table," she informed Dahlia, this smile coming easier. A pleasant morning with friends would distract her from Zack's departure—at least for a little while. And as she walked in the door, her heart lifted at simply knowing her kitchen and sunroom would soon be filled with laughter.

The inn had been her home since the age of twenty-four. And it had been her beloved grandmother's home before that. It got quiet during the long winters. Quieter still it seemed when Zack took to the water, even though she knew it wasn't really any quieter than before he'd arrived in her life. She just noticed it more now, and maybe she was happy to postpone that quiet a bit longer.

But this is what you signed up for. She'd taken over the inn after her grandma's unexpected death in her early sixties, and at a dark moment in her own life when isolation had seemed…safe, and easier than other alternatives. And though it wasn't the life she'd planned, she'd never regretted the decision. Even if it meant a very particular, secluded sort of existence.

But soon the ferry would begin bringing tourists for the season and the streets would bustle with bike and foot traffic and the house would be filled with guests, old and new. The lilacs and honeysuckle would burst into fragrant bloom, their sweet scents competing with the aroma of fresh corn on the cob and hamburgers from the grill on the back patio.

Trevor Bateman would be back at the Pink Pelican playing his guitar for tips on the little stage above the bar and Cooper Cross would begin making his daily morning runs past the inn. Mr. Hankins would bring his fresh produce over from the mainland on Mondays, Wednesdays, and Fridays, selling it at the little wooden stand near the bicycle livery. Now-empty flower boxes would overflow with color, and Adirondack chairs would be filled with people escaping their busy city lives somewhere far away.

Summer brought life of so many kinds back to the island, and if *she* needed a little more life, summer would bring it back to her, as well.

Just past noon, Meg stood on a small ladder, attempting to unscrew a peeling white shutter from the front of the sunny yellow inn and trying not to be angry. She shouldn't have waited so late in the season to paint, but she couldn't put it off any longer. And in fairness to Zack, she'd only mentioned wanting to start the project once a few weeks ago, in passing, so he had no way of knowing she'd been counting on his help.

Nor had she told him about the steak. She'd bought

two New York strips at Koester's Market a week ago to surprise him with a special dinner to celebrate their five-year anniversary.

Anniversary of what?

They weren't in a committed relationship. They were…undefined. When his fishing boat was docked here, he lived in the apartment above Dahlia's—and he spent a lot of nights in Meg's bed.

Though everyone on the island thought of them as a couple. "Are Meg and Zack coming?"

"I saw Meg and Zack at the Pink Pelican."

"Meg and Zack put in a gorgeous new firepit on her patio."

And he'd been there for her when Aunt Julia had gotten sick. And sicker. And then died. He'd been her rock in those days. Maybe that was when they'd become Meg and Zack. So many times during Aunt Julia's illness just over two years ago, she'd wanted to crumble, but he hadn't let her.

"You'll get through this, Maggie May," he would say. He'd long called her that, at first teasingly, from the old Rod Stewart song, but then it had become habit. "You'll get through this because you don't have a choice. That's how these things work. But I'm here. And you don't have to be strong when it's just you and me, honey."

And he'd squeeze her hand and hold her tight and let her cry until his shirt was wet, and it had made all the difference not to have to go through it alone.

So it's almost ironic that here you are now, fretting about being alone.

He was there when it counted, after all.

Or…doesn't it *always* count? Being there?

Still, she tried to push down the rise of anger swelling in her chest.

She didn't begrudge him his work. He'd been a commercial fisherman long before he'd been half of Meg and Zack. Despite a serious decline in the Great Lakes fishing industry, he caught boatloads—literally—of lake whitefish, supplying restaurants and seafood distributors all along the lengthy Lake Huron coastline. She just hated when he left with so little warning.

This morning it had come before dawn—with a kiss on the cheek.

At first, she'd thought the kiss was about sex, that he'd woken up wanting it. But then she'd realized she lay in bed alone and opened her eyes to find his ruggedly handsome face above hers, his body bending over her, fully dressed. "I'm heading out, Maggie May," he'd said softly. As if not really wanting to wake her, as if slipping out quietly like a thief in the night would somehow make it better.

"Oh—I..." She hadn't needed to ask heading out where. Her heart had sunk.

When will you be back? How long will you be gone? She'd wanted to ask—always wanted to ask, because they were reasonable questions—but she knew better. There was a reason he'd become a fisherman. He liked being alone for long periods. It wasn't about her, it was about him. He'd assured her of that many times. And if she'd asked those questions on the tip of her tongue, he'd simply have told her he didn't know.

But this time hurt worse than usual. Because of tonight. Their anniversary. Of...something. Meeting. Their anniversary of meeting. And it had been...a *memorable* meeting. Filled with a palpable chemistry.

Which had lasted. Grown. It was powerful still—had never faded.

Perhaps because absence made the heart grow fonder, because reunions kept things feeling somehow new and fresh? Or was it because she loved him? And she did. She loved him like crazy. And she'd wanted this evening to be something special. Even if they were... undefined. So she'd heard herself saying, "But what about tonight?"

He'd blinked. Let his brow wrinkle, just a little. "What's tonight?"

And something inside her heart died a little. He was a guy—guys didn't remember dates, so she shouldn't be hurt. "Nothing. Never mind."

He'd hesitated. Tilted his head slightly. The first hints of daylight had shone in the window behind him just then, making him look a little ethereal. "You sure?"

She'd swallowed back anything else she might have wanted to say and left it at, "Yeah."

"Bye, honey," he'd said, and then he'd lifted one warm, rough palm to her cheek and lowered a long, slow kiss to her acceptant mouth. Always acceptant, always hungry for a little bit more, even in darker moments like that one. *Maybe with a man you know will always eventually leave again, you feel the lack even before it comes.* And then he'd walked out the bedroom door.

She'd gotten up behind him, tossed on jeans, a tank, and a cotton blouse, covering it with her blue sweater, and wandered out onto the porch a few minutes later—in time to watch the water carry him away. She still didn't know why she'd bothered. Maybe seeing the *Emily Ann* drift into a distance that grew greater each second made it more real, made it so that she wouldn't accidentally expect him to be here later.

Even so, she still felt that kiss on her lips—and knew she would miss it tonight when there were none.

She let out a frustrated breath, still struggling with the shutter—then fought down the sudden urge to violently stab her screwdriver into the window frame. *Because he left, damn it. Again. And this time* did *hurt worse. He's thoughtless. Selfish. And somehow managed to arrange things so that, technically, I can't even be mad at him.*

But she was anyway. She was mad as hell. Despite the cool temperatures, the work had her sweating.

You took care of this place long before you had Zack's help, though—you're a capable woman and can take down some shutters on your own.

This morning's breakfast in the sunroom had indeed had the desired effect of brightening her spirits—at least for a while. "So what has you up and at the griddle so early today, my dear?" Dahlia had asked as she'd forked a bite of pancakes into her mouth. Her lips had been painted a shade of pink few women in their sixties could pull off, but she managed it fine.

Meg had hated to answer—but it was useless not to. Though she'd tried to smile as she'd said it. "I was watching the *Emily Ann*…go." She'd pointed vaguely east.

Suzanne had let out an audible sigh as Dahlia admitted, "Thought it might have something to do with my nephew leaving."

Bristling inside, Meg had attempted not to sound resentful as she asked, "Then you knew? That he was going?"

"Told me yesterday."

Another stab at a tight smile. "Well, he didn't tell me until about thirty seconds before he walked out the door."

"Oh…" Dahlia said.

"More like—oh my God," Suzanne added, rolling her eyes, and despite herself, Meg appreciated someone just putting it on the table and acknowledging that it was a crummy thing to do.

"I just…have to wonder sometimes how much he really cares," Meg confided in them. Both were good enough friends that she could do that.

But Dahlia was quick to reply as she always did when the topic came up. "He loves you, honey. I know he isn't always the steadiest sort, but trust me, he's steadier with you than he's ever been with anyone in his life."

This time, though, Meg lifted her gaze and met the older woman's. "Are you saying this is as good as it gets with him?"

Dahlia peered back at her through tiny silver spectacles. "I'm saying he's a work in progress, so give him more time to be the man you want him to be."

Meg took that in. She knew Zack had grown up in a troubled environment and left home young. She knew he had commitment issues. She knew that Dahlia was putting it lightly—he was more than a work in progress; he was…broken in ways Meg had never quite gotten to the bottom of, because he wouldn't talk to her about it. She'd accepted all that because she loved him and did believe he could grow and change.

And he always came back. He always left again, too, but…he always came back. Always. That was the flip side to a man who was always leaving—when he came back, you knew it was because he wanted to be there.

But Suzanne was rolling her eyes again. "No offense to Zack, Dahlia, but sometimes waiting is overrated. If I wanted a man around all the time—and I don't, mind you, which is why I came here—but if I did, I'd…want him around. Not just coming and going without warning."

"His job is on the water," Dahlia pointed out.

"And I knew that from the start," Meg had added—even as she wondered why she was defending him. *Maybe because it defends me, too. Defends my staying in this situation.*

Yet Suzanne had shrugged. One of the things Meg loved about her friend was that she never pulled any punches. "I just want Meg to be happy, and I'm not sure Zack is making her that way. I mean, he's a great guy in a lot of respects—but…"

She hadn't finished. And so Meg had concluded, "He is who he is. And it's…fine. And I invited you two over to get my mind off the big lug, and yet here we are talking about him, so let's chat about something else, okay?"

And so they had. They'd speculated on the coming tourist season. They'd agreed that one afternoon soon they'd take the ferry to the mainland and see a movie at the old theater in St. Simon. Suzanne had updated them on her current project of refurbishing several of the little greenhouses on the hill behind the shop that had always allowed Aunt Julia to grow her own flowers despite the long winters here. And Meg had never once mentioned that there were two steaks in the fridge, and that today was an anniversary no one would celebrate, ever.

After a lot more concentration, perspiration, and the fresh fury she'd apparently tired of pushing down, she finally succeeded in getting some of the screws out of the first shutter. Oh, how she regretted not keeping the electric screwdriver in the toolshed charged. How she regretted not having done this when Zack was still here. And she refused to think about the fact that there were over thirty more shutters on the inn.

Drawing the ladder away from the house since the last screw could be reached from the ground, she wiped the sweat from her brow with the back of her hand, then struggled out of her shirt to the plain tank underneath. A little sun plus some exertion had her drenched and exhausted already.

But also determined. Maybe the anger was good for *that* part.

Because sure, there were people around town she could ask for help and they'd gladly give it. Only right now she needed to prove something to herself. Simply that she could do this. That she was no less strong or capable than she'd been before Zack had entered her life. That she didn't need to depend on anyone. She'd gotten in the habit of counting on him, a mistake she intended to rectify. There'd been a very long time, after all, when she'd counted on no one but herself—and she'd done just fine that way. *I don't need you, Zack. I don't need you, I don't need you, I don't need you.*

Drying her palms on the thighs of her blue jeans, she took another look at the task before her and approached it, screwdriver in hand.

As the last screw in the shutter loosened, though, she

realized just how large her shutters were, and that she didn't exactly have a grand plan to keep this one from slamming to the ground when the last screw was removed. So she began trying to support its weight with one hand while still awkwardly freeing the last screw with the other.

But it was heavy, and trying to keep control of it challenged her—she was only just now realizing that each shutter was as tall as her, and awkward to manage. The truth was, when the shutters had been painted in the past, it had been more of a family project, with her father taking them down—and he'd made it look much easier than this, so she'd just assumed she could do it.

Damn you, Zack Sheppard. This wasn't his fault—and yet somehow it was. Misplaced anger—maybe. But anger just the same, making her want to drop the stupid thing, send it crashing onto the lawn, kick it, stomp on it, rip it to pieces with her bare hands.

Only she was far too practical of a woman for that—like it or not, she couldn't afford a damaged shutter. Not only financially, but she didn't think her ego could handle it today, either. She felt stuck in place, her body lodged against the massive old shutter, wondering how much longer she could hold it up, but fearing the result if she let go.

She let out a growl of frustration.

And that was when a smooth, deep voice came from directly in back of her, saying, "Whoa now—looks like you need a little help with that, darlin'," just as the warmth of an unfamiliar male body pressed into her from behind.

CHAPTER TWO

MEG TENSED FROM head to toe, sucking in her breath as she saw two masculine hands close over the shutters' edges on either side of her body. Then instinctively turned her head to take in light hair, a strong, stubbled jaw, and blue eyes—no more than an inch from hers.

"I... I..." He smelled good. Not sweaty at all the way she surely did. The firm muscles in his arms bracketed her shoulders.

"I think I got it if you just wanna kinda duck down under my arm." Despite the awkward situation and the weight of the shutter, the suggestion came out sounding entirely good-natured.

And okay, yes, separating their bodies was an excellent idea. Because she wasn't accustomed to being pressed up against any other guy besides Zack, for any reason, not even practical ones. And a stranger to boot. Who on earth *was* this guy and how had he just magically materialized in her yard?

The ducking-under-his-arm part kept her feeling just as awkward as the rest of the contact until it was accomplished. And when she finally freed herself, her rescuer calmly, competently lowered the loose shutter to the ground, leaning it against the house with an easy, "There we go."

He wore a snug black T-shirt that showed his well-muscled torso—though she already knew about that part from having felt it against her back. Just below the sleeve she caught sight of a tattoo—some sort of swirling design inked on his left biceps. His sandy hair could have used a trim, and something about him gave off an air of modern-day James Dean.

"Um... I..." Wow. He'd really taken her aback. Normally she could converse with people she didn't know—she did it all summer every year at the inn. But then, this had been no customary meeting. Even now that she stood a few feet away, she still felt the heat of his body cocooning her as it had a moment ago.

That was when he shifted his gaze from the shutter to her face, flashing a disarming grin.

That was when she took in the crystalline quality of his eyes, shining on her like a couple of blue marbles, or maybe it was more the perfect, clear blue of faraway seas.

That was when she realized...he was younger than her, notably so. But hotter than the day was long. And so she gave up trying to speak entirely, and settled on just letting a quiet sigh echo out, hoping her unbidden reactions to him didn't show.

"Sorry to sneak up on ya like that," he told her. "But I was passing by and when I saw a pretty lady in distress, I couldn't very well keep going, could I?" Again with the grin, and this time he added a wink.

She knew instantly that his brand of charm worked well on women—it was working on *her*, even when she saw through it for what it was.

"Well, thank you—you definitely came along at the right time." She then glanced toward the troublesome shutter because it suddenly felt easier than holding eye contact with him. He had a way of looking at her so intently that it was a little unnerving. Though she suspected most women *liked* that—because it gave the impression she was the foremost center of his attention. Something that might have appealed more if she hadn't been such a hot, sweaty mess. "I, um, apparently bit off a little more than I could chew here. I didn't realize the shutters would be so heavy."

"No one to help you with this?" he asked, motioning vaguely toward the inn.

"Not…at the moment, no." But rather than get any deeper into that, she decided to ask the obvious question. "I hope it won't sound too nosy if I ask where you were passing by *to*. We don't get many strangers around here until summer—so if you're a tourist, you're early." She ended with a smile, to sound *less* nosy, but on an island so small that it could only be reached by ferry, strangers were downright rare before late May or June.

He tilted his handsome head back, letting out a small, deep laugh before he said, "No, not a tourist—more on the flip side of that, in fact. I'm a handyman by trade, and hoping to find work here for the spring, helping businesses get their places fixed up for the season—and maybe stay the summer, too, if the work holds out."

Ah, a handyman. He wasn't the first fix-it guy to come to Summer Island in spring looking for employment—he was only the youngest, most handsome one she'd ever seen. He didn't fit the usual mold.

"Where are you staying?"

"Rented a little cabin from a fella named Walt Gardner."

She tipped back her head in recognition. She knew Walt and she knew his three cabins—aging bare bones structures a twenty-minute walk from here that could be rented cheap due to the poor shape they were in and the proximity to town. On an island without motor vehicles, distance was measured a little differently than in most places.

"Seth Darden," he said, holding out his hand.

She wiped the sweat off her own once more before taking it, feeling the warmth of him again, even if only through his palm this time, and actually, that was potent enough. "Megan Sloan. But my friends call me Meg."

He lowered his chin, his eyebrows raising in speculation. "Do I make the cut, Megan Sloan?"

She'd set herself up for that, so said, "Sure."

"Well, it's nice to meet you, Meg. And now—" He glanced to the house again, this time more toward the second story, from where she officially had no idea how she'd possibly remove the shutters. "Would it be too bold of me to offer my services on the task at hand?"

Meg drew in her breath. In one sense, the question came as no surprise. But it also meant that this strange, awkward, and somehow heated little encounter—heated for her at least—might be more than a five-minute thing.

"No pressure, darlin'," he said with another sexy wink, "but I could use the work and you could surely use the help."

She couldn't argue the point. And while she could indeed ask around the island for assistance, she didn't particularly want to bother her friends and neighbors. Nor was she inclined to have to tell everyone that Zack was gone again—even if no one would judge the situation as harshly as she did—and she wanted to get this project done in the coming few days. "How much would you charge to remove the shutters and put them back up if I handle the sanding and painting?" It was the one aspect of this she still felt equipped to accomplish.

And true, she hadn't planned to pay for any help this spring as she did in some years—but when he answered with a reasonable price and she weighed it, it sounded better than having tacky-looking shutters all summer, something that simply wasn't done on Summer Island.

Just before his arrival, she'd been determined to do this on her own—but maybe it was time to accept a little help.

SHUTTERS LAY IN a neat row on the long canvas drop cloths she'd unrolled in the front yard, each being buffed with the electric sander, then getting two coats of the same white paint they'd had before. Every now and then, she looked up from her task to glance over at him, watch him working. Seth Darden. Now he stood on a tall ladder, detaching the shutters from second floor windows, one by one. Even that he made look easy and she couldn't help being impressed. He handled the big shutters like they were feathers.

She'd finished sanding the last shutter in line and had just opened a fresh can of white paint when her cell phone buzzed.

Her first thought—Zack. But no—she didn't hear from him much when he was working, and never this soon. Thinking it was him was only a habit—and an annoying one at that. *A man who you're always trying to get out of your head when he's not around—is that a good thing or a bad one, a help or a hindrance in the big picture of life?*

Setting the brush down on the can's lid, she made

sure her hands didn't have any paint on them, then reached for the phone in her back pocket.

It was a text from Suzanne: Who's on your ladder?

Damn. She'd been hoping no one would notice she had a visitor. In the summer, no one would even bother asking—they'd all be too busy with their own businesses and lives. But in the spring, anything out of the ordinary on the island became a question worth investigating.

She texted back. A handyman I hired to help with the shutters.

Where did he come from?

I don't know.

Do you know him? Is it safe to have him working on the inn?

Meg sighed, peering at the phone. Suzanne was still a relative newcomer to Summer Island and she still often thought in mainland ways. The island was virtually crime-free because it was hard to hide here and even harder to make a quick getaway. No, but yes. And she left it at that.

Which didn't fly with Suzanne. So you just hired some stranger? You islanders are too trusting.

You're an islander now, too. Get with the program and quit being so suspicious.

It's a dangerous world, Meg.

What's he going to do, steal my shutters and make a run for it?

Just be careful.

Cross my heart.

He looks cute from my window. Is he? Or have I just been on this island too long?

At this, Meg glanced again from the phone to the

man on the ladder. Took in the muscles in his arms. Sweat had his black T-shirt sticking to him a little more than when he'd started. When *she* sweated, it was gross, but when he did, she didn't mind it so much. He didn't see her watching and appeared very serious as he worked the large screwdriver she'd handed over to him—much more serious than she'd seen him look so far—and she found herself wondering what thoughts floated around his head.

He's cute, she typed. And young.

Hmm. Young can be good. As in fun.

Meg wasn't sure if Suzanne meant fun for Meg or fun for Suzanne, but knowing her friend, the former. And she almost replied by reminding Suzanne that she was taken—but then she remembered that she, in fact, wasn't. And that the one time she'd ever said anything in front of Zack to that effect, he'd quietly corrected her in a good-natured way. "We are what we are, Maggie May, and it's good that way," he'd said on a deep laugh. "Don't complicate it."

So instead she typed: Nice enough change of scenery, I suppose. But mostly I'm looking at the shutters I'm painting. Back to work. And don't you have some flowers to tend to or something?

The view out my window is a little more interesting right now, but you're right—a fresh shipment of azaleas are calling my name.

As she picked the paintbrush back up and resumed working, she did the math in her head—the guy on the ladder was an unplanned expense, but cheaper by far than a bunch of broken shutters if she'd started dropping them. And having his help would make this project go much more efficiently even if she *could have* done it all on her own. In a couple of days, all the freshly painted shutters would be rehung and she'd feel ready for her summer customers.

Keeping the place up wasn't only about business, though—she did it for her grandma, too, who she suspected was peering down at her from some cloud or other floating across the sky today, smiling. She'd loved this house in a way Meg had seldom seen anyone love anything. That had been at least part of why she'd chosen to stay here, run the inn, keep it the way Gran had. The other reasons had been more complex.

"Got another paintbrush?"

She looked up to see Seth Darden casting the same alluring grin as before. Not so serious now. Turning on the charm again.

She smiled in reply, but reminded him, "I said I'd do the painting, remember? I can't really afford to pay you more than we already agreed to."

He tilted his handsome sandy-haired head and said, "I'm more charging you for the time I figure the work will take than the particular kinda work, and you're sorta backed up here." Then added a wink that moved through her in an unexpected way.

Young can be good. As in fun.

Or…maybe it could be a reminder of roads not taken. *Refocus.*

She did, and realized he'd detached the shutters way faster than she could sand and paint them.

"Don't much care what work I'm doing," he told her. "It's all the same to me as long as I'm making some cash. So I can stand around and literally watch paint dry, or I can help you out to get more of it drying. And besides, I figure if I do right by ya that maybe you'll be good enough to recommend me to your neighbors when I'm done." He ended with another grin, another wink. They fell from him like promises from a salesman.

Even so, though, Meg's own smile relaxed—it had been manufactured up to now, a thing she'd put in place to be cordial—but for a stranger, salesman or not, he somehow made her feel at ease.

Well, when his body wasn't plastered to hers anyway. The memory brought a fresh heat to her cheeks—thank God the day was bright and hopefully made the blush seem like a result of the sun.

And blushing aside, she couldn't argue with what he was offering. She'd always found that dealing with charmers was fine as long as you remembered you were being charmed and didn't agree to anything you wouldn't have otherwise. So she stood up, offered her brush to him, and said, "I'll go find another."

She rummaged in the toolshed, selecting one from the drawer where she kept them stored. She stayed a minute longer than necessary, though, trying to clear her head. He was cute—more than cute, *hot*—and he knew it. And it was fine to be friendly, but she still hoped he wouldn't pick up on her unwitting responses to him. She wasn't some lonely older woman in need of male attention and she didn't want to risk coming off that way.

Though as she approached him through the yard while gazing out over the vast waters in the distance, the red-and-white-striped lighthouse off the south shore in view, she was glad he'd come along. Not only for practical purposes—but for personal ones he didn't know about. Doing all this alone would have kept her fretting and fuming over Zack's morning's departure. As it was, working alongside Seth Darden was keeping her on her toes a bit, distracting her, making her day a little more interesting—just like the view from Suzanne's window.

"Always been yellow?" he looked up to ask.

The question caught her off guard. "What?"

"The house. Has it always been yellow?"

"Yes." But then she remembered. "Well, no. When my grandmother was growing up here, it was blue with black shutters. I have a few pictures of it from back then. But when she turned it into an inn after my grandfather died, she painted it yellow with white trim, just like it is now. It's like the sun, she always said. The color of a perfect summer day."

Seth paused his paintbrush, tilted his head. "That's nice," he said. "A nice idea."

Meg smiled. "She used to say the color kept her warm in winter, and always reminded her that summer would come back eventually."

"Gets awful chilly up here, huh?"

"You could say that."

"Surprised me at first," he said. "How cold it is, even now, at the start of May."

"It always used to surprise me, too," she confessed. "Year after year. We usually came in summer, my family, and it was beautiful most of the time. But whenever we visited in any other season, I always forgot how cold it would be until we got here."

"You stay here all year round?" he asked, squinting slightly at her under the afternoon sun. Just like on neighboring Mackinac Island, many residents didn't winter here, which he must have already discovered.

"Yes. My great-grandparents lived here all year round when they built the place, and my grandparents after them. And my grandmother never even thought of leaving for winter, even after my grandpa passed. So I guess sticking out the winters here is…kind of a family tradition." She ended on a shrug and a smile.

In fact her younger sister, Lila, in Chicago, and her parents in Ann Arbor as well, always offered her a place to stay. "Why go home right after the holidays?" her mother asked every single year. "Stay for January. Or longer." But something about it had felt wrong. To leave the inn for that long. Her grandmother never would have, so she didn't, either.

It surprised her, though, to hear her handyman say, "That must be nice."

She shot him a glance, eyebrows rising. "To stick out the winters here? Most people think it's a little crazy."

He only laughed in that easy way she'd noticed about him. "No, I meant just to…have a history like that someplace. Strong ties to where you live."

Maybe she took that for granted. It struck her that most people who had that probably did. And it begged the question. "Where are *you* from?"

The inquiry—one which, as an innkeeper, she asked people commonly—drew from him another of those captivating grins. "Here, there, and everywhere," he told her. "Pennsylvania as a little kid, but raised mostly down south—Mississippi and some other places. And since then, I just see where the road takes me on any given day."

Hmm. So he was a true drifter. The kind you saw in old movies.

Only this was now. And someone with no ties like that, no real home…surely it came with a story. And maybe—probably—not a happy one.

If Suzanne were here, they'd probably be exchanging glances right now, because perhaps a guy who made the road his home was, in fact, someone to steer clear of.

And yet…it seemed a little too late for that, didn't it?

But he's only doing a job for you. He doesn't need to be a saint for that. So it's fine.

As the day wore on, the sun grew hotter and they made more conversation. She checked the thermometer mounted near the front door to see it was over seventy— and explained that the day had grown extraordinarily warm for May. He said it was nothing compared to a Mississippi spring, reminding her he was used to far more heat than he'd find on Summer Island any day of the year.

The shutters on the ground got painted, two coats, front and back.

When he resumed removing more from the house, she sheepishly confessed that she had an electric screwdriver but just hadn't thought to charge it and would do so overnight. He smiled and told her he had one of his own he'd be happy to bring tomorrow with the rest of his tools to make getting the shutters back up a little easier than getting them down had been. It made her realize that he'd never once complained about it all day, not with all the hundreds of turns of that screwdriver he'd had to make.

She learned he'd only arrived yesterday and that other than picking up a few groceries at Koester's on the way to his cabin, today was his first real visit to town. "Farther than I thought from looking at the map before I came," he told her. Then grinned and said, "Good thing I like to walk."

"Most people here ride bicycles. There's a rental," she added, pointing up the street.

And when he just nodded and left it at that, she decided maybe he didn't look much like a bike rider. Unless it was a Harley-Davidson.

When she recommended a few places to eat, like Dahlia's, he said, "Thanks, but mostly I'm just living off sandwiches, saving money. Until I make some anyway." He punctuated it with a quick wink.

By the end of the day, all the shutters were down, most were sanded, and half were painted. Every time she glanced at the inn, she thought it looked strange, naked, without them, and was glad when Seth said he thought they could have them all back in place by the end of the day tomorrow. "As long as we get an early start."

"Sounds good to me," she told him, still a little caught up in how odd the house looked this way, like part of its identity had been stripped away. She always forgot that. This was the third time she'd taken down the shutters to repaint them since owning the place, but only when they actually came off did she remember how strangely dismantled and barren it made the inn appear.

"What's wrong?" he asked her.

She tossed him a glance along with a small, tentative smile. "This may sound crazy but…"

"I've probably heard crazier, so go ahead."

That was how he did it, how he made her feel at ease. So she said, "Well…my grandma always said that every house has a soul. And I guess I was just thinking that *this* house is feeling kind of embarrassed right now—like it wants its shutters back."

He let out a lighthearted laugh, then stood back and

looked himself. "I think you might just be right. But it'll be okay for one night. Good for it to get out of its comfort zone a little, don't ya think?" The almost suggestive raise of his eyebrows landed right in her solar plexus.

Yet she shook it off with a laugh and a smile, same as she had with everything about him so far. Players gonna play; charmers gonna charm.

Though as they set a time for him to come back in the morning and he turned to head down the front walk, he still had her thinking about comfort zones. He tossed an easy glance over his shoulder to say, "Thanks for the work, darlin', and the hospitality, too." Then flashed what she already thought of as a typical Seth grin.

"You came along at just the right time," she assured him, "so it turned out well for both of us."

Then, as he walked away, she shifted her thoughts to what came next. She was tired and her muscles ached—a hot shower and a book sounded good. Though she still had two steaks in her fridge to deal with. She supposed before the shower she'd take the time to grill them both—eat one, save one. Though the very notion made her scrunch up her nose. *What fun.* The first night alone was always the hardest.

Unless…she found a way to make it *less* hard.

Maybe the same way the day had been less hard?

She never usually minded eating alone, but…tonight she didn't want to.

"Seth," she called once he'd reached the street. She hadn't thought it through, at all, but he'd round the bend soon and then it would be too late.

He stopped, looked back.

And she said, "I have an extra steak and some wine. If you want to stay for dinner."

CHAPTER THREE

AN HOUR LATER they sat across from each other at the small tiled café table for two that she had already pulled up next to the firepit, planning for the anniversary dinner with Zack. Eating the same steaks, drinking the same red wine, sitting next to the same small blaze, everything the same as it would have been—except being with a different man, a stranger, left Meg feeling a little off-kilter. Part of her couldn't believe she'd invited Seth to stay. But on the other hand, she couldn't come up with one single reason why it was a bad idea. At least Zack's steak wasn't going to waste.

Of course, she hadn't gotten to shower, but she had run upstairs and changed her sweat-soaked tank for a fresh, clean tunic, which she'd topped with a pastel cardigan sweater. Though not the big, thick kind that Gran swore made living here easier—a thinner, prettier one in yellow that she sometimes wore over a sundress on cool summer evenings out with Zack or Suzanne.

Dusk fell over Summer Island dramatically on this particular night, bringing a sky slashed with streaks of purple and pink. Seth had offered to do the grilling, claiming with yet another grin that he possessed mad skills in that department, so she'd merrily handed him the supersize grill spatula and tongs with a challenge: "Prove it."

Now they sat over plates brimming with seasoned steaks, baked potatoes wrapped in tinfoil, and early corn on the cob that had been grilled in the shucks, and all she'd had to do to contribute was uncork and pour the wine.

"Warm," he'd said after his first sip.

"Red isn't supposed to be served chilled," she told him. "Though some people do anyway."

Across from her, Seth Darden playfully raised sandy eyebrows. "Didn't know Summer Island would be so fancy, educating me on serving wine exactly the right way." He laughed. "And I didn't know *any* wine was supposed to be served warm." Then he took another sip. "But I guess it's okay this way."

She pointed toward the house. "There's beer in the fridge if you'd rather. Chilled," she added teasingly. Zack's. But if he wasn't here, it didn't really matter who drank it.

Seth declined, though, with a shake of his head. "Nah, I'm good, darlin'. Funny thing I've always found about pretty much any alcohol—the more you drink of it, the better it tastes." Ah, that grin again. "And if it doesn't, you know you've got hold of something really bad."

She laughed because she'd actually found the same thing to be true, though she'd never admitted it to anyone before.

And then the conversation fell away, leaving silence other than the chirps of birds in tall trees and the crackle of a fire she'd built while he'd manned the grill. He smiled at her and she smiled at him—but she suddenly felt bashful about that and let her gaze drop. After which she raised it cautiously back—to find him still looking. And she realized this was…flirting.

Which wasn't at all her intention.

Was it?

"So tell me, Seth Darden," she asked—maybe simply to move on from the moment and not have to think about it too hard, "what brings you to Summer Island?"

He used a table knife to run a small slab of butter over his corn until it melted. "I told you earlier—work. And it seemed like a nice place to spend a little time."

But she shook her head. "No, I mean—why here? There are a million summer tourist haunts where a handyman could be handy this time of year—Mackinac is bigger and busier and right on the other side of the pass. What made you choose *this* place?"

He didn't rush to answer—seemed totally comfortable taking his time. He even cut off a bite of steak and ate it while she waited.

"Suppose I liked the idea of so much solitude," he finally replied. "Aren't many places you can't get to by car."

"You have to ferry to Mackinac, too," she pointed out—then feared it sounded like she was interrogating him.

Yet he seemed unfazed. "I actually almost went there instead—but I heard Summer Island was quieter and more laid-back in comparison. Maybe I thought it seemed like…a simple place to be."

Meg had, in fact, always thought of the island as Mackinac's smaller, less popular sidekick in the Great Lakes. She nodded knowingly and said, "If that's what you came looking for, you're in the right place." But she'd noticed the way he'd said *maybe*, and she'd thought it sounded…vague, like he was making it up as he went. "No other reason, though?"

He stopped eating, took a sip of the Merlot she'd poured for him, met her gaze, and leaned back in his chair. When he began to speak, she almost got the feeling he was about to tell her a secret. "Truth is… I think it's possible I came here once, as a little kid. Can't remember it much, but figured if I was right, it'd be nice to go back. And besides—" he shrugged easily "—everybody's gotta be somewhere. I just happen to be *here*. No real reason, I'm afraid."

She took that in, turned it over in her head. She wished there *were* a reason—but she wasn't sure why. Maybe she wanted him to have some direction, more purpose behind his drifting than just…drifting. Because she liked him. And didn't want to find reasons not to.

"And what brought *you* here, Meg Sloan?" he asked, back to eating again.

She took a sip of wine and laughed. "I thought we already covered that, more or less. The place was my grandmother's."

He pointed at her with his fork and said, "*More or less* being the key words in that answer. How'd the place become yours? Where were you before you were here?"

Meg thought back to a girlhood that felt like a lifetime ago. "I grew up in Ann Arbor. Got a degree in marketing from Michigan. Wasn't sure what I planned to do with it—but that's how it is with marketing degrees for a lot of people. It's like taking business classes in high school—you just figure it'll cover a lot of bases and get you a good job somewhere. Even without being sure what I wanted to do, though, I was…ready to take on the world back then." She remembered that precise moment in time—fear and excitement mingling. A whole future ahead of her and a million different directions it could go in.

"And did you take it on?" he asked, brows lifting slightly. He appeared sincerely interested—making her sorry her reply would be a letdown.

"Yes and no," she said softly, with only the slightest hint of self-deprecation. Mostly, she'd let that go. And she'd let go of the girl who'd been so ready to be brave and adventurous. Other things had gotten in the way, taking the brave and adventurous right out of her. "Afraid it's a long and fairly tragic story."

Across the table, Seth tilted his head—and looked a little sad. Because she was letting too much leak out here. Damn wine. "Will you tell me?" He asked it softly, as if hoping he wasn't stepping on her toes.

"You might be sorry you asked," she warned.

"I'm tough—I can take it," he assured her, his expression somehow both playful and supportive at once, encouraging her to go on.

She took a deep breath, thought about where to begin. She actually seldom had to tell the whole story—most people here knew at least parts of it, and it was such old news. A thing that was with her always, dwelling quietly, and yet she didn't often have occasion to think through the details. They might be hard to say. But something in his eyes made that okay.

"Well, at first I had it all. I got a great job with an ad firm in Chicago. And within a year I was engaged to an up-and-coming executive and we moved in together." Drew had been the man of her dreams, everything she could want in a guy, their courtship the stuff of fairy tales. And just mentioning him had, that easily, brought back certain pangs—painful memories of how good things had been between them. Blips of recollections flitted through her brain like images in an old-fashioned slide show—picnicking at Grant Park, Cubs games at Wrigley because he was a big fan and had turned her into one, too, hanging curtains together when they'd rented their apartment. Life had stretched before them so grandly, with plans for buying a condo after the wedding, and eventually a house in the suburbs when it was time to have kids.

"I'll admit I'm intrigued to hear how you went from there to here. Seems like two different worlds."

A sardonic laugh escaped her. "You can say that again." Then she cut to the chase. "I thought I had life all figured out, but then I was diagnosed with leukemia."

Funny thing about that word. It had a way of draining all the energy from a room, or a conversation, or a moment—like this one. Her own heart felt heavier in her chest for dropping it on him that way, like a bomb. But he'd asked.

He stayed quiet for a moment, just looking at her, and his voice came gentler than she'd heard it so far. "I'm real sorry to hear that, Meg." Then he went on, a little more quickly. "But…you must have beat it, right? Because here you are. Taking down shutters—even if you did it pretty badly." A slight grin. "And running an inn and drinking wine with me, and everything normal. Right?"

"Right." She could tell he wanted to be assured—people usually did and she understood that. "I'm fine now. But…it took a while. And things got worse before they got better."

He nodded, and she saw him steeling himself—just a slight thing, almost imperceptible, but she'd witnessed it before when telling the story. Usually to someone she knew better than Seth Darden. But maybe, in a way, telling it to a stranger was a little easier somehow, and again, he *put* her at ease. Or the wine did. Whatever.

So much at ease, in fact, that she decided not to skip over the hardest part. Well, it had *all* been hard—but the rotten cherry on top had made it so much worse. It was really an easy enough part of the story to leave out, or gloss over, yet she heard herself saying it anyway. "The night before my first chemo treatment, my fiancé deserted me."

Across the table, her dinner companion's jaw dropped. But he kept his eyes on her—and she tried to maintain the gaze, too, but couldn't. It fell to her plate as she kept talking. "I came home to a note on the bedside table telling me he was sorry but he just couldn't handle it. He'd packed his bags, moved out, and pretty much disappeared from my life all in a single afternoon when I was having a last outing with girlfriends before my treatment started."

She stopped then, swallowed as her throat thickened—damn, she still felt it. After all these years, she still felt the abandonment.

"That's… God, that's awful." Seth was shaking his head. "What a bastard."

She nodded. Drew's bastardism had long been confirmed. "The plan had been for him to take me to chemo—you know, be there for me, help me through it. So to just make things all the more crummy, I had to call my mom and tell her what happened, and she had to pretty much drop her whole life to come be with me.

And she didn't mind doing it—she'd offered already—but the lack of warning, plus dealing with a heartbroken daughter with cancer…" Meg stopped, shook her head. It was all…heavy. Just talking about it, remembering it, was heavy.

Well, that was *enough* heavy. She took a deep breath, let it back out. Tried to wear a pleasant expression as she went on. "The upshot is that I got through it. It took months of chemo and radiation, and it was rough, but I got through it and got better, and it's never come back."

Now he was smiling again, reassured again. And she was reminded of how immeasurably grateful she was for that, for having it be only a distant part of her past, a bad thing she went through, but that life had gone on and cancer hadn't defined her.

"I still don't know, though, darlin'…"

She finished for him. "How I ended up here."

"Right."

"There can be a pretty long recovery period after chemo and radiation, so my grandma suggested I come stay with her for some R and R."

"Can't think of a more peaceful place for that."

"It was perfect for that time in my life," she agreed. "An easy place to let my body heal and my hair grow. I'd had to give up my job, and so I gave up the apartment, too, and just saw it as a time to recover and then start over. And as I regained strength, I started helping around the inn—it was a good sort of therapy for…getting back to the business of living. I could tell my grandmother enjoyed showing me how she ran the place, and I liked learning from her." She stopped, remembering that time, remembering it in her heart, her bones.

"When I think back on it, I cherish those months with her."

"And then what?" He sounded so truly interested in her life that it made it hard not to want to keep going. Except...

"You might be sorry you asked." She was both serious and teasing.

He smiled. "I'm tough—I can take it."

She made *herself* smile then. That sad sort of bittersweet smile when you're finding the good in the bad, when you're realizing you can't have it all and have to make tough choices. "She died. My grandma. Three weeks before I was setting off to Chicago to look for a new apartment and start back at my old firm. It was sudden—a heart attack. She was on a bike ride with a group of friends from the island when it happened. We didn't get to say goodbye."

"God. Sorry," he whispered.

And oh dear Lord, what had she just done here? She didn't even know this guy and she'd let things get terribly personal very quickly, and terribly maudlin. So it seemed wise to just barrel through the rest. "It was a hard loss. But in the end, after all the crying, someone had to take over the inn. It was my grandmother's second love behind my grandpa, after all. And my sister was only eighteen at the time, and wouldn't have wanted to do it anyway. And my parents weren't up for that kind of lifestyle change—plus my mother was raised here and didn't want to come back permanently. So that left *me*."

Seth tilted his head in the other direction. "So you... gave up your big city plans to stay here and run your grandma's inn."

She nodded, then acknowledged the obvious. "It was a major change in direction, certainly. But when it came down to running the inn or selling it and letting go of the place entirely, I couldn't do it. And so…an unwitting innkeeper was born." She tossed off a light laugh, hoping she sounded okay with the decision—because she was.

And the further truth she didn't share—finally finding the wits to hold something back—was that it had been a choice, not an obligation. Because the moment she'd decided to stay, a rush of relief had raced through her body like wildfire. And she'd realized it simply felt easier. Life here. The peacefulness. The isolation. She wouldn't have to risk running into Drew on a busy city street. She wouldn't have to risk needing someone the way she'd needed *him*, and then possibly have them leave her. She'd never have to risk feeling that alone again—because Summer Island had already turned into a home to her; she'd already become part of the fabric of the community.

"Any regrets?"

She shook her head. "Never."

And to her surprise, Seth lowered his chin and narrowed his gaze on her, playfully challenging her. "Never?"

She smiled at that, took another sip of wine. It continued to draw out honesty. "Well, let's just say…if there are any drawbacks to living in such an isolated place, I long ago accepted them. And I really love running the inn. And I'm happy to keep the place the way Gran would have wanted."

"Ya know, it's none of my business, Meg darlin', but…did Gran ever *say* she wanted you to run the inn when she was gone? Did she ever make you feel like it was expected of you?"

Meg shook her head. "No. She wouldn't have wanted to put that burden on me or my family. Only...she died fairly young. Early sixties. So she never really...had a chance to tell us her wishes. We all thought she'd have a lot more years."

She drank more wine then—mainly to fill the space when she quit talking, and he didn't say anything more right away. She'd accidentally told him so much so fast. And she somehow felt he'd taken in even more than she'd actually said. That he perhaps already knew life for her was a little bit hard here. And that it hadn't held all she'd hoped.

But you have a full life. A better life than so many people. You have everything you need.

That was when she noticed Seth staring at her. Even more intensely than usual. He didn't let his gaze waver. It went so far as to make her a little nervous—enough that she drained the last sip from her glass and poured another. Part of her wanted to call him on it, say: *What the hell are you looking at?* It was so...direct. And again, intense. Yet another part of her...liked it. She wasn't sure any man had ever seemed so dedicated to studying her before.

And finally, when her heart was beating too hard and she didn't feel she could stand it another second, she widened her eyes on him, and playfully said, "What?"

He drew his gaze down, but only for a second before raising it back to her eyes, flashing the slightest of grins. "Just questions running through my mind is all."

"Are you going to ask them?"

He made a slight face, as if weighing it. "Probably

shouldn't. They're nosy and personal as hell. And I'm probably getting a little drunk on this warm wine of yours."

And since she was, too, and he'd made her day—and now her evening—far more interesting than she could have anticipated this morning, she said, "I've just told you some of the most personal stuff in my life. So ask your questions."

"Okay," he agreed, leaning back in his chair, food seemingly forgotten now. "Guess I'm just wondering what such a beautiful woman is doing here alone. But then I gotta think—*are* you alone? Why were there two steaks? Why am *I* eating one of 'em and not some other guy?"

Beautiful, he'd called her. Charmers gonna charm. But she didn't mind.

Had Zack ever called her beautiful? She wasn't sure—and it seemed like a thing she'd remember. Moreover, it seemed like a thing he should have said.

She pointed to the near empty wine bottle sitting between them and told Seth, "Okay, because of this, you get full disclosure. Even fuller than you just got."

"Sounds like it's my lucky night," he said with that slow Southern drawl—and she tried not to read too much into it or think too deeply about that, either. Possibly he was flirting with her, but her bigger concern at the moment was that full disclosure she'd just promised him. She'd already spilled so much. Maybe she'd *never* really been very good at holding information back or knowing how to keep things private. Her adult life, spent in the same place with the same handful of people who already knew everything about her, had held so little need for it—if she'd ever known how to play her cards close to her chest, it was a skill she'd obviously lost somewhere along the way.

"I'm not always alone," she explained. "I'm alone right now because the man I was going to have dinner with tonight left this morning, unexpectedly. The steaks were already thawed."

"Some kind of emergency?" he asked. She couldn't read his expression—he, on the other hand, was clearly as skilled at holding things back as he was at taking down shutters.

She shook her head. "No. He just…left. Because… sometimes he does. That's the nature of our relationship." Then she tried for a smile, as if to say that was just fine with her, but was pretty sure she didn't pull it off.

"So you're not, like, married?"

"Heavens no," she confirmed quickly with a vigorous shake of her head. Zack would probably faint if someone thought they'd taken vows, after all.

"And so, then you're…" He was fishing, curious, trying to figure it out.

And she'd promised him full disclosure. Even fuller than leukemia and desertion. So she said, "To be entirely honest, I'm not exactly sure *what* we are. Sometimes we're a couple   sometimes not. It's…ambiguous."

"And you wish it was…more spelled out."

She nodded. "Sure."

"And he won't give you that."

Another nod.

"Well, that's a shame," he said. "For you, I mean. Not so much for me."

He gazed across the table at her through sexy, half-closed eyes now, delivering a look she felt down below, squarely between her thighs. Part of her wanted to stare back, hold that gaze, let herself be entranced by it—but again, it was too intense. So she looked to her plate, picked up her corn on the cob, and took a bite. Eating corn on the cob was not sexy.

Yet despite trying to desex the moment, she then heard herself ask, "And just how do *you* fit into the equation?"

"Like I said, you're a beautiful woman. And I'll be around for a while. That's all." But his eyes on her said that *wasn't* all. That wasn't even *close* to all.

And she didn't want to be that woman who couldn't take a compliment, but she saw herself as more of a pretty-on-her-good-days type and seldom beautiful— and charmers gonna charm, so she found herself saying, "Are you sure that's not the wine talking?"

"Yeah, I'm sure—you've been beautiful all day, darlin'," he said without missing a beat.

She smiled—it was hard not to like that, especially under the influence of some very potent alcohol—but it was probably time to shut this down. "Are you flirting with me, Mr. Darden?"

"Yes ma'am, I do believe I've advanced to flirting," he answered, that slow, confident grin still firmly in place.

So she asked him pointedly, "How old are you?"

"Thirty-one."

Well then. She'd been right earlier about him being younger. "Afraid I'm way too old for you."

Yet he argued. "I doubt that, darlin'. How old do you think is too old?"

"I'll turn the big four-zero on my next birthday."

And to her surprise, he released a hardy burst of laughter, as if she'd told him a great joke. "Thirty-nine is far from old, and even if it wasn't—haven't you heard that age is just a number?"

Okay, sure, it wasn't as if they were light years apart—but maybe Meg felt older than the candles on her birthday cake indicated. Or maybe it was about knowing he was a charmer—likely a seducer. She didn't like letting anyone think that sort of thing worked on her. Again, charm was fine as long as you didn't buy into it too much.

And of course, there was Zack. Even if…well, as she'd just told Seth, she didn't know what they were—or, for that matter, what they would ever be. Her instinct was to behave as if she had a boyfriend, but the truth was, she actually didn't.

"Nonetheless, flattering though it is, I'm afraid you're barking up the wrong tree if you're looking for some kind of summer fling with an older woman."

"I actually hadn't thought that far ahead," he said coolly, "but sounds like a damn good idea."

And she saw it in her mind then, unbidden—their bodies moving together, naked, sweaty.

Whoa. She pushed it down. It was too startling. Exciting maybe, but startling. And insane—an entirely crazy idea.

She rewarded him with another small smile just for the repartee he was so skilled at. But then she brought things to an end. "We should say goodnight. Lot of work to do tomorrow, after all."

To which he let out a slight laugh and replied, "That we do, that we do." Good—he got the message. "Can I help you clean up?"

"Not necessary," she said quickly. It really felt like time for him to go. That vision in her head was too recent and still had her body tingling.

And he looked almost like he was tempted to argue, try to insist, but instead, after a long pause he simply said, "All right." Still wearing that same comfortable little smile that so often graced his handsome face.

As he swiped a napkin across his mouth, then set it atop his plate, she stood up. To move this along.

And when he pushed to his feet as well, she told him, "See you in the morning. And be careful walking back in the dark." Night had fully descended at some point when she'd been busy being flirted with on the last evening of her life when she'd have expected it.

"Moon's shining bright—I'll be fine," he promised. She just nodded.

"Thanks for dinner—best damn thing I've had to eat in a while and I appreciate it."

She found herself casting a soft smile. "It was…nice to have the company." *Ugh, shut up. "You're welcome" would have been just fine.*

He started to go then, walking toward the edge of the patio, where a paved stone path led around to the front of the inn—but he stopped and looked back. "The stuff you told me, from when you were younger—I'm sorry you had to go through that."

A short nod from her. *Keep it simple.* "Thanks."

Then the corners of his mouth curved up, just a little. "And I hope I didn't make you uncomfortable. With the flirting," he said. "If I did, I apologize."

"No worries," she told him. "I'm sure it was just the wine and all will be forgotten tomorrow."

That was when he narrowed his gaze on her one last time to say, "Not a chance, darlin'," just before he disappeared around the corner of the house.

CHAPTER FOUR

TURNED OUT THE walk back around the island the next morning was downright nice. Nicer than yesterday anyway. Nicer because today there was less guesswork. Nicer because he'd already gotten what he'd come for—a paying job. And…a foothold at the Summerbrook Inn.

He'd known that it had always been yellow. But he'd asked just to make sure. To test his memory.

The morning air was cold and fresh with spring, and the lush foliage along the small road that circled the island felt new, like it had probably just burst to life in the last few days. His eyes fell on two herons standing in ankle-deep water at the shore's edge, and a small faded red rowboat someone had tied to a weathered post twenty yards out.

He hadn't noticed his surroundings so much on the walk yesterday—because he'd been too busy coming up with a plan. He'd been busy dredging up old skills he'd tried for a while now to bury—and suddenly he was using them again, for better or worse.

But in the end, it hadn't taken a plan at all—it had only taken showing up at the right time to find Meg Sloan struggling to control a tall shutter too heavy for her slight build. It had only taken stepping up to help.

She'd made it easy and he appreciated that. For both their sakes.

He'd always known how to talk to women without even trying—his father had called it his love potion. "Get out that love potion of yours."

"Just sprinkle your love potion on her." It came instinctively, but with someone like Meg Sloan, even more so. She was attractive. And genuine. And honest. He felt all that just dripping from her.

His father hadn't believed him that he didn't try with women—his father thought everything every person on the planet did was a scheme, a strategy. And he'd taught Seth an awful lot about scheming over the years, that was for damn sure—but when it came to women, Seth just did what came naturally.

And so all that flirtation hadn't exactly been part of the plan—because, again, she'd taken his plan away, made it so he didn't need one. The flirtation had just… happened. And maybe more would happen than just flirtation. Time would tell. There were things he'd come here to do—but she could add an element of pleasure to that he hadn't expected.

She struck him as a woman who needed to loosen up a little, have some fun. He'd be willing to help her with that if she let him. And given that he needed to get inside the house, have some time to look around… well, it just seemed like fate was smiling on him for a change. And if he seduced Meg Sloan in the process and they had some hot summer fun together, all the better.

Rounding the bend in the narrow road, he came on to the south shore where most of the businesses and homes were located. The cool morning air smelled fresh with spring and the sun cast a bright, sparkling ribbon of light onto the easternmost tip of Lake Michigan. Soon enough, the sunny yellow inn on the outskirts of town came into view.

MEG HADN'T SLEPT WELL. But for entirely different reasons than she'd expected earlier in the day.

She'd sent Seth and his flirtations away, but the effects had stayed with her.

She'd tried all day to simply write off her responses to him. Sexy younger guy who turns on the charm and has a rocking hot body—it's normal to notice that. Maybe even *feel* that in certain places, experience particular sensations.

But when he was long gone and she was still feeling them in the shower, and when she lay down to sleep a couple of hours later to find herself still unwittingly contemplating that vision, of the two of them naked, writhing together in the dark—she had to face a certain truth. She was attracted to him. And not just in that momentary way she'd been trying to fluff off. It was more real than that. *And you have to own that, not pretend it isn't there.*

He was still too young for her, and she still wasn't going to do anything about it—but the upshot was…last night had opened her eyes. Last night Seth had shown her…everything.

You act, in your heart, like someone who is stuck— stuck in situations you have no control over. You hide on this island from the rest of the great big world, afraid of being abandoned and alone. And maybe she had good reason for that. Plenty of people *had* left—albeit in many different ways. Drew. Gran. Aunt Julia. And Zack—over and over again. *But you aren't stuck at all.*

You can do and have anything you want. And staying on Summer Island hadn't kept anyone from leaving.

Now she'd eaten breakfast and dressed, and she found herself walking from room to room in the big house, peeking inside them all, *feeling* them all. The blue room, where Lila had always stayed when they'd come to visit as girls—with its two pretty twin beds. The lilac room, which had become her parents' over time when they were on the island, mainly because it had been her mother's as a girl. The yellow room, where she herself had stayed. "Because you need the sunshine, my Meg, to help keep you bright inside," Gran had said to her once as they'd stood by the window, the sun beaming in through white sheers, the wall color seeming to reflect and illuminate it even more. She'd said it privately, like it was a secret. And perhaps a gift. It had been Gran's favorite room. And even now, Meg only gave it to guests she felt warmly toward.

And she hadn't really known what Gran meant about keeping her bright, but there had been some concern in her family when she was young that she was too serious, didn't have enough fun. She'd always argued that Lila was frivolous enough for both of them, and she'd meant it. She loved her sister, but someone had to be the responsible one.

Her family had been so happy for her during the two short years when she'd moved to the city, loved her job, and gotten engaged. Her parents' relief had been palpable. *Look, she's not so serious after all—she's going to be fine.* But then cancer had come along and turned everything pretty damn serious again.

As she stepped into each room for a minute—now the mint room, and then the rose room—a certain love emanated from each for her. This inn was her world, and her grandmother's world before her. She'd played here as a child, she'd healed here as a girl, she'd matured here as a woman. Gran had been right about the house having a soul—Meg felt connected to the inn. Connected enough to refuse to let it go at a time when that would have made all the sense in the world and been, by most people's standards, the sane and reasonable thing to do.

And coming here to recover and ultimately never leaving had…limited her. She never wanted to admit that—she always wanted to insist that she loved her life in every way—but in truth it was an existence that came with limits. Limits she'd let herself accept and believe in over time. Her life came with limited views, limited scenery. Limited places to shop, limited places to eat or drink or have fun. Her life came with a limited number of people, social options. Her life came with… a limited number of men.

Over the years, she'd had a few boyfriends—usually due to the matchmaking skills of various island folk. Mostly her romantic interests had lived on the mainland, though, and putting miles of Lake Michigan between herself and a guy she was dating had usually made it feel challenging, less than ideal. And she'd never found one who'd made her want to change her lifestyle to help the relationship progress. Of course, maybe having only the tiny old town of St. Simon as a dating pool had been part of the problem, too. The only reason St. Simon really even existed anymore was the ferry.

And then had come Zack. Whom she loved deeply. But who disappointed her time and again. He'd never made promises. But maybe that was the problem.

Maybe she *wanted* a man who made promises. Maybe she wanted the luxury of meeting *more* men, of not feeling like she had to settle for one who, love him though she did, broke her heart a little more each time he left.

It wasn't that Zack wasn't enough—it was that he didn't want the same things as her. She kept thinking he would. That what he wanted would change. Or what *she* wanted would change. That they'd meet in the middle somehow. But the middle didn't seem to be getting any closer, no matter what Dahlia said.

And last night Seth had shown her: Her choices were only limited by where she chose to be. This lovely, quiet, empty place. This lovely island of few options.

Even if a product of manufactured charm, Seth's attention had made her feel brand new in a way, braver in a way, and more alive than she could have imagined when Zack had left that morning.

This one meeting with a handsome stranger was giving her the courage to think about...changing things, changing her life. It was making her think about...doing something new, *being* something new—starting a new life somewhere else and leaving this isolation behind. Once upon a time, she'd had good reasons for staying. Taking care of her heart, wrapping this island around it like a protective pillow, at a time when it was fragile. But maybe those reasons were gone now.

She'd been on Summer Island her entire adult life, and more than an attraction to her handyman, another thing she had to face was that she'd begun to feel trapped here. Her love for the place had made her lie to herself about that for a long time, but last night with Seth, she'd realized it—Summer Island had caged her in. And a part of her had begun to stagnate; a part of her had begun to feel as if she wouldn't know how to function anywhere else.

And Great-Aunt Julia was gone now, so what was really holding her here? Zack? He wasn't here himself half the time. And maybe she was tired of wanting more from him than he was willing to give.

She was standing in the orange sherbet room—Gran had refused to refer to it as the peach shade it really was; for her it was always orange sherbet—when she caught sight of Seth Darden approaching up the road. Today he wore a navy blue T-shirt that hugged his body just as nicely as yesterday's black one, and he carried a red toolbox. Good thing, too. She winced, smiled to herself, realizing she'd still forgotten to charge her electric screwdriver.

She supposed she'd been a little distracted. Contemplating life-changing decisions. And being reminded she was a vibrant, alive woman who could attract a handsome, younger man.

He looked good, and even from that distance, she suffered a twinge of awareness.

Lord. You'd think I'd been deprived of good sex. But she hadn't. Zack, when he was here, made her very happy in bed. *That's how I know this counts for something, that it's real chemistry.*

Too bad he's so young.

Yet…if he wasn't, would that change things? Would she be more tempted? She'd never been one for frivolous affairs. No, that was more Lila's department. Sex, for her, required a certain level of comfort with a man, not something she built over a night or two.

Well, except for with Zack. With Zack it had happened fast. It had just felt right. She'd let herself be swept off her feet in a way she never had before.

Otherwise, though, it had always taken some time for her—a build-up.

Though she had a feeling if her grandmother were here, she'd say: *Go ahead, be a little frivolous.*

Her instant response: *But what about Zack?*

And she could hear her sweet grandma's voice in her head, clear as a blue sky, answering: *How often has he made it obvious that there's no permanent tie between you? You owe him nothing. For all you know, he's with someone else right now.* A thought that always stung—and always hung in the air in an uncommitted relationship.

She pushed the unpleasant thought aside—it was time to go work on shutters. And to…keep exploring this new idea. Of leaving Summer Island.

Descending the long mahogany staircase to the foyer, her eyes fell upon…a penny. Faceup. At the bottom of the stairs, dead center. She bent down, grasped it between forefinger and thumb. *See a penny, pick it up, and all the day you'll have good luck.* Funny, though— where on earth had a penny come from? She wasn't exactly carrying pennies around the house. Maybe from Seth, from a pocket, on one of his bathroom trips? She stuffed it in the hip pocket of her blue jeans remembering the notion of a penny being a message that someone in Heaven was thinking of you. Gran? Aunt Julia? Either way, a nice idea.

As she stepped out onto the front porch, she realized it was less foggy than yesterday—the sun was out early and had already burned the hazy moisture away.

She could already see the old South Point Lighthouse offshore, its red-and-white stripes gleaming.

"Mornin', darlin'," her handyman said. Normally, it annoyed her when men she didn't know used that kind of endearment—but from him, there was something about it that appealed, even if just on a visceral level.

"Good morning," she answered with a smile.

As he came up the walk, he slanted her a grin and said, "Afraid I got some bad news for ya."

She blinked, went a little rigid. "What's that?"

The sun made him squint up at her as he got closer. "I still think you're beautiful."

A warm flush ran the length of her body. *You don't have to hide from it, though.* She gave her head a tilt, tried to embrace that bit of newness and courage she'd just acknowledged. "Is that bad?"

His eyebrows shot up. "You seemed to think so last night. You reconsider that?"

"I can appreciate a compliment," she assured him. "But it doesn't mean anything's changed." *Remember, charmers gonna charm—yet maybe it doesn't hurt to just relax into it a little, enjoy it.*

It surprised her that he wore an almost cocky expression. "Early days yet. Not even June."

His confidence made her laugh. And also made her like the idea of…being pursued. Even if she had no intention of letting anything happen between them, perhaps she did enjoy the notion of the flirtation lasting. For a while anyway.

"Ready to get started on these shutters?" he asked, lowering his toolbox to the thick spring lawn.

"Yep. I'm ready to paint." She'd put the painting supplies on the porch last night and now held up the last can they'd been working from in one hand and a brush in the other.

"And I'm ready to start putting some shutters back up so your house won't feel so naked." He winked. Lord, those winks. She didn't even deny to herself that she felt that one right in the crux of her thighs. But she hoped like hell it didn't show on her face.

They worked in companionable silence after that, due to the fact that she was in one place—painting on the drop cloth—and he was busy moving from window to window, sometimes with the ladder in tow, other times just toting a freshly painted shutter. But they still made light conversation from time to time.

"How's it look?" This after he'd rehung the ones around the first floor windows that faced the front yard and street.

She'd smiled. "Great! The house feels better already—I can tell."

By lunch he'd replaced all the shutters they'd finished painting yesterday and he rejoined her at the drop cloth to help with the rest. Today the crisp blue sky was dotted with more fluffy cotton clouds that kept the temps a few degrees lower than yesterday and the sweating to a minimum. And despite herself, she liked that he was nearer to her now. She *felt* the nearness. She was still getting used to that—but she liked it.

"Which windows are yours?"

"All of them," she said on a laugh.

He slanted her a look. "I meant which ones go to your bedroom?"

She stopped painting and glanced over, let her face express a mild suspicion. "Why do you ask?"

He shrugged. "I don't know. Curious where you

sleep." The words held more than sleep, though. The words held sex.

So much that she considered not telling him. He was somehow taking a very simple thing—the location of her bedroom—and making it…intimate, personal. She bit her lip—but then thought, what the hell? If this meant he was going to peek into her room when he rehung the shutters there and envision her in the bed…was that horrible? Or just…another compliment in a way? "The corner room with the turret."

"I thought that," he said.

"Why?"

"I don't know. Just thought you seemed like a woman who'd be drawn to that sort of thing, the tower."

"It's the best room in the house. I *should* use it as a guestroom—people always ask for it and are disappointed it's not available. But it was my grandmother's room, and when I took over the inn, I figured I should give myself the one I wanted."

"Always a good decision, giving yourself what you want," he said. More sex in the words. *He's saying I should indulge. In him.*

She tilted her head. "Always?"

"As long as it's not hurting anybody—always." He sounded so sure. She liked that about him—he always seemed certain of things. No wavering.

A little while later, she lay down her brush to go inside and make sandwiches for lunch. "Need help?" he asked.

She gave him another smile. "Thanks, but I'm good. Frankly, I can handle making lunch easier than I can handle painting sixty window shutters."

He scrunched his brow a little to ask, "So do I get a

grand tour of the place when we're done? Feel pretty acquainted with the exterior now—kinda curious to see it from the other side." And when she didn't answer right away, he added with a playful look, "That way I can recommend your place to all my friends here."

She laughed lightly and said, "Sure, I guess." He'd used the bathroom several times, but it was near the front door so it was true he hadn't really seen the house. And she was flattered he wanted to.

She carried their lunch out in a picnic basket because it was the easiest way to transport sandwiches, chips, and drinks, thinking they'd just eat quickly on the front lawn. But Seth pointed to a wooden bench that faced the water across the street and said, "No offense to your drop cloth, Meg darlin', but seems like a nicer lunch spot over there."

She glanced up Harbor Street, still and quiet as usual in May, but she knew there were eyes everywhere. "I don't need the whole town thinking I'm on a date with my handyman."

He arched one brow, a lock of sandy hair dipping over his forehead. "Why not?"

Hmm, good question. Given that she'd told him too much about her relationship with Zack last night. "Fine, but we're eating fast," she said. "I want my house fully clothed by nightfall."

He took the basket from her and they crossed the street to sit on the bench peering out on the lighthouse. White-capped waves frothed around the sandy edges of the tiny island it sat upon. "Is that still in use?" he asked.

She nodded, biting into a ham sandwich. "It's not manned, but has a working light. There are others, too, off different points of the island. And one on a ridge above the western shore that's open to visitors."

He grinned. "Think I've seen it from the road. You should give me a tour sometime."

When she tossed him a sideways glance, a beam of sun peeked from behind the edge of a cloud and shone down behind his head, making him look like some sort of fallen angel. But no. Fallen angels were...bad; the devil had been a fallen angel. "That sounds suspiciously like a date," she said. "And again, I don't need people thinking I'm on a date with my handyman."

"And again, I don't see why not. Since you're in an open relationship and all."

She thought that through. And she kind of liked being reminded once more that she was free to do whatever she wanted. Though she explained, "Most people don't really know Zack and I aren't exclusive. So it could make me look bad."

Now it was him with the sideways glance. "Oughta get that cleared up then. Not really fair to you otherwise."

He said it so matter-of-factly that she almost felt foolish. Because it made so much sense. She'd just never before had a reason to concern herself with it. And maybe she'd *liked* people assuming Zack cared enough about her to make it exclusive.

Seth Darden was definitely forcing her to rethink some things—even if having a fling with him wasn't one of them. "You're still too young for me," she said bluntly. Already, she could be blunt with him. She supposed last night's wine and accompanying confessions had opened that door.

But like earlier, his answer came out fully confident. "I don't think you really feel that way."

Lowering her Coke can from her lips, she let her eyes go wide on him. "You don't?"

He shook his head. "In fact, I think you seem…" He stopped, narrowed his gaze on her, as if trying to size her up. "Different than you did last night. Ever since I got here today. More…relaxed. Or open. Or something."

Maybe that was showing a little more than she'd meant it to. But maybe she also didn't really mind. In some ways, she didn't feel she had much to hide with Seth—at least not after last night, after she'd bared her soul in so many unexpected ways. "Maybe I am," she said. "But not about dating you."

"Then about what, darlin'?"

Borrowing a page from *his* book, now it was she who took her sweet time answering. They'd finished eating and had just stood up to start back across the street. She carried the picnic basket looped over one arm. And as she glanced up at the Summerbrook Inn and thought of the summer about to begin, a summer that suddenly seemed destined to be about change, she said, "I have a proposition for you."

CHAPTER FIVE

"Now that's what a guy likes to hear."

She glanced over to see his grin and returned it. Because it was hard not to; there was something infectious about him. "I told you, it's not about that."

He appeared intrigued. "What's it about then?"

She stopped on the front walk, again to peer up at the inn her grandmother had made a staple on this island, the inn she had made a vacation home for so many guests over the years, some who returned every summer. She looked up at this house she loved, this house that really was a home, in so many ways to so many people, past and present, herself included. And she gave voice to the notion that had been floating around her brain through the night and this morning—though it was difficult to actually say it out loud. "I'm thinking of selling the inn."

When he looked at her, she sensed he felt the gravity in her words. After all, she'd told him enough last night for him to know this was big. "I didn't see that coming."

"Neither did I, actually. But...maybe it's time for a change."

He continued eyeing her. Possibly with admiration. Perhaps she suddenly seemed adventurous, or unpredictable. "Where would you go?"

She shrugged. "I have no idea. Just somewhere new."

Then she drew her eyes fully down from the house and onto him, to get to the practical part. "But it's a new idea, so I'm not going to rush into it. I'm going to use the summer to think it over." *Use the summer to see if anything changes. With Zack. With my feelings. With anything else relevant here.* "And I'll decide for sure at the end of the tourist season."

"What's the proposition part, darlin'?"

Ah, yes, the proposition part. "I keep the place in pretty good repair, but if I were to put it on the market, I'd need to spruce some things up to get top dollar. So I want to hire you to do some more work." She wasn't rolling in dough, but if she was serious about this, investing in improvements would be worth it, especially since she'd surely get it back when the inn sold. It would be worth dipping into her savings for. "Are you interested?"

He cocked his head and shot her an amused look.

And she lowered her chin, her expression chiding him as she added, "In the work. Are you interested in the work?"

In reply, he laughed and said, "It'll be my pleasure to do whatever you need done, Meg darlin'. On the house—or otherwise."

He winked, and she rolled her eyes at him—but a flutter of warmth rippled through her stomach and headed south, right into her panties.

By the end of the day, all the shutters were rehung. The muscles in Seth's arms and shoulders ached, but it was a good ache, the ache of an honest day's work. He found himself smiling down at Meg from the lad-dcr as he tightened the last screw. She was turning out to be an interesting woman, and the smiling came easy.

Not only because she was interesting, though. Because she was helping him out more than she knew by hiring him to make improvements on her house. He watched as, down below, she gathered up paint supplies and started carrying them away. This morning, he hadn't known much about his future beyond today, or at least he hadn't known how he was going to get access to the house, but this was working out better than if he'd planned it, proving that sometimes plans just got in the way. Seemed downright serendipitous, in fact.

Serendipitous—that was a word his grandpa used to use. His grandpa on his mom's side. Funny that he remembered certain little things about his maternal grandparents—he hadn't seen them since he was ten.

But he remembered his grandpa had liked those kinds of big words. Liked sounding smart, but not in a pompous way. Liked feeling as if he was teaching you something that might help you out along the path of life. And game shows. The man had loved game shows. Liked trying to say the answers before the players could.

He remembered his grandma puttering around the kitchen, sweeping the floor all the time—she'd swept that floor every day, and had sometimes made him do it, too. She'd made pie crusts by hand while he'd watch. Their house had been tiny, not big and sprawling like this one, but she'd kept it nice and always had it smelling good with something from the stove or oven. Country food like cottage ham and green beans or chicken and dumplings or homemade pie from fruit the whole family would go picking from an orchard. Peaches, apples. Or from the blackberry bushes along her back fence.

He and his mom had lived there after his parents broke up when he was little. He didn't even remember them being married—his whole childhood had been at his grandma and grandpa's in a little town in northern Pennsylvania he couldn't recall the name of.

Memories were funny things. They could play tricks on you.

Sometimes you think you know something, but it turns out to be wrong. And other times what you remember is spot-on, exactly the way it lived in your head.

He remembered his mother's smile. Her hugs, the kind that came with a little extra squeeze at the end. He hugged people—women—that same way, a habit she'd left him with. Because he'd always been aware it made the other person feel a little bit more special.

Her voice had been deep for a woman, throaty. She'd smoked. But then she'd stopped after a big fight with his grandma about it. He remembered the perfume she wore, too. Not the name of it, but the smell. Musky. Nothing light or flowery—not a girl's perfume, but a grown-up woman's.

He and his grandfolks had gone away for a week every summer, whether they could afford it or not, because, "Ya gotta have special things in life, Seth, special moments and special places," Granddad would say. "Ya gotta do things and see things that expand your horizons and make ya a little more than you were before." That was what he'd said, wasn't it? That was what Seth remembered anyway. But he had reason to doubt. Not having seen the man since he was ten.

He hadn't seen his mother since he was ten, either. That was when she'd died. And everything had changed. Everything.

He backed down the tall ladder, then carefully pulled it away from the inn, maneuvering it until it lay on its side in the thick spring grass. A soft breeze danced across his skin and drew his gaze out to the water, to that lighthouse. He could see why Meg felt isolated here, why she might want to leave—but at the moment he thought he wouldn't mind staying awhile. It felt so far away from…everything else. And it felt like a place where someone could start over. Meg had done that here, after all.

But don't go getting ahead of yourself. He had no idea what his future held—only what it didn't. Only the bad shit he'd walked away from. And that the coming few weeks, or maybe longer, would be spent in this quiet place that felt much farther away from the rest of the world than it really was, making some money—and looking for what he'd come to find.

He'd taken something from Meg's family a long time ago—or at least his memory told him he had. And it seemed pretty damn ironic that now he had to take the very same thing a second time, right when he wanted to *stop* taking. But sometimes life held necessary evils.

Hefting the ladder up into one hand, he carried it around the back of the house toward her storage shed. She didn't see him coming; kneeling, she folded up the drop cloth very neatly with precise little movements he couldn't help thinking were damn cute. He didn't like having—at least in certain moments—to see her as a pawn, a target, but if things went well, she'd never find out he was anything more than a handyman.

"This go back here somewhere?" he asked.

She looked up, her brown hair tousled, falling in her face. He liked it.

She pushed it back from her eyes and pointed. "There are hooks on the back wall in the shed."

He wasn't surprised to find the shed—situated near a little stream behind the house and also painted yellow with white trim—possessed a tidy and organized interior. Like her. He barely knew her, but he could already tell that about her.

"Ready to give me that tour?" he asked, stepping back outside.

"Sure."

They entered through the front door into the same foyer he'd been in several times already to use the bathroom. He'd caught glimpses of a living room with antique furniture, but now got a better look. "Gran always called this the parlor, so I do, too," she said. "I use it as my living room during the off-season, but during the summer I open it to the guests." The flat screen TV on the back wall blended in shockingly well to the decor—he'd almost failed to notice it.

Across the parlor another door opened into a small circular room—the bottom of the tower, underneath her bedroom. "This is the library," she told him. Curved built-in shelving from ceiling to floor held books of all kinds, old and new, and he instantly found himself scanning them, trying to take them in, read the sideways titles on all the spines. The room boasted several small easy chairs and two windows that overlooked rosebushes.

From there, she led him back to the hallway, pausing at a wall full of pictures beneath the stairs. She pointed to the largest, most central one in a polished wood frame. "This is Gran." The woman's hair was white, her eyes kind, and the frame boasted a little gold placard that read:

Margaret Adkins.

Founder—Summerbrook Inn.

The other pictures included family photos and one that looked to be from Margaret Adkins' wedding, but his eyes stayed locked on the big portrait of Meg's grandma. He'd seen her before, a very long time ago, and until this moment, her face had been a vague blur in his mind. The photo filled in the gaps.

From there, Meg showed him a couple of small guestrooms on the first floor, and a little space she called the reading nook, which came with more bookshelves, doorways on both ends, a tall window, one overstuffed easy chair covered in a flowery print—and a calico cat. "Meet Miss Kitty," she said, reaching out to scratch behind the cat's ear. It sat on the shelf like a knick-knack.

"Like from *Gunsmoke*?" he asked, scrunching his face slightly. He thought he was remembering that right, but wasn't sure.

Meg smiled, clearly surprised he knew. "Yes. My grandma was a fan, and she had a soft spot for the saloon girl."

He grinned. "I think I used to watch reruns with my grandpa when I was a little kid." Then he touched a finger to the white molding around the built-ins. "Paint's starting to peel some here."

"I know. It's exactly the kind of thing I figured I could put off awhile longer, but now I want it taken care of."

From there, they entered a sunroom that held a white wicker sofa and chair to one side and a coordinating wicker table with four chairs. "I use this space mostly as my dining room, and to soak up some warmth all through the year on bright days. Gran added it to the house in the nineties. And last but not least on the first floor…" Then she led the way into a large eat-in kitchen that looked well kept but outdated.

"I could paint those cabinets for ya way cheaper than replacing them. If you're into a rustic, weathered look, I know some techniques you might like. And same for that table."

She stopped, glanced around the room, obviously weighing it. "Hmm—yeah, I might be interested in that." After which she peered down at the floor, then back up at him. "Have you ever refinished hardwood? There's wood under this linoleum—but Gran covered it up back in the seventies."

"Yes ma'am," he answered her. "And do a pretty damn good job on it if I say so myself."

From there, she showed him her small office at the rear of the house, then led him back to the foyer, where they ascended a wide, dark wooden staircase with a turn and a landing halfway to the top. "Up here," she said, "only guestrooms." And she began pointing them out fairly quickly compared to the downstairs part of the tour. Which was a shame because he was trying to re-member, remember which one he might have been in a long time ago—but they flashed by too quickly. All he took in was that they were decorated in quaint decor and springy colors that fit the mood of the island, and he wondered why she suddenly seemed in such a hurry.

And then he understood. *Oh, it's the beds.* And the quiet sense of seclusion up here that he hadn't felt so much downstairs. Being empty of guests right now, it was a more intimate space.

So he followed the urge to add, "And *your* room," saying it low, over her shoulder—just in case she'd forgotten.

When she turned to look at him, it put their faces close. "No need to show you that one," she said smoothly. But underneath the smoothness, he thought she was a little nervous. About beds.

"Why not?" he asked, giving her a grin. "I'm curious." He truly wondered what sort of room Meg Sloan chose to sleep in. Frilly and soft? Simple and practical? Something in-between?

She'd started to walk on, but now stopped, glanced back at him. He pulled up short—and again, it put them close. And something invisible moved between them— like the slight pull of a magnet. He knew she felt it, too.

Her mouth curved into the smallest of smiles. "You seem a little too interested in my bedroom."

And he laughed. Because she was so up-front with him in ways. His grandpa, back in the day, would have called that being guileless. Seth called it keeping things real, and he couldn't claim he was an expert at that—he knew how to keep his secrets but he admired people who were comfortable enough in their own skin to just say what was on their minds.

Despite the rebuff, he wanted to flirt with her. "What's wrong with me being interested in your bedroom, darlin'? It's just another room." He arched one brow.

And her eyes dropped bashfully just before she turned away and said, "End of tour. Let's go back downstairs."

He was sorry he hadn't seen her room. But that magnetic tug between them remained, even as he followed her back down the wide steps, polished with time. It was a blunt awareness; he knew they were noticing things about each other—*feeling* things about each other—that came from a stark sense of attraction. Her eyes were the warm green of deep forests, her lips thin but pretty, the palest shade of pink. She wore her nails long but unpainted—though a few were short and had probably broken during the last couple of days working on the shutters. A small mole dotted her neck, a larger, darker one her chest. She concealed her breasts in modest clothes—another tank top covered by an open blouse today—but he could still see they were ample, round, touchable. Same with her hips—blue jeans covered them, but he'd found himself watching her ass nearly every time she'd walked away from him the last two days.

And as they stepped back out on the front porch and she turned to face him, he knew with complete certainty that she'd noticed just as many things about *him*. She was taking in the color of his eyes right now, maybe noticing the width of his mouth, or that he hadn't shaved today and that the stubble on his jaw came in darker than his hair.

She was *looking* at his mouth, in fact—possibly wondering how it would feel to be kissed by it—until he asked, "About the work—tomorrow?"

Her gaze rose to his. He almost regretted having shaken her from that silent connection.

"Um, let me take a day to think through some of this," she said then. She'd come back to herself—put her game face back on. Guileless, but in control of her moves. "The idea of selling, and of fixing the place up, is brand new. Day after tomorrow, though?"

He answered with a short nod. "It's a date."

"No, it's a work arrangement."

He laughed lightly. Guileless about everything except her attraction to him. "Whatever you say, darlin'."

And then he suffered the compulsion to kiss her goodbye. Odd that it passed over him that way, like she was someone he knew better, like it was the normal thing to do. He'd even begun to lean slightly forward when he realized—no, this wasn't a woman he kissed. Not yet anyway.

"'Night, Meg darlin'," he said.

"You can...bring an invoice next time if you like. For the last two days."

The suggestion forced more laughter from his throat. "I don't really have...that kinda system."

Her pleasant expression stayed in place. "Well, I'll need invoices for my taxes, so you should come up with one." She ended on a smile, then tacked on a quick, "Goodnight, Seth," and disappeared back into the house, that fast.

He stood looking after her, amused, tired. It had been a long day. But a good day. Better than most in his life.

Dusk settled over Summer Island in thick layers of darkening blue as he began the walk back around the western perimeter toward his empty little cabin. Unlike at lunch, the water looked smooth as glass now—everything seemed still but for the occasional call of a bird. A few of the brightest stars grew visible in the sky as he walked, punctuated by a pale white moon.

He didn't know Meg well, but he knew instinctively that a fling would be good for her. She clearly needed something she wasn't getting, something she didn't have. But in truth, he thought it could be just as good for him, too. A good distraction from some of the more serious shit in his head right now—some of the stuff he was trying to remember, and some of the stuff he was trying to forget.

CHAPTER SIX

MEG SPENT THE next morning thinking. About cabinets to be painted. About floors to be changed and redone. About repairs to the walkways that led through gardens where roses and lilacs planted by her grandfather would soon bloom, adding fragrance and color to her world. And about Seth Darden.

But every time Seth came to mind, she diverted her thoughts back to cabinets and the like. And she decided she'd employ her new handyman on a project-by-project basis—doing the bigger things first, seeing how much it cost and how long it took, and then deciding from there if more work was warranted. And maybe as a little time passed, she'd know whether or not she was going to stick to her plan to sell the inn.

It all depended on Zack really. She didn't want anything from him that he didn't want to give. And so whenever he came back, she didn't intend to serve him up any sort of ultimatum or anything—she simply set an internal deadline in her head, same as she'd alluded to Seth. If nothing happened to change her mind by the end of the tourist season in September, she'd put the inn up for sale and start a new life somewhere else by next spring.

She only hoped Gran would forgive her from up on that cloud. But at the same time, she knew Gran would want her to be happy—and she just thought her life could be richer; she thought there could be...more. And once you thought that, if you didn't go after it, how did you live with yourself?

Though she wasn't going to tell anyone about this, not even Suzanne. She didn't want anyone influencing her decision. She didn't want anyone telling her no, that her life was here and how could she ever want to leave? Or telling her yes, that much bigger and better things awaited her out there and she should give up on Zack and throw caution to the wind and just do it. This had to come from inside her, in her heart.

Of course, fishing season ran from April to December on the Great Lakes, and summer kept Zack away longer than other parts of the year for practical reasons. The weather was nicer for life on a fishing boat, and fish was more in demand at restaurants and chains up and down the shores and beyond when temperatures were warmer. So he probably wouldn't be back for a while—for better or worse when it came to this decision.

Would he care very much if he knew? Maybe he wouldn't. Maybe he'd just tilt his handsome head and say: *Do what ya gotta do, Maggie May.* And maybe that would be the worst possible thing to know, to hear. It would make the decision easy. But the heartbreak worse.

Just after noon, she fed Miss Kitty, who was the perfect inn cat—she kept to herself, a quiet little furry statue in a corner of the room or curled up asleep on a shelf. She didn't run from the guests for the most part, and didn't even mind occasionally being petted by a visiting child. She was content and tolerant.

Like me. The similarities had never occurred to Meg

before. Though she thought the traits sounded more pleasing in a cat than a woman.

"Sorry to tell you, though," she said to the kitty as she lowered her food bowl to the floor, "wherever *I* go, you go. You don't come with the inn." She'd adopted the cat as a kitten—who'd come mysteriously walking up onto her doorstep one rainy spring morning eight years ago. She hadn't been in the market for a cat, but very quickly discovered she enjoyed having her around. A quiet companion who fit in the quiet house, and sometimes, if Meg was lucky, Miss Kitty would curl up beside her in the nook or next to her in bed.

Just then, she heard the buzz of her cell phone in the next room, and soon found a text. Still not from Zack. Suzanne. Lunch on Dahlia's deck?

She'd been just about to make herself a sandwich and step out on the patio to eat it. After two days of Seth Darden shaking up her world in more ways than one, she welcomed the quiet. *See, you've become too conditioned to that. A woman who has to force herself to be social—that's not who you want to be.*

So for the sake of not letting herself begin the slow morph into a cat lady who never went outside, she texted back: Meet you there in ten.

She walked to a mirror in the hall, glancing quickly at her reflection, then proceeded on to the mirror in her bathroom. She looked plain to herself—*felt* plain. Long winter plain. Cat lady plain. She needed to brush her hair, put on a little makeup.

I didn't even do that with Seth here. Even when I knew he was coming back yesterday.

She always tried to look reasonably pretty for Zack when he was around—just the normal stuff like makeup and a little grooming. But she'd forgotten that entirely with Seth. And he'd treated her like the most alluring creature on earth anyway. Charmer or not, there was something lovely in that.

Peering into the glass, she bit her lip, thinking that over, taking herself in. She looked at her eyes, her lips, her complexion, her hair. She was getting a few wrinkles under her eyes, lines around her mouth. She had crow's feet now when she smiled. She thought her features appeared a bit sunken before she highlighted them with mascara and lipstick. But Seth hadn't? Seth had seen something pretty there? Something she couldn't?

Or maybe he just wanted the work. *Maybe a handsome young handyman drifter learns that flattery will get you everywhere—or at least to a bigger paycheck.* Maybe it was all talk.

But it hadn't felt that way.

She didn't want to be naive—she didn't want her disappointments with Zack to make her susceptible to any line of crap from another man—but it just hadn't felt that way.

If he was faking it, he was damn good.

Because there was chemistry there. Something electric. With stronger currents the second day than the first.

How strong will they be on the third day he's here? And the fourth?

Maybe that was why she'd taken the day in between—to just…calm her body down. Calm her reactions down. Calm her thoughts down. *If he's going to be here working, you really have no choice—you have to stop having physical reactions to him.* So that was what she would do.

It felt good to walk up the street to Dahlia's, and to see more people out and about. Residents who wintered on the mainland returned all through May, and it was becoming evident the island was more populated than even a week earlier.

Just then, Cooper Cross went running past her in the direction of the inn. "Meg!" he called with a wave and a smile.

She returned it. "Good to see you!"

She didn't know him well—only that he was a handsome professional type who summered here in one of the large stately old homes on Huron Hill and went running faithfully every day.

And as she approached Dahlia's, other businesspeople around the town could be seen nearby. Trent Fordham, who owned the bicycle livery, was out getting his stock ready for the season, and Mr. Wittleston, owner of the Bayberry Bed and Breakfast, was leaving the flower shop with a flat full of pansies, the bell on the door tinkling behind him.

"How's my girl?" Dahlia said in greeting when she stepped inside.

"Good," Meg answered with a smile. *Oh Dahlia— I fear you want Zack and I together as much as I do.* How would Dahlia feel if she knew Meg was considering selling? Well, that was just one of many reasons to keep the whole thing to herself.

"Suzanne's out back." The older woman pointed.

Although the temps still warranted sweaters—worn by them both, Meg noticed as she approached the table where Suzanne waited—it was the kind of day that made the island feel as if it were coming back to life. White pelicans, with their black-rimmed wings, perched on the docks below, and ring-billed gulls fluttered and cawed in the distance. Just to see a small lunch crowd on the deck, just to feel the sun warming her face in a way it seldom did in winter, brought summer a little closer than it had been yesterday.

Dahlia had already delivered them both iced teas in tall glasses. Meg sat down, gave her friend a "Hey," along with a quick smile, then glanced at the menu—though she wasn't sure why since she probably could have recited it.

"What's up?" Suzanne asked in greeting.

"The shutters. And they look great."

"That's a shame."

This drew Meg's gaze. "It is?"

Suzanne's lips curved into a mischievous smile. "He made the view nice out the shop window."

But Meg cast an accusing look. "He was really too far away from you to have made the view all that nice."

With a tilt of her head, dark curls blowing in the breeze, Suzanne mused, "Well, maybe the *idea* of him made the view nice. But I'm sure he made *your* view much nicer, being so much closer."

"Yeah, okay, my view was nice." She saw no reason to lie. "But I'm glad the job is done."

"I was going to ask you to lunch *yesterday*, but I saw you were already engaged."

Now Meg sighed. Eyes everywhere. "I made sandwiches for us both—no biggie. What was I supposed to do, starve him?"

Suzanne tilted her head the other way. "I think most paid laborers provide their own lunch."

Yet Meg just shrugged. "He's new here—and sure, I could have sent him marching up the street to the deli or the Skipper's Wheel, but that seemed silly. And inefficient."

Suzanne studied her with a sizing-up look. Appeared a little let down. "So you're really not into him."

Meg sipped her iced tea. "Why would you think I would be? I mean, I have Zack."

"Sort of. But not right now," she pointed out.

Their gazes met across the table. Acknowledgment that she wasn't bound to Zack—even if most people didn't realize that.

Dahlia arrived then, pad and pen hand, and they both clammed up on the topic and ordered their lunch. As comfortable as Meg usually was with Zack's aunt, this wasn't a conversation for her ears. Even if Meg was saying all the right things. Because that didn't mean she was *feeling* all the right things.

After Dahlia's departure, Meg looked back to Suzanne and said, "Even if I was in the market for a man, he's too young. And too…a lot of things."

Suzanne pursed her lips. "A lot of things, huh? Like what *kind* of things?"

"Flirty," Meg admitted. "Forward."

At this, Suzanne's eyes widened. "He's flirting with you? And you're not leaping on that? Are you crazy?"

"No, I'm very sane, thank you. Crazy would be leaping on it. He's a self-proclaimed drifter who I know nothing about. He's thirty-one and doesn't seem to have a home—or at least made it sound that way. He might be cute, but there are *so* many reasons *not* to leap on that and to instead just be content to let him work on my house." Then she narrowed her eyes on her friend, remembering. "Besides, two days ago you thought he was dangerous and that I was too trusting. What's with the about-face?"

Meg watched as Suzanne took all that in, weighed it. "I guess I got used to the idea." She shrugged. "And decided I was being too…wary on your behalf, like you said. And the upshot is…" She switched her expression back to an admonishing one. "There aren't a lot of a viable, single, attractive men on this little island, my friend."

"Then it's good I have Zack," Meg replied without missing a beat, "who is at least single and attractive. And if you're so into my handyman, I happen to know he's available. So maybe *you* should leap on that."

"You know I'm not in the market for a man," Suzanne said—and though she made the statement often, today sounded a bit more wistful about it than usual.

So Meg let her off the hook. "I know. Never mind. I'm just saying—you're hardly in a position to be scolding me about this."

Though Suzanne had come to Summer Island less than two years ago, she and Meg had bonded quickly and already knew each other well. Suzanne's husband had died five years earlier and she still wasn't ready to move on—and was, in Meg's opinion, far too fond of saying that maybe she never would be.

She'd dated a couple of guys since then and it hadn't gone well—one had turned out to be married and the other had been a world-class player. She'd moved here to retreat—same as Meg once had—and was also too fond of making it clear she had no interest in dating and that she generally considered men more trouble than they were worth.

"I'm not suggesting you marry the guy and have his

babies," she said now. "I was more thinking you could just enjoy him a little while Zack's away."

"*You* could enjoy him a little just as easily if it's only about…that," Meg said, her voice laced with a slight discomfort.

"He hasn't flirted with *me*," Suzanne aloofly pointed out. "Or been forward with me."

Meg raised her eyebrows. "He hasn't *met* you. But again, if you're so into him, I'd be happy to arrange an introduction when he comes back tomorrow."

At this, Suzanne appeared unduly pleased, albeit clearly ignoring the part about *her* and keeping the focus on Meg's connection with the guy in question. "He's coming back? Pray tell whatever for."

Meg sighed, blinked. She almost hated to fill her in. "I've decided to have him do some more work."

"Smartest thing I've heard you say in days." A wide smile unfurled on her friend's face.

"There are really quite a few little things that could stand to be repaired. And bigger things that need updated."

"This seems sudden," Suzanne remarked with a saucy slant of her head.

Another shrug from Meg. "He seems to know what he's doing, so it makes sense to take advantage of that."

When Suzanne simply smiled, Meg reheard her own words. And was grateful when one of Dahlia's servers, a quiet teenager named Catelyn who Meg had never seen minus her ponytail, delivered their food.

"Now let's change the subject to something more sane," Meg suggested as she picked up the cheeseburger from her plate.

"Okay. Have you heard from Zack?"

Meg flicked her gaze from the burger to Suzanne. "Something other than men, period." Truthfully, the very mention of Zack—at least in terms of reminding her that she *hadn't* heard from him—was annoying. "How's the flower business?" She raised her eyebrows pointedly, very ready to move on from this.

As they ate, she learned that traffic at Petal Pushers—the flower shop and nursery Suzanne had bought and cutely renamed after Aunt Julia's passing—had picked up predictably in the last week or two. Before coming north, she'd run a similar establishment in Indiana, a place that had allowed her business to thrive in more seasons—but having the only stop on the island for plants or flowers of any kind, she did just fine here, as Julia had before her.

From there, they discussed the idea of Suzanne buying a new bicycle this year. It was a practical discussion—bikes were to Summer Islanders what cars were to mainlanders. They weighed the merits of having a basket on the front versus a larger one in back, and Suzanne informed her Trent Fordham had a few nice used ones for sale as he was weeding out his stock, adding new bikes to take their place. "I have my eye on a fun aqua three-speed," Suzanne concluded.

Meg let out a soft laugh. "We lead such wild lives."

In response, Suzanne gave her a quiet, almost gentle smile. "The difference between you and I, Meg, is that I'm very content with the peace and quiet here, and you're not. I know you once were, but that's changed. Deep down, you want more."

Meg had never said anything to Suzanne about that, wanting more—in fact, the revelation still felt very new to her. So she was taken aback to hear it stated so absolutely.

And the truth, the truth she couldn't share even with Suzanne, was that talking about Seth had her reliving certain moments from yesterday—remembering how drawn to him she'd been, how her body had felt like molten lava that wanted to flow all over him. But also remembering just as much, at the same time, how insane it was to feel that way.

Meanwhile, Suzanne went on. "I know you once made the choice to come here, and to stay. But that was a long time ago. So… I guess that's why I just feel compelled to urge you to…take a chance when one comes along. Me—I like to look at a hot guy out the window, but I don't really want the emotions or complications involved with anything more than just the looking. I think you do."

Meg took that in. Suzanne really did know her well—maybe better than she'd thought. But she was still barking up the wrong tree. "I have enough complications, which are currently sailing around Lake Huron on the *Emily Ann*."

Suzanne screwed up her mouth. "I've always meant to ask—who *is* that floozy, *Emily Ann*, anyway? Uncommitted or not, I say you put your foot down and demand that boat be renamed the *Megan Marie*."

"I don't actually know," Meg confessed, scrunching up her nose.

Suzanne blinked. "And you've never asked?"

Meg shook her head. "At first I guess I wanted to be aloof about it, not act like I cared. And then later I realized maybe I didn't want to know. In case it's some great lost love I can never compete with."

"I'd have asked anyway. In fact, next time I see Zack, *I* might ask. And then recommend that name change."

"Don't you dare," Meg warned. "And besides, it's bad luck to change the name of a boat, so I would never even suggest it."

But Suzanne's eyes had fixed on something across the deck, clearly more interesting than Zack's fishing boat and leaving her to appear truly astonished.

"What?" Meg asked.

Suzanne lowered her voice. "Tall drink of water at eleven o'clock."

Meg let her brow knit, thinking aloud. "If I'm calculating correctly, eleven o'clock would be behind me."

"Then be sly when you look."

Meg sighed. "Sly might be outside my skill set."

Her friend just shrugged. "Then this is good practice."

Meg turned her head, pretending to peer beyond the tall drink of water toward the masts jutting upward into the sky from the harbor. Tall drink indeed. He was dark haired and wide shouldered with a muscular build, and classically handsome. "Wow," Meg whispered, turning back to face across the table.

"I take back what I said about not having enough attractive guys on this island. He's attractive enough to make up for ten men who aren't."

Just then, Dahlia happened past after having just seated him, and Suzanne reached out to grab her wrist. "Who's the human Ken doll?" she asked, voice low.

Dahlia chuckled in reply. "That's Beck Grainger, owner of Grainger Construction and Development and stately new island resident." She glanced back at him.

And reading Suzanne's obvious interest asked, "Shall I introduce you?"

"Oh—no," Suzanne said, drawing back slightly. "I mean, sometime—when it will seem more natural."

"He's new," Dahlia said. "That makes it natural." And with that and a conspiratorial nod, she was off to his table, hauling the poor man up by the sleeve of his plaid flannel shirt.

Meg and Suzanne barely had a chance to exchange glances before Dahlia had dragged him to their table. "Beck Grainger, this is Megan Sloan, who owns the Summerbrook Inn up the way and dates my nephew, Zack, and Suzanne Quinlan, the owner of Petal Pushers, the lovely little flower shop and nursery you may have noticed across the street."

When Suzanne didn't speak right up, Meg said, "Pleased to meet you," and held out her hand.

He shook it. "Likewise." He was a man-of-few-words type, like Zack—she could tell that already.

He then reached for Suzanne's hand, too, which she gave him, but she didn't quite meet his eyes. And her nod came off as distant and even shorter than his.

So he surprised Meg by saying, "Hope to see you both around—and maybe I'll stop by your shop some time soon." Gaze intent, he directed the last part toward Suzanne.

Who just quietly said, "Great," and looked back down.

Once Beck Grainger was gone and they were alone again, Meg leaned over and said, "What was *that*?"

"What was what?" Her friend tried to sound innocent.

"The man said something nice to you—like maybe

even expressed interest in you—and you were barely more than rude."

Suzanne met her gaze, then gave yet another shrug. "I felt weird, nervous. He was too handsome. And I'm too emotionally crippled." Then she shook her head. "But it's fine."

Now it was Meg casting the disappointed look. "So you really aren't interested in maybe getting to know him? A little? In case he might want to ask you out or something."

Her friend appeared only a tiny bit sad, and frightfully at ease about the situation, as she said, "Not really. All in all, I'd rather pick out a new bicycle than pick out a new man."

CHAPTER SEVEN

THE MAJORITY OF lake whitefish in the Great Lakes were gone, along with a once-thriving commercial fishing industry. And perhaps surprisingly, it wasn't about pollution or an oil spill or any other contaminate getting dumped in the water—it was about invasive species.

Overfishing during much of the twentieth century might not have helped the situation, but the real culprits were the zebra and quagga mussels, which consumed the plankton most Great Lakes fish fed on.

The upshot? A decimated ecosystem, resulting in a decimated and now highly regulated industry. And over time, the whitefish had finally started feeding on the mussels themselves—nature had a way of adapting and correcting itself—but the intense regulations made it hard for a fisherman to earn a living these days. There weren't even many of them left. But Zack Sheppard was nothing if not stubborn.

A brisk north wind cut right through him as he stood on the deck, sorting the catch from a trap net, releasing anything that wasn't a whitefish—as well as the ones that were too small—back into the water alive. The rest were tossed on ice and kept belowdecks in plastic bins until he docked at the end of the day, where he'd negotiate with a wholesaler ready to take the fish off his hands.

He didn't feel the frigid winds much anymore. Again, nature had given birth to creatures who adapted. When he'd climbed aboard his first trawler at sixteen, he'd thought his skin would freeze solid. Now, if anything, the cold only made him feel alive.

And all around him…peace. Not another boat, or human, or any land—for at least twenty miles in any direction. Sometimes sorting the fish—or any other aspect of his work—was like a trance for him, or what he guessed some people would call meditation. He did it without thinking—he watched his hands now, and the fish that passed through them. The only sound was the occasional call of a passing bird and the ripple of water against the hull as the *Emily Ann* floated, anchored, while he emptied the net. That and the *plop, plop, plop* as he returned small fish to the great lake.

He wasn't a religious man. He believed in the here and now. And such moments were about as close as Zack got to praying. Lake Huron was his church.

Only…there was a little sin in his heart today. Not that he believed in sin. But something felt a little wrong. Had yesterday, too. Damn it.

He didn't let himself think much about Meg when he was out here working. She was that nice, soft place to go back to when he was through—when he'd had enough solitude, when his own company began to feel stale. But she'd stayed on his mind after leaving this time.

Five years. May fifteenth, five years ago, Dahlia had dragged him up to her in the Pink Pelican, him grousing at his aunt the whole time—until he saw the woman she'd been so insistent he meet, and then he'd shut up. And thought: *Okay, maybe I'm interested.* She'd been wearing blue, his favorite color. Because of the sky.

And though he wasn't much of a talker, he'd already been drinking some that night and had found her easy to be with. She'd had the nicest smile of any woman he'd ever met.

He'd known good and well it was their damn anniversary when he walked out that door.

The problem with anniversaries being—they meant something. They marked something. They celebrated something. And he just hadn't wanted to make a big deal out of it. He hadn't wanted to be forced to think about what they were or where they were going or any of that shit. Just like when sorting fish, he was a one-day-at-a-time guy, an appreciating-the-moment guy. And he knew Meg wanted him to be more than that. But he just wasn't.

So taking off had seemed like the simplest thing to do—for both of them. Just removed any big question marks from the day.

Only he hadn't expected it to leave him feeling like shit.

Swallowing back his regret, he tried to refocus on what he was doing. Trouble with not having to think when you did your job was that it didn't always provide a distraction when you needed one. At sixteen, it had taken every ounce of concentration and fortitude he'd had to work on a fishing rig. But once more the thought struck him that nature made you adapt over time.

An hour later, the sun began to sink and Zack hauled up the anchor, started the motor, and sailed for Port Loyal. It was his home base of choice for the moment. Most fishing boats docked in one place permanently, but Zack had built a network of ports along the Eastern Michigan and Canadian coasts where he could always get a slip, connect with a wholesaler he knew there, and bargain for fresh ice the next morning.

A vague melancholy always settled into his bones as he turned for shore, though. Even when he wanted to go, even when he decided he'd had enough fishing for a while and wanted to head back to Meg. It was an old habit. Since his teenage years, the water had been his freedom, his escape. Nothing bad could happen when he was on the water. Nothing bad ever had.

And so even now, as the *Emily Ann* cut through the vast, dark waters, leaving a soft wake behind her on a brisk but bright day, that slight sense of being sorry to leave dropped over him like a blanket.

It would fade; it always did—life necessitated that, made it happen naturally enough. But it was always there, under the surface, making him wonder sometimes if he'd been born in the wrong time or place, if he just wasn't meant to exist in a world that required mingling with society. He knew Meg didn't understand that about him—*most* people didn't get that about him. Most people just didn't get that we aren't all wired exactly the same way.

The sun dipped toward the western horizon by the time he reached Port Loyal, a small, simple fishing town that had fallen into economic decline over the past ten years. A series of gray dilapidated docks, most of them unoccupied these days, lined the shore—above them, gray equally dilapidated buildings. A fluttering flock of gulls and the glow of dusk softened the landscape as he maneuvered into the slip he rented by the night from a paunchy old man with an unlit cigar always chomped between his teeth.

The few other fishing boats that called Port Loyal

home were already in for the evening, and the dock bustled with life, as it did for a brief period every morning and night. The scent of fish filled the air, though Zack was surprised he even noticed the smell anymore.

After he left the boat, walking the planked dock, a scrawny kid of about twenty in a sock cap approached him. "Looking for work," he said. "Used to help my dad on his boat, but we're out of business. You need any help, mister?"

A lot of loss shone in the kid's face. And there had been times when Zack could use a hand—times in the past, *better* times, when he'd hired on another guy or two for a week here or there. But besides the fact that he valued his time alone on the water, those days had vanished, along with the fish. "Can't afford it," he said to the boy. "You know how it is."

The kid pressed his lips together, flattened them out. Nodded. Trying not to let one more disappointment show. "Yep," he said.

And part of Zack wanted to give the kid some advice, tell him to go somewhere new, learn something, go to school of some kind, build a better life than you could fishing the Great Lakes these days. But it wasn't advice *he'd* have taken as a young man. And everyone had to travel his own road. So he just said, "Wish ya luck," and walked on.

What the Port Loyal Bar and Grill lacked in originality it made up for with cheap prices and decent food. It was one of the weathered gray buildings that stood near the docks, and Zack had eaten many a meal here over the years. He thought some fish and chips sounded good as he walked in the door, then found himself sidling up to the bar—first things first, he needed a beer.

A bartender he didn't know had just delivered it in a tall glass when a waitress he knew *very* well appeared at his side. Tonya was apple-cheeked and petite, sweet and a little too hungry for life. One more person who should've gotten the hell out of here a long time ago.

"Why, Zack Sheppard—aren't you a sight for sore eyes."

As sweet, and even cute, as she was, she hadn't crossed his mind since the last time he'd seen her, and he had no idea how long ago that was. "How's it going, Tonya?"

She flashed him a flirtatious grin. "Better *now.*" Then she leaned in close, close enough that he could smell her musky perfume, close enough to rub her breasts against his arm.

He'd passed the night with her on more than one occasion. Another good thing about freedom and having no ties.

Now she rose on her tiptoes, whispered in his ear. "If you're here for dinner, I could get off early." Then she drew back slightly, licked her heart-shaped lips. "Dessert at my place?"

Zack wondered for the first time why she wasn't married, why she wasn't making some guy's night as "dessert" every evening, why a slight air of desperation lurked underneath her seductive confidence. But then he understood. She'd been waiting for someone better. Someone better than she could get in Port Loyal. And he still hadn't come along. And life had probably gotten pretty disappointing for her by now.

Because she wasn't free at heart like him. She was more like Meg. She wanted more from her relationships than they were giving her.

And though he didn't like hurting her feelings—hell, he didn't like hurting *anyone's* feelings; he just seemed to do it a lot—he said, "Thanks, hon, but I'm beat—few long days on the water—and I'm gonna have a quiet night." He ended it with a wink. To assure her it was nothing personal. And it wasn't. But he'd lied—he wasn't overly tired.

"I'll be here 'til ten if you change your mind and wanna buy a girl a drink," she said, looking undaunted. He supposed a string of seasoned sailors toughened a gal up over the years.

"Maybe I will," he said.

But he was pretty sure he wouldn't.

And as she walked away, round tray in hand to collect empties from abandoned tables, he found himself pulling out his cell phone. And typing in a text: What's up, Maggie May?

He'd drunk half his beer, chatting on and off with the bartender about the weather, when her reply made the phone buzz on the bar. Not much. Had lunch with Suzanne today. How's the water?

He was pretty sure Suzanne didn't like him. But she was Meg's friend, so he always kept that to himself. And he'd never seen life as a popularity contest. He typed back: Good. Brought in a decent haul today.

Good, she answered.

He thought about what else to say. Most men would be more suave, or maybe just plain…considerate. He could say he missed her. He could say he loved her. Both were true. But he usually thought it was better to just keep that to himself, rather than build up expectations he wasn't ready to fulfill. The two of them were good the way they were, like he always told her.

Except maybe for that damn anniversary. Guilt niggled at him again as he spotted the wholesaler he dealt with entering the restaurant. Zack raised his hand in a wave and they talked business as he finished his beer and paid. Twenty minutes later the two worked together to transfer Zack's fish into a freezer truck the guy had pulled up to the dock, and they shook hands, agreeing to meet tomorrow night—same as tonight, same as last night. And on it would go until he decided to head to a different area, a different port town. Probably within another couple of days.

Most nights he slept on the boat. He didn't need much, liked things simple that way. But first he'd have to find dinner, and suddenly the fish and chips didn't seem like the wisest idea. He liked Tonya's company well enough—and even as much as he enjoyed his solitude, a little supper conversation wouldn't be bad—but he didn't want to give her the wrong idea.

So he walked to a Subway sandwich shop instead, thankful that it provided a whole different sort of solitude than the water. No one talked to him while he tried to eat—no one propositioned him and made him think about the reasons he'd turned Tonya down.

Unfortunately, though, he kept thinking about that anniversary anyway.

Wishing he'd waited a day to go now. Just one more day. Meg was a good woman and she deserved a good man. And he thought he *was* a good man, mostly—he just didn't always let it show.

He texted her again. You take care and have a good night, Maggie May.

It was an hour later, as darkness fell over the docks.

and he turned out the light over the cot in the *Emily Ann*'s wheelhouse, that he realized she'd never replied.

BY THE TIME Seth came walking up the road the next morning, emerging from the fog like a magician, Meg had prioritized tasks, and knew where she wanted him to begin. She felt organized about getting the inn into selling shape—if indeed that was the route she ended up taking.

"Mornin', darlin'," he said with that cool smile of his.

"Good morning," she greeted him, stepping out onto the front porch, her cable-knit sweater wrapped warm around her to ward off the chill.

That was when she noticed, realized, that he never wore a jacket or anything with sleeves—today the T-shirt was gray with some sort of insignia on it in navy, and like the others she'd seen him in, it fit well. "Don't you ever get cold?" she asked.

"Guess I'm just a hot-blooded animal," he told her, grin still in place. "And guess I thought it'd be warmer by this time of year."

"A lot of places maybe," she told him. "But not on Summer Island just yet."

How many women had he seduced with that smile, that Southern drawl?

As she pondered that, though, while they entered the house together, another question came to mind: What would it be like to *be* one of those women? A woman who lets herself be seduced? With no further idea of where things will go, with no further *care* about it, either. What would it be like to be that woman—the one who just lived in the moment, appreciated the passion for what it was worth?

And then a certain irony struck her. *If you could do that, you'd be Zack's dream woman.*

Only it was too late with Zack—she already loved him. Once you loved, it all came with stakes.

"You decide what you want me to do first?" Seth asked as they stepped into the foyer.

She pointed toward the kitchen. "The cabinets. And kitchen floor. I have some ideas to run by you."

"Sounds good," he said. Then chivalrously held out his hand. "After you."

He followed her with his toolbox, and only when they reached the kitchen did she remember scrambled eggs still sat in a skillet on the stove, left over from the breakfast she'd made for herself a little while ago. "Um, have you eaten? There are extra eggs."

She watched his face, wondering at the indecipherable emotions flitting swiftly across it. And when he finally said, "I'm not much of a breakfast eater, but thanks," she understood.

Pride. That was what she saw. One of the things anyway.

She wondered if he was hungry. And wondered a million other things, too—among them, where he'd really come from and what his life was about. "They'll go to waste," she said, "so I wish you'd eat some. But if you really don't want them, I'll throw them out."

She tried not to look at him then. Because of the pride. She didn't want him to feel studied. Men were so...odd about that. Zack was the same way. So she moved toward the counter, started tidying things up—lowering her dirty plate into the sink, brushing some toast crumbs into her palm—acting as if she couldn't really care less if he ate the eggs or not. But there was something about men, men who in ways were surely still little boys inside, that made her want to take care of them a little.

"Well, if you're gonna throw 'em away, I'll eat 'em," he said. As if he were doing her a favor. And in a way, he was. She liked that he'd let the bit of pride go. And that he'd let her give him something he'd at first been reluctant to take.

"Good," she said, turning to him with a quick, short smile. "I hate to waste food. And this way I won't have to hear your stomach growling up until lunchtime."

And with that, she dumped the remaining pile of eggs on a plate, and without asking him, dropped two slices of bread in the toaster.

Rather than argue about that, he was gracious. "You're a mighty fine hostess, Meg darlin'."

She blew it off. "I run an inn, so it's second nature to me."

A minute later, she set the plate before him, along with a fork—and then went so far as to pour him a glass of orange juice, also without asking—indeed following that innkeeper's instinct to attend to people's needs and make them comfortable. But after that she joined him at the table and began telling him her ideas for the room's makeover while he ate.

"I'm thinking of having you do the cabinets and table in a pale farmhouse vintage sort of yellow—lighter than the outside of the inn but in the same general hue—and adding some sort of antiqued or distressed look like you mentioned. And then refinishing the hardwood, maybe staining it a warm, matte pine shade. Does that sound like...it works at all?" She wasn't sure and truly wanted his opinion.

He shoveled a forkful of eggs into his mouth while appearing to think it over. "Yep, I like it. It'll bring a lot more character to the space. I can show you some treatments—glazes and such. Might have to order 'em online, but shouldn't take long to get 'em." Then he glanced in the general direction of town and pointed with his fork. "Anyplace to buy paint here?"

She nodded, smiled. "Fulton's Hardware."

"Good—I can start painting while we're waiting for other supplies to arrive." And though he'd sounded all business for a minute, now his expression softened, and he looked at her more like…like he was really trying to see her. "So after a couple days' thought, you're still moving forward with this? Putting the inn up for sale?"

She pursed her lips, remaining uneasy at the idea but remembering that moving forward in life often meant pushing beyond one's comfort zone. And maybe she'd gotten far too comfortable here. And far too comfortable with the circumstances and options life on the island had afforded her. "Yes. Though, just for the record, I'm not telling anyone yet."

"Except me," he pointed out.

"Except you." The unwitting decision, she realized suddenly, made him seem…important. Like someone she confided in. No, not *like* someone—just someone. She'd made him her confidant without quite planning it. And now he knew a secret about her no one else did.

"It's none of my business, darlin', but…what about your aunt you mentioned? If you move, won't she miss having you here, having family nearby?"

Meg swallowed back a lump of old mourning and shook her head. "No," she said, the word coming out in a lower, darker tone than intended. But she pressed

forward. "She died. A couple of years ago. Cancer."
She stopped, blinked, nodded. "I know. It's touched my
life more than once. But so it goes. And in fact…" She
tried to smile. "Her being gone would actually make it
easier to leave."

He tipped his head back solemnly. "Sorry about that.
You loved her."

Stated as certainly as the fact that the sky was blue.
And it reminded her how transparent she was in ways.
"Yes," she confirmed shortly. "And I have a lot of good
friends here, but losing her changed things for me. After
my grandma was gone, Aunt Julia was kind of…my
cornerstone, you might say."

"Cornerstone," he repeated, clearly taking that in
and thinking it over, and she could tell the metaphorical concept was a new one to him.

And in an odd way, it was new to her, too—at least
in terms that were so personal. She'd not realized before she said it that Aunt Julia had been the linchpin,
the thing that held her so firmly here. That and the
memories of her grandma. But memories were…mist.
You couldn't touch them. You couldn't hold on to them
or depend on them.

She loved her friends and neighbors. She loved
Dahlia's unique and quirky nature and the easy way
she looked at life. She loved Suzanne's affection, her
irreverence, her loyalty, and even sometimes her advice. She loved the sense of community she felt all
around her here. And she loved the coming of spring,
and further, the arrival of summer—perhaps more than
she had before she lived here because it was so long
in coming that it made you value it more, hold on to

it with greater reverence. But despite all she had here, she still missed her aunt.

Meg sometimes even puttered around in Petal Pushers, watering flowers and such. She pretended she was just being helpful to Suzanne, killing off-season boredom. But it was really about memories of being there with Aunt Julia over the years, and it always forced her to think about the passage of time, and that no matter how much things stayed the same, anywhere, they were really always changing, a slow and constant shift of circumstances that moved forward whether you wanted them to or not.

"I'm beginning to realize," she said to Seth, "that no matter how simple a life you build, nothing stays the same forever. So I think I'm ready to…start something new."

"Well, darlin', you know I'm more than willing to help you out with that." And when he ended on a playful look, she realized she'd set herself up for it, and that peering into his sexy eyes right at this moment made it—him—seem like…a possibility. A thing that could be easy if she let it.

But even as she suffered a tender ache in her breasts that rippled all the way down through the small of her back, she again pushed the notion aside. For all the same reasons.

His youth. Or maybe the fact that she felt older than she really was.

And that she already had a man. Sort of.

Reasons that actually didn't sound very convincing. No wonder Suzanne had argued.

Rather than respond to that, she asked him, "Who are *your* cornerstones, Seth Darden?" He'd finished eating, so she stood up from the table, picked up his empty plate, carried it to the sink.

"Not sure I've ever had any, darlin'," he said, and though it struck her as sad—sad enough that she turned toward him, unplanned—he wore his usual confident, pleased-with-life expression as he wiped his mouth with a napkin. "And if nothing stays the same, just fine with me that I don't."

Could a man really be that content to have no ties? She tilted her head, looked him in the eye, deciding to dig a little. "No family?"

"Not really."

She teased him. "So you, what, hatched from an egg?"

A small grin curved the corners of his mouth. "Well, let's just say none worth making cornerstones of—how's that?" He softened it further with his trademark wink. Sometimes that wink was a flirtation—but other times, like now, it was an assurance, his way of promising you everything was okay, that he had it all under control.

"You don't talk much about yourself," she boldly pointed out. He was bold as hell with *her*, after all.

"Not much to tell," he claimed, tossing his napkin on the table.

"I don't believe that," she countered. "And I feel like I've told you a lot about me, so it hardly seems fair."

But her handyman, true to form, just replied with an arresting grin that moved all through her. "You're a far more interesting subject to me, darlin'."

It wasn't self-deprecation—he was paying her a compliment. It felt thin, since he was diverting. But charmers gonna charm.

"Now let's talk about this kitchen. You have your yellow picked out yet or do we need to walk down to Fulton's and get some paint swatches?"

CHAPTER EIGHT

THE THING SETH remembered most about this house was the nooks and crannies. Loose floorboards, secret holes in cupboards. Places to hide things.

At ten, creating mysteries had seemed like important business. Now he was more concerned with unraveling them.

The truth was, it was a beautiful old house filled with details. Unique hand-carved crown moldings. Built-ins throughout. A home clearly constructed with loving care, and though he'd had few attachments in life, he could understand Meg's to the inn. Part of him was even sorry she might sell it. If he were ever going to let himself be attached to anything—a place, a home like this—seemed worthy of it. Safer. Than other things. Like money. Or people.

After giving the kitchen a thorough looking-over, they'd decided he'd redo the floor first. Taking up the linoleum and sanding the hardwood would give Meg a little time to select colors, and also clear the cabinets and counters. Fortunately, the fridge could be moved into her office and stay plugged in.

And though he liked being around her, he was glad that at the moment she'd gone outside to work in a flower bed by the mailbox. It was important she get comfortable leaving him alone in the house. It was important he earn her trust, and with it the private time he'd need to look for what he'd come here to find.

It was likely upstairs somewhere, though. In one of the bedrooms. He wasn't sure which, because he couldn't remember any details other than a hiding place. A good hiding place for secret things. So he hoped she'd have some work for him to do on the second floor after he finished other projects.

Though it seemed like a good idea to take a hard look at all the house's bookshelves, too. Just in case. If someone else had found the book—and they might have, because he'd hidden it a long damn time ago—possibly it could have ended up in such a spot. And hell, by that logic, he supposed any room in the house was fair game.

As he pried up the old linoleum with a crowbar, he was glad to see the hardwood remained in great shape. In fact, he might even recommend to Meg that she leave it as is, without stain. Refinishing the aged wood in its natural colors would make it feel even more rustic. Hard to understand why someone would cover it up. He liked the idea of letting it see the light of day, making it new again.

It was something that sustained him these days—bringing things back to life, putting damaged things back in good repair. He wished he'd appreciated that all along, but at least he did now. Better late than never.

He soon opened a door to a small broom closet, which Meg had already emptied, and began ripping up the linoleum inside. And that was when he felt something peculiar—the wood giving way beneath the pressure of the crowbar. Once the linoleum was gone, he could see that two corner boards were loose, broken.

Funny, it brought back a memory. Of that hiding place of his. Only on the wrong floor of the house. And he supposed he would need to repair the boards to do a good job, but part of him wished he could just leave them as they were—a further little piece of character, history, authenticity.

Slipping the edge of a large screwdriver in beside one of the planks, he applied a little leverage and it raised freely. Lifting it out, he set it aside, then easily removed the broken piece next to it, as well.

Underneath, a subfloor, about four inches down. And a dark shadow toward the cupboard's edge, underneath adjoining boards.

Grabbing a flashlight from his toolbox, he shone it on the shadow—and made out a flat wooden box, an old cigar box. Rose-o-Cuba.

He pulled it out. And knew he should probably give it directly to Meg, because it was technically her property, but he was too drawn to the mystery of it—so he opened it up instead.

Inside, he saw the belongings of…well, he'd guess it was the keepsakes of a young girl. Ribbons tied around letters. A couple of very old greeting cards, including a vintage-looking Valentine. Two pictures of Elvis Presley cut from a magazine, one from the blond hair days. And a small red leather book with the word *Diary* embossed in faded gold on the front.

He closed the lid. Now that he'd seen what was inside, his curiosity had been fed and he'd give it to Meg. But he felt an instant if unlikely kinship with the girl who'd once hidden the box beneath these floorboards. How odd to know he wasn't the only one who'd ever hidden secrets in this house.

MEG PLANTED WHITE alyssum and lavender petunias around the white wooden mailbox post, the loose dirt cool on her fingers. As she worked, she thought about other outdoor tasks for the coming weeks—more flowers to be planted around the porch and in the bed along the brook, garden paths to groom, lilac bushes to be pruned after their blooming season. But she was getting ahead of herself. The lilac buds were just now taking full shape, hadn't even opened yet. She loved the lilacs—they were a special part of the place, and a real measuring stick in her mind. They marked the transition of spring into summer, and by the time all the blooms faded each year, summer had begun in earnest.

She thought more about the colors for the kitchen, the precise yellow hue for the cabinets and the exact shade of stain for the floor. Digging in the dirt always grounded her, helped her make good decisions—and it wasn't long before she knew which shades from the swatches were the winners. And nothing about that digging was changing her mind about moving forward with this plan.

How strange it had felt to walk up Harbor Street with Seth to the hardware store. She'd felt obligated to introduce him to a number of people who'd been out and about, including Dahlia, who'd been busily planting her usual, colorful trademark dahlias around the café's white wooden sign and front walk. And a pattern had developed. She'd felt people's stares, confusion, that she should suddenly be strolling through town with a handsome guy they didn't know. But the second she introduced him as a handyman doing some improvements on her place, the muscles in their faces relaxed, all the tension fading away. And when Seth shook hands and turned on the Southern drawl with all the nice-to-meet-yous and offers of his services later in the summer, most people were welcoming—while just a few stayed pleasant but notably, visibly, more wary.

Which surprised her at first. Islanders were usually trusting, just as she'd tried to explain to Suzanne over and over. But then she understood. He was a little too handsome. A little too perfect. A little too good to be true. Even with her vouching for him. And that…said something. Reminded her. *Was* he a little too good to be true? And what made him so secretive about his family, his past?

Of course, if he's just your handyman, as you keep claiming to yourself and everyone else, his past is none of your business and why should you even care?

It was just impossible not to be curious. There were ways in which they'd gotten…personal rather quickly, after all. But the better she got to know him in some ways, the more of a complete mystery he seemed in others.

She'd tried to read Dahlia's reaction to meeting him, but hadn't been able to. If she thought anything was fishy about Meg's new handyman, she hadn't let it show. And she, more than some people, probably understood that Meg might need some help since Zack had left without warning, as usual.

And so the seed has been planted. Just like the flowers she'd picked up at Petal Pushers a little while ago. The seed had been planted around Summer Island that Meg had a new handyman, and word would travel down Harbor Street and beyond quickly. What remained to be seen was if anyone thought there was any more to it than that.

"I missed him?" Suzanne had groused when Meg stopped in for her first batch of flowers for the year a little while ago.

"You can come meet him if you're dying to so badly," Meg had offered.

But Suzanne had simply shaken her head. "I'm sure it'll happen soon enough—but I do look forward to seeing what I think of him."

"I hope you'll be friendlier to him than you were to Beck Grainger," Meg said offhandedly as she'd wavered between varieties of petunias.

Standing behind the shop's counter, her friend had sighed. "Yeah, that was insane, I know. I felt like I was in high school or something." She rolled her eyes. "I wasn't good with boys then, either."

In a way, it surprised her to hear that. Suzanne was usually so confident. "Well, just try not to be mean. To either of them. Just be your normal self."

"It was so easy with Cal." Her late husband. "That's what I miss most about him. The ease. Since then, most men have just made me want to shoot them."

"I know, but…even the men here?"

"Well, okay, not most of them. Most of them are married or not particularly attractive. For some reason, the attractive, available ones just make me feel threatened or something. Just by virtue of having the same traits as the last jerkwads who shit all over me." She shook her head. "That's why I came here. I didn't think I'd have to deal with handsome men who made me want to do things with them. And just between you and me, I hope Beck Grainger keeps his distance."

"Well, sounds like if the poor man comes anywhere near you again, you'll inspire him to."

Suzanne had shrugged. "A girl can hope."

Finishing up, Meg pushed to her feet and peered down on the happy flowers. Petunias had been her grandmother's favorite annuals. "Always so vibrant," she would say. "Like happy little trumpets announcing that summer is here." And so, although she added other types of flowers to the beds and pots and gardens, the lawn and grounds of Summerbrook Inn were thick with petunias every year. In honor of Gran.

Stepping inside, she made her way to the hall bathroom downstairs to wash the soil off her hands since she hadn't worn gardening gloves. Life as an innkeeper had long since made her give up on manicures, and she felt closer to the earth—and somehow to Gran—by actually sinking her fingers into the dirt.

She walked out of the bathroom—and practically collided with Seth as he exited one of the first floor guestrooms. "Oh!" Then pulled up short, then blinked, glancing toward the doorway he'd just passed through. "Were you in…?" She pointed. Because no work was taking place in that part of the house. No work was taking place outside the kitchen, in fact.

He grinned. "Caught me," he said. "Heard something fall and sounded like it came from there, so I went to check it out."

"Ah." She tipped her head back. "Did you find anything? Every now and then, Miss Kitty swishes her tail the wrong way and sends something crashing."

"Nah—false alarm." He gave his head a short shake. "Or I misjudged the direction of the noise—maybe that tail swish happened someplace else, so be on the lookout."

She smiled. "Will do." Then motioned back toward

the front door. "I have some gardening tools to put away out front, so I'm headed back out."

It was probably less than a minute later, though, as she stooped down to collect her trowel and some empty plastic flower trays, that the front screen door slammed and she looked up to see Seth on the front porch and heading her way, carrying a box of some kind.

"What's that?" she asked.

"Almost forgot—I actually *did* find something—just not from a tail swish or in that room. This was under some loose boards in the kitchen, under the linoleum," he told her.

"Really?" She squinted to look harder.

"Guessin' it's been there a long time."

She blinked, studying the wooden box as he came closer down the front walk. A cigar box. So strange and surprising to know it had been hiding beneath the kitchen floor longer than the linoleum had been there— her whole life. All this time, literally right under her feet, without her knowledge.

And yet, on second thought, maybe not so strange at all. Maybe it made all the sense in the world, in fact. Especially if she could determine that it had been put there by Gran.

She took the box, then motioned back toward the porch. "Let's sit down on the steps."

Once there, she cautiously lifted the lid—then smiled, her heart lighting up. Yes, the cigar box had been Gran's. She could tell by a mere glimpse of the contents. And it actually made her let out a laugh.

"Something funny in there, darlin'?" Seth asked next to her.

She shifted her glance to him, then back to the box.

"My grandma loved hiding things in this old house," she told him. "She was famous for sending my sister and me on treasure hunts on rainy days—and sometimes they even led outdoors if the day was nice. We were always finding little gifts and notes tucked here and there—and trust me, there are a million little hiding places." Then she shook her head, still smiling, happy, feeling connected to Gran. "But I never knew it went back that far, that she'd been hiding things all the way back to when she was a young girl. Or that there were hiding places I've never even known about." She met his gaze again. "Looks like this house has secrets even from me, after all these years."

"Dare I ask what was so precious that she hid it away?" her handsome handyman asked.

"My grandma loved Elvis," she told Seth, picking up one of the cutout pictures of The King between her fingertips. "But she told me her parents didn't approve—rock 'n' roll was new and controversial back then, and the way he moved his hips was considered scandalous." She let her eyes widen playfully on Seth, then peered back down at the magazine pictures. "So she must have hidden these little pictures just to steal away and look at privately when she could."

"Sounds like she was a rebel," he imparted with a grin.

The suggestion made Meg chuckle, and she somehow felt a little closer to Gran than ever before—albeit in a slightly sad way—to envision her as a young girl with a secret crush she couldn't share with the grownups in her life.

Next she reached for a Valentine featuring a cartoon-type puppy holding a big heart in his mouth that said,

Be Mine, Valentine. She opened it up and read the inscription: "To the girl I love. J.T." "This…looks like it's from my grandfather. They started dating in high school." It made her laugh a little and tilt her head, though, as she mused aloud, "But…we knew him as John. I think his middle name was Thomas, but I never knew he went by J.T."

Then she realized there was another smaller card stuck to the back of it—pulling them apart, she saw that this one was a birthday card, the front showing two white kittens playing with a ball of yarn. Apparently baby animals had always been in vogue in the greeting card world. And she flipped it open—to find an entirely different handwriting than on the other. "To my best girl! Ace."

She flinched. *Ace?* Who the hell was Ace?

"What's wrong?" Seth asked.

She kept staring at it. "This *isn't* from my grandfather." She held up the first one. "This one is. But this other one isn't." She shook her head, still studying the words, as if it would somehow make the past clearer.

"Looks like maybe your grandma had more secrets than just a couple pictures of Elvis," Seth put forth.

Meg nodded slowly, still taken aback. "Yes, it does. Though…" She let her brow knit. "Who knows—maybe it wasn't a secret at all. A girl, even back then, could go out with more than one guy. And I guess grandmothers don't sit around telling their family about every boy they ever dated. But…it's interesting to me. To find out she had romances, boyfriends, I never knew about."

Next to her, Seth shrugged. "Guess it's hard to know *everything* about anybody. Guess every person has their secrets."

She met his gaze, wondered if he could read her thoughts. *What are yours?*

But he looked away, down at a book in the box—a diary. "Probably find out more about Ace in there."

She flattened her lips together, thinking. "A diary is such a private thing. I don't know if I should read it."

"Ever keep one?" he asked her.

She shook her head. "Never saw the point. Just a bunch of words no one else will ever read."

He cast her a speculative look. "Guess if you read *this* one, there'd be a point. Maybe there's stuff in there she'd want you to know."

"I WAS THINKING of grilling hamburgers tonight—if you'd like to stay." She'd been waffling about whether to issue the invitation, but she was in the mood to grill again, and something about Seth delivering up lost parts of her grandmother had her feeling grateful…and a little more connected to him as well, mysterious or not.

It struck her that between him and this Ace character, mysteries suddenly abounded at the Summerbrook Inn.

He knelt next to his toolbox on the kitchen floor, now bare but for leftover patches of old glue from the linoleum. Despite having picked a color, she'd decided, on his suggestion, to leave the floor bare of stain. He took a moment before replying, but then got to his feet to say, "You're a generous woman, Meg darlin', but you don't have to feed me every meal."

His eyes said he thought it was charity. And breakfast—maybe that *had* been some combination of charity and that urge to take care of someone who might need it. But this was…more selfish. "Maybe I'd like the company," she said gently. Wondering as the words came out if he would read something into them, think she was growing more open to his pursuit.

She wasn't. She really wasn't.

Even if the way he was looking at her right now made her a little weak in the knees. Even if something in the scent of his sweat actually turned her on a little.

When he didn't reply, she added playfully, "If it'll make you feel better, I can always deduct it from your pay."

It brought a laugh. And a better answer. "Okay, you talked me into it. I'll have a burger."

"Good."

"As long as you let me do the grilling."

"I know—you're a grill master."

He nodded. "Damn straight, woman—now point me toward the tongs."

Half an hour later they sat on the patio eating. She'd again kindled a few flames in the firepit while he'd cooked—and she'd added more corn on the cob to the menu and baked beans from a can that she emptied into a small, shallow pot on the grill. Dusk dropped a shadowy veil over the island that came with the need for a sweater, even next to the fire. But as usual, Seth didn't seem to notice the chill.

"I've decided I'm going to read it," she informed him of the diary after they'd finished eating.

In fact, she hadn't been able to stop thinking about it since he'd found it. And she'd concluded that he was right—maybe Gran would want someone to know whatever she'd had to say about her life back then. And already it had begun to feel like a rare gift—this opportunity to look at the world through her grandma's teenage eyes.

"In fact, I'm going to start tonight. I'm going to curl up in bed with it after you leave."

Something in that made Seth chuckle.

"What's so funny?" she asked.

"Nothin'," he said. "Guess I can just think of better things to be excited about curling up in bed with, darlin'—that's all."

She tilted her head, gave him a look. No wine tonight—they were drinking soda. She'd decided that maybe wine and her didn't mix if Seth Darden was in the equation. But she still followed the urge to say, "Just when I think you're done with this topic, that you're all business—I'm wrong and you're not."

"What topic is that?" he asked, all sly-faced and clearly egging her on.

"Your…pursuit of me. Or brash flirtation," she added—in case it was, in fact, only that and she was making too much of it. "Whichever it is."

He leaned back in his patio chair, looking relaxed and confident. "Pursuit's a fair way to describe it."

Okay, that answered that.

Then he grinned. "And I do manage for fairly long stretches, in my personal opinion, to behave at least somewhat professionally with you. But what can I say? You bring out the devil in me."

She saw that in his eyes just then—the devil. Seduction. Sex.

That magnetic chemistry she experienced with him never went completely away when in his presence, but at that moment, it was strong as ever, so strong that she felt locked in place, held down tight, by his eyes. She couldn't look away. And wasn't sure she wanted to.

She felt almost as if she *had* drunk some wine.

Maybe Seth was intoxicating enough without adding alcohol.

Questions flitted through her mind. *How long can this go on? How long can this simmering tension last before...something happens?* Before the temptation to be "that woman"—the one who lets herself be seduced, the one who could enjoy a hot fling—made her give in? Could she keep wearing her practical, no-nonsense face all summer—at least at long enough intervals to hold the attraction at bay? Or would there come a moment, like this one, or like the other night, when the pull, the curiosity, the scorching chemistry, would become too great?

Maybe he *was* a fallen angel. Maybe his secrets, his mysteries, were bad ones. Maybe, for all she knew, he was dangerous as hell.

But maybe in the end, none of that would matter. Maybe in the end, the devil in him would win.

She was torn from her thoughts, from the heat seeming to sear her skin—both from the fire and Seth's eyes—when a deep, familiar voice cut through the silence.

"Where are you, Maggie May? Out here?"

Then the back screen door slammed and Zack was walking toward her—his expression darkening in the firelight when he realized she wasn't alone.

CHAPTER NINE

MEG HAD NEVER been so stunned in her life. Zack *never* came back this soon. *Ever.*

And the scene on the patio looked far different than it was. Well, sort of. It looked like a date—which it wasn't.

As she instinctively pushed to her feet, she heard his name spill from her lips. "Zack."

And saw the stark confusion still coloring his face. Not much caught Zack Sheppard off guard or left him looking befuddled, but this had. "Um—maybe I should have called first?" The words came out low, with just a hint of sarcasm—but also with the unspoken acknowledgment that, shocked as he was, he didn't have the right to be angry.

And maybe Meg took a tiny speck of pleasure in that—but at the same time, she impulsively rushed to explain the situation, which felt extremely awkward all the way around.

"This is Seth—he's doing some work around the house. He's a handyman."

Zack's gray-green eyes flitted from her to Seth, to the fire, then back again to her. "Um, okay."

"I invited him to have a burger after a long day of work," she went on. Thank *God* there were no wineglasses—for more reasons than one now.

"Okay," he said again.

That was when Seth stood up as well, came forward, and offered Zack his hand. "Seth Darden," he said. "Good to meet you."

Zack hesitated. And Meg wanted to kill him. Seth was trying to do the right thing, be a decent guy, and Zack wouldn't let him.

But Seth kept his hand out, even as the cool evening air thickened with tension. Meg's stomach churned.

And finally Zack accepted the handshake. Gave a curt nod instead of words.

But it all still felt just as awkward for the grudging way it was done.

"Thanks for the burger," Seth said to Meg, "and I'll say goodnight. I'll swing by Fulton's to pick up the sander tomorrow morning."

She nodded. "Goodnight." And tried to tell him with her eyes that she appreciated everything he was doing—leaving graciously, and validating her explanation through his comment about renting a sander.

As Seth disappeared around the corner of the inn on the stone walkway, she thought Zack should feel embarrassed, or apologetic, but she could see he didn't. And she wondered if he could feel it, too—the chemistry between her and her handyman.

She didn't know what to say and they stared at each other for a long, strange moment. Her heart beat too hard. She considered defending herself some more, but why should she? No matter how you sliced it, she'd done nothing wrong.

Finally he said, "You know you can do what you want, Meg. I'm just caught off guard, that's all."

She let her eyes widen on him. "I know I can do what I want, too, but I'm not doing what you clearly think.

I'm getting some help on some things around here, and being nice enough to offer the guy something to eat because he seems a little down on his luck."

Zack still looked entirely perplexed by it all. "Where the hell did he even come from?" He gave his head a slight shake.

"He's here for the summer, to work."

Now it was Zack whose eyes widened. "And you're just…letting a stranger have the run of the place? Letting him come and go in the house?"

She tried to give him a little perspective. "I let strangers come and go in the house all summer, Zack."

He tilted his head, clearly thinking all this through. Then pointed vaguely in the direction Seth had departed. "Since he seemed to be leaving…he's not staying here?"

"No." She let out a harrumph, tiring quickly of being grilled. "But what if he was? It's an inn."

His critical look implied that she was being foolish. "There's a big difference between summer vacationers and one lone guy you don't even know."

"I'm capable of handling those types of decisions on my own, thank you very much."

He tipped his head back in sarcasm. "Ah—well, sorry I give a shit about your safety." He stopped, ran a hand back through his wavy hair—then looked at her again, clearly still trying to wrap his head around this. "What on earth is it he's doing for you?"

"He helped paint and rehang the shutters. And now I'm having him refinish the hardwood under the old linoleum in the kitchen."

He drew back slightly at that—maybe since she'd never mentioned wanting that done before, or because he'd apparently walked right over the newly revealed wood without noticing.

"If you needed help, Meg, why didn't you just ask me?"

"You weren't here."

He stayed quiet and she knew they both felt the weight of the statement.

"What are you doing here *now* anyway? I mean, you *never* come back this fast."

He looked down at his work boots, then back up—to earnestly meet her gaze. "Would you prefer I hadn't?"

"I didn't say that. I'm just surprised."

"I came back…because I felt bad about the way I left."

Meg sighed. This was new. And maybe it meant something. Something good. Maybe it was the kind of change she'd spent a long while hoping to see in him. And yet, at the moment, she felt weary. Weary of feeling neglected. Weary of their relationship operating on his whims. So she quietly pointed out, "That's *always* the way you leave."

A small glint of guilt flickered in his eyes, but he moved past it quickly. "I came back because I know it was…our anniversary. And I felt bad about it. Regretted going when I did."

Hmm. If Zack had ever felt bad about any decision he'd made regarding her, this was the first time he'd bothered to tell her. So, again, it seemed almost like… a breakthrough of sorts. In fact, the confession left her downright shocked.

But so did all of this. Seeing him when she'd least expected it. Having him find her eating with Seth. She pursed her lips, and asked, "Did Dahlia tell you that? That it was our anniversary?"

He looked a little thrown by the question, but said, "No. I knew."

"It's hard to decide if I should be happy you knew and came back—or hurt that you knew and left."

He tried for a sweet smile. "The first one."

It had always been difficult to stay mad at him for long, and his eyes on her now turned her heart full, heavy in her chest. Her emotions for him felt more confusing than ever, but the fact that he'd come back counted for something. She looked toward the grill, beside which rested a plate with two extra hamburgers on it. "Have you eaten?"

He shook his head.

"Want a burger? I can toss it back on the grill for a few minutes, heat it up. And there are extra beans."

"Sounds good," he said solemnly. "Thanks." Then he stepped closer, lifted one hand to her cheek, and lowered a small kiss to her lips. The familiar taste of him moved through her like something comfortable, safe.

But was it? Was it safe to love a man who was always leaving?

Sadly, she couldn't be certain she was happy to have him home. Maybe the damage had already been done. And to find out he'd known about their anniversary and still left—that wasn't much better, and was maybe actually much worse, than when she'd thought he didn't have a clue.

She reheated the leftovers while he went back inside to wash up. After flipping the burger, she pulled her sweater tight around her, and for a short moment, hated it here. Hated the often relentless chill. Hated the dearth of options—about anything, from men to hardware stores. Hated feeling trapped. And wanted to be anywhere else in the world.

Or…maybe she just didn't want to be where she was in this moment—with a man she both loved and resented, in a situation where she didn't know how to find complete happiness. A few minutes ago, laughing with Seth, life had seemed simpler.

But only because he's new, like a new flavor of ice cream, and you don't really know him yet. Everyone has issues; everyone comes with baggage. Hell, Seth won't answer simple questions even after you practically told him your life story. You were only happier being with him because he's never hurt you.

So Zack had come back.

And that meant something even if she wasn't sure what.

And thus in the time it took for him to wash his face and hands, she resolved to be pleased about that, and to see where it led them.

He, too, seemed calmer and more contrite when he exited the back door again, carrying a can of soda from the fridge.

"That hardwood looks to be in good shape," he said, pointing over his shoulder to the kitchen. "I didn't even know it was there."

She nodded as she handed him a plate, complete with the burger on a bun, and they moved to the same table where she'd sat with Seth a few minutes ago. "Gran put the linoleum down before I was born, but I always knew there was hardwood underneath. A shame she covered it—I think it's going to look great."

He gave a nod as he dressed his burger with lettuce,

a tomato slice, and some mayonnaise. "Seems like everybody was covering up hardwood in the sixties and seventies."

She asked how the fishing had been going, and he caught her up on the past few days on the water—he'd set some nets the first day, had a small catch the next day, better the day after that. He'd been fishing off the coast of Port Loyal, below Michigan's thumb.

She told him she'd started planting flowers, and she'd taken some new room reservations. Without going into detail on the work Seth would be doing, she said the kitchen should be finished in plenty of time for the first guests' arrival in a couple of weeks. She added that she thought Miss Kitty might have gone into hiding with all the activity in the house. "I put her water and food bowls in the hallway, but haven't seen her all day." The closest she'd come was the mystery sound Seth had reported earlier.

"She's on a shelf in the nook right now," Zack informed her. "Probably happy to have some quiet in there."

She nodded, glad the cat had surfaced.

And then he said, "I forgot about the shutters. Sorry, Maggie May."

"It's okay," she lied—she saw no point in dredging her anger back up. "But…you understand why I hired someone. I tried to do them myself and it was too much."

"I get it," he said. "My fault for forgetting. And leaving."

"It's nice," she acknowledged softly, "that you came back."

"I didn't want you to think the anniversary didn't matter to me at all."

"Does it?" She wasn't trying to be snide, but the words left her before she could stop them. "Because… I mean, if you knew, why'd you leave?"

He didn't answer right away. Took a big bite of his burger. A forkful of beans. Washed them down with a long swig of Coke. "I want to be honest with you."

"Good," she said. Though the words sounded ominous.

"It's been five years, right?"

She nodded.

"I guess I just worried that…you'd see it as a big thing, like…a turning point or something. I was afraid you might decide it was time to start pushing for a commitment. One I might not be ready to make."

She took that in, nodding slowly the whole time. Just what every girl wants to hear—*I'm not ready to give you a commitment after five years together.*

"But I love you," he added.

He didn't say it often. Only occasionally.

You love me but you ran away from me because you don't want to commit to me after five years. She just nodded again, though, because the words seemed…silly to say. Almost redundant, since he was saying them already, just in a more roundabout way.

And though she hadn't planned on telling him this, now it made sense. "I'm thinking of selling the inn at the end of the summer."

His fork paused midair, on the way to his mouth, the baked beans falling off and back to his plate. "What?"

"I'm thinking of selling the inn. And going somewhere new."

"Somewhere *new*?" He'd repeated it as if the word were offensive. "Jesus, Meg. *This* is sudden." She could see she'd given him yet another huge shock—but there was no other way to say it.

"That's why I'm taking the summer to think it over," she calmly replied. Though even as she'd voiced it, it hit her...that this wasn't really so sudden at all. Maybe it had been coming for a very long time.

He was blinking at her now, fork still in his hand but seemingly forgotten. "Where on earth would you go? I mean..." He shook his head, clearly dumbfounded.

"I have no idea," she told him, the very concept actually making her feel gleeful, carefree. "I just know that... I'm not really happy here. Not really fulfilled. Not the way things are."

Because of you. She didn't have to say that part—he heard it anyway.

So she added, "Perhaps we should both use the summer to think about what we want."

Across from her, he nodded. And she could sense this brand new idea sitting between them on the table: What would life be like without each other? *Completely* without each other. Even with Zack's frequent absences, they had become comfortable habits in each other's lives. She'd become his home base, the place he always returned to. And she'd become the proverbial woman who stood out on a widow's walk, watching for her sailor to come home—far too often.

Zack's brow knit and he glanced down at his plate, then back up at her. "Damn, this is big, Meg."

"I know. I don't mean to drop it on you when you came back trying to be nice."

Their gazes met, seeming to cement the strong connection between them—but how strong could it be when he couldn't even say he wanted her to be the only woman in his life?

He blew out a breath. "I wish I could stay longer, honey—give us some time to talk more about this, work through it."

And her heart dropped. She wished that, too. Until this second, she'd thought maybe he would, since he clearly grasped the gravity of her announcement. "So you're...not? Staying?"

His gaze fell away from hers, a small sigh escaping him. "I can't."

"When?"

"Tomorrow."

"Oh." She tried to sound unaffected, but didn't pull it off.

"It's almost June, Maggie May—high season. I set more nets before coming home. I can't afford not to put decent weather to use."

She nodded. "It's fine."

"I know it's not and I'm sorry."

But she insisted, now shaking her head. "Really, it's fine. I understand." And with that, she stood up, ready to end the conversation—since nothing more needed to be said. "I'm going to start cleaning this up—you should finish eating before it gets cold."

And then Zack was on his feet, as well. Reaching out to grab her hand, squeeze it in his, step close to her. "I don't care about eating. Let's go upstairs so I can show you how much I miss you when I'm gone."

And it almost came as a surprise to her when she was the one now saying, "I can't."

She sensed his whole body going rigid with yet one more little shock. He blinked. "You can't?"

For more reason than one, not the least of which was the undeniable attraction she'd suffered for her handyman less than an hour ago. But the part she could tell Zack, maybe *should* tell Zack even though she never had before was, "I don't know if you'll understand this, but…every time you leave, I have to adjust to you being gone, to sleeping alone. I have to miss you. And then I get used to it. Until you come back and eventually leave again, and then I have to adjust all over again. And it's fine, but…if you're already leaving again tomorrow… I just don't think I want to put myself through it—you know?"

He looked at her for a long moment before quietly saying, "Okay."

He'd never realized that—she could see it in his eyes. It was clearly not a problem they shared. He didn't get attached to her presence the same way she got attached to his.

"Then I, uh…should head home for the night?"

"That would probably be best."

He nodded through an expression that hovered somewhere between taken aback and troubled. "All right. But I'll come say goodbye in the morning. If that's okay."

"Of course," she said shortly. Still a little amazed that she was sending him away. But it was what her heart told her to do right now. And she was going to start following her heart—her seemingly braver-than-ever-before heart—trusting it to lead her where she was supposed to go.

CHAPTER TEN

March 13, 1957

Dear Diary,
I hate it here! I hate it, hate it, hate it! Why, of all the places on earth, do I have to live here, on this stupid island? Someday I'm going to leave and never come back—you can bet your bottom dollar.

Mother calls me an ingrate whenever I complain about it, but she just doesn't understand! She was a mainlander before she married Father—she chose to come here! God only knows why. We live like Pilgrims here—no cars, no radio stations, no place to buy a pretty dress. But maybe that doesn't matter much—because there's also no place to wear one.

At least I got a record player for my birthday! I think it's the only thing keeping me from going off my rocker! Though Mother doesn't like the records I buy, and I have to listen to them with the sound turned down low. I have records by Fats Domino, Little Richard, and Frankie Lymon and the Teenagers, just to name a few.

We got a television set for Christmas last year! The channels are snowy, but it still feels like magic to me, like having a picture show right in our front parlor. Mother says it's trouble—that it's giving me pie-in-the-sky ideas about life. She doesn't even think Ralph Kramden is funny. She tries not to enjoy any of the shows we watch—I can tell—but the other night I saw her laugh out loud at Lucy.

Elvis was on The Ed Sullivan Show back in January, and Mother crossed her arms and looked critical the whole while. They only showed him singing from the waist up since his dancing is so scandalous, but when even Mr. Sullivan said Elvis was a decent, fine boy, Mother seemed to relax a little.

She's so old-fashioned. Father says it's because she lived through hard times and that hard times make you grateful to be someplace as peaceful as Summer Island. They say it's peaceful—I say it's boring, with a big, fat capital B.

Father says people who lived through the depression and the war were affected a lot of different ways, and that for Mother, it made her want to retreat and find a safe place. She thinks Summer Island is safe. But my teacher, Mr. Hardy, said that when they drop the big one, we won't be any safer here than anyplace else. He wants to build a bomb shelter. Mother thought it was outrageous when I told her and Father about it over dinner last week—that he was filling our young heads with fear. Father just laughed and said to take it all with a grain of salt and remember that no one knows what tomorrow holds but the Lord.

We're taking the ferry to St. Simon on Saturday.

I'm going to use my allowance to buy All Shook Up from the record section at Bergman's! And next weekend I'm going to a sock hop! Also in St. Simon. J.T. and I are double-dating with Mary Ann Hoskins and Carl Kaneally. Other kids from our school are going, too, and a few who already graduated. The ferry is even going to make a special run to bring us all back at midnight. Mother frowns every time I talk about it, but she's adding some lace to my green dress to make it look more fit for a party, so deep down she must want me to have a good time.

I hope it doesn't snow. I hate snow. And ice. And cold. Someday I'm going to go to Florida. Or maybe Mexico. A place where it's always summer. I always tell Father they named our island wrong—it should be called Winter Island, since it feels like that most of the time. He said if it was called Winter Island, no one would come, even in summer.

It's true that the summers are nice. I just wish they lasted longer. And that Mother would let me wear shorts like the girls we saw in St. Simon last August. She said only saucy girls would wear something so brazen. I didn't think they looked brazen at all. And if that's so, maybe I want to be saucy, too.

> *Yours, wishing for eternal summer,*
> *Peggy*

MEG SAT CURLED UP in an overstuffed easy chair in the library, staring at the old diary in her hands. She wore cozy flannel pajamas, and Miss Kitty lay curled contentedly at her side now that the house was quiet and still.

She reached down to touch the ink, the handwriting, with her fingertips. It was as close as she could come to touching her grandma now, and reading her words, seeing the way she signed her name—the girlish flourishes in her penmanship—made her feel somehow even more connected than she'd expected to when she'd opened the leather-bound book. But what really caught her off guard were the words themselves.

She barely recognized her own life the past few days and this only added to the surreal quality her existence had taken on. First a handsome stranger enters her world, making her feel new and interesting things. Then Zack comes back when she least expects it, forcing her to realize exactly how new and interesting the things she's feeling *are*. And now this—she discovers her grandmother hated living here as a girl!

She let out a breath, still staring at the page. She'd *never* heard her grandma complain about Summer Island or talk of having ever wanted to leave. Until this moment, she'd have sworn on a stack of Bibles that Gran had loved this place always, had valued and even cherished the beauty and serenity of it her entire life.

She thought again of the odd discovery that her grandpa had once been called J.T. instead of John. And now she found out her grandma had once been Peggy and not Margaret, the only name Meg had ever known her to go by.

Her thoughts returned to the mysterious Valentine from the mysterious Ace. She'd always just assumed, knowing her grandparents had married young, that there'd never been any other romance in either of their lives. Suddenly that seemed dreadfully naive and short-sighted. Since, clearly, even as isolated as her grandma had found this place, she'd known at least one more suitor. And now Meg wondered just how important this other boy had been to her.

How much else about her grandmother didn't she know?

And maybe the bigger question—at least right now—should be: What had changed her mind? About the island? What had made her fall in love with it and happily stay her whole life?

She read on. Entries from days that followed revealed that "Peggy" had gotten her new Elvis record—amazing to think of a time when "All Shook Up" had been brand new—and that snow was indeed predicted for the coming week. "I guess it can snow all it wants," she wrote, "just as long as it doesn't get much colder. Too much ice and the ferry won't be able to get through."

Yes, Meg knew all about ice and ferries and why the dead of winter was definitely the starkest of times here.

Of course, Zack's entry into her life had made winters a lot warmer. Ice and bitter cold kept fishermen at home. A season she'd once dreaded had become one that felt more…dependable now, one where she knew what to expect. Nights in his arms. Sex. Cuddling.

He wasn't there all the time, of course—they maintained separate residences and separate lives and that was fine. She wasn't the clingy type actually. She just liked consistency. She just liked knowing what tomorrow held.

He could be here with you right now. He'd come back because he wanted that, wanted to show her he cared. That still blew her away, being a first. But she stood by her decision. To watch him sail away in the morning with no more of a promise between them than there'd been the last time, or the time before that, made it feel… empty. Like a slow road to nowhere.

She and Suzanne joked that the road circling the island—more of a wide paved path really, given the lack of cars on it—was just that, a road to nowhere. There were plenty of stops along the way, but ultimately, it led you in a big circle, back to where you'd started.

Suzanne liked that. "No surprises," she'd said. "I like knowing it will always bring me back, that I know exactly what to expect."

"I guess what it comes down to," Meg had replied, "is whether the place it brings you back to is fulfilling enough that you always want to be brought back there."

And they'd gotten into a philosophical discussion of whether places that never changed were more good than bad, and whether a world with definite boundaries gave you security or hemmed you in. Obviously, from her grandma's diary, it was a topic that had long been a point of contention here.

And maybe it always would be. Maybe mothers and daughters and granddaughters and friends would be weighing all the pros and cons of it for generations to come. The only real uncertainty in the mix for Meg being whether she'd still be here to take up the discussion or would leave Summer Island in her wake and never look back.

DESPITE BEING IN his own bed, Zack slept poorly. Or maybe that was the problem—being in his own bed. He'd expected to be in Meg's, after all. And he'd spent the better part of the night tossing and turning, still trying to wrap his head around the fact that he wasn't, and the confusing reasons why.

He'd thought she'd be happy to see him.

But then, he'd thought she'd be alone, too.

It had never crossed his mind that he'd walk out that door to find anyone but her on the patio. His Maggie May.

There she'd been, smiling, laughing, with some young guy who was too good-looking for anybody's good. He was like a guy you'd see in a commercial, or a magazine. A guy who could sell stuff to gullible women.

And turned out he'd sold *himself* to Meg—at least in a manner of speaking.

And Meg was thinking of selling the inn? Leaving? Now, as he walked down the stairs outside his apartment and into Dahlia's for breakfast, he shook his head, still trying to convince himself he hadn't somehow hallucinated the whole damn thing.

His aunt opened the restaurant early this time of year—earlier than was probably necessary until the tourists arrived—so he found her there alone. She wore a purple sweater that made her look younger and more stylish than her years. She had a flair about her, Dahlia. And she was blunt as hell. "Well, look what the cat dragged in. And you do look like you've been dragged, nephew." She tilted her head, eyed him from behind her little spectacles that made him think of early seventies hippies. He suspected she'd probably been one. She planted her hands on her hips. "Didn't you just leave?"

"I came back," he muttered. His head hurt the same way it would from a night of heavy drinking—without having had the pleasure of the drinks.

"So you weren't dragged. Just look that way."

"Didn't get much sleep."

She arched a brow. "And not for a good reason, I'm presuming, or you'd be in a better mood."

"Shouldn't have come," he said, trudging past her to a table. "Headed right back out."

She turned to look at him, but he didn't return the gaze. "What brought you home?"

He thought about how much to say. As little as possible. But enough to keep her from prying. "Thought Meg was mad about me leaving. Turned out she was doing fine without me."

It surprised him when Dahlia laughed. "Then you've heard she hired some help."

He raised his eyes, spoke drily. "Don't really see what's so damn funny about it."

Dahlia moved to the drink station, started pouring him a glass of orange juice without asking. "Guess it just amuses me to see you jealous."

"Well, now, wait just a minute," he said, holding up a hand in protest.

"No, you wait." She lowered the glass in front of him. "You may not want to put a label on it, but the fact is, you're unhappy and Meg taking control of her life without you is clearly the reason why. But considering that you come and go at your leisure, why would you expect her to do anything else?"

What the hell was his aunt babbling about? He had no idea. And his head continued to pound. He squinted up at her. "For your information, I don't care who she hires to do what, but that guy rubbed me the wrong way. She doesn't know him from Adam and here he is, hanging out on the patio with her like he owns the place."

Her wrinkled face twisted into another smirky smile. "Jealous," she said softly. "Like I said."

He rolled his eyes. Only then it hit him to ask, "There's nothing going on between them I don't know about?"

"Not that I'm aware of. But I doubt Meg would run down here and tell me if there was. And…if there was, would there be anything wrong with that?"

Aw hell. She was backing him into a corner. Because no answer was the right one here—he couldn't win. So he settled on saying, "I'm not gonna discuss this with you, old woman."

Her eyebrows shot up critically. "Watch who you're calling old, nephew, or you won't get the waffle I know you're waiting on me to make."

They both knew good and well the other was teasing—even if the remarks hadn't necessarily come out sounding that way. "Fine, I take it back. But I'm still not gonna discuss my relationship with Meg."

She shrugged, then turned toward the kitchen. But as she started to walk away, she paused, looked over her shoulder. "You may not want advice from your old lady aunt, Zachary, but she was hurt when you left. She's always hurt when you leave. And I think you already know that. But the point is, if you care about that woman, you could just stand to…let her know, that's all."

Zack considered the many ways he could reply. He could point out—again—that he'd come back, for God's sake. He could point out that their relationship was none of Dahlia's business. But he'd just told her he wasn't discussing it and he meant it. And he knew she had good intentions, but…hell, his head hurt. "I have the situation in hand," he said quietly. "And yeah, I would appreciate breakfast."

She nodded and said in just as calm a tone, "You know I'm happy to make it for you."

She started toward the kitchen again, and almost against his better judgment, he said, "Dahlia."

"What?" She looked back once more.

"I meant it when I said the guy rubbed me the wrong way. And not just for the reasons you think. I know there are strangers in the inn all the time—she reminded me of that—but…this just feels different. So, uh, maybe keep an eye on that situation while I'm gone?"

She looked uncertain—whether about the request or his judgment he didn't know—but finally said, "To the degree that I can. She's not an incapable woman, though. You know that, right?"

He nodded. "Of course I do."

And he did. He truly did. And if he'd ever thought she was too attached to him, she'd blown that theory right out of the water last night. He still felt a little off-kilter about it.

An hour later, he'd let Dahlia's apple-strudel waffles revive him and had shut the apartment back up, ready to leave. As he walked the short distance down Harbor Street to the Summerbrook Inn on a clear morning, he wasn't sure how to say goodbye. And that was new.

Stepping up on the front porch, he heard music playing, loud, over the also loud sound of some sort of machinery. Since the front door was open, he reached for the screen door handle and stepped inside, hoping to find Meg before he found her handyman.

No such luck. A quick search of the downstairs led him to the kitchen, where the guy he'd seen on the patio last night used a large sander on the newly revealed wood floor. He didn't notice Zack's approach amid the various noises, allowing him to walk right past and out the back door—but still no Meg, damn it.

Only when he came back in did the sander go quiet as the stranger's blue eyes—too blue to be real, he thought; his mother would have called that movie star blue, Paul Newman blue—turned his way. "Mornin'," the guy said.

At just that moment, Meg emerged from her office, carrying some color swatches as she began, "I was thinking—" And then, spotting Zack, stopped. Like he was interrupting.

"Morning," Zack said, to both of them. It came out stiff, brusque.

She didn't quite smile. "Hi." And despite himself, that stung a little—that not-quite-smile. Usually, she smiled.

"Stopped in to say bye," he told her. But that came out stiff, too—because he had to announce it in front of this other guy, and it felt awkward, strange. The handyman's presence put everything out of whack.

In response, Meg—thank God—stepped around the guy and the sander toward Zack. "I'll walk out with you." She led the way into the hall, past the nook where the cat lay sleeping in the sun-filled window, and out to the foyer.

Once there, she said, "Be safe."

He nodded. "Always am." Then he took in certain details about her. The pale pink of the top she wore, The messy ponytail she'd pulled her hair back into. And mainly…the confidence she gave off. Dahlia was right—she was a damn capable woman. So maybe he shouldn't worry, should let all this go and assume things were fine. Maybe.

"It was nice of you to come back, Zack," she said, looking up at him. "I'm sorry…things were weird."

"I'm sorry, too—if I overreacted."

"Thank you for that," she said softly. Seeming sweeter now, but still a little distant. And he had the feeling he'd really messed up somewhere along the way, only he had no idea what he'd done.

Still, maybe he should take Dahlia's words to heart. "Listen, Maggie May, you know I love you, right?"

She pursed her lips, looked almost sad. He didn't get it.

"Is that a bad thing?" he asked.

She shook her head. "No—of course not. It's a good thing."

"Good," he said, not completely convinced, but he'd take what he could get. And then he followed the impulse to lift one hand to her silky cheek, look into her gentle eyes, and lean down to kiss her. Not a heavy, passionate kiss—no, it was slow, lingering, a connection of mouths that he tried to make last, that he wanted them both to remember after it ended.

He looked back into those green eyes afterward and felt better than before he'd come. And he sort of wished he could stay longer, but just like last night, he knew she didn't want him to if he was only going to leave. And if he went now, he could lay some more nets on the way back to the Port Loyal coastline and be ready to start bringing in the catch from the ones already there first thing tomorrow.

"I'll see ya soon, honey."

She nodded.

He squeezed her hand.

And then he walked out the door.

MEG STOOD ON the front porch watching as the *Emily Ann* sailed off through the cold, deep waters of Lake Huron toward its next catch. This time, though, everything felt different.

She wasn't wearing her grandmother-prescribed sweater, because today no barrier of fog hung between the sun and Summer Island—the days were slowly getting warmer, brighter.

Her heart wasn't breaking—because she'd stopped letting it. She had projects and plans to see to—things to do, things to fix, things to think about.

And she didn't know all the coming summer would hold—but one thing it would definitely deliver was answers. Big ones.

As a light breeze wafted across the porch and the boat disappeared beyond the horizon, summer felt a mere heartbeat away.

Part 2

"The true courage is in facing danger when
you are afraid, and that kind of courage
you have in plenty."

—*L. Frank Baum,*
The Wonderful Wizard of Oz

CHAPTER ELEVEN

IN THE DAYS that followed, she fell into a routine of sorts with Seth. She welcomed him in the mornings, sometimes with a light breakfast—or not. At lunchtime, she made two sandwiches and they ate together, albeit quickly, usually at the table in the sunroom. She hadn't offered him dinner, though, since the night Zack had interrupted them—something felt officially awkward about that now. As if she had somehow turned it into a date. Or he had. Or they both had. Wittingly or unwittingly—it didn't matter. She didn't want to confuse him. Or herself.

He kept her updated on the work and consulted her on any decisions to be made. The kitchen floor was done within a few days and looked amazing. Now he had started painting the cabinets and would move on to the kitchen table after that. Most of the inn felt quaint and lovely to her, as such a place should but the kitchen had rocked a bit of a seventies vibe her whole life, and the changes Seth was making would bring the room into sync with the rest of the big, beautiful old house.

While he worked, she did, too—just on other things. More flowers, more planting. Multi-hued verbena and vinca in pots on the back porch, clumps of Solenia begonias in coral, yellow, pink, and cream in shady spots, along with impatiens at the bases of some trees—although they were annuals, she'd had some luck with them coming back, cross-pollinating, taking on the look of wild-growing blooms. She also trimmed the hedges, tidied up bushes in the rose garden, and scrubbed down the patio furniture—and today she had moved indoors to clean guestrooms. Her first visitors of the summer arrived in only a week and there were always a million things to do to get ready. She was giving the rooms a thorough dusting today, one by one, currently the rose room with its classic white furniture and a style just a little more pristine than shabby chic.

Of course, when they ate lunch, they talked about more than just the work.

He flirted. Outrageously. With those eyes of his. And that grin.

"Sure you wanna leave this place, Meg darlin'?" he asked her one day over lunch, grin in place, eyes half-shut, head cocked to one side. The noon sun shone bright behind him, again giving him that angel-with-a-dark-side look.

She regarded him with a small, pleasant smile—a smile she'd learned to reserve for him. It didn't flirt back, but it didn't push it away, either. "No, actually, I'm not—you know that. I'm just considering it. And preparing for the possibility."

"'Cause it's none of my business, but something I can't help thinking, all the time, is that…you fit here."

She wasn't sure how to take that, but it made her smile drop away. Had he decided she was boring? Quiet? Old-fashioned? Or…did the leap she made to that conclusion just indicate she thought that about *herself*? She lowered her chin slightly. "How do you mean?"

It surprised her, though, when his grin faded as well, and he appeared to be thinking very hard. "There's such a thing as…simple beauty. It…doesn't try too hard—it just is. This island's like that. This house is like that. And you're like that."

As they looked at each other in that moment, she suffered the oddest, most unexpected, most compelling urge to kiss him. It rose up from deep within her solar plexus like a flower growing as fast as Jack's beanstalk, and the bloom burst open somewhere around her breasts.

She still thought he was a player, a charmer—by trade in fact, almost as much as he was a handyman—but he was so damn skilled at it that it almost didn't matter. It was impossible, even in her awareness of such, to know where the charm became the truth. *This* felt true. Like he really saw that in her. One more reminder of how good he made her feel—with only a tiny bit of effort. Regardless of where the line of truth lay, she couldn't help thinking his charm made the world a nicer place.

She hadn't kissed him, of course. She'd simply let that small, practiced smile come back and said, "Thank you," as a bit of warmth rose to her cheeks. Then she'd picked up both their empty plates and walked away. And now she tried not to feel the memory too much as she cleared the few items off the white dresser and sprayed some furniture polish.

Conversation also went in other directions.

She learned which of Walt Gardner's cabins he was staying in. "The third one, farthest back the lane, with the dip in the porch roof. It's rustic as hell, but I don't need much, so I don't mind. It's got a tin roof—good for sleeping when it rains like last night."

He assured her he still didn't want to rent a bike when she brought it up again. "I like the walk, even if it takes a little longer. See more, hear more, that way. Gives me more time to think about your pretty face and wish you'd give me a chance." That came with the usual grin, and she'd been tempted to ask *a chance for what exactly*? but thought better of it.

She'd learned that he enjoyed working outdoors and had also done some construction in his day, he didn't drink coffee, he had calluses on his hands, he preferred ice cream to frozen yogurt, and dogs to cats—though he liked Miss Kitty fine because she mostly kept to herself. "And she's named after a saloon girl," he added with a grin.

He asked her about Zack on more than one occasion. The first time being the very day Zack had left. "Darlin', I'm sorry if I caused any trouble for you last night."

She'd tried to blow it off as nothing. "It's fine," she told him with a quick shake of her head. "He just expected me to be alone—not with a handsome younger guy."

His eyebrows had lifted, his expression playful but smug. "Careful there or I'll start thinking you like me, too."

"I do like you," she'd said, all confidence and grace, "just not in the way you're talking about." *Liar, liar, pants on fire.*

His eyes had told her he knew that. But he said nothing, let it go.

And just yesterday, out of the blue, as he'd been brushing pale yellow paint onto one of the doors currently detached from the cabinets, he'd said, "You and that guy…"

The doors and drawers were spread on a drop cloth stretched across the backyard between the patio and the stream. She'd been headed back inside when his words had cut through the gentle sound of water trickling overtop rocks and around roots, stopped her, made her look over her shoulder. "Zack?"

"Yeah."

"What about him?"

He'd hesitated, and she'd thought maybe he wasn't quite sure what he even wanted to ask. "What's the… uh…deal with you two? How serious is it?"

Talk about a tricky question. But then she remembered there was an easy answer for that these days. Which she delivered with her same little Seth-all-purpose smile. "It's complicated."

He laughed lightly—then met her gaze. Challenged her. "Too personal for me to ask?"

She pursed her lips, thought a moment. "Too complicated for me to answer."

"In my experience, 'it's complicated' usually means there's a lot of serious shit there, but that all's fair."

"All's fair?"

The corners of his mouth curved slightly and his eyes went sexy, seductive. "That if something happened between you and me, you wouldn't be breaking any rules."

Maybe she should have been dishonest about that, to keep his advances at bay, but she wasn't used to having to think that fast, or be deceptive. "I wouldn't be," she told him, "but nothing's going to happen." And she'd disappeared through the back door before he could say another word.

And despite all this conversation they'd been having on so very many topics, still Seth revealed little to nothing about his past. Even when she asked.

"Where in Pennsylvania did you say you lived when you were little?"

He shook his head, smiled easily. "Just some little podunk town—nowhere too interesting."

"What did you do in Mississippi?"

"Pretty much the same thing I'm doing here." Then he'd let his eyes drift down her body and back up. "But here the view's better."

Now, as she finished the rose room, noting that she still needed to change the bedsheets and towels, she picked up her dusting supplies and padded down the hall into the sherbet room.

Then gasped, flinched—to find Seth there, kneeling between the bed and the far wall.

He looked up, eyes wide, like he'd been caught at something. But that quickly his face changed, trying to cover it. "Uh...sorry to scare ya, darlin'."

She drew in her breath. "What are you doing up here?" Because there was no reason for it whatsoever. His work remained strictly in the kitchen. And certainly not up here. Where it was way too far away to have heard a noise, as he'd claimed the other time she'd found him in one of the rooms.

He flashed his usual grin. "Snoopin'?"

She just looked at him, waited for more. Her heart beat harder in her chest.

"Was just takin' a little break—doing a little sight-seeing, I guess. Liked it up here when you gave me that tour and wanted to see some of the rooms again, that's all. And then I caught sight of a loose baseboard here."

He pointed to a spot beside where he still knelt. So she walked around the bed toward him, glancing down. The board did bow slightly from the wall in a way she'd never noticed. "I'll put in a couple finishing nails—see if that fixes it—and touch up the paint."

And then he stood up. Which put them face-to-face, body to body, only a few inches between them. Why had she stepped so close? *Because you were trying to see the baseboard.* But it seemed like a mistake now.

Because that magnetic thing was happening between them again, that chemistry that felt like something physically connected them even when it didn't. It had continued all along, of course, but the closer she was to him, the worse it got—or the better, depending on how she looked at it.

She raised her eyes to his only for a second—but then lowered them because the sensation was too intense. Her entire body tingled. She wore a purple tank top with lace at the edges over shorts. Typical summer day outfit—but now she suddenly felt exposed somehow. Maybe because her breasts physically ached just being so near him. She wondered if her nipples were hard. And if he could see.

Though it hardly mattered since he surely didn't need to see her nipples to feel how moved she was. Questions flitted through her brain. *Does he have this effect on all women? Does he feel it, too, as strongly as I do? Is this mere sport for him—am I prey? or could he possibly really like me? Or both.*

"That sounds fine," she said.

Then turned and walked out of the room, furniture polish and dusting rag still in hand. No smile, no graceful exit—this was pure escape, no hiding it. Ugh.

Her first thought: *Go to your bedroom*, her most private haven.

But no—he might come there, knock on the door, ask her why she'd run away, start kissing her or something.

So she headed downstairs instead. Although that also seemed like a bad plan—since he'd likely come back down to resume painting in the kitchen.

And what the hell was he doing in the sherbet room anyway? Sightseeing? Really?

Grabbing a can of soda from the fridge, she followed the instinct to walk out the back door, cross the patio, and head for the lilac grove, one of several garden areas that dotted the expansive yard at the house's side, stretching for fifty yards or so before the grounds gave way to woods. The small grove of tall bushes, some now large enough to consider trees, was a place of peace and refuge for her—because her grandmother had loved it and so did she. The lilacs were ready to bloom any day now.

She sat down in a white Adirondack chair and let the surroundings calm her. The day was bright with a light breeze that whispered across her skin. Pink roses were budding, ready to open in the distance, and purple clematis climbed a nearby trellis. She reminded herself to take some time to enjoy the lilacs in the coming few weeks—no matter what else was happening. She waited all year for them, every year, and didn't want to miss it.

There was a certain kind of woman she aspired to be—someone who was always calm, cool, and collected, someone who had her life well under control, someone who handled every situation with grace and aplomb. And she thought she pulled that off most of the time. But there were, undeniably, certain elements in her world that stole her grace away.

Every time Zack left in his unceremonious fashion it stole a little of her grace.

And just now—being so close to Seth that she could almost feel his breath on her skin, and then racing away—that had stolen a little of her grace, too.

The second instance seemed more pleasing than the first, even if not ideal. But even so…

I want my grace back—all of it.

And wasn't grace just…self-possession? Being your best self? Living your best life?

At night, she thought about him. Some nights more than others, but always at least a little. She imagined what it would feel like if he touched her. Different than with Zack? More exciting—because he made her feel more like a prize to be won and cherished? Because it felt more daring, more wild? She asked herself those questions in the dark—but let them drift away on sleep, nearly forgotten by the next morning.

Yet now she asked herself a question in the daylight of her garden for the first time.

What would happen if you quit running from Seth?

What was so wrong with her reaction to him? What was so wrong with his desire for her?

Zack loved her, he said. But love could be so nebulous. How much did a man really love you if he couldn't promise you…anything?

And still, Seth remained…such an unknown quantity. So secretive in ways. And there was a serious possibility that she'd just caught him sneaking around her house. *Snoopin'*. Said so innocently. How innocent was he truly?

Then again, what could he be looking for in her inn? Maybe he really *had* just been taking a break. He'd expressed an open appreciation for the house, and she'd told him a lot about it, including it having an abundance of cubbyholes and hiding places that added to its charm—so maybe he really *was* simply exploring. She'd sometimes done the same as a girl, back when the place was new to her, too—a habit brought on by Gran's treasure hunts.

The upshot of it all: She wasn't certain she would even know *how* to have an affair.

Though she was pretty sure he'd be happy to show her.

Could I?

Really?

Outside of my little bedtime fantasies?

She glanced toward the house. He was somewhere inside.

As another soft May breeze wafted past, an answer settled over her. *Maybe.*

SOME YEARS THE impatiens beneath the shade trees in the east yard reseeded themselves in the sandy soil there—and some years they didn't. This year she'd seen little sign of regrowth, and since it seemed like a good time for a walk anyway, she headed to Petal Pushers.

"How's your handyman?" Suzanne asked from where she stood loading red geraniums into small plastic pots for selling. It was the usual greeting these days, and of course she'd long since filled her friend in on the little drama that had ensued with Zack's unexpected return.

"Fine," she said as usual, approaching her friend. Then, not as usual, she heard herself confess, "We had a moment a little while ago. A moment when we were standing very close and I wanted to kiss him."

Suzanne looked up, her hands dark with dirt, jaw dropping. "Um, um…wow. I knew you were into him, no matter what you said." Meg had continued to deny more than the passing attraction most women would have toward him. "But somehow I didn't see this coming. What did you do?"

"I didn't, couldn't." She gave her head an uncomfortable shake. "So I ran away. It was very mature." Then she rolled her eyes. "Almost as mature as your response to Beck Grainger."

Suzanne ignored that part. "I could use more details," she said, wiping her hands on her large canvas apron, emblazoned with the Petal Pushers logo.

"There's definitely…chemistry between us. It's just that I'm not sure if I want to act on it." Then she scanned the shop, remembering why she'd come. "I need impatiens, by the way—hot pink ones."

Just then, the bell above the shop door tinkled, announcing a new arrival. They both looked up to see the tall drink of water known as Beck Grainger walk in. Think of the devil—though Meg didn't think him devilish at all really. But her heartbeat doubled on Suzanne's behalf—she could feel the nervous energy just spilling from her, that quickly.

"Hi," Beck said, locating them in the back. Though he looked directly at Suzanne.

She said nothing. So Meg replied, "Hi."

"I was, uh, looking for a big pot of flowers, for my front porch."

Meg glanced from the very handsome construction mogul—Dahlia had recently referred to him that way, as a mogul—to her apparently mute friend. She even nudged her ankle with one tennis shoe when she still didn't answer.

"Do you have any?" he asked.

And finally Suzanne pointed toward a door that led out back. "There are pallets of them outside, to the left."

"Maybe you could…help me pick one out."

"There aren't many. Everything I have is right outside that door."

And with that, Beck Grainger looked properly shot down and left through the appointed exit.

"Holy God," Meg said. "Could you not see that the man is trying to engage with you?"

"I don't know why," Suzanne replied. "When I clearly don't want to be engaged with."

"'Clearly' is the right word." Meg simply shook her head.

And that was when Suzanne announced, "I'm going to go get your impatiens from the greenhouse. Would you mind ringing him out if he makes a purchase."

Meg knew how to work the register—she'd helped Aunt Julia and had kept the shop running for a few months after her great-aunt had died. But she still rolled her eyes and said, "Are you serious?"

Suzanne pressed her lips into a flat line. "I am. Sorry. And thanks." With that, she made a beeline toward a different door than the one that had led her customer to the pallets outside, leaving Meg standing there shaking her head.

When Beck returned carrying a large pot brimming with a combination of yellow Solenia begonias and some fuchsia, she smiled and asked, "Is this for a shady spot? These can only take an hour or two of sun a day."

He nodded. "Yeah. I read the sign that said so, but thanks for checking."

As he lowered the pot to the counter and Meg rang up the sale, she said, "I apologize for Suzanne. She's not feeling well today."

But he shook his handsome head and answered shortly, "No worries." Then completed the transaction, added a quick, "Thanks," and was gone.

A minute later, Suzanne conveniently returned carrying a large tray of bright pink impatiens.

"I'm pretty sure that man didn't even want flowers for his porch," Meg informed her. "I think he came just to see *you*."

Suzanne only shrugged—and Meg tried not to feel infuriated, but it was difficult.

"Just FYI—your bad behavior," she informed Suzanne, "is making it hard for me to want to take advice from you."

"Do as I say, not as I do," Suzanne said, lowering the flowers to the counter. "Surely you've heard that one before."

"Yes, and it's never held much water for me."

"Look," Suzanne told her, heading back to her work stand, "let me be an example of what not to do so you won't end up a bitter, lonely woman like me." She smiled then, though. "Good thing I *like* being bitter and lonely."

"You do seem to." Meg crossed her arms. "Since Beck Grainger is giving you every opportunity to change that."

But again, Suzanne just shrugged as she scooped

some potting soil into a plastic container with a trowel, then added a geranium. "Like I keep saying, he's too… startlingly handsome. That type is usually up to no good in my experience—can't be trusted."

"Isn't Seth that type?" Meg asked.

Suzanne shook her head. "No, he's more…mysterious." Then narrowed her eyes, looked pleased. "I dig that." And as she glanced down at her potting soil, added, "No pun intended."

"I'm not sure I do. Dig it, I mean. It makes me nervous."

"Still can't get any personal information out of him?"

"No. I even Googled him—but I got nowhere." She'd done it last night at bedtime, on a lark, more curious than suspicious at the time, but now wondering if she should give suspicion a little more credence. "And today, our moment occurred because I found him in the sherbet room—when he was supposed to be downstairs. He claimed he was just looking around, but it seemed weird."

Suzanne tilted her head. "It's a pretty house, Meg— if I were working there, I'd probably wander around a little, too. There's something very comforting in the guestrooms—maybe he was just drawn there. By the comfort."

Meg mulled that over. It echoed her earlier justifications on the topic. And was part of the reason it was so hard to imagine leaving—the house made you feel relaxed, safe, like a home should. She thought of her grandma's diary—the part about her great-grandmother feeling safe here. Maybe the house's soul had been part of that.

"So say you kissed him. Or…more," Suzanne sug-

gested gingerly, as if they were both tiptoeing into un-
charted territory. "What's the worst that could happen?"

"I don't know," Meg answered with a speculative tilt
of her head. "Maybe that's the scary part."

Suzanne eyed her suspiciously. "But you're thinking
of doing it anyway."

"Am I?" she asked coyly.

"Yes," Suzanne said with full certainly. "Yes—you
are."

CHAPTER TWELVE

SETH STOOD IN the library, raking his gaze over the spines of all the books, once again trying to take in titles, but they all ran together. After a quick glance out the window, up the street, to make sure Meg wasn't on her way back, he stepped closer, looked harder. Needle in a haystack. If it was even there at all. And he knew it probably wasn't. But if you're attempting to find a book in a house that actually has a library, it only made sense—as he'd thought upon first seeing the little room—to look there.

He was sorry the heat between the two of them had sent her running—damn sorry—but when he'd caught a glimpse out the window of her walking up the street a little while later, it had felt like an opportunity he couldn't squander.

Still, he soon concluded that what he sought wasn't in the library—and it wasn't in any of the other rooms he'd checked out so far, either. Of course, he hadn't gotten to explore them as thoroughly as he wanted because he'd been on edge, couldn't take his time. And then she'd walked in on him.

So it *could* still be here somewhere. He just wished he had a firmer grip on what room it had been in. As he departed the library through the parlor, a caustic chuckle left him. It was almost ironic that he'd found her grandmother's secrets, but not his own. And maybe he deserved that, considering exactly what his secret *was*.

He hadn't imagined the whole thing, had he? He hadn't just somehow made it up in his brain, leaving that book here? Along with what he'd put inside it.

Hell, sometimes the past was hard to piece together. Sometimes you thought you remembered something absolutely perfectly and then had it proved wrong.

He'd spent most of his life remembering a ride to Mississippi when he was ten in his dad's brand new bright red Mustang GT. Black leather seats that almost swallowed him, engine that revved and purred, little horse emblem on the glove box. It wasn't even something he'd ever questioned—he'd just known. But when he'd mentioned it in passing a few years back, his dad had said, "No, son, we were in a rental. A Honda of some kind." And Seth had argued the point, thinking his dad had lost it, until he said, "Son, you were only ten and we didn't get that car until '01, the year it came out. Think about it. Don't add up."

And to his astonishment, his dad had been right. The Mustang had been a 2001 model, making it physically impossible to have been the car they drove south.

He stood in the inn's foyer now, thinking his way through the rooms, thinking through them all as he'd come to know them the last few days—versus any memories of them. But doubts crept in big-time now, enough that another sardonic laugh escaped him. *If I came here looking for something that doesn't even exist, that's hilarious.*

Frustrated, he swiped a hand back through his hair. *Maybe I should go back upstairs, keep looking there.*

Doubts aside, his gut told him that was where he'd left it. It had to be true. Had to.

Get caught up there again, though, and it might not be so easy to talk your way out of it.

Unless…maybe you're just looking for more loose baseboards. Or floorboards. Trying to unearth more old, lost treasures for her like the box from her grandma. Thin, but maybe she'd buy it. She seemed trusting and she assumed the best of him, so that helped.

He swung past his toolbox—parked in a kitchen corner on the newly varnished hardwood—to grab a hammer and a few nails to carry with him, to back up his story. Then he took another look out an eastern-facing window up Harbor Street to see Meg nowhere in sight —before ascending the stairs.

Once at the top, he headed down the open hallway toward the rooms at the front of the house. They were all numbered, though their doors were open right now— since the vacation season hadn't started, he guessed. Well, they were all open except for one—which, instead of a number, had a little sign on it that said, Private. With a daisy painted at the end of the word. Only on Summer Island would an innkeeper attempt to make the word *Private* seem friendly.

He shouldn't go in. For more reasons than one.

But for all he knew, what he sought was inside, under another loose floorboard *there*. Again, he only wished he could remember more about the hiding place.

Reaching down, he quietly turned the knob. Though his heart beat too fast. Too fast for a guy who'd done this before. Too fast for a guy who'd been taught to take what he wanted no matter what rules it broke.

If she comes back now, catches you in here, there's no talking your way out of it.

Unless...you tell her you wanted to see where she sleeps. Where she takes off her clothes at night. Her personal space.

It was only as he took in the room that he realized it wouldn't even be a lie.

The sun shining in through old-fashioned white sheers gave the bedroom a gossamer glow. The sheers, edged by curtains sporting purple blossoms, blew in the breeze that came through open windows. The walls were lavender—but a shade more warm than soft. And the space *smelled* of lavender, too—but maybe the scent came from the bathroom off one corner. It was many things, this room: It was warm and inviting, but clearly someone's private space. It was soft and feminine, but also sophisticated and mature. It was a girl's room. It was a woman's room.

It was everything he saw in Meg—shades of light and dark, fun and serious. He'd known his fair share of women, and he'd seduced his fair share, too—but this one, this one was more of an enigma than any he'd ever met. In one moment carefree, innocent, open, with adventure shining in her warm green eyes. In the next, the staid, responsible innkeeper who never got ruffled.

Well, except for when he stood too close to her. *That* ruffled her. That ruffled her like crazy.

And damn, he liked that. With a woman who he could tell normally had it all under control, it escalated his attraction to her even more. Because if just standing close to her affected her that much, what would it be like if he kissed her? What would it be like if he took her to bed?

Most women he could read. Most women made it easy. Hell, most women wanted to be seduced so bad they could taste it.

But Meg was different.

And when he got to see her soft, sweet sides, or— Lord—her ruffled side, he thought… *I'm getting pieces of her that not everyone does.* Just standing here, seeing *this* piece of her that few people did, and thinking about the quiet innkeeper who'd nearly started trembling with him not long ago, made his groin tighten. Damn. He wanted more of that, more of her.

But you came in here to look for something, not to stand around lusting for your current boss.

Like most of the house, the floors in this room were hardwood, not covered with carpet. If Meg's grandma had ever covered *these* floors, Meg had removed it, leaving only throw rugs and area rugs behind. But as he ventured deeper into her bedroom, inspecting the parts of the floor that were visible, he didn't see any signs of loose boards. And for the first time it occurred to him that what he'd hidden could have long ago had a repair done *over* it, in effect sealing it up in its secret place, making it virtually undiscoverable. Shit.

He leaned back his head, shut his eyes.

But don't get discouraged. Still might be here.

And…maybe she never had those types of repairs sought out or done. Because he thought she liked the idea of the house having little hiding places as much as her grandma had. It was part of their family history, and he could tell preserving that mattered to Meg.

And the truth was, even if what he'd once hidden *wasn't* still here, even if he never found it…well, he guessed it wasn't the end of the world. He wouldn't be any poorer than he'd started out. It had been only an idea, a way he'd thought he could get his life moving more rapidly in the right direction. He'd had no place else in particular to go this summer—and this place had held the possibility of a brighter future. As well as the added appeal of maybe finding out if his memories were real...or just wishful thinking.

Taking one last look around Meg Sloan's room, the first hint of guilt crept over him like a shadow and he decided he should leave. Guilt—that was the thing that kept him at least a little in line these days. He only wished he'd learned to feel it sooner.

Though when he thought of all the things he shouldn't have done in the past, it heaped up enough guilt and regret to eat him alive. And as the heaviness of that dropped over him with all the weight of a smothering blanket, he forced himself to push it away. *Don't let it in. Can't go back and redo anything. Can only try to do things better from here on out.* And being here, working for Meg, working for anyone who wanted to hire him on Summer Island, and looking for what he'd left behind, was a way to move on and put the past behind him—and well, maybe resolve some of it, too, if he ever found that damn book.

Pulling her bedroom door quietly shut, he heard the twitter of a bird and—through open doors and windows—caught sight of spring green foliage on tall trees towering on the other side of the house. It reminded him that Meg had said there was a garden area he hadn't yet gotten a good look at—at least this time around. He recalled playing in the big yard as a kid.

Just then came the sound of the front door opening, closing. She was home. And he was still upstairs. Shit.

You've gotten careless. His dad would call it soft. Or stupid. It took a certain sort of man, with a certain sort of hardness inside, to live the way his father did. Always on the take. Always. And never careless about it.

He made calculated movements and said a prayer he'd time this right. That she'd head for the kitchen and not the stairs.

A peek down revealed no sign of her, so he moved briskly but quiet as a cat. His father had always said that: Not quiet as a mouse, but quiet as a cat. And it was true, cats moved in silence and you only heard them if they chose to let you.

The foyer lay silent and still, stately and quaint, but he almost turned the corner from the foot of the staircase too soon—glimpsing a purple tank top disappear through the kitchen door.

He caught his breath, then took a few more quiet steps—into the hall bathroom.

Where he flushed the toilet, stepped back out, and headed to the kitchen.

She looked back at him from the doorway to her office. "There you are." A whisper of a blush colored her cheeks a little, though, and he knew why—the last time they'd seen each other, they'd been standing too close for comfort and suffering a heat more intense than Mississippi asphalt in July.

What was it about her? She wasn't his usual type. But again, it was those layers, those pieces of her—the really good ones under the straitlaced innkeeper shell.

He gave her a smile, hoped it would set her at ease. Well, mostly. Because he liked the heat and wanted her to keep feeling it, same as he did. "Here I am."

"How's the, um, work coming?" She pointed vaguely

toward the cabinets and he got the distinct feeling she'd forgotten for a minute what exactly he was even doing there—besides turning her on.

That kept his grin in place. "Good. I'll finish painting tomorrow and can start the antiquing process the next day."

She nodded and he walked closer to her. It was instinct mostly, but convenient when he looked down and realized his paint tray rested on that side of the room.

And that was when his gaze fell on something behind her—something he'd never noticed before. A bulletin board hanging on the wall of her office. More notably, photos there. And one in particular.

"What's this?" he asked, pointing.

She looked over her shoulder at it and smiled. "Pictures of some of my regular guests—the ones who come back every summer."

He broadened his view to take in the whole board and found photos of couples and families, some standing by the Summerbrook Inn sign, others next to bikes in front of the house, still others sitting around the firepit. But his eyes were drawn quickly back to the first snapshot that had caught his eye.

In it, a slight woman with white hair, likely in her seventies, wore a sun visor and fanny pack, and stood next to a heavyset gray-haired man with a big mustache. And maybe he was crazy, but they looked familiar. Older than he remembered, of course. But familiar.

Except that…hadn't he just acknowledged that sometimes his memory played tricks on him? And sure, seeing something like this right here, right now—of course his mind would go there. So he was probably imagining it.

"Who are *these* people?" he asked, pointing. Without even caring that it might seem weird to ask. But at least their picture was front and center on the bulletin board, and taken more close-up than most, with the nearby lighthouse in the distance behind them.

"Funny you should ask," Meg said. "Mr. McNaughton is one of my first arrivals, due in about a week. Comes up from Pennsylvania."

McNaughton. As his stomach lurched, he tried like hell not to let it show.

"They…look happy," he said. Because they did.

"A sweet couple," she told him. "Friendly as can be. And he's a real talker. But she never seemed to mind. She always struck me as…content with her own thoughts. Like she didn't need to share them, was happy just keeping them to herself." Meg let out a soft trill of laughter. "At times, they didn't seem like they should fit together—and yet they did. Perfectly."

He tossed her a sideways glance. "That's kind of a… good thing to keep in mind, don't ya think? That sometimes people you wouldn't expect to work together do." He ended on a wink.

And she responded with a simple smile. A smile that said *I know you're flirting with me*. And that he hoped also said she liked it. Either way, though, any smile from Meg made him happy and seemed like a good sign.

"They apparently used to come here years ago, when my grandma was still alive, but then stopped for a while. Now they come every June like clockwork. Or, well, *he* does," she amended. "She died a couple of years ago. But I know it's really summer when Mr. McNaughton checks in."

Seth kept his eyes on the picture, pressed his lips together tight, hoped his expression didn't change.

But he couldn't keep looking at it. He couldn't keep standing here, in fact. "You mind if I take a quick break—just to stretch my muscles some?"

She looked a little surprised—maybe his expression *had* changed. Or maybe his whole demeanor. Which was why he needed to walk away for a minute, get his head wrapped around this. "Sure," she said anyway. "Of course."

He tried for a smile, but knew it came out tight. "Thanks, darlin'."

Then he pushed through the back door, out into the fresh air and sunlight, striding briskly. To anywhere.

His first impression had been right. The people in the picture were his grandparents. And the last time he'd seen them, he'd been ten years old, attending his mother's funeral.

CHAPTER THIRTEEN

THE FOLLOWING AFTERNOON, Meg curled up in one of the Adirondack chairs in the garden, wrapped cozily in a thick plum-colored cardigan sweater, her grandmother's diary in hand. The day had brought clouds—a few drops of rain with them. But the drizzle had ended early, leaving only the rich, damp scents of spring-ready-to-be-summer. Now clouds still hovered overhead, keeping the air cool but tolerable without a breeze.

Gran had loved this garden, a love she'd passed on to Meg. Meg's grandpa had planted most of it over the years, adding bits and pieces right up until his early death from a heart attack—same as what had stolen Gran from them—at forty-eight when Meg had been just a little girl. She possessed vague memories of him, in most of which he was digging or mulching or planting, just like his sister Julia—and the image of him in her mind came with a cigarette between his lips and a trowel in his hand.

The first lilac blooms had finally begun to open, so before sitting down, she'd stepped up to cup a dark lavender blossom in her palm, bending to drink in the sweet aroma. She remembered her grandfather planting these particular ones—the Pocahontas Canadians, which always bloomed first and possessed a slightly deeper hue than others—when she was little, but now they towered over her head.

Grandpa John. Or Grandpa J.T. For all she knew, maybe having the right "grandpa name" had even brought about the change in moniker since Grandpa J.T. lacked the necessary music in her opinion. She remembered him being such a responsible, quiet man. Not a J.T. Definitely a John. Gran had once said this garden was his love letter to her, and that he wrote a little more every year.

She wished she could freeze time—keep the lilacs here longer. In a few days, the rest would start blooming as well, lasting for a couple of fragrant, beautiful weeks, and then, that quick, they'd be gone until next May and June. When she didn't even know if she would still be here. *So this might be my last time seeing them, smelling them.*

But quit wishing for impossible things, things you can't change. Quit trying to hold on to things that can't be held.

The thought brought Zack to mind. They'd exchanged some texts since he'd gone. The usual. Weather reports. Safety reports. And an unexpected goodnight from him that had somehow felt bittersweet—like a thing she wanted, but somehow it only made her sad for all the nights she'd never gotten it before.

Work going okay on the house? he'd asked a couple days ago. So careful not to ask specifically about Seth.

Yes—great, she'd told him. I think the kitchen's going to look amazing when it's done.

Good, he'd said.

She opened the diary to the red ribbon she'd used to mark her place. She'd found it toward the back of the book, where her grandmother had quit writing. She couldn't believe it had taken her so long to get back to reading it, but life had felt less than normal lately—and this was the busiest time of the year, which her grandma would certainly understand.

March 25, 1957

Dear Diary,
It snowed a little, but didn't get cold enough for the lake to refreeze, so the ferry was able to take us to St. Simon for the sock hop. We all had to bundle up for the ride, and we huddled together behind the wheelhouse trying to keep warm. You'd think that would be awful, but J.T. put his arms around me and I was on Cloud 9. I've known him all my life, but only in the last year did I start noticing how handsome he is. He asked me to go steady at Christmastime and I said yes, of course. I know it's only been a few months, but I'm over the moon for him!

And do you know what else, diary? He hates it here as much as I do! We both hate how hard it is to get anywhere, and we both want to live on the mainland. He works with his dad in their garden up on West Bluff and he's applying to Michigan State University in the fall to get a degree in horticulture. Father says he's really on the stick!

So even though I was freezing half to death and worried I looked like an oddball in the thick winter hat Mother knitted for me last year, I'd already had a wonderful time before we ever reached St. Simon. We could even see the gigantic new bridge they're building across the pass—it's going to connect the upper and lower peninsulas!

The sock hop was keen! They'd decorated the hall with crepe paper, and a handsome fellow in a red jacket played Elvis, Sam Cooke, Chuck Berry, Buddy Holly and lots more! It was fun to be with other kids none of us knew, and they all thanked us for coming over. Funny—I wanted to be around them and their mainland lives, and I think they thought we were the interesting ones, living on the island. I still want their life. And they might think they want mine—but they wouldn't after one winter here. Or even one summer. They don't know how small your world can be when it's surrounded by water.

J.T. and I tried to jitterbug. We need to practice and may ask his sister to give us lessons. But it was good for a laugh.

Next, we got some punch and stood drinking it in one corner where the lights were low—and next thing I knew J.T. was kissing me. We've necked before, but this was different. It made me feel hot, even with snow falling just outside the window. If we'd been somewhere alone, I think we could have gotten carried away.

And if we're going to be together, forever, maybe it's okay. We've talked about leaving the island after I graduate, too, and then getting married. But my girlfriend Barb Norris said to to tell him no. She went all the way with Donny Barker last year after he said he loved her and wanted to marry her, but then he started ignoring her and told everyone she was fast. I know

J.T. would never do that to me—but Barb never thought Donny would, either.

I'm sorry to say the night took a sour turn after that, though. It started when this boy named Ace came in from the cold wearing nothing but a thin jacket as a coat. The kind James Dean used to wear. And he just stood against the wall being churlish with his ducktail and a thick lock of dark hair dipping down over his forehead. He was very good-looking, but you could tell he was a hoodlum. The St. Simon girls said he was bad news and they didn't know what he was even doing there. One of them told me he robbed a liquor store!

Toward the end of the night, I was leaving the bathroom and he blocked my path and wouldn't let me pass. He said, "What's your tale, nightingale? I've been waiting all night for you to come back here so I could get a better look, and I like what I see."

I've never had someone be so forward, but I thought my answer was very smart. I said, "If you've been paying such close attention, then you can see I'm with someone else."

But that didn't slow him down at all! "Maybe you should be with me," he said. "He looks like a square."

The nerve! So I said, "You're rude."

And he said, "You're a dolly." And looked all smug.

"Leave me alone," I told him.

And he said, "Especially when you're scared."

I claimed I wasn't scared, not by the likes of

him—and I still can't believe what happened next. He kissed me, diary!

Of course, I should have pushed him away—I certainly meant to. But even though I had been afraid—the strangest thing happened. I let him. Kiss me. Just for a moment. I don't even know why. The shock of it, I guess. He smelled of whiskey but tasted like spearmint gum. It was so different than being kissed by J.T.—I felt him all around me and it somehow took away all my thoughts and left only the kiss in their place.

But almost instantly, I realized how terrible that was, and I pressed my palms to his chest and gave him a big shove backward. I yelled at him to leave me alone as I marched away. And he had the gall to call after me, "A shame you don't mean that."

But of course I did!

I went straight back to J.T. and the others right as the Bunny Hop Mambo began, so we all fell in line—but the whole time, I stayed shaken. As we were hopping around the floor, I wondered if anyone had seen me kissing him. Even though I looked at other people or down at my socks or up at the fluttery decorations, I kept seeing his face. And I kept remembering that kiss.

After that, I didn't feel well the rest of the night. But I didn't tell anyone why, not even Mary Ann or Barb. It was too hard to explain, especially the part where I let him kiss me. And I still don't know why I did!

But I'm trying to forget all about that. Especially since the rest of the dance was such

*a dream! J.T. walked me home from the ferry
after, and when he gave me just a small, soft kiss
goodnight on the porch—out of sight from where
Mother and Father could see—it was exactly what
I needed in that moment. Another reason why he's
the perfect boy for me.*

> *Yours, thankful for her boyfriend,*
> *Peggy*

After finishing the long entry, Meg just stared at
the book in her hands, the page still open to her grandmother's written words. At first, she'd marveled over
things like never having known her grandfather had
officially studied horticulture, though perhaps it made
sense given that he'd ultimately run the nursery with
Aunt Julia until his early death. But that had quickly
been overshadowed by learning that her grandma had
had a tryst with a bonafide bad boy! Who drank whiskey and forced kisses on girls in secluded hallways.
And maybe even robbed liquor stores? Behind Grandpa
John's back. It was a hard notion to fathom.

"Is...this a bad time, darlin'?"

She flinched, looked up. Seth stood peeking around
one of the tall slender arborvitae trees that stood like
sentries near the street side entrance to the lilac grove.

She smiled. "No." It felt good to see him—she'd
grown accustomed to his smile and it brought her back
from being so jarred by what she'd just read. "I was
just...digging into this." She held up the diary.

His grin widened. "Anything juicy?"

The question made her laugh when she least expected
it. "Yes, actually."

He gave his sandy head a thoughtful tilt. "I hope I wasn't wrong suggesting you read it."

She thought about that and said, "No—or at least I don't think so. But I just found out about the night my grandmother met the mysterious Ace. From the birthday card."

He raised his eyebrows. "Oh?"

She wondered how much to tell him. Her hesitation wasn't about it being private to her grandmother—Seth had never known Gran, after all—but maybe it came from the very concepts feeling…awkward, intimate. A kiss that was far from romantic but had still moved her grandmother in some way that she'd perhaps been too young to articulate. And…clearly her grandma had been torn between two boys, enough that she'd made out with both of them on the same night in the winter of 1957. All things considered, that seemed a topic worth not bringing up with her sexy handyman.

"He was…just a little rough around the edges, not someone I'd expect my grandma to be drawn to. And she was already dating my grandfather, so it was kind of…forbidden, you might say. I'd never pictured her youth this way." She decided to leave it at that.

Seth gave his head a slight tilt and said, "Maybe that just makes her a more interesting gal." And as he ended on a playful shrug, she couldn't help thinking he was right. And what a nice way that was to look at it. After all, Meg knew the outcome, and that her grandparents had been very happy together.

Just then, Seth seemed to inhale the garden scents. "Smells nice out here."

"Lilacs are starting to bloom," she said, pointing. "My grandpa planted them."

"The good guy who won the girl in the end?" He grinned.

And a soft trill of laughter left her throat, unbidden. "Yes, him." She'd closed the diary now and it rested in her lap. "The weeks the lilacs are in bloom is my favorite time of year."

He eased down into the Adirondack chair next to her, wearing a white T-shirt and faded blue jeans, both spattered with bits of paint. "Yeah?"

She nodded. "In a few days, they'll all be in full bloom. And the air will smell like perfume." She laughed. "And me—I'll be walking outside every chance I get, trying to soak it up and drink it in before it's gone."

He didn't answer for a long moment, but it was oddly comfortable—comfortable in a way she normally only got with someone over time. Finally, though, he said, "Hard to really enjoy something, isn't it, if the whole time you're already worried about it being gone?"

She took that in, turned it over in her mind. She'd never viewed her feelings about the lilacs precisely that way before. She stayed aware of how quickly they came and went, but the idea that she might be cheating herself out of a pure enjoyment because of that was a new one.

Though when she looked over at him and their eyes met, she wondered if they were talking about lilacs… or something else. Did he think she'd declined his advances because his presence here was temporary? And even if that had been the case, was there anything so wrong with that? She already had one temporary man in her life.

"It's true," she ventured tentatively, "that I often

value permanent things more than fleeting ones. I guess I like…dependability."

He lowered his chin, gave her a look. "Not everything's meant to be permanent, Meg darlin'." And something in the words made her chest grow warm within the confines of her sweater and the blouse underneath. She'd tipped her hand—he knew she was talking about more than lilacs now, too. "Flowers, for instance. They have their seasons. Up this far north, everything is all about seasons. Guess it surprises me you're not good with that. I mean, living here and all."

"Maybe I'll head south in the spring," she said with a small smile, "where the flowers keep right on blooming. Where summer doesn't end, or at least where it lasts a hell of a lot longer."

He was smiling back at her now, in his easy way. "Something like lilacs, though—you appreciate 'em more because they're not around as long. And to my way of thinking, that makes their season just right."

Meg didn't answer. Instead, she sat quietly—contemplating the idea of a fling. With Seth.

Something she'd appreciate more for knowing it would be temporary?

Or that she'd *fret over* knowing it was temporary.

Maybe she never fully enjoyed her time with Zack, being aware that every day might be the last for a while and that she shouldn't get too comfortable having him around. Kind of like the lilacs.

Was it possible to see the temporary nature of a relationship as something to savor with one man but resent in another? Was that even fair?

And why was she even weighing this at all? *It's not like you're going to suddenly hop into bed with Seth.*

No matter how drawn you feel to him in moments. Like this one, the ease of it underwritten with that same magnetic force she'd been unable to break free of with him from the start.

"Well, I'd better get back to work. Those cabinets aren't gonna antique themselves, are they?" He stood up.

And she smiled. "How's it coming in there?"

He returned it. "Looking pretty great if I do say so myself. You'll like it, darlin'."

She pulled in her breath and hoped he didn't see. *You'll like it, darlin'.* The words stayed in her head long after he'd walked away, punctuated by the sweet, fleeting scent of the lilacs planted by her grandfather—not the liquor store robber.

SETH PICKED UP a small sanding block, ready to distress the kitchen table he'd painted this morning. After buffing fresh paint off edges and curves in the spindled legs to let the darker wood show through—making it appear as if it had happened naturally, over years of wear—he would add a pale antiquing glaze to heighten the effect. But before he started on the table, now situated on a drop cloth, he found himself stepping into Meg's office, peering again at the bulletin board.

It wasn't the first time he'd studied the photo since first noticing it. It was closer to being the tenth. He didn't want to care, but it was strange seeing his grandparents over twenty years older than the last time they'd crossed paths. He was taking in the lines on their faces, the joy in their eyes. The two things didn't match. He'd mostly seen people grow surly, bitter with age. He didn't expect someone to get happier as they got older. But he could see in their eyes that it had happened. He wondered how.

And to learn his grandmother had died...well, he shouldn't have cared about that either since he'd never expected to see her again anyway—but it still stung.

It shouldn't matter. None of it. Whether either one of them was dead or alive. Whether his memories of them were right or wrong. Whether his *dad's* memory of it all was truer—just like it had been about that damn Mustang.

Though the fact that, right now, it *felt* like it mattered made him angry at himself for coming here at all. He could have gone anywhere. Anyplace in the whole damn world. Sure, this place had held the maybe of finding that book, the maybe of cashing in. But it also held a memory. And that had him thinking through *all* the memories. And wondering which ones were real.

After all, how did a man quantify his life if he didn't even know what the hell had happened, how he'd gotten to where he was?

Maybe it matters more than you want it to.

His grandpa would be here in less than a week. And part of Seth wanted to run. Finish this job for Meg, get paid, and disappear from this island forever. That was what his father had taught him. Running. Running kept you safe. Running kept you one step ahead. No one catches you when you run.

But that alone was reason enough to ignore the impulse. Break that cycle—because it had come from his father and was a shitty one.

And there were other reasons to stay, too.

He'd come here for answers he hadn't quite found yet. All in that damn lost book. Answers that would help with his future. And answers that would help with his past, too.

And while he had no intention of introducing himself to his grandpa, at least he could see what the man was really about. Maybe he could somehow…figure out why things had happened the way they did.

Small world. He comes back here. His grandfather comes back at the same time. He shook his head. Small damn world.

More reasons to stay?

Money. Meg still had work for him to do. And if she ran out, he might find more.

Rest. Most people might not call working every day rest, but when you were always running, always moving, it took a hell of a lot of energy, mental as well as physical. The little cabin across the island wasn't much—four walls, a roof, and a bed, about as sparse as you could get—but the longer he was here, the more he liked the routine of it. Liked knowing what each day held. Liked knowing where he would sleep that night. Of course, he'd stayed plenty of places longer than he'd been here—but he liked that the choice was fully his now, not brought on by circumstance. He liked knowing that he could leave if he felt like it, but that he could also stay as long as he wanted to.

And then there was Meg. Such a puzzle in ways. He thought she hadn't had many lovers. He thought she needed at least one more.

He was learning *he* liked dependability, too. Patterns. Knowing what to expect. But life was all about taking chances. And he wasn't sure Meg Sloan had taken many. And nothing was forever. If Meg could just let go with him…

What would that be like—Meg letting go? A ripple of desire arced across his chest as he began gently distressing the pale yellow table, rubbing away the top surface to reveal what lay underneath. If Meg could just let go with him, let this thing between them reach its natural destination, it would surely make for a summer to remember.

CHAPTER FOURTEEN

THE LILACS CONTINUED to blossom. The ones in the garden. The ones behind the patio. The ones across Harbor Street that grew wild along the shore. The French lilacs, the President Lincoln lilacs, and the Wonderblue lilacs. And like neighboring Mackinac to the east, the entire island brimmed with them, boasting far more than just those on the grounds of the Summerbrook Inn—they bloomed in yards and lined stretches of picket fences and grew in stray clumps, as both trees and bushes, along the road that circled the small coast. Summer Island was awash in their sweet perfume.

And Meg was still busily readying the inn for guests—it was time for fresh towels and linens—but as she did at this time every year, she took quick breaks outside, brief walks through the garden during which she would stop to cup a dainty lavender or white blossom in her palm to breathe in the scent. Though it was still chilly through the nights and most mornings, when weather permitted, she opened the windows to let the lake breeze carry the fragrance inside.

Seth continued diligently working in the kitchen and she stayed almost painfully aware of him. She felt him in the house—even when on an entirely different floor. And she realized she *liked* feeling him there.

They still ate lunches together, as well. It had become

a new routine in her life—and maybe even something she'd started looking forward to: The few minutes when they'd catch up on how his work was progressing, or just discuss random tidbits about the inn or the island or the weather.

"Am I gonna be in the way when your guests show up?" he'd asked one day when they'd taken their sandwiches and sodas to the patio.

"No," she'd told him. "I can arrange the work I want you to do so that it won't hamper anyone's stay." Then she'd glanced toward the back screen door, thinking of the room on the other side. "But the kitchen will be done by then, won't it?"

"Absolutely," he'd promised with his usual confidence. "With time to spare."

Two days after their discussion in the garden, he came outside to find her late one afternoon. She sat in the same Adirondack chair—not with the diary this time; only a cup of tea instead because she still had so much to do and only enough time for a short break. He peeked around the same arborvitae as before, to ask, "Out here soaking up the lilacs again, darlin'?"

He stood in the shade of a mostly cloudy afternoon with only a few patches of blue showing through. And she realized that a man who had, for a while, made her feel slightly on edge with his mere presence had gotten much easier to be with. *I've grown used to the chemistry, the magnetism.* That same energy still flowed invisibly between them, but it felt…safer to her now, less intimidating. A little time always changed everything.

"Guilty as charged," she answered with a soft smile.

"Don't worry—I'm not the lilac police," he said on a teasing wink. "Your secret's safe with me."

"Join me?" she suggested without quite planning to, motioning toward the adjacent chair.

He glanced at the chair and then back at her. "Normally I would—but got somethin' to show ya."

She sat up a little straighter, her very posture asking him what.

"Kitchen's done."

Together they followed the garden path, paved with brick by Grandpa John, toward the stone walkway that led to the patio, then stepped inside. She'd witnessed the whole transformation taking place every day for a while now, but seeing the finished room took her breath away. It was the perfect change, the perfect kitchen for her quaint, homey inn.

"I love it," she whispered, absorbing all the details. Every cabinet door and drawer had been uniquely antiqued—her old kitchen table, as well. What had before looked outdated now felt as warm and inviting as the rest of the house, as well as considerably more rustic. Seth had even gone to the trouble to hang the new curtains she'd bought for the window over the sink and return things that had been moved to other rooms during the work, like Miss Kitty's bowls and the salt and pepper shakers from the table.

"The kitchen feels like…it's wrapping around me now or something, like it's holding me."

"Lucky kitchen." The glance he slanted in her direction brought heat rising to her cheeks.

Their eyes met, but she looked away quickly, turning her attention back to the room even as she tried not to smile. "This is amazing, Seth. Truly." Knowing already that she would enjoy time spent here much more now, she said to him, "I'd better be careful. You might make the place look so good I won't want to leave."

Just then, her phone buzzed with a new text. Pulling it from the back pocket of her blue jeans, she found a message from Suzanne: You're late.

"Crap," she whispered.

"Something wrong?"

"I totally forgot an early dinner date with my friend Suzanne." She glanced down at the work clothes she'd been in all day. "I need to run upstairs and change—I'm sorry."

"Nothin' to be sorry for, darlin'—I've just got a little more cleaning up to do and I'll head back to the cabin."

"You don't mind if I rush out?"

"Not at all."

The dinner wasn't anything special—just burgers and drinks at the Pink Pelican—but it was Trevor Bateman's first night back on the island. He'd be performing mostly for locals, though Meg knew a few early visitors had arrived on the ferry over the last couple of days as she'd begun seeing tourists on bicycles, and a few meandering up Harbor Street. And given the lack of social options on the island, even just common catching-up sessions felt noteworthy.

Meg texted her friend a quick apology, then ran upstairs and changed—albeit without showering. She threw on a long, flowy summer skirt and coordinating top, and grabbed a sweater for later.

Heading back down, she popped her head into the kitchen, where Seth was packing up his toolbox. "Goodnight," she said. "See you in the morning—and I love the kitchen, Seth." She flashed him a bold smile, something she didn't often do, but seeing the room again made it hard to hold back her happiness.

"I'm glad you like it, darlin'," he told her. "Should I lock up or anything on the way out?"

Now that mainlanders were starting to arrive, this was the time of year when she started actually doing that, but one night of unlocked doors wouldn't hurt anything. "No need," she assured him.

Which was when he told her, "You look real pretty tonight."

The simple compliment sent a fresh burst of heat through her chest, and as on other occasions, she wondered if her nipples might be getting hard, showing through her top and bra—but she had no intention of glancing down to check right in front of him. "Thank you. 'Night."

And after that she rushed out.

She made the walk quickly, drinking in the transition from day to dusk. The scent of lilacs in the air plus the few tourists wandering about town made it official— summer had arrived and Summer Island was open for business. Though she'd all but forgotten tonight's plans, now she found herself looking forward to seeing Suzanne and other friends, and to hearing Trevor's set. And she also found herself…feeling pretty. Because Seth had said so.

She didn't walk around feeling ugly by any means, but those few simple words made the lilacs' fragrance a little sweeter, the darkening air a little softer, the coming night a little richer.

IN THE LAKE HURON port town of Newfork, Zack sat in a dark booth with cracked vinyl seats downing a deluxe cheeseburger and fries. He'd never met the waitress before but she'd flirted with him enough that she felt like an option. An option he didn't want.

What was it with waitresses having a thing for him? *Or maybe it's because they're the only women you come into contact with when you're on the water.*

The burger was good, and the day's catch had been surprisingly good, too. He'd got a good price for it almost the moment he'd docked. And the restaurant was warm on a cold Great Lakes spring night, a good, cozy enough place to be for an hour or two. So if everything was so damn *good*, why the hell did he feel like shit?

Normally, a night like this would seem peaceful to him, the solitude comforting. Places where you didn't know anybody didn't require you to talk much and he liked not talking just fine. Usually anyway.

But something wasn't right.

And it had to do with Meg.

With how much he didn't like having left her there with that handyman flitting around. No matter what she said, the guy felt like trouble.

And with how much he didn't like the new uncertainties between them. Would she really, actually leave the island? Leave *him*? He wanted their relationship to stay the same, be like it had *always* been. She was damn nice to come home to. And maybe he didn't tell her that enough.

He'd tried to say the right things before he'd left. But she hadn't seemed to want to hear them. Or maybe he just didn't know the *real* right things to say.

He found himself thinking back to the night they'd met. He'd known in five minutes that she wasn't the easy, breezy, carefree kind of woman he usually ended up connecting with. He'd known she would be more to him than that, and require more *from* him. Even with her drunk on too many Sea Breezes consumed too fast at the Pink Pelican, laughing and giving him come-hither looks he'd felt in his groin, he'd known she was a steady, sweet sort of woman.

And he'd gone home with her anyway. And never regretted it, not for a moment. Not even when she wanted more from him than he knew how to give. Not even when she got angry or put out, making it clear he let her down. She was worth trying to please. Even if he seemed to do a crappy job of it.

He'd never been good at staying, at having a real home. His mother's fault.

Of course, maybe it was weak to lay blame. He'd known by the age of five that his mother wasn't like other people's. It had been an awareness—observing other moms with kids, seeing that they weren't all furious, or yelling, or hitting. He'd realized that young that he'd gotten cheated in life somehow.

But shit—why was he thinking about that? He'd survived, gotten away, and it was long in the past. And while Dahlia wasn't exactly the maternal type, his MIA dad's sister had given Zack a sense of family, a sense of someplace to belong, that he was grateful for.

Try harder with Meg. When you go home, try harder. Just figure out what she needs from you. Without having to give up what you *need. Surely there's a middle ground there. Just find it.*

She'd been wearing yellow that first night—a spring night, unseasonably warm and sweet and full of moonlight. "Meg runs the big, pretty inn up the street from my place," Dahlia had said by way of introduction.

They'd drunk. And talked. Drinking made the talking easier for him with someone he didn't know. He'd talked about commercial fishing—because he didn't know much else. She'd talked about her inn, and her family, and her late grandmother. Her smile had nearly buried him. So earnest. But…ready. For something. He'd sensed that. It was a natural attraction, the kind that makes *you* ready for something, too, when you least expect it.

"Are you gonna invite me home?" he'd been so bold as to ask after lots of drinks and talking, and a little touching of knees under the table and hands on top.

"I never do that."

"But are you going to tonight?"

Their eyes had met. And she'd looked as surprised as *he* was when she whispered, "Yes."

They'd walked up the empty street—it was late, past one—holding hands, leaning flirtatiously on one another. And she'd risen up on her toes to whisper in his ear. "I have a confession to make."

He'd turned to peer down on her in the soft evening air. "What's that?"

She continued to whisper. "I've never been very fond of fish."

A laugh had erupted from his throat. And he'd teased her. "Then we can't go on. I can't come home with you."

"Really?" Her eyes had widened, intoxicated and innocent.

He'd narrowed his gaze. "Well, you're pretty enough that maybe I can make an exception."

She'd smiled, flashing one more of those come-hither expressions that had him counting the seconds until they were behind the closed doors of her inn. "Then I'm a lucky girl."

And he'd wanted to wait until they reached her bedroom, but he in fact had only made it to just beyond that closed *front* door before he'd started kissing her. He'd kissed her and undressed her all the way up the stairs, leaving a line of clothing that trailed from the foyer like bread crumbs.

The house had been empty of guests—just before the season started. He'd been so damn happy to find out they were alone, didn't have to be quiet. And he'd made her moan and cry out in ecstasy before they'd fallen asleep in each other's arms.

"Anything else, handsome?"

He looked up. The waitress was young. Too young. Tattoos on both her arms, displaying the names Brandon and Austin. Boyfriends or babies? Maybe one of each? He didn't much care as he said, "Just the check."

"You a fisherman?"

He gave a brief nod. Still not interested in chitchat.

"We get a lot of fishermen. Hard work."

"Mmm." Disinterested agreement.

"Lonely, too, I bet. Sort of like a long haul trucker, but on a boat." She giggled, amused by her own analogy.

"I like my own company."

The mere way she tilted her head told him he'd said the wrong thing, given her an opening. "Might like mine, too," she suggested. "I get off soon."

He kept it simple. "Got someone at home."

"That's too bad."

And for the first time Zack realized he *liked* having someone at home. And that it wasn't bad at all. It was pretty damn good actually. If only he could figure out how to make his someone happy.

He didn't answer the waitress. He'd already made his position clear.

In response, she tore a ticket from her old-fashioned order pad and placed it on the table. "You have a nice night now."

He left money next to his empty plate, then pushed past the heavy front door out into a brisk night made more biting by the wind blowing in off the lake. Stuffing cold hands in his coat pockets, he thought of calling Meg.

He didn't have much to say, but maybe that didn't matter.

Pulling out his phone, he placed the call. And got her voice mail.

"Hey there, Maggie May. Just wanted to say hi." *And I miss you.*

He didn't add the last part, though—just disconnected. He didn't know why. Maybe he didn't like admitting it, and didn't like admitting to himself or anyone else not being absolutely happy and content with where he was in this moment.

Though, in fact, he *was* content. He liked his work. And he liked knowing she was there to go home to when his work was done. The only thing he didn't like was realizing something had changed recently, and that he wasn't sure how to fix it.

But I love her and she loves me—that's all that matters.

THE CROWD AT the Pink Pelican, situated on the ground floor of the Huron House Hotel, surprised Meg at first—but it had been a long, cold winter on the island and she supposed everyone was ready to officially welcome summer.

As she slid into a chair across from Suzanne at a small table near the bar, Clark Hayes, who owned the place, came to greet her. "It's awful nice to see you out and about, Meg."

And it hit her—she *hadn't* been lately. Out and about. Was that because of Seth and her conflicted feelings surrounding him? Or did she always get a little reclusive when Zack first left? Deep down, she supposed it embarrassed her for people to know she put up with a man who was always leaving. Even if no one else saw it that way.

A waitress she'd never met—Clark always hired college girls from the mainland for the summer—brought her a drink she hadn't ordered along with a menu. "It's something Clark is calling an Island Splash and has rum in it," Suzanne informed her. "I decided we should both drink tonight. You know, cut loose a little."

"Be careful," Meg warned her. "You might let your guard down and start talking to Beck Grainger if he shows up."

Suzanne peeked up from her drink, clearly alarmed. "Crap, I never thought of that. But surely he won't."

"I hope he does. Would do you good."

Suzanne appeared belligerent. "Then I hope your handyman shows up."

Meg slanted her a look, then tried the drink. It was sweet, tasty—with fruit juices mixed in. "He won't. He's headed home for the night."

"Is that why you were late? Couldn't tear yourself away from him?"

"No. I just…lost track of time." That sounded a lot nicer than "forgot altogether." Though maybe Seth *had* played a part here. In the forgetting.

If she was honest with herself, he stayed on her mind a lot. She arranged her days around his comings and goings now. Not on purpose. Not because he was so important. But just because he would be there. It was impossible not to plan for that, to make sure she was up and dressed before he arrived, to organize her work around his.

"You should have invited him."

The very suggestion made Meg let out a laugh. "As if I need the entire town talking about me and my handyman."

Suzanne lowered her chin, hesitating briefly before saying, "Maybe they already are."

Meg's stomach churned. "What do you mean?"

"Nothing bad," Suzanne was quick to assure her. "A few people just asked me about him—that's all. Said they'd noticed you had someone working at the inn."

"But they didn't think there was anything…funny going on, right? Because it's not."

"I don't think so," Suzanne said in answer to the first part. "And I still think it *should* be," she said to the second.

Before they could discuss it further, the waitress came back, and though Meg hadn't had a chance to look at the menu, she ordered one of her usual choices. Then Trevor Bateman arrived, guitar in hand, chatting with them as he set up his speakers on the bar. The handsome thirty-something singer was a semi-local, returning every summer from some point south—Tampa Bay if Meg was remembering correcting.

Soon dinner arrived, the music started, and she had the most fun she could recall having in a while. Unless she counted the night she'd grilled out with Seth on her patio. And some of the moments with him since. And maybe she *should* count them. Being around him made her feel good, plain and simple.

The only islander to ask her about him personally all night was Audrey Fisher, who ran the Rosemont Inn, a five-minute walk in the opposite direction from Meg's place. "Bob said you had some young guy doing work for you." Bob was Audrey's husband. "Is he any good?"

Suzanne nearly choked on her third Island Splash at the question—while Meg tried to act normal. "Yes—he just redid my kitchen cabinets and floor and they look amazing. You'll have to come by and see."

Audrey nodded. "Well, when you're done with him, send him our way."

"Might be a while," Meg heard herself say, sounding almost proprietary.

They talked a few minutes longer, and after Audrey departed, Suzanne said, "Planning to keep him around all summer, aren't you?"

Meg considered that. "I haven't thought that far ahead. But I have more he can do."

"I'll say you do," Suzanne replied.

Meg rolled her eyes and kept right on acting as if she were offended at Suzanne's ongoing innuendos. But *did* she plan to keep him around all summer? She wasn't sure, and she wasn't even certain she wanted to keep thinking about it. Maybe she'd thought about it too hard and too long already. Maybe she should just live in the moment—as her grandma likely would have advised if she were here—and see where those moments led without worrying about it so much.

She supposed, as shocked as she remained by how Gran had let the ruffian Ace kiss her, that even then her grandma had lived in the moment. Margaret Adkins had always immersed herself in experiences without looking forward or back, for better or worse.

Beck Grainger never showed up, though Suzanne kept a nervous eye on the door all night after the suggestion that he might.

And they were both a little drunk on too many Island Splashes by the time they strolled home, in different directions. One of the upsides of having no cars—you could drink like a fish on Summer Island if so inclined and never have to worry about driving afterward.

She wanted him to touch her. As she made that slightly tipsy walk up Harbor Street, quiet and lit only by the moon and a few streetlights, she couldn't deny that desire. She wanted Seth Darden to touch her. And if he'd been there, she might even have told him so. *Good reason to never, ever drink with him again.*

Pushing the unlocked front door open, she indulged in a small fantasy. *What if he stayed earlier, never went home? What if he's in here right now waiting for me?*

In her current condition, the idea sounded…almost appealing. On every level. Like there'd be no reason to say no, no reason not to follow her impulses.

And as she stepped into the foyer, it struck her that he was so bold sometimes that it actually seemed like something he might do. *Could he? Would he?* She even called out, "Hello?"

No answer. *Okay. I can keep breathing.*

But as she padded into the kitchen and flipped on

the overhead light, she caught the scent of lilacs—and found something that hadn't been here when she'd left. Three billowing sprigs of Pocahontas lilacs jutted from a bud vase she kept in the cabinet above the fridge. The vase rested atop a slip of paper that read:

So you don't have to go outside to enjoy them.

CHAPTER FIFTEEN

THE NEXT MORNING found her curled up in the easy chair in the nook in drawstring pajama pants and a tank top, morning sun at her back, cat in her lap. A hint of lilac perfume hung in the air, and outside, birds sang. It was a new day.

She'd decided to have Seth paint the woodwork in the nook today, even though it wouldn't make Miss Kitty happy. Although the cat roamed the house freely, the nook was her favorite area, and also where her little cat bed resided, right next to the chair. Meg stroked her fluffy calico fur and said, "You're going to be so mad at me." She'd had to lock the cat in one of the downstairs guestrooms during some of the kitchen work, letting her out only when surfaces being painted or glazed or varnished were completely dry. "But it's for your own good. You don't want paint-covered paws, trust me."

The cat responded by standing up and pouncing down onto the floor, swishing her furry tail as she sauntered away.

Cats. They were so aloof and self-sufficient.

I should be more like her. She likes me, but she doesn't care much if I'm not around. She doesn't get lonely. She doesn't think too much. She's endlessly content. Well, except for when she was locked in a room for a long time, but anyone would have a right to feel disgruntled over that.

Meg had fallen asleep fantasizing about Seth being here when she'd come home last night. However, she'd awakened resolved to put such silliness behind her. Suzanne acted like it would be so easy to indulge in some wild affair with him, but there were so many reasons not to.

He was younger, and somehow, in her mind anyway, younger equaled wilder. He intimidated her. Sexually. She knew without having to ask that he'd been with a lot of women and she felt inexperienced in comparison.

And then there was Zack. It had surprised her to find a short voice mail from him while walking home from the Pink Pelican last night, and she couldn't deny that it was nice just to know he'd been thinking about her. Sometimes it took so little to make someone feel cared for. She owed him nothing, she knew. But having loved him for so long kept a soft spot in her heart for him despite everything—it kept her remembering the hurt in his eyes when he'd found her with Seth on the patio. She had nothing to feel bad for, and yet she still did—a little.

And then there was the whole island. Dahlia. Clark. The Fishers. Cooper Cross. Everyone. They would talk. Maybe judge. They'd assume she was cheating on Zack—because they assumed Zack was hers to cheat on. Of course, maybe they already did, if people were asking about it behind her back.

Even so, though, the idea, while pleasant to think about, would be a lot more complex if she let it become real. It would make an already complicated situation even more so. And who wanted that?

That was when she heard the front door open. Damn—he was here already? Time had gotten away from her. She was usually dressed when he showed up. She instinctively pushed to her feet—just as he approached down the hall and caught sight of her in the nook. "Mornin'," he said.

She wasn't wearing a bra. And knew it showed. As their eyes met, her arm rose on impulse to cover her chest. His gaze dropped there. Then rose back to her face. "Am I early?"

"No—I'm late. Sorry. I'll be back down in a minute." She rushed past him to the stairs, warmth filling her cheeks.

Oh Lord. She felt like a little girl. Or worse, an irresponsible woman. How hard was it to watch the clock and make herself presentable by the time he arrived for work? And covering herself with one arm had seemed a better alternative than letting him see, but neither felt like the height of class. And there had been heat. And awareness. Undeniably. Even as she'd wallowed in quick embarrassment and then made her escape, there'd been heat.

Shutting herself into her bedroom, she hurried to dress. Usual "uniform" for this time of year—blue jeans and a tank with an unbuttoned shirt over top. She hurried to wash her face, brush her hair, reach for a ponytail holder.

But then, catching sight of her reflection in the mirror, she stopped. *Be like a cat. A cat wouldn't sweat this. A cat would just go about its business acting as cool and confident as usual. So he caught you in your pajamas. Big deal. Life goes on.*

And for some reason, she put the ponytail holder

down and let her hair hang loose. Because she thought it looked sort of pretty, even if in a messy way. Tousled. And then she even reached for a little makeup. Her makeup bag remained on the bathroom counter from last night, when she'd rushed to meet Suzanne. She typically didn't wear any with Seth, but, well…maybe she would today. Just a little. A touch of eye shadow, a bit of mascara. A quick swipe of lip gloss.

"Hi," she said after walking back downstairs. She found him in the kitchen, Miss Kitty weaving figure eights around his ankles. Uncharacteristic clingy behavior. So much for wanting to mimic the behavior of her cat.

"Hi," he returned. He grinned a little, perhaps acknowledging the awkward moment just past. "Sorry to catch you off guard." Now *fully* acknowledging it.

She gave her head a slight shake and tried not to worry if she was blushing a little. "No problem. Ready for a new project?"

"Yes ma'am. Your wish is my command."

She dropped her gaze, tried not to hear the double entendre in that, and pointed toward the nook. "I'm going to have you do a little touch-up painting over the next few days, before the guests start arriving."

"And when is that?" He pointed vaguely over his shoulder toward the bulletin board just inside her office. "When does that old man come?"

"Mr. Carmichael, an elderly gentleman whose granddaughter and her family live here year-round, is due late Saturday morning. And Mr. McNaughton arrives Saturday afternoon," she said with a smile. "Then the Eastmans, a family of four, on Sunday. And another couple, younger and first-timers here, are due a few days after that."

Leading him to the nook, she pointed out all the woodwork to be painted in the small room. Then she asked him to walk up to Fulton's and get a gallon of white, explaining, "Just tell them it's interior trim for the Summerbrook Inn. They have all my colors on file."

Together, they unloaded the books and knick-knacks from the built-in shelves, carrying them into the foyer to stack them on tables and the edges of some of the lower stairs. When they were done and the cat still shadowed Seth, Meg bent to scoop Miss Kitty up into her arms. "And now I'm going to put this young lady in the same room she's already been shedding in lately."

Seth reached out, scratching behind the cat's ear. It put his hand close to Meg's breasts. "I think she likes me." His voice came out a little deeper than usual.

"Seems that way."

"Hoping she'll put in a good word for me with her owner."

Meg started down the hall then, but tossed over her shoulder, "You don't need a good word. I already like you, too."

He called after her, "Well, maybe I'm hoping you'll get more affectionate, like her."

She stopped at the guestroom door and glanced back to find him standing at the end of the hall, looking cute as hell. "Are you saying you want me to rub up against your ankles?"

He gave her a grin. "Something like that. But I can think of better places to rub up against."

She met his pointed gaze for only a second—before carrying the cat into the room. She could have just lowered Miss Kitty to the floor and shut the door on her, but she needed to escape him for a moment after that.

Yep, no way could she handle sex with him. No way at all. She looked down at the cat she still carried and whispered, "Afraid I'm gonna have to leave the affection to you."

A moment later, she'd exited and closed the door, securing the now-meowing kitty inside. The hallway was empty, and she assumed—hoped—Seth had headed for the hardware store. She'd wondered the whole time they were together if he was thinking about her breasts—because of her covering them so openly earlier. And when he'd petted the cat while she held it, *she'd* certainly thought about them.

She was glad guests would soon arrive—for many reasons. The house felt so alive in the summer—when people were here, enjoying it, inside and out. It made the island feel less isolated when the seasonal visitors came. And it would be much harder to entertain the idea of having a summer fling with Seth once there were guests sleeping right down the hall from her bedroom.

SETH ENJOYED PAINTING. It was among the simplest kinds of work he knew how to do, but he did it well and liked the methodical act of it. Maybe it quieted his brain watching the brush go back and forth, applying just the right pressure, giving just the right touch at edges so that the paint wouldn't seep under the tape. Mostly, in all his work, he found it satisfying to make something new again. And a big old house like this one—well, nice to think he was helping to keep it in good shape.

Funny thing—most people hated work as far as he could tell, but his whole life, working was when he'd been the happiest. Or at least found the most peace. Getting lost in the brushstrokes—or whatever else he was doing.

But he'd found more peace in other things lately, too. Even just those walks around the island. Even just going to sleep at night with a clear conscience. As clear as it *could* be anyway, under the circumstances. He wondered if his grandfather's arrival would mess that up—the peace part.

Damn, why had he come here again? But once more he told himself: *Just get whatever answers there are to get. Then you can move the hell on from it forever.*

Unloading all those books, he'd watched for the one he'd been looking for. But still no sign of it. Still a lost memory.

He'd opened the window behind the easy chair to let some fresh air in, and now a soft breeze carried in the sweet scent of Meg's lilacs. He'd heard the door a while ago—and wondered if that was where she'd gone, out to smell her lilacs some more.

He liked thinking about Meg a hell of a lot better than some of the other shit in his head right now, so when he finished the first coat and it was time to reload the paint tray, he decided to take a break. A glance at a nearby clock told him she would probably be making sandwiches for lunch soon. Sweet how she did that.

He still wanted her in bed. And every time he was sure it wasn't gonna happen, that she just wouldn't let it, something renewed his hope. It was the chemistry between them that did it, over and over. He wondered how long she'd keep fighting it.

Deciding to turn the tables on her a little just now, he headed to the pantry, then the fridge, and made a couple of ham and Swisses. He knew his way around her kitchen at this point.

He even knew where she kept the picnic basket, so he got it from the cupboard and loaded it up with the sandwiches, a big bag of corn chips, and a few pieces of fruit. A couple cans of soda and a picnic blanket, also from the closet shelf, finished his packing.

He wasn't surprised to find her sitting silently in her usual white Adirondack chair. But he didn't walk right up—for some reason, he stopped quietly and watched her for a minute. He took in the curve of her cheek, the waves in her hair. She wore flip-flops with jeans. He'd noticed her toenails were painted pink. Not a bright pink, but a soft shade, like cotton candy.

When he entered the lilac garden and she lifted her gaze, he held up the basket and raised his eyebrows hopefully.

A smile made its way onto her pretty face, but it came with cautious eyes. "Why, Mr. Darden, I do believe you're trying to seduce me."

"Is it working?"

Rather than answer, she kept eyeing him speculatively, drawing her chin down. "I meant to thank you for the lilacs this morning. The ones you brought in."

He offered up a soft grin. "Guess they didn't do the trick, though, since here you are." He lowered the basket to the carpet of grass beneath his feet, then spread out the thin blanket he'd carried under his arm.

"Silly, isn't it?" she said thoughtfully, gazing off into the blossoms, thick and abundant now. "I'd never thought about it before we discussed it, but I've realized it's true that every year I mourn their demise before they even bloom. Because their season is so short and they're so lovely."

She stood, then joined him to sit on the blanket. "They remind me of my grandmother. She loved them so much, and she tended them faithfully after my grandpa died. She never wore perfume because she said nothing a man could invent in some laboratory could ever smell as good as spring on Summer Island—and that anything less would be settling."

As Seth passed her a sandwich and a drink, then got out his own, he took in her words. He didn't want to be some guy who thought he had all the answers, but... "Have you ever thought about making lilac water? To keep the scent around even after they're gone?"

She gave her head a short shake. "I've never had much luck with that. The water never really holds the fragrance."

Narrowing his eyes on her playfully, he said, "Maybe you're just doing it wrong."

"Are you telling me you're an expert on lilac water now?" She arched one skeptical brow in his direction as she popped the top on her soda can.

And he almost felt a little embarrassed admitting this, but the truth was, "Believe it or not, I know an old family recipe. I used to help *my* grandmother with it every spring when I was little."

He couldn't read her expression when she said, "Here we've had all this discussion about lilacs and you never mentioned it."

He just shrugged. "A lot of people like lilacs, darlin'. Guess it's something our grandmas had in common."

"And you still remember how to do it?"

He tilted his head, thought back. "Been a while, but

I think so." His memories from that time were spotty, sparse, but for whatever reason, this one had stuck. "We made it for my mother's birthday every year—it was my present to her, something that didn't cost anything."

Across from him, Meg smiled. "I bet she loved it more than anything you could have bought."

A notion that made Seth offer up a wistful smile. "Fact is, I don't recall. I just remember making it, and bottling it up, and writing on the labels."

"Why didn't you tell me this before?" she asked, seeming more intent on the issue than he would have expected.

He gave another shrug as he reached for an apple, taking a big, crisp, crunchy bite. "Don't know. Didn't seem important."

"You never tell me much about you. I feel like I tell you a lot about me, but you never reciprocate."

Oh—*that's* why she was pressing on this. Most people didn't call him on that. Most people weren't as observant as her. Or maybe most people were more self-involved, happy to talk about themselves, happy to have someone listen and ask and give them attention. "Maybe I think you're more interesting than I am," he told her, adding another grin.

"I think *everyone's* interesting," she said. "Fifteen years of running this inn has taught me that everyone has a story worth hearing. And…maybe I'd be more open to…um, being seduced…if I knew more about you."

Damn, look at her, just putting it on the table like that. It impressed him. And created one of those moments when he thought maybe something hot and heavenly could still happen between them. Maybe when he least suspected it.

"Is that a promise, darlin'?"

She reached out to pick up an apple that rested between them near the basket—and he took the opportunity to reach out as well, to run the tip of one finger down the back of her hand.

She drew it smoothly away, along with the apple, and said, "No. Just...something to keep in mind."

But he knew she'd felt that electricity between them the same as he had. Just from that tiny little touch.

"So what do you say? Maybe after I finish painting today we make some lilac water?"

When her eyes met his, they were still cautious, tentative—but she slowly said, "Sure. Let's."

CHAPTER SIXTEEN

"Okay, we're gonna need a brick, a stainless steel bowl, and some kind of big pot—with a concave lid. I think my grandma used a canning pot. You have anything like that?"

It was nearly dusk by the time Seth had finished the second coat of paint and they'd let Miss Kitty out of hiding, then grilled burgers for a quick dinner.

"A brick?" Meg asked, squinting slightly at him in the kitchen where they'd just put dirty dishes into the sink, wondering if she'd heard him correctly.

"I know it sounds weird, but it'll make sense soon—trust me."

Trust him. She supposed she did now—mostly. Charmers gonna charm, but she grew less wary of that by the hour. He'd made her no promises other than doing good work for a fair price. And she didn't necessarily want any. They were making lilac water. And there was a mutual attraction between them that she'd probably never have the guts to act on—even if he did suddenly become some kind of open book. That was the extent of their relationship.

As for the times she'd found him in odd places in the house—she still didn't know what that was about, but maybe he'd truly just been exploring, like he'd said. Or checking out a noise as he'd claimed the first time.

The truth was—it bothered her wondering; added to any remaining wariness she suffered. But she *must* trust him—or she wouldn't have left him alone here last night. And obviously he hadn't hurt anything, nor stolen anything—there wasn't much to steal, and he'd shown up at work today like normal, even if she hadn't been as prepared for him as usual. She suspected thieves didn't generally return to the scene of the crime.

"I have stainless steel mixing bowls," she said, stooping to remove the nested bowls from a lower cabinet. "As for the pot... I think my grandma did some canning, and I even sort of remember a blue speckled canning pot, but it might require a trip to the attic."

"And the brick?" he asked.

She pointed toward the back door. "In the toolshed. There's been a pile of them there as long as I can remember—left over from when my grandpa laid the brick pathway that leads into the lilacs."

"Tell you what, darlin'. Why don't you show me the way to the attic and I'll go pot-huntin' while you round us up a brick."

"This is getting involved," she teased him.

"But it'll be worth it." He winked.

And she wondered just what kind of miracle lilac water they were going to create—or if it would actually just turn out the way hers always had in the past when she'd tried, not very potent nor worth the effort put into it. Or maybe the end product didn't matter much— maybe this was one of those moments when life was about the journey, simply the doing of something, the sharing of something with another human being.

She led him to the upstairs hallway where a square in the ceiling pulled down to reveal a foldable ladder.

Then she made her way back down and out to the shed. After a little cobweb removal, she had an old red brick in hand and carried it back toward the house. And when she stepped onto the patio, she caught sight of... *Hmm*, another penny. Just lying there on one of the flat inlaid stones.

This one was shinier, but faceup, same as the last. She stooped to pick it up. Read the year it had been minted: 2017. Nothing particularly noteworthy about that, though it had been when Aunt Julia died. She suddenly wished she'd noticed the year on the last one—although she wasn't sure why. Nor was she certain what had become of it. Perhaps it was still in a pocket somewhere, or had gone through the wash. She couldn't remember exactly what she'd even been wearing that day now to check.

And this penny gave her a little more pause. One had seemed random; a second felt like...well, okay, probably nothing. Sure, only Seth and she were here, but he could have dropped it, same as she'd speculated about the last—and Zack had actually been here, too. And for all she knew, the penny had been lying here unnoticed for weeks. Even if that seemed unlikely given that she and Seth both passed by this area pretty frequently lately. But still, it could happen.

Brick and penny in hand, she entered the house, lowering the coin into a small dish by the door next to an old key for the shed, which she usually locked up once summer came, just to keep curious kids from wandering in when playing in the yard. The brick she laid gently on the counter near the stove.

When Seth hadn't returned after a few minutes, she headed back up the wide polished wooden steps, past the books that still rested there, and called up into the attic from the bottom of the ladder, "Any luck?"

"Not yet, darlin'. Still lookin'."

Deciding she might as well go up and help him, she quietly climbed the ladder, and when she poked her head up into the attic, saw him rifling through a box of her old college books. Odd—since there obviously wasn't a canning pot inside.

And yet…it hardly seemed like the act of a criminal.

"I'm pretty sure you won't find it in there," she said, attempting to sound light.

His glance darted from the box to her. "Probably not," he said with his usual grin. "Just got distracted. These yours?" He held up a philosophy textbook.

"Yes. From college." She shook her head, then took the last few steps up into the attic. "Not sure why I kept them—I like books, so I guess I'm a bit of a pack rat in that way."

"I kinda like that—people who save stuff." He lowered the book back into the box, closed it up. "I haven't managed to hold on to anything from when I was young myself. Moved around too much, I guess."

And as he put the lid back on the banker's box, she realized that the word "Books" was even written on the side and top—clearly. It was no place to look for a pot. Which made his actions all the more confusing—and yet still harmless. Maybe he was just drawn to her way of life since his own sounded so transient.

That was when her eyes fell on the same large blue speckled pot from her memory, sitting on a shelf—in plain view. She pointed. "Found the pot."

He laughed. "If it had been a spider, it woulda bit me."

It was hard to understand how he hadn't seen it.

But then, she supposed that happened to everyone now and then.

Don't be completely naive. He had to have seen it. But he'd gone digging into a box of books anyway. What the hell does that mean? And are you sure you want to keep trusting him?

"It has exactly the right kinda lid," Seth declared about the pot.

"The lid matters?" she asked, drawn back to the task at hand.

"Yes ma'am—it's key to the process," he said with a grin, and she couldn't help thinking he liked the mystery he'd created around this recipe of his.

After they returned downstairs to the kitchen together, Seth set the pot on a stove burner and said, "Next, let's go gather up some lilacs."

Together, they walked out to the garden. Seth carried the largest stainless steel bowl and Meg toted a pair of garden clippers from the shed. "The only bad part of this," he said, "is you have to cut down some of your blooms. But it's a trade-off. And pick the ones you like the smell of the best."

Meg chose the French lilacs—they had the sweetest, most common and most potent scent, and she relished it even as she chose which blossoms to cut. She tried to draw from large clumps where a few blooms wouldn't be missed as much, and Seth held the bowl as she took cutters to the stems. They stood close to each other, maybe closer than necessary. So close that if the air hadn't been perfumed with lilacs, she would have smelled *him*—his skin, his sweat.

She'd seldom been as aware of a man's presence as she was of Seth's—always. Of course, maybe it would have felt the same with Zack in the beginning if their courtship had been slower, more drawn out.

Darkness fell around them, the sky fading from lavender to a deeper purple, stars and a half-moon beginning to appear up above. Sometimes their arms brushed together, sometimes their hands as she placed the lilac sprigs gently in the bowl.

Returning inside, full bowl in her grasp, it was necessary to turn on a light in the kitchen. Seth took the brick Meg had left on the counter and lowered it into the big pot, then reached for one of the smaller stainless steel bowls, which he placed, empty, on top of the brick.

"Next, the lilacs," he said.

"What do we do with them?"

"Come here and I'll show you."

She approached, bowl of blooms in one arm, as he said, "We're just gonna place 'em in the pan here, around the brick, in a circle. Help me."

And again, they stood close to one another. Reaching into the same bowl. Their hands touched, their fingers. She still smelled the lilacs, but now she *did* smell him, too. Just a faint, musky odor. A man who'd been working. A man who smelled like a man should.

Their arms brushed, and when he said, "Yeah, darlin', like that," it came out lower, a little raspy. She felt the words, their sound, in her breasts, and even in her panties. Occasionally, he raised his gaze, his eyes sparkling on her.

She was almost sorry when all the lilacs had been placed in the pan around the brick.

"Now we add some water," he said. "Got a pitcher?" But his voice still came out sounding sexy somehow. He might as well have been saying: *Now we take off our clothes.*

"Yeah." It left her in a whisper and required more effort than it should have to draw back from his nearness and get the pitcher from a cabinet a few steps away.

"Fill it up," he told her softly, and she did. The silent tension in the room made her hear the noise of the running water more than usual—made it seem loud, somehow more intense to her ears.

When she stepped back up to the stove, and to Seth, he said, "Pour it in—enough to mostly cover the blooms. But stop at the top of the brick."

She did so, and Seth used his fingers to press a few of the bulkier blossoms down into the water. After which he turned the burner on high. Then tossed her a sideways glance. "You ready to find out the secret, darlin'?"

It felt like a big question. The secret. She suspected he had many, even though she knew he was only talking about the lilac water. "Yes," she said.

He answered by taking the blue speckled lid and placing it upside down on the pot.

She just looked at him. "That's your secret? An upside-down lid?"

He chuckled softly. "Yep. Secret is…most people just boil blooms and bottle the water when they're done. What's gonna happen here is, the water's gonna absorb the scent but then start evaporating—and it's gonna make condensation on this lid." He pointed. "And then those little drops are gonna run down to the center of this lid and drip into our bowl. We're actually distilling the water, not just boiling it. Then we'll take our bowl of distilled lilac water and bottle it up, easy as that."

Meg stared at the pot, a little in awe. There *was* a secret. Distilling the water. "Amazing," she said.

It didn't take long for the water to boil—they could

hear it—and Seth used potholders to gently lift the lid
once, straight up, to show her the process in action, and
indeed, the distilled water dripped from the concave top
of the lid into the bowl below. "You get a lot less this
way, but it's good stuff." He raised his eyebrows in her
direction, then lowered the lid back into place.

The whole time, Meg suffered that magnetic pull
between them. *This would be simpler if I didn't. We'd
just be...platonic friends.* As it was, she didn't know
what they were, how to define their relationship. She
told herself over and over that he was only a guy doing
some work for her. But that was a lie and she knew it.
He was more.

She seemed to have an easier time accepting that
when under the influence of alcohol. Yet she wasn't
drinking now. And here she was, acknowledging it anyway, not running from it. Well, not completely, at least.
She still wasn't sure what she wanted to do about it, but
it was hard not to like the way he made her feel.

Standing there, literally watching a pot together, listening to the boil inside it, filled the air with anticipation. But it somehow felt more like waiting for...
seduction—or something—than just for the water to
finish distilling into the bowl.

When the boil died down, Seth turned off the burner.
And once again picked up potholders to lift off the lid,
this time giving it a little shake to drain any remaining drips of condensation into the fragrant lilac water
below. Indeed the potent scent filled the room when he
looked over to say with his usual grin, "I hope you've
got an empty little spray bottle handy for us to put this
in. I shoulda thought about that sooner."

"No worries," she said, and soon returned with one

from her bathroom. "I use this for shampoo when I go to visit my parents at Christmastime, but it's empty right now."

"Perfect," he said. It was the kind that came from the travel section of the drugstore.

"And…" she added, opening a cabinet door to reach under the sink, "I also have a funnel."

Seth let out a soft laugh and said, "That was my next question."

Working together, back to standing enjoyably close again, they poured the cooling lilac water into the bottle, after which Seth screwed on the cap. "Now you see it didn't make much, darlin', so use it wisely." He added a smile. He added a smile to *most* things, making everything he said seem…a little special.

"Next," he said, "the finishing touch. I'm gonna need some paper, scissors, a pen or marker, and some tape. For the label."

She blinked, then added a coy smile herself this time. "I can remember what it is without a label."

But Seth would have none of it. "No ma'am—this is nonnegotiable. It's not so much to help you remember as it's just part of how this is done." It came with his signature wink, and she realized that he was taking more fulfillment from this than she'd understood up to now—reliving something from his childhood, making this for her the same way he'd made it for his mother. Apparently there were certain sacred steps to be followed.

So she gathered the items he'd requested and watched him work at the counter, carefully writing and cutting and taping with the quiet intensity of an artist creating a masterpiece, until he handed the bottle back to her with an intricate little label affixed.

The words *Eau De Lilac*, written in a neat print with the purple Sharpie she'd handed him, were embellished with a little flower over the *i* and a decorative flourish underneath. A tool line rimmed the four edges of the label he'd cut from a white sheet of notepaper, as well.

"That's how it's done, ya see," he told her, his tone punctuated with a certain boyish humor she couldn't help finding appealing. "How we always did it. The lilac water wasn't finished until I'd drawn the special label and put it on the bottle."

She smiled. Because it wasn't much, but it was something—some little window of insight into his soul, his past, his memories. And perhaps a hint that there would be more if she was patient. And she wanted that, now not only to dispel mysteries about the stranger she'd let into her life but because she simply yearned to know him better.

"I bet your mom loved it," Meg said with a heartfelt smile. She found herself trying to imagine Seth as a little boy, wondered if he'd been as much of a charmer even then—if it was a natural trait or a learned one.

"I do believe she did, darlin'," he replied with a nod that struck her as wistful. Uncharacteristic for him. And this time he'd gone so far as to acknowledge his mom's reaction instead of claiming he didn't remember. Another little window cracking open.

"Do you ever…make it for her now?" A fishing expedition.

The answer came with a quick shake of his head as he looked away. "No." The word came out short, barely there, and he turned his attention to the sink, beginning to rinse out the little stainless steel bowl.

"Why not?" She knew from Zack that fishing sometimes took persistence.

"Aw, times change, Meg darlin'—you know that." A quick grin, not as sincere as most, and a glance her way that returned to the bowl in his hands almost quicker than she could catch it. "It's getting late, so we best get all this cleaned up."

"I can do it," she assured him, "if you want to get going."

"Naw, no rush—I'm happy to help." He seemed more relaxed now, his usual mode, since she'd let the subject change.

And despite herself, she was glad he wasn't leaving just yet. Though she didn't love feeling that way. When getting just a few more minutes with a man became a thing you wanted, it risked being a little depleting, meant you weren't quite as in control of your emotions as seemed wise to her. This was how she felt about Zack; she didn't need to feel it for another guy, too.

Though Suzanne would say it was okay. Miss Do-As-I-Say-Not-As-I-Do would tell her it was about flirtation and letting herself go with the flow—no biggie. She'd probably even call it healthy. So Meg tried not to overthink it. Tried to just relax into the gladness that the night wasn't yet ending.

Together they tidied up the kitchen. Meg loaded the dishwasher with dinner plates and glasses while Seth emptied boiled lilacs into the trash and washed the big blue canning pot in the sink, along with the steel bowls.

"Think I'll run this brick back out to the shed while

we're on cleanup duty or I'll forget and it'll sit here for days," she told him as he dried the pot with a dish towel.

He nodded and said, "I'll put this back up in the attic for you, too."

As she stepped out the back door, brick in hand, she tried to decide if she found that offer suspicious or not. Silly to, perhaps. There was nothing to find in the attic, after all—just attic stuff. So if for some reason he wanted to snoop around up there some more, he could have at it.

TIME. IT WASN'T on his side in this particular moment, but when else would he get the chance to be back in the attic? *So use it wisely.* Shoving the blue canning pot back onto the shelf it had come from, he scanned the area, hoping to catch sight of more books, or boxes labeled that way. Of course, maybe that made no sense— to think a book he'd hidden would end up in the attic, a place he'd never been when he was here before. But when he thought through all the variables, he still concluded it could be anywhere. Or nowhere.

Keeping one eye on the entrance where Meg could pop up anytime as she had a few hours ago, he did his best to quickly rifle through things without messing them up. Some boxes contained old bric-a-brac, empty picture frames, Christmas ornaments. Another old papers, folders, maybe from Meg's school days. He succeeded in finding another box of books, but they were more in the church hymnal and Sunday school study line. He looked quickly through them just the same, but of course didn't find the volume he sought. Damn it.

Letting out a sigh, he dropped the lid back on the

box. And disliked himself for a second, for all this damn searching through this woman's home.

A victimless crime, though. Most of his crimes hadn't been that way, so by that standard, this was nothing.

The heat between them was downright palpable. He'd never dreamed making lilac water with someone could be so sexy—and he gave a soft chuckle thinking that making it with Meg had been a damn sight different than with his grandma. He'd never imagined standing over a pot together would be so tempting. But something about him and Meg together…just being with her brought out that side of him.

Of course, some would argue *all* women did, that it was just how he was put together. Was there something different about this one? Hell. He didn't know, and it wasn't like him to over-examine such things. And this was a bad time for it anyway.

A glance back toward the square of light that opened down into the second floor hallway made him decide it was time to go, not get caught here again looking through her belongings. He quietly descended the drop-down ladder, then folded it back up into the ceiling, feeling better for being back out in the open.

The house lay still and quiet—no sound from below. Maybe she was still outside.

And so it made sense to just head back downstairs—if she was outside, it would be good to have her find him back in the kitchen when she returned.

But maybe it wouldn't hurt to take just one quick glance into one particular room.

MEG DRIED THE stainless steel bowls resting in the dish drainer, then put them away in a bottom cabinet. She took in the sunny rustic look of her kitchen, soaking up the yellow. Then she bent to pet the calico cat who had just sauntered up to rub against her ankle.

After which she lifted her gaze ceilingward, aware that Seth had had more than enough time to return the pot to the attic and come back down. She'd been waiting a few minutes now, in fact. Long enough that she felt herself drawn to the stairs.

By the time she reached the landing halfway up, she could see the attic door was no longer open. And something about that made her heart beat a little faster. Snooping in the attic was one thing, but... She let out a sigh, reminded that the snooping had *already* extended beyond the attic, and that maybe she'd just been trying to forget about that or believe she'd misinterpreted it.

As she reached the top of the stairs to find him nowhere in sight, she thought better of calling his name. If he was snooping, she wanted to catch him at it. Catch him at it enough that he wouldn't be able to fluff it off with an excuse, enough that he'd have to explain himself.

Zack wouldn't like this. He might even tell her it was dangerous to go trying to catch someone in the act of doing something potentially wrong in her house, that it might endanger her. But the more time she'd spent with Seth, the less wary of him she'd felt, and the more she believed they were building a real connection.

Don't be naive, Maggie May. Serial killers and psychopaths lure people with their charm all the time—that's how they get you. That was what Zack would say. But Zack wasn't here.

She walked quietly down the hallway, careful not to make any noise. Most of the upstairs doors were closed, same as when they were occupied by guests, but one stood open—as it often did during the months the inn stayed vacant.

She approached the entry to her bedroom, stopping in the doorway. Seth stood across the room, on the far side of the bed where the turret created a curved space that held a cozy chair and a special rounded bookcase Zack had had built for her birthday two years ago— this was not a casual peek into the room. Seth looked up, and indeed appeared caught.

"What are you doing?" she asked. Her voice came out smaller than intended, more worried than she wanted to sound.

His Adam's apple moved as he swallowed. "Something I shouldn't be, I guess."

She simply stared at him, stuck for words. Because she'd expected more of them from *him*. He looked caught yet not quite guilty, leaving her as perplexed about him as ever.

That was when he crossed the room, circling the bed, coming toward her.

Zack would think he meant her harm. But again, Zack wasn't here. So she stood her ground—until he was upon her. Until he was taking her face in his hands. Until he was kissing her. His mouth came down on hers with more passion and intent than any kiss she'd ever received.

Her hands rose instinctively to his wrists, closing around them, as she grappled with herself amid the kiss—let this happen, or push him away?

But he kept kissing her, soon pressing his tongue into her mouth.

That was when a wave of surrender passed over her,

consumed her, and her own tongue came to meet his. She gave up any internal struggle she'd been putting forth and let a stranger kiss her. Just as her grandmother once had.

And she understood why now, fully.

CHAPTER SEVENTEEN

HER GRANDMOTHER HAD always told her that life was full of surprises. And while life on Summer Island had perhaps held less of them than she might have expected, they did indeed come along from time to time—and the fact that she was letting Seth Darden undress her was a big one.

One minute it had only been kissing, kissing that felt at once wild but grounded, urgent yet moving in slow motion in her mind—and then he started to take off her clothes. First, his hands went under her shirt, exploring the planes of her back, his touch warm on her skin—almost even hot—as he smoothly began to push the fabric up, higher, higher, until he was removing it over her head with the help of her lifted arms. And then his fingers were at the opening to her jeans, and soon he was pulling them down, then closing his palms over her hips, fingers splayed—again heating her flesh with his touch. Every move seemed like slow motion in a way, and she felt a little outside herself, like she was watching it happen to someone else, maybe because she couldn't quite believe she was letting it take place.

But maybe all the messages of the last week or two had settled deep inside her—messages from Suzanne, messages from Zack—simply leading her to do what she wanted, what felt good and right in the moment.

Of course the rightness lay *not* in the fact that she kept finding him in places she shouldn't and that she still knew nothing about him other than that he was a skilled handyman who had a way with lilacs and smooth talking. The rightness was about the way he looked at her, the way he smelled, the way his clothes hung on his body, the grin, the wink—and now, his touch.

It spiraled all through her—and came as no surprise at all that the man knew how to use his hands on a woman's body as well as on a paintbrush or screwdriver.

The glide of his palm across her stomach, the graze of his fingertips down her arm, was as intoxicating as the scent of lilacs still filling her kitchen and now wafting vague and light through the whole house, rising the same way heat did, up and into the turret room as he lay her back onto her bed in only her bra and panties.

Part of her wished she'd worn nicer ones, but how could she have known? And Suzanne claimed that most men didn't really care about that anyway—they just wanted you naked.

Soon enough she *would* be—and the mere knowledge, along with everything else happening, turned her breath thready. From both excitement and nervousness. But the former overcame the latter enough that she found herself pushing up his T-shirt as well, running her own hands over muscles—in his arms, on his chest, stomach—that she'd only admired with her eyes up to now.

When he was shirtless—beautifully so—her hands dropped to the button on his blue jeans, as well. She bit her lip, aware of the hardness beneath her fingers, aware that she might luck the boldness to reveal it herself. When she hesitated, he took over, lowered his zipper, pushed the denim down. Her heart pounded against her rib cage almost painfully.

"I'm a little nervous," she confessed on a shaky breath. They lay face-to-face on her bed atop the covers.

And he lifted his fingertips to her cheek, brushed hair back from her face as he looked into her eyes. "'Cause we haven't known each other long, and my body is new to you," he said.

"Exactly," she said around a slight lump in her throat, at once surprised a guy could grasp the issue so clearly and unable to articulate it further herself.

"I love that about you, darlin'," he said, "that it makes you a little nervous. But thing is—you can relax because…well, this is something you can't mess up."

His soft smile wafted warmly through her, the perfect reassurance. It made her kiss him. It made her ready. For more.

And as he removed her bra, raining dewdrop kisses across her breasts, she gave herself over to pleasure and forgot to be nervous anymore. As he lowered her panties, she found herself tugging his underwear down, too—driven more now by instinct than thought or decision. And yes, some instances still felt a little awkward—because here they were, two people who didn't know each other well, suddenly connecting in the most intimate of ways. But the reassurance he'd given her made it okay.

It had been like that with Zack, too—some awkwardness the first time—because it had happened even quicker with him. With Zack, it had come with bits of nervous laughter, aided by alcohol. With Seth, though, no laughter of any kind, no acknowledgment on his part that anything was any less than perfect. Which maybe *made it*…perfect.

As he kissed his way down her stomach, that struck her. That perfection, as much as beauty, was in the eye of the beholder. That she could look for flaws in this moment, reasons it shouldn't be, reasons to feel unsteady or lacking or worried or regretful—or she could choose to see the perfection in this man who had walked onto her island and into her life and into her bed all so easily.

And that was how it stayed from that moment forward. When he parted her legs, it became easy to feel herself truly opening to him, opening *for* him. When he entered her, it became easy to accept him there—the pleasure, the fullness. When he began to move, it became easy to rise against him, meet his thrusts.

He put her at ease with every touch of his hand, every kiss on her skin, every deep stroke inside her hungry body, every time his eyes met hers in that dark, warm way, reminding her once more of a fallen angel…who was taking her to heaven.

And it was good.

MAYBE IT SHOULD have also surprised her how easy it was to lie cuddling with him afterward under the covers in her bed. She still had no idea what he was snooping around her house for, and that made him seem suspicious, no matter how you sliced it. And given that she'd been fretting over the hurt by another man mere days ago—hurt that lingered still now—it somehow felt tawdry to her that she'd slept with him. This wasn't who she was, how she saw herself. So it seemed to her that lying silently with him afterward, the room dimly lit by her grandmother's Tiffany lamp on the bedside table, should perhaps be even more awkward than the sex itself should have been.

But just like the sex, it wasn't.

Neither had spoken since their last gasps of passion a few moments before, and when she saw him tilt his head toward hers on the pillow in her peripheral vision, she waited for the grin, the wink. So perhaps the biggest surprise of all was when neither came, and when, instead, he lifted one fingertip to a spot high on her chest, and asked in a low whisper, "What happened here, darlin'?"

Though she didn't have to look down to know what he was asking about. It was a scar so pale and thin now that she no longer saw it in the mirror, or thought about it. Gran had once called it her badge of courage. "It's where my chemo port was." And—odd—just saying the words took her back there in time, to the strangeness of having something under her skin that didn't belong, and what it had been there for.

"Chemo port?" The inquiry came with caution, like he wasn't sure he should ask more, and she couldn't help thinking how blessed he was to have never known someone who'd gone through chemotherapy. And how she was about to ruin that in a way. Because it was a loss of innocence, cancer. A threshold that, once you cross it, for yourself or someone close to you, you can never really go back to the simplicity of life before it. The scars it left behind were more than just physical.

But she wanted to put him at ease, and it was an old subject, so she didn't mind explaining. "When you have chemo, they surgically implant a port under your skin that leads directly into the veins. You get your chemo through it and any other injections or medicines you need—it keeps your veins from being damaged."

"I never knew that," he said, then ran his finger the length of the thin white scar. "Did it hurt?"

"It hurt when a needle was put in, and sometimes it just ached a little. Even when it didn't hurt, though, I never really got used to it. Some people don't mind having them, but I was always aware of mine—it protruded through my skin, like a hard bump. I tried to think of it as…well, like a friend, because it was the portal for medicine that would save my life—but I was so happy when they finally took it out."

He lifted his gaze to her eyes then, and something in his expression made her realize how open she'd just been. But she'd never thought about being any other way. Because hell, she'd just had sex with him, and she liked him, obviously, and whether or not it was wise, she felt a connection with him now. So being honest about this had come naturally.

"What…was it like? Having cancer. Getting the treatment." This question came in an even lower tone, like something forbidden. He clearly didn't know if he should ask.

And God knew it wasn't a pleasant subject, but…had Zack ever asked her? About this? She'd told him stuff, especially around the time they'd been caring for Aunt Julia together—but had he ever actually asked, wanted to know, wanted to hear? It was long in the past, and yet also still a part of her, who she was—anyone who'd walked that road knew that; it became a part of the fabric of a person. So despite the darkness of it, she liked that Seth wanted to know.

"It was the worst time of my life," she confided.

"Scary to be so young and suddenly not know if you're going to live or die. And it was…humbling. I had everything going for me. One day I was wearing designer suits and heels to a high-rise office building, feeling on top of the world, planning a wedding, and looking forward to everything the future held. The next, all that was gone and I was lying on a couch just trying to hold on to any little bit of strength I had left inside me to keep going."

She watched him take a breath, let it back out. It was heavy and he was feeling that weight. But he didn't look afraid of it, and he didn't back away from it. "The chemo—it was as hard as people say?"

She nodded against a lavender pillowcase. "It affects everyone differently, but for me it was rough. It zapped all my energy, and all my thoughts. The best way I can describe it is that it makes you feel like…nothing. I would just lie there, without the energy to even think. It's hard to explain, but for me that was even worse than the physical depletion."

"Did you lose your hair?"

Another nod. Another memory of what it was to be stripped down to your very core.

Yet the weight of it all was getting *too* heavy now, even for her. She didn't mind going back there on occasion, but no need to wallow in it. "The good news, though, is that I tolerated radiation better, and my hair grew back, and here I am, healthy and strong with all of that far behind me. When I came here to recuperate I was still pretty fragile, but Gran took good care of me, and the peacefulness of the place was very healing—it was an easy place to be at a hard time." Talking about all this was reminding her of that part of it, too—restful afternoons curled up in a chair in the garden, wrapped in an old quilt, smelling flowers, listening to birds sing, reading books, and wearing one of Gran's floppy sun hats over slowly growing hair.

"Even if I'm thinking of leaving now, I'll always be grateful that this island, and house, were both here for me when I needed someplace to retreat to."

"Seems like it really…changed your life. I mean, more than it does even for most people. It changed… everything *about* your life."

She blew out a breath, thinking what an astute observation he'd just made. Because truly, it was as if she'd been one person before leukemia, and another after. Nothing had ever gotten back to being the same for her. Somewhat by choice. Staying here had meant selecting a different path than the one she'd been on. But it had changed her in less obvious ways, too—she'd become less ambitious, less assertive, and she'd wrapped herself in a cocoon of sorts here. Maybe…afraid to become a butterfly. Because the cocoon felt safer.

But this reply she kept simpler. "Yes—in some ways for the better and in some probably for the worse. But I try to focus on the better parts. Of pretty much anything."

Did his eyes turn a little sad then, or just wistful? "Sounds like a wise way of looking at life, Meg darlin'."

"Why do you seem sad?" she asked. Not even a fishing expedition—just an honest question.

"Do I?" She saw him attempt a grin and fail.

"Yes."

He blinked, sighed. "Maybe I'm just real sorry you had to go through something so awful. Sad *anybody* has to go through such bad things. But I'm kinda awed by how strong you are about it all."

The simple sentiment made her heart expand a little in her chest. Had anyone ever called her that before—strong? Had anyone ever noticed that about her? "Thank you," she whispered.

And reached up to touch his bare chest with her palm. A smattering of light brown hair trickled to a line that led down his stomach. She took a second to let herself just soak in the masculine beauty of him—and to feel that this really *was* okay, what she'd done with him. It wasn't reckless; it wasn't tawdry. And it came with extra, unexpected gifts. Like being recognized as strong.

"Can I ask you something?" Her voice floated through the mid-evening air, as cautious as his had been asking questions. The faint perfume of lilacs still graced the room.

"What's that, darlin'?"

"You…never tell me anything about *your* past." She bit her lip. "And you don't have to if you don't want to, and I don't mean to pry. But…" She stopped, smiled. "I just spilled my guts to you. Because I feel comfortable with you. So I hope you can be comfortable with me, too. That's all."

Seth took his time replying. It was something his father had taught him. *Most people answer ya fast, feel they gotta fill that air up with talking. But speak before ya think and it can get ya in trouble. Truth is, people'll wait for your answer, so ain't no need to rush it. You just take your time and choose what you mean to say.* Slow, well-thought-out answers were a tool of his trade. His old trade. But he'd learned they served him well in life most of the time regardless—it was good to choose your words carefully, and this was a moment when that applied.

"Well, what is it you want to know, darlin'?" He flashed a smile to try to lighten things up. Even if he was the one who'd turned them so serious. He hadn't meant to—and yet he wasn't sorry. He liked that she'd shared so much with him. He liked knowing her better, knowing more about where she'd been and what made her tick. And that made her question seem fair, and made him begin to think, wonder…could he tell her? The truth? At least part of it?

"I've never really known anyone who…didn't live anyplace in particular," she went on. "It intrigues me, I suppose. It makes me think…you must have a story you're not telling me. And I'm curious. I mean…we just had sex. And maybe this is a leap, but I'm guessing it might happen some more. And we've been spending a lot of time together. It's only natural that I would wonder."

Yep, all that was true. And he was quick to answer at least one part of her questioning. "I'm sure as hell *hoping* it'll happen some more, darlin'."

She responded with a pretty smile that reached down into his stomach—but left all her other questions hanging in the air, waiting for answers. And the way she made him feel seemed…like something to be damn cautious of, the kind of thing that could probably make a man sell his soul—if he let it.

But at the same time, she was so guileless that it left him feeling rubbed raw in a way, like she was peeling off layers he used to protect himself and getting down

to where there wasn't much of that left. All with her
honesty, all with her trust.

And maybe he didn't *want* to be trusted. Not *that*
way. So many people had trusted him before, and almost every one of them had lived to regret it. He'd seldom been there to see it—he'd already moved on. And
he'd long since learned to put up a wall that wouldn't let
him think about the damage left in his stormy path—
but behind that wall it all still lurked, waited, for him
to feel it someday. He didn't want to make Meg regret
her trust. And he was pretty sure he would before this
was all over.

And so he had no earthly idea what he was thinking
when he said, "My mom died when I was just a kid,
and after that I was raised by my dad. Down south. In
Mississippi, like I told you. And...a lot of other places."

"Oh Seth, I'm sorry." He could hear that sympathy in
her voice, sympathy he wanted to avoid. Because it had
been a long damn time ago and he'd gotten over the loss
a long damn time ago—because he'd had to. He could
hear her...caring. About him. Which was why it was a
bad idea to go down this road. For her sake. "How old
were you? When she died?"

"Ten."

She gasped. The way women will do over tragedy.
Such soft hearts. *Don't be soft for me, Meg. Be strong.
Like you were with leukemia.*

"How?" Not "how did it happen?" but just the one
simple word.

"Car accident. She was hit by a drunk driver on her
way to work."

That part she didn't reply to—not with words anyway so much as her eyes. It relayed a certain under-

standing. That she wasn't the only one who'd suffered; that he, too, knew what it was to have life pull the rug out from under you.

At last, she spoke quietly. "I'm guessing that changed pretty much everything about *your* life."

"More than you know." *Shit, shut up. That's what happens when you answer too fast—words come out that you didn't intend to say.*

"How do you mean?"

Stop. Think. Choose your words. It just came harder right now than usual because he never told anyone this stuff. Usually it was just about charming them. Being strategic. Getting whatever he wanted from them. This felt different.

He drew in a breath, slowly let it back out before answering. "I never saw my grandparents again—my mom's parents. We'd lived with them, her and me. And I know Dad moved me a long way south, but…well, it was weird that they weren't around after that. Never even a phone call or a birthday card—nothing."

Under the covers, she squeezed his hand in hers. "You must have missed them terribly."

Why was that hard to admit? Even to let himself feel? But he did, because it was true. "Yeah."

"And you don't know why? Other than the distance?"

He swallowed back a small lump in his throat. Damn. Then pushed aside memories that tightened his chest in order to reply. "Not really. When I would ask my dad, he'd say it was just him and me now, so I guess he was trying to…you know, deflect the question, protect me. I imagine it was too far to travel. For them. Or for him to take me." He shook his head. "But it was a long time ago and life goes on, Meg darlin'." He reached for a smile, pulled one up. The effort was slight, natural, the way he moved through life.

"Like my leukemia," she said knowingly.

"Exactly." They'd both walked hard roads, they'd both survived—and now they could talk about other, better things.

"So your dad moved you around a lot. Was that for work?"

So much for better things. And despite himself, the question drew out a quick laugh. "In a manner of speaking," he told her. Again answering too damn soon. Saying leading things that would make her ask more. Hell.

"What did he do?"

At this, Seth stopped, stopped everything—stopped talking, stopped thinking about the best way to reply. He just looked at her, looked into her eyes and really saw her. This kind, strong, vulnerable woman. He'd always thought it was a bad trait, vulnerability—but she made it look good. Made him want to be like her. So damn open. Cautious in some ways, but ultimately brave enough to trust him to work in her home—when she shouldn't have, when he had an ulterior motive.

Maybe he should see her like any other mark, not as a person but as a means to an end—and maybe he should view her trust as weak or dumb. But instead there was something kind of beautiful about it. Something that made him think she was amazing—to trust, to still believe in the good in people, after what her fiancé had done to her when she was young. He only wished she'd picked someone else to believe in, someone worthy.

And hell. That was when something broke inside him, some kind of dam that held in all the secrets—

because he just wanted to let it all out, be honest with her. At least as honest as he *could* be.

"Meg darlin', my father was a con man. And before I knew it, he'd made me into one, too."

CHAPTER EIGHTEEN

MEG'S HEART FROZE in her chest. She tried not to let the shock and horror show on her face. She was in bed with him, after all. And despite certain concerns, she'd seen so much good in him. But what he'd just said raised more questions than she could fathom.

He went on, saving her from having to reply. "Not anymore, though. I've left that life behind. Left *him* behind, altogether."

Now she managed some words. Just a few. "Left him behind how?"

"Just packed my bags one day when he wasn't around, got in the car, and started driving. North. Didn't look back. We were in Alabama at the time. Threw my cell phone out the window somewhere on I-65 so he couldn't even try to reach me. Kinda dramatic, I guess—but it seemed like the simplest way to just cut all ties, just like that, ya know? That was six months ago."

"Six months," she murmured. Wishing it had been, say, six years. Six months wasn't long. Six months was yesterday.

Her head still whirled at this unexpected turn of events. Though…was it *totally* unexpected? Hadn't she known there was something not entirely aboveboard about him? She'd tried to believe the best about him, tried to let Suzanne's encouragement make her think wariness was silly, tried to remember she was always safe here on the island—but now some cold hard truths hit home. Drifters didn't drift because their lives were amazing and stable. The world was filled with people ready to scheme and trick and take advantage of trusting, innocent people. Zack's concern had been valid. Zack, Zack, Zack. Always in the back of her head, even now—such a fixture in her heart. And so far from perfect—yet not a con man, not a drifter, not someone who would ever hurt anyone in the way Seth was telling her his father had hurt people. And maybe he had, too. It was all so nebulous and sketchy at this point.

She would be wise to ask him to leave. Right now. No more tiptoeing into the unknown here. It was dangerous.

"I shouldn't have told you," he said quietly. "You're worried now."

She wasn't sure how to reply. She only knew her chest had gone tight, her whole body more tense than a minute before. "Should I be?" she whispered.

"No." Spoken quickly and low. "I'm sorry. So sorry, darlin'. I'd never want to scare you or make you worry. But you asked, and so I'm just being honest with you. Because I want to do that. Be honest."

"Because you aren't *usually* honest with people?" she dared ask.

He pinned her in place with his eyes, trapping her in that warm, warm gaze of his. Even now, something in it buried her, owned her a little. "I am now. I have been for the past six months." He looked so intense; she could feel him wanting so badly for her to believe him...and she did. At least in this moment.

"I spent the winter picking up odd jobs through Tennessee and Georgia," Seth told her, thinking maybe it would help to keep talking, help make her under-stand, "but when the weather broke, guess I found my-self wanting to keep heading north."

"To find your grandparents," she said. Stated, not asked.

"No," he told her. But ironic as hell she thought that, since he'd unwittingly found them anyway—on her bul-letin board. "Just...to get farther away."

Turned out distance had been as necessary as time to make him feel fully separated from his father. Like the man would somehow be able to track him down, drag him back to the life he'd always known. Both were impossible, and yet some ties were hard to break, even when you knew it was best. Or hell, maybe it was just his past in general he needed to get further away from, however he could.

"Seems like you'd go to your grandparents," she said. Sounding thoughtful now. Calmer. More like the com-passionate woman he'd come to know.

But he shook his head. He'd gone down a reckless road here, but he couldn't see any other way than to just keep being real with her now that they'd come this far. "No idea if they'd be happy to see me, or vice versa, all things considered."

"I'm sure they would. I mean, if your father is the kind of guy you say, it makes sense that he would con-nive to keep you away from them."

"Maybe—never could be certain. But...not sure I'd be proud to let them see how I've turned out." Hell. Something else to scare her. It was as if opening this door had taken away every ounce of sense he had. *Choose your words carefully and you know when to shut up. Don't—and this happens.*

"How *did* you turn out, Seth? I mean…what kind of things have you done?"

Asked warily, but a fair enough question. One he had to figure out how to answer now. Still wanting to be honest, but also make her see that he'd changed. Mostly anyway. Some people thought a person *couldn't* really change. And he thought he had. Or he was trying like hell to. And…shit, he still wasn't sure he wouldn't hurt this woman, still knew he couldn't tell her the entire truth about why he was here—and yet he wanted to earn her respect, her faith in him, more than he could understand. It was the epitome of being stuck between a rock and a hard place, torn between good and bad, right and wrong.

"You know how sometimes on the news you see stories about workers who ask for payment up front to do roofing or plumbing or home repairs, and then they disappear with people's money?"

Next to him, she nodded.

"That was us. What my dad's always been, and what he taught *me* to be. We lived mostly in motels, moving from town to town before anybody could figure out what was up. We'd get enough money to take it easy awhile—then it would run out and we'd be on to the next scam. Sometimes we'd lift a credit card here or there, a wallet from a restaurant table, but mostly we started work we didn't finish even though we'd already been paid for it.

"I'm not proud of it, darlin'—not any of it. Damn ashamed actually." He shook his head against the pillow. "Not even sure why I'm telling you. Never planned to tell anybody, ever. Just planned to do better, walk the straight and narrow, make an honest living—learn how to do that. That's why I'm here, working for you. Just trying to live right."

"And are you? Living right? I mean, have you been honest with me?"

"I've been doing honest work, haven't I? Haven't asked you for anything I haven't earned. And would I tell you all this if I was up to no good? Though I guess... damn, I wouldn't blame you if you don't want anything more to do with me, if you send me packing."

"You're telling me the truth here?" she asked, still clearly needing that confirmation, still appropriately wary of a guy who'd just admitted he'd spent his whole life being a crook.

"Every word I've said is the truth, darlin'." Even if he hadn't told her everything. And the part he couldn't tell her she really didn't need to know. It would never affect her.

And hell—the way things were going, he wasn't gonna find what he'd come looking for anyway. Which was discouraging, but...maybe he'd been meant to come here for other reasons. Life worked in funny ways sometimes, and he'd be damn sorry if he never found the book he'd been searching for, but he'd found Meg instead. A woman who made him feel something brand new: A desire for her respect.

Even so, though, he had to make the offer to go. Because he wanted to *earn* her respect, not try to force it. "If you want me to leave, darlin', just say the word."

"Why *did* you tell me all this?"

He thought through that. "You asked. You asked me to open up to you the same way you did with me. Maybe I shouldn't have. Or maybe I should have made up a lie, something that sounded better and would make you comfortable. But I'm trying my damnedest to be out of the lying business these days, so… I just answered your questions, for better or worse."

He peered up at the ceiling of the dimly lit room, thinking of the evening just past. Lilac water. Sex with a good woman. Sweet scents in the air. Even now, a partly open window across the room admitted a breeze that lifted the curtains and smelled like spring. A good night by anyone's standards, and maybe one of the best of his life, coming in only behind fond childhood memories that grew dimmer with each passing year. And now he'd dropped something ugly onto it, changed it into something less than it had been.

"I'm sorry if I ruined the evening, Meg darlin'. You just made me want to be real with you. And that's a compliment, by the way."

She stayed silent for a long moment. He let that silence fill the space around them, let himself get comfortable with it. He usually was. Waiting to hear Meg's next words, though, made it harder than usual.

"I…don't think I want you to go," she finally said. "At least not right now." Voice soft as that spring breeze, more delicate than normal and maybe a little unsure. But still an answer that left him feeling…bolstered, like all was not lost here, like maybe it would all be okay.

"Thank you," he said, just as gently. "I'm glad."

She lifted one brow. "But if you suddenly start trying to get me to sign over the inn to you, I'll know something fishy's going on."

He laughed. Then connected their gazes in the shadowy light. "I hope you believe me, Meg. I hope you know I wouldn't tell you all this if you couldn't. But again, I understand if you decide you don't."

"I'll… I'll be thinking about it all."

"Of course, darlin'," he said, and then he leaned over and kissed her forehead. And she reached to turn out the lamp next to the bed, bathing the room in darkness save for a small square of moonlight admitted through the open window.

As he rolled over to go to sleep in Meg's bed, he basked in the comfort of it—of getting to fall asleep in this house with this woman, of her trust even if only tentative. And he wished he felt as sure of himself as he wanted to, as trustworthy as he kept telling her he was. He'd felt so damn sincere asking for her faith, as if it was real—when he still kept secrets from her.

WAKING UP THE next morning was strange. Maybe a part of Meg wished Seth hadn't told her the truth about himself last night—but she was a practical enough woman to know that it was really closer to wishing the truth had just been different, more innocent, less jarring. Maybe having mysteries surrounding him had been better than this.

On the other hand, surely knowing was truly better. Now the questions were answered. Now all she had to do was decide whether those answers were okay with her. He was a confessed con man. A man who cheats, lies, steals. Though one who promised her he doesn't anymore. Of course he *would* say that. But…why tell her any of this if he hadn't changed his ways? It was a lot to puzzle through.

And she was lying naked next to him in bed.

In retrospect, maybe suggesting he go back to his cabin last night would have been wise. But she hadn't— because for the most part, for smarter or dumber, she had believed him. And she felt safe with him—still. Perhaps that was naive—the effects of passion and sex and touches that had felt more natural than weird. But there it was: A sense that all was well here. Even if the morning felt a little awkward anyway. Because she wasn't used to waking up naked with anyone besides Zack. The very thought of which made her heart hurt a little.

Without looking to see if Seth was awake yet or not, she scampered as silently as possible to grab a robe from a hook on her bathroom door across the room. She slid her arms into the sleeves and swiftly tied the terrycloth sash, then turned to see the handsome man in her bed smiling at her.

"Mornin', darlin'."

She let out a small gasp. Then composed herself. "I didn't know you were awake. Good morning. How did you sleep?"

"Like a baby."

She had, too, actually. But chose to attribute it to spring air and weary bones after some tiring days.

"I'd better get at it early if I'm gonna have everything done before your guests show up."

She nodded—though she'd nearly forgotten. The guests were due. She had an inn to run. Life went on despite unexpected sex and the unexpected news that her new lover was an ex-con man. "Are you hungry for breakfast if I make some?"

He flashed his signature sexy grin. "Wouldn't turn it down if you're so inclined."

"I am." She guessed she'd worked up an appetite last night. "Bacon and eggs? Or pancakes?"

"Both sound pretty damn delicious."

"I make a mean pancake," she informed him.

"Well, I wouldn't want to miss out on *that*, darlin'. Pancakes it is."

And so apparently things were going to go on like normal here. Which was good. Easy. What would make them both comfortable. And she saw no reason to belabor his confession—either she believed him and should let it lie, or she didn't and should make him go. So far, the former seemed to be winning out.

So without further ado, she started to head downstairs to get the griddle heated and batter mixed. Though she stopped at the door to glance back. "One question—about the things you told me last night."

She regretted the somber expression that replaced his grin when he said, "What's that, Meg?"

But asked anyway. "You didn't tell me what made you leave your dad the way you did."

"Wasn't happy," he told her simply. "Didn't like my life. Never had. And decided to try and change that before it was too late."

It was a good answer. Though of course now a tiny part of her had to question: *Is he scamming me, charming me, telling me what I want to hear?* Charmers gonna charm and last night's admission gave that a whole new meaning. But again—she had to choose whether to believe him, and for the moment anyway, she didn't have evidence not to. So she just said, "Thank you. For telling me."

Then proceeded down the wide staircase toward the kitchen, feeling that her life had taken a noticeable twist in the night. Just like when leukemia had struck, just like when Seth's mother had died—while less traumatic, this was one of those moments that caused a shift, a difference in the way the very air around her felt, a difference in everything. No matter what happened now, nothing in her world would ever be quite the same again.

"DELICIOUS AS PROMISED," Seth told her half an hour later across the table. The scent of lilacs had been replaced with the aroma of buttermilk pancakes made from her grandma's recipe. And despite everything, it felt nice to eat with him, nice to share a good breakfast in her newly made-over kitchen. She only hoped she wasn't being foolish to trust, hoped it wasn't sex and closeness blinding her.

"Glad you like them."

"I like more than just the pancakes, darlin'," he told her, then pointed the fork in his hand in her general direction. "I'm likin' the view, too."

The saucier, flirting side of Seth was back—and she glanced down to see her robe gaping open in front.

He was fully clothed, and she'd thought perhaps she should get dressed herself—but it had just seemed easy to cook in her robe, and easy to eat in it while the pancakes were hot.

"Only problem," he said, "is that knowing you got nothing on under that is making me hungry for more than just pancakes."

As she rose from the table, pulling the terrycloth together in front and tightening the tie, she smiled inwardly. She hadn't been with many guys, and this was reminding her that a new connection with a man was filled with bits of sexy magic that nothing else in the world could really provide. The newness made every flirtation or seduction more exciting and grand. "Too bad," she said, "that we both have so much work to do."

She glanced over her shoulder at him as she moved to the sink with her plate. "I'm going to clean this up, get dressed, and get busy."

She was rinsing the plate under the faucet when two hands came from behind, sliding warm around her waist. It was like that first day, the day he'd eased up behind her and taken the shutter from her grasp—but oh so different. Smooth and stealthy no matter how you sliced it, though. Smooth and…mmm, sexy as hell, pressing against her in a way that left no doubt as to his desire.

Then she felt him reaching to untie the sash she'd just pulled tight. Felt his hands sliding hot across her skin. Felt her own hands abandoning the plate with a clatter, unplanned.

Moments later he was laying her back across the kitchen table he'd just repainted for her, giving it a use it had never had before. And with that easy surrender came the knowledge that she did trust him, that she wasn't going to think this over and change her mind. She trusted Seth Darden. In her home. And with her heart.

SETH FELT LIKE a man revived as he went through guestrooms looking for walls or baseboards that needed touch-up paint or repairs. Telling Meg the truth about his past had been hard, likely foolish, and damn unsettling. But once he'd realized that she wasn't going to throw him out of her life, it had also felt…like a freedom of sorts.

He'd tried to change his life—and his dad's—before last fall. He'd suggested that they go straight, do fair labor—they both had the necessary skills and Seth enjoyed putting his to work as he'd had the opportunity to do at Meg's. But his dad had been all about easy money. Beating the system. He took no joy in an honest job—it was why he'd turned to a life of conning and scamming. The only real satisfaction he'd ever taken from much of anything in Seth's estimation had been in getting something for nothing, feeling like he was somehow smarter than the rest of the poor schmucks who made their money through work and toil.

And so when it was clear that his dad would never change, he'd told him he wanted to at least change his *own* life, settle down someplace, start his own business, go down a new path. But good old dad…he was good at paying lip service to something only to then get in the way of it. He was needy—and wouldn't let Seth go. Every time Seth had tried, his dad was suddenly sick, or lonely, or just sadly declared he didn't want to lead a life without Seth in it. *It's always been me and you, son—we're a team. Why would you want to leave your old man? You're all I've got, son.* And he loved his dad, even with all his faults. Because his dad loved *him*—even if in some twisted ways.

When he'd left his father behind that surreal December day—having come to realize a clean break that felt like an escape was the only way to really separate their lives—that had felt like freedom, too. Freedom came in a lot of different guises, turned out.

Most of the rooms were in pretty good shape, though the baseboards in the mint room, as Meg called it, needed some touching up, as had one in the rose room.

Now he was in the blue room, where nudging a baseboard in one corner behind a bedside table with the toe of his work boot made him realize it was loose—

so loose that when he slipped the tip of a screwdriver behind it, a section fell off completely, having been held there only by a few finishing nails too small for the nail holes.

The missing baseboard revealed a jagged opening at the foot of the headboard, a couple inches high and nearly a foot across. A great place for mice...or maybe something else.

Perhaps it wasn't wise to stick his hand in a hole that could be home to spiders or vermin or God knew what else—and yet he didn't hesitate, holding his breath with anticipation as he reached inside. Because something about the spot felt strangely...right.

When his hand touched a dusty hardcover book, it was like being able to breathe again.

Like getting new life.

The book. He'd found the book.

He hadn't just imagined hiding it here all those years ago. He'd really hidden it. And no one had ever found it.

Until now. His heart beat faster in his chest.

He pulled it out, brushed a thick swath of dust off the cover. *The Wizard of Oz.* A gift from his grandparents after he'd discovered the movie as a kid, watching it with them one rainy night over a bowl of buttered popcorn and cherry Coke. So magical and scary. And at an age before he'd been too cool to admit being totally drawn into it.

He'd brought the book on their summer vacation here. He wasn't much of a reader, but his mom and grandmother had been trying to get him interested in books, and Grammy had suggested he might like to read it in bed at night or sitting in the garden.

He never had. Instead he'd carefully, painstakingly

damaged it. He'd opened it to Chapter 1, past the first few pages that came before that, and he'd used the tip of the pocketknife his dad had given him that year for Christmas. He could still hear his mother and grandpa talking about that.

He's a little boy—what does he need a knife for?

Oh, relax, honey—Ron meant no harm. Fellas just like to have pocketknives is all. Same way gals like to carry around fingernail files.

Instead of reading the book at night, Seth had used the knife to carve out a small thin slot in the margin—all the way through to almost the back of the book. A hiding place.

It was among the earliest forms of deception his dad had taught him—*See, you can cut a hole into a book and hide something there. Can't be nothin' big, but there's plenty o' valuable things in this world that are little.*

Of course, now Seth would see if the other part of the memory—the thing that had drawn him here—would hold up as true. He realized he was holding his breath again as he opened the cover, then flipped past those first few pages.

And then he saw it. Inside the hidden slot that started at Chapter 1 rested the diamond ring he'd taken from Meg's grandma when he was ten years old.

Part 3

"If I run, I may fall down and break myself."
"But could you not be mended?" asked the girl.
"Oh yes, but one is never so pretty after being
mended, you know."

—*L. Frank Baum,*
The Wonderful Wizard of Oz

CHAPTER NINETEEN

THE KITCHEN STILL smelled like lilacs. And Meg knew that for the rest of her life the scent would make her think of Seth Darden. And making lilac water with him. And having sex with him. She inhaled deeply, breathing it in. Trying to decide if that was a good thing or a bad one.

No, stop it—it's a good thing. No matter what happens now, it was an amazing night.

She was in no way sure what would happen. She wasn't even sure what she *wanted* to happen. Of course, at the moment she was all caught up in the afterglow, almost feeling clingy in a way she didn't want to act on. Because she'd read enough books to know most women were programmed so that sex bonded them to a man. And that it wasn't wise to have sex with a guy you didn't want to feel attached to.

Fine time to remember that.

But you're a big girl—it'll be okay.

Even if it was just a one-time thing. Well, two times if you counted the post-breakfast connection on the table. *But whether this is the end of it or if it happens again—whenever he moves on, it'll be okay.* Although the very thought made her bite her lip as she stepped into the nook and peeked out the window on a bright, blue-sky day. Because if it happened again, she'd become more attached.

But quit analyzing it so much. You're both adults who acted on a mutual attraction. And you're not committed to anyone, and this is exactly the sort of opportunity it's fun to have when not committed.

Just then, her text notification sounded. *Please don't let it be Zack.* A rare and surprising response from her—perhaps a first.

The message had come from Suzanne. The alyssum is here, so I'm holding a tray of white aside for you. Meg wanted to add some to the pots on the patio as companions to other flowers, but Suzanne had sold out of it and had ordered more from a supplier on the mainland.

Meg texted back. I'll come get it in a few. Then added another. Are you busy? If I made sandwiches, could you take a lunch break?

If you're making, I'm eating. Come on down, the weather's fine.

Be there in fifteen.

As Meg made peanut butter and jelly sandwiches in the kitchen—once again awash in lilac scent now that the pancakes were gone—two thoughts flitted through her mind. That it was nice to have a friend you knew well enough to make a sandwich for without having to ask what sounds good. And that getting out of the house was the opposite of being clingy—*so take that, whatever attachment chemical sex lets loose in the body.*

After adding some snack chips and sodas to the picnic basket, she walked to the foot of the stairs and casually yelled upward, "Seth? I'm heading down to the flower shop for a while. But help yourself to whatever you like for lunch."

"Oh. Okay," came his voice in reply.

Did he sound a bit caught off guard, like he'd assumed they'd eat together? It almost made her feel guilty. Yet she pushed it aside. Such politeness was a habit. And one she usually liked in herself—but she had a lot of thinking to do about Seth. And everything he'd told her about himself last night. And Zack. And everything he'd *never* chosen to tell her.

That realization stayed with her as she stepped out into a warm Summer Island day and started up Harbor Street.

Seth's past was…frightening. It made him seem like trouble, like exactly the kind of guy Zack had assumed he was. It created so many questions. Was he truly reformed? Could someone with a past like his really ever be *completely* reformed? *Completely* trustworthy?

And yet he'd told her. She'd asked and he'd told her. Confessed horrible things. She'd known he was holding back, and now he'd trusted her enough to make her understand why. And Zack…never had. Trusted her enough. To tell her about his past, his childhood. For all she knew, he'd been a con artist, too—or worse.

So even while Seth's truth was scary—he'd shared it.

As she retreated from the bright sunlight into Petal Pushers, Suzanne called through a back screen door. "I'm at the picnic table."

Meg passed through the shop's interior and back outside to find her friend seated at the old wooden table that had adorned the concrete patio between the shop and the greenhouses for years, currently a lime green. "I'm feeling lavender this year. What do you think?"

Every summer Meg and Aunt Julia had painted the table a new color, and Suzanne had been happy to go along with the tradition. Meg smiled. "I like it. Painting party later this week maybe? Before my guests show up?"

Suzanne nodded. "I'll get the paint and it's a date. Friday night." Then she dug into the basket Meg had just lowered to the table. "Oooh, PB and J. It never gets old, does it?"

"I felt like something old-school and simple today." She'd confided in Suzanne on previous peanut butter and jelly occasions that it always reminded her of her grandma, who'd fed them to her from her childhood right on up until she was recovering from leukemia. Through her adulthood, she'd often turned to such staple items as a source of comfort.

"What's the occasion?" Suzanne asked. "Still missing Zack?"

Meg pulled half her sandwich from a plastic baggie and bit into it. "No. It's that I had sex with Seth last night."

Suzanne's jaw dropped, along with half of *her* sandwich, to the table. "Wh-what?"

Meg raised her eyes to her friend, then drew them back down. "You heard me."

Suzanne blinked, twice. "Correctly, apparently." Then she narrowed her gaze. "But I'm going to need some details."

"We made lilac water," she began, then relayed the general series of events that had followed. Though she didn't fill her in on Seth's past. Maybe she would at some point, later, once he was gone from their lives. But for now, it just didn't feel like her story to tell. And besides, she didn't want to worry Suzanne, whose original concerns about Seth seemed to have faded in direct correlation with his hotness.

"That's…incredible," Suzanne said when she was finished, still appearing rather agog. "And was it amazing and hot and perfect?"

Meg considered the question. "Amazing, yes. Hot, yes. Perfect—well, as perfect as it can be with someone you don't know very well."

Suzanne's shock gave way to happy approval the longer they talked, and she wore a supportive smile as she asked, "And how do you feel about it now?"

"Confused, I guess. Like… I broke a rule or something. Like I belong to someone else. Even though I don't." She knew it made no sense, but it was ingrained.

Suzanne was shaking her head. "That's ridiculous. You owe that man nothing. You're a free agent. And so is Seth. You should feel nothing but happy and carefree about this."

Meg eyed her critically. "Says the woman who's afraid of Beck Grainger."

But Suzanne only shrugged. "I keep telling you—it's apples and oranges. You want something I don't. And I'm thrilled you've let yourself have it." Her smile returned, grew. "Do you think it'll happen again? Like become a regular thing?"

"I have no idea."

"But you want it to, right?"

"I have no idea."

They both laughed, and Meg let out a sigh. "It's so new, and unexpected—I guess I'll just see where it leads and try to go with the flow."

Suzanne popped a chip into her mouth and crunched it up before announcing, "You're my hero."

"What?" Meg gave her head a tilt.

"Because…maybe there *is* a tiny piece of me that wishes I was more like you in this moment. I'm content that I'm not, but I admire that you're facing life head-on."

Half an hour later, a customer came in, so Meg departed, a tray of tiny white flowers between her hands and a picnic basket looped strategically over her arm. As she walked back down the street, another text notification sounded from her pocket—probably Suzanne, but she'd have to wait a few minutes. When Meg reached the inn, she lowered the flowers to the front porch and checked her phone.

Only this time it *was* Zack. Hey there, Maggie May. How's life on Summer Island? Missing you.

She simply stood there, phone in her hand, studying the words. He was missing her? He hardly ever said things like that.

It's because of Seth. Because he sensed there was more going on than you told him, and now it turns out he was right.

She wasn't sure if that equated to real, true missing. It was hard not to feel skeptical even amid the wisps of self-reproach swirling around her like thin clouds in a summer sky.

It's good, she answered.

Normally, she would say more. About how life was. That she was getting ready for the first guests in a couple of days. That she was planting more flowers. Just easy, everyday conversation.

Good to hear.

How's fishing? It was the least she could do to ask.

Decent. Been doing well off the coast near Newfork and Lawrencetown.

Hmm, that was new. Him bothering to tell her where he was.

I'm glad, she said. But nothing more. Because while normally she would be missing him far more than he was likely missing her, right now things were a little complicated on that front. And she didn't really have anything else to say.

A few minutes later, another text from him. Well, you have a good day, Meg.

You too.

She knew she'd been distant. And part of her wondered if he really did love her more than she knew, and if maybe a little more patience would bring about the relationship she wanted with him. No matter what the reason, it was nice he was thinking of her, and missing her, and bothering to tell her that, as well.

But another part of her decided to do what she'd told Suzanne—just go with the flow. It wasn't her fault he wasn't here. It wasn't her fault they weren't in a committed relationship. It wasn't her fault he'd made it so convenient for her to sleep with another man.

SETH HAD BEEN holding the ring in his hand when Meg had called up the stairs to him. He'd nearly dropped the damn thing upon hearing her voice. But instead he'd shoved it in his pocket—this ring that had been hidden here untouched for over twenty years—then closed the book and put the baseboard back in place.

He didn't hammer it in, though. Because the secret hole in the wall made him think of Meg's grandma hiding things around the house like Meg had told him. Maybe she'd used this very spot at some point before he had. Maybe someone else would use it someday.

Hiding places weren't necessarily bad things—they yielded lost surprises, and this house seemed to have plenty of those.

He wasn't sure what he'd do with the book. Maybe he'd take it with him, finally read it. Or maybe he'd quietly add it to the inn's library and let it be its own mystery—just showing up out of the blue, with a secret slot inside.

He also wasn't sure what he was going to do with the ring.

Once Meg had gone, he'd pulled it back out of his pocket to study. He did the same thing again now, standing in the round library on the first floor. Funny damn thing—he'd come here looking for this, but hadn't thought ahead to what he'd do if he actually found it. The logistics part anyway. Like a plan for the book so that he wasn't holding it in his hand when she came back. For now, this would be a good enough place for it. Maybe he hadn't really thought it would be here. Holding the ring in his hand now, it still felt like a surprise.

Wanna go on a secret mission, son? his dad had asked him that summer before he'd come here with his grandparents for the last time. *I'm gonna give you a secret assignment—make this trip more interesting for ya this year.* His dad had never understood why a trip to a serene little island in the Great Lakes was appealing to anyone—he'd made fun of it. Or maybe he'd been jealous—there'd always been a push/pull over him between his parents from the time they'd split when he was little. His memories of those years hinged strongly on feeling like the rope in a game of tug-of-war. Maybe the secret mission had made his pop feel more like he was there with Seth.

*Bring me somethin'. Somethin' we can sell and buy
ourselves some presents with.* He hadn't said to steal,
but that was what he'd meant. And Seth hadn't quite yet
understood that stealing was wrong—with a dad like
his, who'd made it seem like a skill, a thing to aspire to.

Wanting to impress his father, it had seemed an easy
choice. Like something God had pretty much dropped in
his lap, especially when he'd overheard Mrs. Adkins—
Meg's grandma—talking about it. He could still hear
her cheerful voice sharing too much, being too trusting.
*Only real bit of jewelry I've ever had is my wedding
ring. We didn't have much, but John, bless his heart,
insisted on buying a nice one—far beyond our means.
His parents helped him out on it—we paid them back
over time. And he actually bought it at a pawnshop!
Which doesn't sound romantic by today's terms, but
to me it was, because he wanted better for me than we
could afford. Spent three thousand dollars on it, but
it appraised at seven. And Lordy, with inflation and
all, probably worth quite a bit more now.* Then she'd
laughed. *Not that it matters. Its value, to me, lies in its
connection to John. And it does sparkle so on the occasions I wear it.*

And then he'd found it. Snooping. Somewhere. He
couldn't remember exactly. Would he have had the balls
to go into her bedroom? Hell, probably so—he'd had
the balls to go in *Meg's* bedroom, after all. Which he
guessed, now that he thought about it, was probably the
very same room. And he'd wanted to please his father
so damn badly.

Of course, in the end, he hadn't. He'd left it behind.
Hidden. After an unexpected call about his mother's ac-

cident had sent him and his grandparents racing away from an island he'd never come back to again—until now.

Hearing a nearby electronic beep, he glanced out an open window to see Meg standing on the front walk, typing into her cell phone. He wondered briefly if it was a text to her boyfriend—or whatever that guy was—and a surprising bolt of jealousy shot through him.

But he had bigger things to worry about. Like the ring in his hand.

He shoved it back in his pocket, deciding right there on the spot to keep it.

He wasn't planning to leave just yet, but when he did, taking it only made sense. Meg probably never even knew it existed, and if she had, it was long since forgotten, yesterday's news. It was the reason he'd come—a way to get a new start. One last misdeed that would help turn his life around. Taking it would help *him* more than it would hurt *her*—as he kept telling himself, it really wouldn't affect her at all.

Taking a last look at the spine of *The Wizard of Oz*, shoved into a random spot on a bookshelf, he left the circular room and crossed the parlor, soon stepping out onto the front porch. A flat of little white flowers rested at his feet. "Need help plantin' these, darlin'?"

Looking up from her phone, she gave him a small smile, one that reminded him how much he liked being close to her and made the phone seem forgotten. "That would be nice."

"Then let's do it."

CHAPTER TWENTY

PLANTING FLOWERS WITH Seth was a lot like making lilac water with Seth. Their hands touched in the potting soil, and their faces came close to each other as they bent over the big terra-cotta planters on the patio.

After that, their fingers touched some more in the dirt of the flower beds. She found herself looking at his hands, studying them in a way she hadn't up to now. Big, strong hands. Capable hands.

At one point, she looked up, their eyes meeting. They were both sweating in the sun on the hottest day the island had seen yet this year. He grinned, and kissed her.

Her first thought? *Nice.* It spilled all through her. Her second? To wonder if anyone had seen. She glanced toward the street, thankful no one was passing by.

Why does it have to feel like cheating when it's not?

"You got a lot more to do between now and opening day?"

"Not much. All the rooms are ready."

"Any other big plans before then?"

She lifted her gaze to his, wondering what he was getting at. "Helping my friend Suzanne with a painting project Friday evening, but that's all." Then she glanced toward Petal Pushers to add, "You can come and help if you want. It's more of a social thing, something we do every year. We'll probably come back here afterward to grill out burgers."

She thought he looked pleased to be included. "Well, if I won't be in the way, maybe I'll just take you up on that."

"You won't be." Suzanne would like meeting him, and it felt like a safe way to tiptoe him out into her life a bit more.

Which maybe wasn't even wise, since he probably wouldn't be in it—her life—for very long. And yet the urge had struck, so she was doing that go-with-the-flow thing.

"But why were you asking? About my plans?"

He arched one brow. "Was just thinking maybe when we're done here I should take you to bed."

She drew back slightly, caught off guard by his bluntness.

Yet he went on. "Because once you're open for business, seems like that might be a little harder."

So this would continue. For a while maybe. The fresh knowledge made her heart beat faster as she said, "I'm sure we can find a way."

"I don't know," he said, teasing her. "You're pretty loud."

More surprise at his words—and this time a laugh broke free from her throat. "I can be quiet if I need to."

"Guess we'll see," he told her.

"Guess we will."

The sun slipped behind a fluffy cloud just then, softening the air, and she realized that this all felt…right. The same way it once had with Zack back before she'd understood how he would come and go. Even though Seth had told her just last night that he was a crook and scammer by trade. By any measuring stick, it seemed like dangerous waters to be wading deeper into. And yet, here she was—wading.

EVERY BED IN the Summerbrook Inn was adorned with fresh sheets, every bathroom with clean towels. Trim paint had been touched up, flower beds filled. That's how it usually was—a big rush to get it all done, so big that she finished a couple of days early and could relax with a bike ride or sit in the garden with the lilacs.

The only difference was that now she had…a lover. She'd always thought it sounded sophisticated when people said that. It made them sound so in control of the situation, as if the "lover" were a mere plaything to be cast aside whenever the owner got bored with it. She didn't necessarily feel in control of anything here—far from it—and yet it seemed the word that best described what Seth had become to her, given that he wasn't her boyfriend and she had no idea how long he'd be in her life.

All she knew was that the two days before her first guest arrived were sweeter for his presence than they'd have been without him. After planting flowers, they hadn't had sex—instead they'd rented him a bike and pedaled together around the island. They'd stopped to hike up to one of her favorite spots—a meadow of wildflowers rimmed with a natural rock formation that seemed to spill down the hillside to the road and Lake Michigan beyond. After that, they'd visited the Promontory Lighthouse for that tour he'd requested.

She had chosen to stop worrying about who might see her with him and what they might think. She'd introduced him to Trent at the bicycle shop simply as, "Seth, who needs a bike for the afternoon."

They'd stopped at his cabin for him to quickly shower and change—while she waited outside since it was such a lovely day and the interior of the old shack was drab and uninviting. And part of her felt bad that he'd been staying here—but another part of her remembered he'd spent his life living in cheap motels probably on a par with this place. In short, they were from different worlds.

As they'd biked back into town and onto Harbor Street, completing the circle, she'd waved at people she knew as if she didn't have her handsome young handyman on a bike at her side, and felt better for having done it. And it didn't hurt that summer was truly upon them and had the street bustling—everyone was busy, either catering to the first tourists or preparing for them, and probably had better things to focus on besides who she was keeping company with.

Last night afterward, however, they'd had that promised sex. And now she let herself sink fully into the memories of it. In ways it was like the night before—accentuated with scents of spring and a cool night breeze that made the curtains flutter. Though in other ways it was different, because she was more comfortable with the touching, and the being touched—it hadn't come as such a surprise, hadn't held as many questions. His kisses were like whispers on her skin, his hands those of a skilled craftsman, as gifted at delivering pleasure as they were at painting and repairing everything in her world.

And because it was a little more relaxed than before, it had also become about a loss of inhibition. This time she hadn't been shy about taking his pants off, touching him where he was hard and ready for her, taking him in her hand. This time she'd followed other instincts, too—to explore the rest of his body with her touch, as well. To let herself be fully aroused by the fact that he was all muscle—his shoulders, his arms, his chest and stomach. To let herself go more in other ways, too—her responses became more instinctive and less measured, she'd cried out when he'd sunk deep inside her, and she'd cried out more when he'd rocked her world with deep, hard thrusts that made her forget anything else existed for a few mind-numbing moments.

After, she'd found herself touching the tattoo on his arm. She'd never been much into tattoos and didn't understand the vast fascination with them—but his she liked. "What is this?" she'd asked, running her fingers over it as they lay in bed, limbs still intertwined.

"A mother and son symbol," he answered.

"Oh," she'd murmured, reminded again of his loss, not only because of the tattoo but because she could hear it in his voice. Learning this made it easier to grasp the metaphorical meaning of the Celtic-looking design in which one set of curves and swirls sort of cradled another.

"I got it on my twenty-fifth birthday. Probably silly, but seeing it makes me feel like she's still with me somehow."

Meg had smiled. "It's not silly. I think when people die, they *are* still with us."

Now another beautiful day poured sunshine down onto Summer Island, and they picnicked on a blanket in the lilac grove next to the inn. Clumps of lavender flowers bloomed all around them, filling the air with that heavenly scent she loved. They'd eaten cheese and pepperoni on crackers, along with green grapes, and an apple they'd cut into slices and shared. On a lark, she'd pulled a bottle of white wine from the fridge and uncorked it, even carrying the good wineglasses out into the garden. Because life was for living, and suddenly she seemed to be doing that. She still had no idea how wise her choice of a man was, but she remained inexorably drawn to him and had simply decided not to worry, and to trust life to take her where she was meant to go.

She watched now as Seth rolled over onto his back, peering up at the blue sky, today cloudless and flawlessly clear. "Ah, darlin', I gotta tell ya—this is nice."

"*What's* nice?" She lay across the blanket from him, on her side, propped on one elbow.

"All of this. This place. This weather. You." He shot her a grin. "Not in that order, mind you."

She laughed softly. Liking him more and more. Almost wishing she didn't. Wanting to stay wary. Zack would think it wise to be wary, crazy to be cavorting with him like this. Jealousy notwithstanding. And maybe he'd be right. She wondered vaguely for a moment what her grandma would do.

And she suspected she knew the answer. *Kiss the scary one but stay with the safe one.* And as far as she'd ever been able to tell, Gran had never harbored any second thoughts. She and Grandpa John had always been happy. Ace the hoodlum had apparently become a distant memory.

"Do you miss your father?" she asked without preamble.

Seth's expression didn't change—he appeared to be searching the sky for...something. "Less than I thought," he told her. "I loved him. But I'm not sure I liked him much. There's a difference."

"I guess that does make it easier," she said. "I've never really had that—love for someone I didn't like. When Drew left me, I truly missed him. Because I truly enjoyed being with him. We laughed all the time. We found the same things funny, the same things smart. Sometimes, when I let myself think back on the relationship, I still can't believe he did that to me."

"Probably regrets that weakness every day of his life," Seth suggested.

But Meg shook her head, feeling wistful as she tried to remember Drew's face. "No—probably denies it instead. Probably put up some wall and never even lets himself think about it. Probably married with two kids, living in a big house in the suburbs, some kind of perfect life, and the people around him don't even know he was ever engaged to a girl who got leukemia."

"If that's the case, you're better off without him." He glanced over at her. "You know that, right?"

She did, of course, so she nodded. But it still hurt sometimes to have felt so ultimately unimportant to someone she'd loved so completely. So she'd still missed him when he'd gone. Just as she missed her parents when she hadn't seen them for a while—her sister, too. And if she was honest with herself, she missed Zack even now, darn it.

Yes, it was convenient not to have him around at the moment, given the circumstances, but despite what she'd told herself the other day, deep down she still missed his company. She missed his quiet masculinity. And the fact that it was simply easy to be with him at this point in their relationship. She hated realizing that, but couldn't change it.

"Sometimes I feel like I ran away," she suddenly confessed. "Coming here. Staying here. Like maybe I hid here—and have been hiding all this time. I don't want to be a person who runs from things."

Seth glanced up at her. "Guess by that logic you could say I ran away, too."

"It's not the same." She shook her head.

"Sure it is," he argued. "When you boil it down, I left a life that didn't feel good to me. I went someplace that felt better. Nothin' wrong with that. Nothin' wrong with trying to find what feels better, staying someplace that feels good. Seems to me it's the opposite that makes no sense. What would be the point in staying someplace you're not happy?"

When she didn't reply, he went on. "I can see why you stayed, darlin'. This place feels good to me. Maybe better than any place I've ever been."

"It's cold in the winter. And in the fall. And in the spring."

He laughed and added, "Good in other ways besides the weather."

And she wasn't sure if he meant the landscape—the vast waters and the lighthouses and the bicycles and the pastel-colored buildings…or her. Or maybe even something else entirely.

But she decided not to ask. Because it was good enough simply to know she was part of it, part of why he liked being here. When you broke it all down, it was just nice to be appreciated and wanted in this world.

HOURS LATER, MEG and Seth walked up Harbor Street to see Suzanne approaching from the other direction, a gallon of paint in one hand, a bag from the hardware store in the other, the handles of paintbrushes visible.

"Paint party time!" she said as they met. "You must be Seth—I'm Suzanne. Thanks for being shanghaied into working for free tonight."

Seth chuckled in his good-natured way. "I'm in it for the burgers after," he teased. "And the company of two pretty ladies."

"You were right," Suzanne said with a teasing grin, looking to Meg and then back to Seth. "She said you were smooth."

He let out another laugh. "Sincere," he claimed. But Meg could tell he knew damn good and well just how smooth he was.

Just then her eye was drawn past Seth to Beck Grainger, exiting Dahlia's across the street. Without forethought, she raised her hand in a wave. "Beck!"

The tall, handsome man glanced over, smiled—and headed their way. "Looks like this is the fun side of the street."

Meg smiled, thinking it was a generously playful comment given how coolly Suzanne had behaved toward him so far. "Fun if you like to paint," Meg said.

Beck's eyes dropped to Suzanne's paint can, and despite that she hadn't even acknowledged him, he asked her, "What are you painting?"

And as before, when she didn't answer immediately, Meg jumped in. "The picnic table behind the flower shop." She motioned vaguely in that direction. "It's an annual thing, from back when my aunt owned the place. We pick a new color every year. This year's is—" she bent over to read the label on top of the can "—hot lavender."

He let out a good-natured laugh and said, "I didn't know lavender could be hot, but I'm intrigued."

"Welcome to Summer Island," Meg teased, "where the nights are chilly but the pastel colors are sizzling."

Beck introduced himself to Seth, and as they shook hands, Seth followed suit.

"Well," Beck said, addressing them all again, "if you have an extra brush, I'm happy to pitch in."

"I only bought three," Suzanne announced. And it was all Meg could do not to cringe. She wanted to strangle her friend. And sensed Seth teetering on the edge of offering to go get another at the inn, praying he wouldn't. Since, while it was tempting to continue to try to include Beck, she was afraid Suzanne would only become ruder. If that was even possible.

"Well then," Beck said, "you guys have a nice night—I'll let you get to it."

And then he was walking away. And the three of them stood quietly. Until Seth said, "Did I miss something?"

"I'm socially misfit with handsome men who want to spend time with me," Suzanne replied like it was a totally normal thing to say.

It took him a second to form a reply. Which came as a simple, "Why is that?"

Suzanne shrugged. "Long story. Dead husband, came here to be alone—and don't ya know there suddenly has to be this ridiculously good-looking man who wants to chat me up. Come on, let's paint. I'll turn on some music, pour some wine, and it'll seem fun again."

As they followed her in through the front door of Petal Pushers, Meg and Seth exchanged glances, and she knew they were both back to thinking about people who came here to escape something. And whether or not that was good or bad.

THEY WERE ON the second coat of paint, and second glass of wine, when Dahlia came walking around the corner of the building. "Heard there might be a little party over here," she said.

Meg's first thoughts: *She feels left out since the three of us usually get together more than we have lately. And she's just noticed there's a man here.*

"This gives new meaning to a paint and wine party," Dahlia went on, but her smile was now stiff at best. She looked to Seth. "I'm Dahlia—I run the eatery across the way. And I'm also Zack's aunt. Have you met Zack?"

Okay, so Suzanne wasn't the only person creating awkward moments around here tonight. And it was a shame, because the Beck incident notwithstanding, they'd been having a nice time. Suzanne and Seth had hit it off well and the painting had indeed been fun. It was a pretty *good* little party, if people would stop trying to ruin it.

"Yep—couple times, just briefly," Seth answered. Then stepped forward to offer her his hand, the one not holding a paintbrush with lavender bristles. "Seth Darden."

Her handshake was brisk and short. "You're Meg's handyman, I believe."

"Yes ma'am."

A nod, equally brisk and short.

"Want some wine?" Suzanne asked, apparently trying to relax the situation. "We're almost done, but heading to the inn to grill out if you want to join."

"No," Dahlia said. "Thanks, but just thought I'd poke

my head in to see what was happening. Café's still open another couple hours." Dusk was falling, and Dahlia generally let other staff close up, but it was obvious she didn't want to hang out with Zack's competition. And clearly she considered Seth just that.

And as she started to leave, Meg felt the need to follow her—although she had no plan for what she was going to say, and the two glasses of wine she'd consumed didn't exactly have her feeling quick-witted.

"Dahlia," she said as the older woman started across Harbor Street, the thoroughfare busy with some pedestrian traffic and a few bikes trying to reach their destinations before the sun set completely. A purpling sky loomed above like a ceiling lowering down over them.

Zack's aunt stopped, turned. And in this moment she was definitely Zack's aunt—not just Meg's friend. Her connection to Zack nearly dripped from her right now.

Meg searched for more words. *It isn't what you think.* No, not that—because it *was* what she thought. *I'm not doing anything wrong.* No, that sounded like someone who *was* doing something wrong. Finally, she heard herself say, "Please don't be mad at me."

Dahlia took a step back toward her, looking serious and fraught. "I can't tell you what to do, Meg—you have to follow your heart. But *my* heart breaks for him a little, that's all."

It made her feel defensive. Why was Zack always the good guy in this situation? "He could be here doing this with me if he wanted. He's not. And don't say it's about his work. He could do the same work without being gone for weeks or months on end. He chooses to."

Dahlia let out a sigh, her voice softening. "You're right, you're right." Her expression melted into sadness.

"I just defend him because I love him, and because I know he loves *you*."

Meg took that in, weighed it. A lump rose in her throat. "It's hard to be sure," she said around it. Then turned and walked away. Hating the drama of it. Because it was one more thing that made her question her choices here—the right, the wrong, the safe, the dangerous.

For someone whose life had seemed almost too simple a few weeks ago, it had somehow gotten pretty damned complicated pretty damned quickly.

BY THE TIME they'd cleaned up the grill and Suzanne left the inn, it was late. Both Mr. Carmichael and Mr. McNaughton arrived tomorrow, so a good night's sleep seemed wise. Not that this notion prevented Seth from seducing her. It didn't take much. Touches in the kitchen. Kisses on her neck in the bathroom as she wiped her makeup away. A fingertip on her shoulder, under her top, under her bra strap, as she turned back the covers. She didn't want to tell him no, so she didn't.

As on the previous few nights, they slept naked beneath the sheets.

And she awoke with the sun, well rested and happy.

When her cell phone rang, she reached absently for it on the bedside table, then saw a picture of Zack on the screen. And despite herself, it felt somehow obscene to be with Seth like this, knowing Zack had no idea.

Thoughts raced through her mind as she scrambled up and toward the robe on the bathroom door, phone in hand. *You don't know who he's been with, either. He could be lying naked with someone right now, too.* It just didn't feel like that was the case at the moment, though.

And she knew she didn't have to answer, but she did miss him, damn it. He was part of her now.

"Hello?" she said, stepping out into the hallway, pulling the door shut behind her. It felt vital to put a door between the two men.

"You sound harried, Maggie May. Did I wake you? You're usually up by now." True enough—but it was nice to sleep in when you had a man to cuddle with.

"Yeah—late getting up."

"How are you? Got any guests yet?"

"The first come today."

"Ready?"

"Yes—every towel is in place."

"I'm sure the inn looks great."

"The lilacs are in bloom." She had no idea why she mentioned it. Maybe she was sad that he almost always missed it, and it was pleasant to share something you loved with someone. The way she'd been getting to share it with Seth this year.

"Listen, Meg, the reason I'm calling is…guess I just want to make sure everything is okay between us."

Cripes. "You do?" *Since when?*

"Of course I do."

What to say. Nothing came to mind. But given the naked man in her bedroom, it was fair to say things weren't very okay. "I…guess that surprises me some. You…don't usually seem to care much."

She heard him sigh. "I know I'm not good at showing that. I'm sorry for that, honey." The words made her heart feel like it was bending in her chest.

"Okay." It was all she had.

"I've been thinking," he went on, "about…about all we've been through."

"Yeah?"

"I was remembering the days we spent with Julia, when she was dying."

All the air drained from Meg's lungs. Hard memories. But a time when Zack had been there for her. In the biggest of ways. The illness had progressed quickly, suddenly, in winter when the lake was frozen, and her mother hadn't been able to get there before Julia had passed. It was hard to nurse someone to their death—for Meg, it had been harder in a way even than her own leukemia. Because she'd recovered. And Aunt Julia hadn't.

Meg swallowed. Wandered toward the stairs. "Why… why were you thinking about that?"

"I'm not sure. I guess maybe because…it was a tough time. For both of us. A tough thing to handle. And I was just thinking that…there's nobody besides you I'd want to go through something like that with."

Meg slumped down on the top step, taken aback. And speechless. "It…it meant a lot to have you there with me."

"I'd never let you go through something like that alone."

"I know." Did she, though? Before this moment? Or…maybe she did. Because he *had* been there when she'd needed him. He hadn't run like Drew once had. Maybe she knew that deep down everything Dahlia claimed was true—he loved her, he would be there for her through bad times. But…was that enough? What about being there for the good times, too? The taking down shutters times? The painting picnic table times? The blooming lilacs times?

"I hope so, Meg."

They talked a few minutes more. About his morning—he was off the coast of Finch Bay, taking up nets he'd set yesterday. And about her night—she told him about painting Suzanne's picnic table. But of course had to leave out the part about Seth being there. And in her bed right now.

As they spoke, she cinched the robe tight around her, walked on bare feet down the old wooden steps and into the kitchen, and poured herself a glass of orange juice. Before disconnecting, he told her he'd be home soon.

But he said that a lot—casually, vaguely. Soon could mean so many things, none of them specific. It could mean a week. Or a month. Or more.

Her heart beat too fast, however, with some sense of self-condemnation she couldn't quite escape. Something she shouldn't have to feel here, but damn it, she still did. *Why did you have to pick now to start being so sweet, Zack?*

Of course, maybe it meant nothing. Maybe it was a momentary thing and would dissipate as quickly as the wake behind the *Emily Ann*. But what if it didn't? What if this was a sign of some real, lasting change in him? What if seeing her with Seth had truly altered something in Zack, finally made him realize what he had to lose? What if he came home to Summer Island to stay?

CHAPTER TWENTY-ONE

IT WAS FUNNY how much peace a man could find standing on the wind-beaten deck of a boat sorting through a net full of lake whitefish. It was a peace Zack never seemed to get enough of. It came with a practiced focus that didn't let anything else in, good or bad. Just the job, the work. It occupied his hands and his mind, but at the same time put him out under the sun or the clouds or whatever else the sky happened to bring over Lake Huron, letting him feel the elements, soak them up.

Today it was fast-rolling clouds with occasional peeks of blue in between, and a wind that filled his ears. Plenty of mature fish in the catch this afternoon, most around twenty inches long and covered with silvery white scales. A few zebra mussels, along with some younger fish, and even a healthy salmon—a pretty rare sight in Huron these days thanks to the invasive mussels—were all tossed back, creating small plopping splashes to his left.

Funny thing, though. There was more on his mind. More than the weather. More than the catch. More than the sorting. There was Meg. His Maggie May. He'd meant what he'd told her—he was going home soon. He'd thought for a very long time that the lake, this boat, was his home—the place he felt the most *at* home. But maybe that was changing. Her inn, her arms, were a damn good place to be—and to call home.

The *Emily Ann* puttered along a little farther north today than she'd been yesterday, and even farther north than she'd been the day before that. Summer Island rested up at that northern tip of Michigan's mitten, and he'd found himself working his way in that direction over the past several days without quite admitting to himself that he had a particular destination in mind. Only he knew now that he did. He was working his way home. And when he got there, he was going to make things different with her, going to make things right.

AS MEG WALKED UP Harbor Street in denim capris and a tunic with an open blouse over it to ward off the morning chill, she realized that she'd found herself running to her friend for advice and support a lot lately. She gave Suzanne a hard time about pushing romance away, but as she put one tennis shoe in front of the other, she had to admit that she was in too deep here and it was starting to eat her alive. For the first time, she could almost see Suzanne's side of things—it might require a little rudeness to a nice guy, but at least she didn't have quandaries over which man to love raining down on her.

And whoa—love? With Seth? Was she falling in love with him? Her younger con artist handyman? She'd never even imagined that word entering the picture with him—this was supposed to be a fun summer fling. And yet...she felt more than that. An attachment and affection that went beyond sex. She cared for him.

And maybe the ironic part was her struggle to be fair to two men, neither of whom had ever expressed the wish to be in her life in a committed way.

Maybe she was reading too much into Zack's phone call and other recent behavior. And maybe Seth would leave tomorrow. For all she knew, the joke would be on her—she'd worry and toil over which man to choose only to find out in the end that neither cared about her as much as she cared about them.

After hanging up with Zack, she'd downed her glass of juice and dressed in clean clothes from a laundry basket downstairs that hadn't yet been put away. And now she was walking through the front door of Petal Pushers, in need of her friend.

Suzanne smiled at her from behind the counter. "You look rumpled. Is that because you had great sex last night?"

She sighed. "It's because I got dressed in the laundry room and snuck out of the house without brushing my hair—or teeth."

Suzanne made a slight face and motioned to a small bowl of peppermints on the counter. "Trouble in paradise?" She scrunched up her nose. "I hope not, because I like him. He's fun. And more friendly than Zack, frankly."

Meg unwrapped a red-and-white mint and popped it in her mouth. "Not trouble with Seth exactly," she said around the disc of candy. "Just…confusion." Then she filled Suzanne in, and also added the part about her conversation with Dahlia last night, which she hadn't been able to share at the time.

"Am I crazy?" she asked Suzanne. "To be looking back on Julia's death and letting it count for so much that he saw me through it."

Suzanne tilted her head, sighed thoughtfully. "You

know I'm not a big fan of Zack's, but…stuff like that matters."

Meg nodded. "I know. It really does, right?"

"Did I ever tell you I used to be a nurse in a former life?"

Meg lowered her chin. "No. And that seems like a big thing to have left out of our getting-to-know-you process."

Suzanne just shrugged. "I gave it up after Cal died. I wanted to help people, but I wasn't cut out for it—it drained me emotionally. Taking care of someone who is ill or injured or dying is just plain hard—it takes a special kind of person to do it. So… I do give Zack a lot of credit for helping you through that."

"I just wish," Meg said wistfully, "that he was one way or the other, you know? All the way supportive and into us, or all the way distant and neglectful."

"Most people aren't," Suzanne pointed out. "One way or the other, I mean. Most people are a mixed bag a lot of the time, just doing the best they can on any particular day." She stopped, smiled wryly. "That's what I tell myself when I imagine someday being able to make Beck Grainger understand that I'm not a raging bitch but just a socially stunted widow not ready to move on."

That made Meg sad. "You really don't want to explore his interest in you? At all? Aren't you afraid you might miss out on something really great?"

Suzanne let out a wistful yet acceptant sigh. "I can't handle it. That's all. I just can't handle it." She sounded so sure that finally Meg decided to quit arguing the point with her.

And she had enough problems of her own to worry about anyway. "I'm not sure I can handle what's on my plate right now, either. No one has asked me to make a choice, and yet it feels like one has to be made. I think, deep down, I'm just a one-man woman. Any advice, o celibate one?"

"Yes," Suzanne said solemnly. "On one hand, I think it's pretty clear that any change in Zack's behavior here is a result of being afraid of losing you to Seth."

"Agreed. But does that mean it isn't real? Or that it won't last? Even if the timing is suspicious, maybe it's a wake-up call that really changes things."

"True. To all of that. Because on the other hand, maybe you're right, it's the real thing, and your fishing boat has finally come in here. But only time will tell."

"So you're saying I should trust in it—or not?" For someone who'd acted like she had advice—to give to someone who usually didn't need it—Suzanne wasn't providing Meg with the clarity she sought.

"I'm saying I'm not sure—but that as long and hard as you've loved this guy, maybe it's worth giving him a chance."

Meg sighed. She supposed she couldn't blame her friend for not knowing the mind of an unpredictable man.

"And as much as I'm Team Seth in most ways," Suzanne went on, "I think it makes sense to take a little step back from him right now to help you think clearly."

"Me, too." Meg nodded, having already reached that particular conclusion herself. "That's why I snuck out of the house like an adolescent."

"After that," Suzanne said on a wistful sigh, "all you can really do is follow your heart."

"What if my heart is being pulled in two different directions?" Meg asked.

"See which side pulls harder."

IT SURPRISED SETH to wake up alone in Meg's bed. It surprised him even more to discover she was nowhere in the house. He'd pulled on blue jeans and gone from room to room looking, calling her name. He'd found the cat in the parlor, sitting in the front picture window like a large figurine—but no sign of Meg.

That's when he caught a glimpse out the window of a chubby old gray-haired man trudging up the street wheeling a roller suitcase behind him. Shit—it was Saturday, and the first ferry must have already run because guests were arriving. And where was the Summerbrook Inn's proprietor?

He bounded back up the stairs, taking them two at a time, grabbed the T-shirt he'd shed at the bedside last night, and yanked it on as he went back downstairs. Then glanced down at his bare feet. But the old man was already turning past the mailbox and onto the front stone walk, so he'd have to be greeted with no shoes.

"Morning," Seth said, holding the front screen door open.

"And a splendiferous morning it is indeed," the elderly gentleman replied, smiling up at Seth as he maneuvered the roller bag up the wooden porch steps.

And Seth realized this old man wasn't the Mr. Carmichael Meg had mentioned—this was his grandfather. Twenty years older and grayer, twenty pounds heavier. In fact, he looked considerably older and heavier than even in the picture on Meg's bulletin board.

"I'm…the handyman," Seth began, feeling unexpectedly stymied. His heart had tightened into a knot in his chest, which he hadn't anticipated. He'd somehow thought a life of scamming had drained all the sentimentality from his soul. But apparently some things didn't leave you—they just hid inside until some moment when you least expected it. He forced himself to keep talking. "Not sure where Meg got off to this morning—can't seem to find her." He looked toward the parlor, the window still adorned with a calico cat. "If you want to take a seat on the sofa there, I can get you something to drink while you wait." He thought he'd seen a fresh pitcher of tea in the fridge last night, along with the other beverages she kept on hand. "Can I get you a glass of iced tea, water, a Coke?" He glanced toward the kitchen, thinking out loud. "I don't believe there's coffee." Meg wasn't a coffee drinker, he'd learned—same as him—though she'd mentioned often keeping a pot made during the summer for guests.

"Thanks, Seth—but I'm here now. So sorry I wasn't here to say hello myself, Mr. McNaughton. I wasn't expecting you until this afternoon."

Seth turned to see her entering the front door with a smile, and now looking to her guest—his grandpa. Who he'd never expected to see again. Until showing up here. He probably should have given more thought to how that would feel—but getting all wrapped up in Meg the last few days had made it seem like...well, like a thing that wasn't real, wasn't really gonna happen.

"No problem at all, my dear—I just decided to make the whole drive up to St. Simon yesterday and get an early start on my excursion. And my, the entire island looks to be in glorious bloom!"

"I've got your usual room all ready for you," she said. "And Mr. Carmichael should be right behind you. I heard Seth offering you something to drink—what can I get you?"

That was when his grandfather turned to look at

him, harder than before in a studying sort of way. And he knew that quickly that he was trying to put pieces together, so quickly that he could barely form another thought before his grandpa remarked, "Seth, did you say?"

Meg nodded. "Yes, Seth has been doing some work for me around the inn and has become a good friend. Seth, this is Stanley McNaughton."

She hadn't used Seth's last name. "Pleased to meet you," Seth said. That was all it would take, his last name, to confirm what his grandfather was surely trying to figure out. Yep, he should have given this some thought. It would seem that Meg had truly stolen all his powers of logic. And now here he stood without the slightest of plans in place.

Well, here was a plan. Extract himself from the situation. "I'm gonna do some work outside," he said—and slipped out the front door before Meg could even reply.

There wasn't actually anything outside that needed doing. But he'd find something.

As he moved briskly down the porch steps, another old gentleman came up the walk. "You must be Mr. Carmichael," Seth said with a grin, thankful for the timing. A second guest would surely distract his grandpa from wondering if he'd just seen his long-lost grandson.

Of course, he didn't know how long the man could stay distracted from such a thing. He'd have to figure out how to handle this.

But as he plopped down into one of Meg's Adirondack chairs in the lilac grove, he glanced toward the sky and had to laugh at himself just a little. Ron Darden would hang his head in shame if he could see how fast and far his son had fallen. He might have a valuable diamond ring in his possession, but his conning skills had clearly been wiped clean from his brain by the charms of Meg Sloan.

He'd come here feeling so damn in control, so clear on what he was here for and how he was going to get it. Now everything had changed and any control he'd had was a thing of the past. And he saw himself as just… floating. Floating like a lost blow-up inner tube in the choppy Lake Michigan waves. He'd try his damnedest to stay afloat here, get through this unscathed—but his fate would largely be a matter of where the waves carried him.

MEG HAD NO idea why Seth had gone rushing out—one minute he'd been the consummate gentleman, going above and beyond the call of duty welcoming Mr. Mc-Naughton, and the next he'd made an awkward exit that had filled the room with tension. Or maybe the tension had been there before—she wasn't sure. Or hell—maybe *she'd* brought the tension; God knew she was experiencing enough of it.

But now both of her guests had been checked in and were resting in their rooms. Mr. Carmichael, she'd learned, planned to meet his granddaughter and her husband for lunch at Dahlia's in an hour, and Mr. Mc-Naughton intended to unpack and then rent a bike for a leisurely ride around the island.

So her hostess duties were done for the moment, though she did promise both men a pot of coffee would be waiting upon their return. After starting the coffee, she began thinking about lunch. She had fresh cold cuts in the fridge—as more guests began to arrive, more lunches would be eaten on the run—and a hot ham and cheese sounded good on this partly cloudy, breezy day.

Of course, it begged the question: Should she make one for Seth? Normally, she would, but she was supposed to be pulling back. And for all she knew, his rushing away had something to do with her sneaking out of bed this morning. Or maybe not. Her mind was in too much of a whirl to have a firm grasp on the situation. And what on earth was he doing outside anyway when everything was already done?

She made only one sandwich, and decided to carry it out to the lilac grove where maybe she could do as Suzanne had suggested and clear her head.

Only as she entered the area with her lunch and a glass of iced tea in hand, she found Seth bent over part of the brick walkway that passed through the garden. Unduly alarmed by the sight, she snapped, "What are you doing?"

He looked up. Appeared a little sullen. "Thought I'd fix this walk. The bricks are loose. I can mix up some grout and repair it."

"No," she said quickly.

"Why?"

Good question. But then she understood her unmeasured response. "It's one of the places my grandma used to hide things—under the bricks. It's silly maybe, but I guess I just…don't want it sealed up."

He gave his head a solemn tilt, looking serious—no sexy Seth grin charming her today. "I thought you were moving and wanted the place spruced up. So what does it matter?"

She pulled in her breath. Moving. Leaving. Somewhere along the way, that plan had fallen to the back of her mind. With Seth falling into her bed, perhaps. Yes, somehow what had started out to be about leaving and finding a new life had morphed into feeling torn between two men *here*, on the island.

"I never said I was leaving for sure, and I'm definitely *not* sure. Maybe you were right. That it's okay to be someplace that feels safe. Maybe… I don't want to leave after all." She shook her head. "Or maybe I do. I'm a little confused about some things right now."

His expression softened as he pushed to his feet. "Things like what?"

"You. And Zack. And going or staying." Another more pronounced head shake. "I'm usually so much more grounded than this, steady—but lately that's left me."

"Funny," he said, "since that's what I'm trying to get to—grounded and steady. You…make that seem possible for me."

"I do?" She met his gaze, surprised. "Why?"

"Even at your most frazzled, Meg," he said, that grin coming back now, reliable as lilacs in June on Summer Island, "you feel steady as a rock to me. A safe place to lean. But…don't let me lean on you if you're not comfortable with that."

She drew in her breath. She hadn't planned on telling him any of this—she'd aspired to be more distant. But just like most everything since his arrival, it wasn't going as expected. "I'm not sure. Because… I think I care for you both. And Zack's not here right now, but he will be sooner or later, so…" She stopped, sighed. "There's my confusion. Which maybe is pointless, because I don't know your plans and maybe you'll leave tomorrow and it's silly of me to be trying to sort through all this anyway." Yep, so much for pulling back.

"I'm not leaving tomorrow, Meg," he informed her. Sounding pretty damn steady himself. In a way that made her believe in him all the more. That he was changed. That he was worth…considering. And maybe taking risks for. "But I need to ask you a favor, darlin'— something important."

She lowered her chin, surprised. "What's that?"

"Mr. McNaughton in there," he said, motioning vaguely toward the house. "Don't tell him my last name."

She blinked. "Why?"

"He's my grandfather."

CHAPTER TWENTY-TWO

MEG LOWERED HERSELF onto the edge of an Adirondack chair. "What did you just say?"

"He's my grandfather. The one I told you about."

She stared at him, dumbstruck. This man was just full of surprises. "How is that even possible?"

"Remember I mentioned I'd been here as a kid?"

"Oh." That was how it was possible. But... "You didn't tell me. When you saw his picture and I told you his name."

A spark of guilt flashed through his eyes before he said, "I don't know why. Just didn't expect it, I guess, and wasn't sure I was happy about it. And I'm still not. Which is why I don't want him to know who I am."

She shook her head. "I don't understand. I mean, you made your grandparents sound like the best part of your childhood. Why wouldn't you want to—"

"This part I *did* tell you, remember? I'm not proud of where I am in life, Meg. And I guess... I guess I'm pretty pissed he wasn't in it. Because I missed him—missed them both. And maybe if they'd been in my life, it woulda gone better."

She pulled in her breath—feeling the pain in his words more than in any he'd ever said to her before. "But that seems like all the more reason to tell him you're his grandson. To talk things out. To have him back in your life."

"No," he said. Low and swift. So very sure. "Do this for me. It's the one thing I'll ask of you that you don't want to do—nothing else."

Secrets. She hadn't had many in her life. But she was keeping one now, from Zack. And it was making her understand that, for better or worse, it had to be hers to share if and when she chose to. Secrets were seldom good in her opinion, but the one they were discussing wasn't hers to tell—much as she hated knowing this and not being able to run up to Mr. McNaughton's room right now screaming the news.

"I think it's a huge mistake," she told him, "but okay."

He gave a short nod. "Thank you, darlin'. It's what's best—for me." He placed his hand on the back of her head then and bent to kiss her forehead.

And her thoughts whirled. Maybe it wasn't best for Seth's grandpa. Maybe she shouldn't be letting Seth kiss even her forehead if she was trying to pull back. Maybe her life was beginning to spiral out of control.

SETH HAD HEADED to his cabin for a while. She'd asked if he'd be back this evening without even knowing if she should want that, but—for better or worse—she'd gotten used to having him around. And the idea of making dinner for herself alone, without him, suddenly felt… bigger than it should have. *You barely know him. And he promised you he'd told you everything when he hadn't.* And then there was Zack—changing, learning to express himself, making her feel valued. So why did she want Seth back here?

She truly wasn't sure. Because—chemistry and passion aside—she felt more uncertain about him than ever. She kept thinking all the questions about him were answered, but that never turned out to be true. At least not so far.

Mr. McNaughton was right—spring was bursting all around them. Even though it was technically summertime now, Spring came later to the island than in most parts of the United States. Pink tulips her grandma had planted the year before she died had opened below the parlor window, and white and blue hyacinths bloomed with their burst of perfume near the back patio. Redbud trees had just passed from purple to green, but the blossoms on the pink-and-white dogwoods across the street, skirting the lake's edge, had outlasted them.

All those colors were how this island came back to life after a long, cold winter. And something in Meg had come back to life, too—because of Seth. Maybe he really *was* her Ace, her adventure, her dalliance, her brief moment of grabbing on to something that wasn't good for her. And if so, maybe it was time to let go.

She went inside to find that all remained quiet— even with a couple of guests in residence now, only Miss Kitty greeted her with a swish of her calico tail as she walked in the front door. So she grabbed up her grandma's diary from where she'd been keeping it on a shelf in the nook, and took it back out to the garden.

May 5, 1957

Dear Diary,
It's almost summer even though it barely feels like spring here. But I got my bicycle out and J.T.

tightened the chain for me, so I'm all ready for better weather. I got a new pair of pedal pushers, too, in St. Simon two weekends ago—they were on sale at Bergman's.

We also bought the prettiest yellow fabric I've ever seen—Mother is making me a new dress! I hear the sewing machine going right now, so maybe it will be ready for Mary Ann Hoskins' birthday party on Saturday. J.T. is taking me and there will be party games, food, records, and dancing.

Though I'm sorry to say that getting this dress made came with a price. Last week, Mother sent me to the Five and Dime up Harbor Street for some thread—we forgot to get matching thread at Bergman's, so I took a swatch of the fabric with me. And when I went to the counter to pay, a new boy was working the soda fountain and register. He was smiling at me in the funniest way—until I finally recognized him. It was Ace! That awful boy who practically manhandled me at the dance in St. Simon!

Imagine my surprise at seeing him here, on the island! I barely recognized him without the James Dean jacket. I asked him, "What are you doing here?"

And he just laughed—the nerve of him!—and said, "Aren't you glad to see me?"

I told him no, of course!

And yes, perhaps I have thought more about that kiss than I should. But only because it was so jarring and strange.

And do you know what he did then? He walked

*over to the soda fountain and gave me a free black
cow! Without Mr. Lyman's permission! I've been
going to Mr. Lyman's store as long as I can remember and I would never want to steal from him!
I tried to refuse it, but Ace wouldn't take no for
an answer and I eventually realized it was just
easier to drink the stolen soda than to argue the
point. And the creep wouldn't ring up my thread
until I did!*

*He tried to lure me into conversation the en-
tire time, but at least I got him to explain what on
earth he's doing working in Mr. Lyman's store—
it turns out that Mr. Lyman is his uncle! Ace is
spending the entire summer here on the island
working for him.*

*I smartly told him he hadn't seemed like the
type of fellow to put in an honest day's work, and
that his insistence on giving me a free soda only
made me think all the worse of him. And the lout
laughed! Then he told me he was saving up to buy
a car. A '47 Chevy hot rod. Although I didn't let
it show, I admit this caught my interest because
of never having been around cars much. I've ridden in a few on the mainland, and it's rather fun.*

*Before he finally rung up the thread, he told
me I'd stayed on his mind. I said, "You don't even
know me." And he said, "Yes I do, Peggy Sue
Winters." I couldn't keep from gasping, and then
I demanded to know how he knew my name. He
said he'd asked around after the dance. And I
asked him why.*

He said because I kissed so good.

And diary, I'm pretty sure my face turned beet red! I mean, the gall of some people!

Then he said that was part of the reason he'd agreed to come to Summer Island, because he knew I lived here. And he was glad I'd come to buy thread. And he wanted to see me again.

My heart was beating so hard by this time that I could barely breathe. But I told him, "Look, Ace or whatever your name is, I have a boyfriend! And we're getting married and leaving this stupid island!"

And he said, "That dunce you came to the dance with?" He seriously called J.T. a dunce. So I said, "J.T. is far smarter than you'll ever be!" And he said, "How do you figure, Peggy Sue?" And I very smartly said, "Well, he's got me for a girlfriend, doesn't he? And you don't." And then I took my change and walked out.

I felt pretty pleased with my parting line, but inside I was shaking. There's something about him, diary, that just makes me nervous. Even without the jacket and the liquor on his breath, he feels dangerous to me. Just standing behind the counter at the Five and Dime.

After I got home and gave Mother the thread, I went to my room and shut the door for a while, just trying to calm down. He didn't kiss me this time, thank goodness, but...maybe it felt the same as when he did.

Later, I went to J.T.'s house. His mother made us tomato soup and grilled cheese because it's chilly out, even for May, and then we played Sorry with his sister. He walked me home and gave me

*a nice kiss goodnight on the porch. Everything
seemed right again. And it made me look forward
to a life far away from here.*

*I thought of telling him about this Ace char-
acter, but decided it would only create trouble.
It will be easier if I just figure out how to keep
my distance from the Five and Dime while Ace
is on the island. Though it might make for a long
summer.*

*J.T. graduates next month already, and he got
into horticulture school and will go to Michigan
State in the fall! And next year I'll graduate, too.
I can't wait to move to the mainland and marry
J.T. and have babies, and a car, and begin our
happy life. One without unpleasant surprises in
James Dean jackets.*

> *Yours, impatiently awaiting the future,*
> *Peggy*

Meg stopped reading, drinking in the scent of lilacs
on a passing breeze. Then she looked at the diary in
her hand and shook her head. Clearly, her grandma had
been smitten by the bad boy, and Meg had been just as
surprised as young Peggy to see "this Ace character"
turn up on the island.

She wished she'd had the chance to read the diary
before her grandmother had passed—she had so many
questions. Though it was fun to envision teenage ver-
sions of Gran and Grandpa and Aunt Julia sitting around
a table playing Sorry or Monopoly. And she supposed
her main question was one she already knew the answer to. While part of her wondered if Gran had ever
harbored any regrets about staying with Grandpa John

over exploring the forbidden, ducktailed Ace, the rest of her *knew* her grandparents had been happy and totally devoted, like two peas in a pod.

She turned the page, eager to see what other tidbits of excitement her grandma's summer had held. Was the dress done on time for the party? And had she managed to stay out of the Five and Dime? Maybe it was a nice distraction from her own problems to delve more deeply into her grandma's in 1957.

May 12, 1957

Dear Diary,
Mary Ann's party was such fun. J.T. surprised me with flowers when he came to the door, and Mother went on and on about it. She found the perfect vase for them and took them up to my room.

He also surprised me with how good he's gotten at jitterbugging just since the sock hop! He and his sister have been practicing because he knows I like to dance. We ate a delicious yellow butter cake Mary Ann's grandma made, then played Pin the Tail on the Donkey and had a three-legged race in her yard. And after that, we spun records and danced all night!

J.T. suggested sodas from the fountain at Mr. Lyman's on the walk home, and I had to pretend I was full from cake even though it had been hours since we'd eaten. I hate fibbing to him, but it was for the best. And when he kissed me goodnight, I thanked him for being the most wonderful boy-

friend in the world and he gave me the sweetest smile.

Only then the craziest thing happened, diary. I had just put on my pajamas and turned out the light in my room when I heard something on the window pane—a knocking sound. I walked over to look out—and that crazy boy Ace was sitting right there, on the roof outside my window!

You better believe I opened that window and gave him what for! I asked him what the devil he thought he was doing and told him he was going to break through onto the porch. Then I demanded he get down right that instant.

But, diary, you know Ace well enough by now to guess that's not what he did.

He said I didn't belong with that straitlaced boyfriend of mine, that I belonged with him! Belonged, he said! Like he had the right to say something like that! I pointed out that I don't even know him, and he said I knew him enough, and that he wanted to know me much better. He doesn't lack for confidence, that's for darn sure!

When I told him again that J.T. and I planned to leave Summer Island and never come back, he caught me off guard, saying it seemed like a nice place, and that maybe I wouldn't like the outside world so much once I got there. He's so presumptuous!

I said I wanted freedom, to be able to go places and drive a car. And he said, "Sure, I get that way of thinking, Peggy Sue. Got to have someplace to drive my hot rod when I get it, after all. But I'm just saying this place ain't so bad."

We talked about other things then—he told me

about his family, and where he lived; he claimed to be a card shark, and told me he likes to shoot pool. He laughed and said that was the one thing this island was missing, a pool hall. I told him nice places didn't have pool halls. He said he guessed he couldn't have his cake and eat it, too.

I admitted that saying had never made good sense to me, and he said, "That's 'cause we're all saying it wrong." He claimed the original way it had been said back in historical times was: A man cannot have his cake and eat his cake. Which maybe makes a little more sense, but not much. Anyway, I asked him how he knew such a thing and he said he'd read it in a book. I said, "You don't strike me as a fellow who would do much reading." He said I shouldn't make assumptions and that maybe there was more to him than met the eye. And that intrigued me, just a bit.

So I asked him, "Did you really rob a liquor store?"

He looked at me—and I would be lying if I said he didn't have nice eyes—and asked, "What's the right answer, yes or no?"

"The truth is the right answer," I said.

He told me, "No, Peggy Sue, I didn't rob anyplace. Just got into an argument with the owner for opening a bottle before I paid for it."

"And drinking it without paying for it?" I asked pointedly, remembering that black cow.

He just shrugged.

And I said, "You're bad. You do bad things."

And he said, "Maybe I just need a good girl to make me want to be better."

My heart fluttered at that, but I don't know

why. And it had been almost like we were friendly there for few minutes, but then I remembered everything that was so wrong about the situation and demanded again that he get off my roof. I said if my father found him there, he'd be in for it!

And do you know what he did then, diary? He said, "All right, but I'll be seeing you again, Peggy Sue, real soon." And then he leaned right through the window and kissed me! Just like at the dance. Not a little kiss. A deep, hard kiss. It left me shuddering afterward.

I put down the window and got back in bed and tried to pretend to myself that it hadn't left me all shivery inside. But when I caught sight of J.T.'s flowers on my chest of drawers in the moonlight, I felt terrible. For talking to Ace at all. And for letting his kiss make me shiver.

I'm not sure what will happen, diary. What do you do about a boy who keeps turning up in your life without your permission? Yesterday Mother insisted we get egg cream sodas together and what could I say? And there he was, serving them up to us, giving me sneaky grins when she looked the other way. It made me feel his kiss all over again.

I love J.T. and I know he's the boy I want to spend forever with and have a life with and a family with. But if that's true, then why does my heart beat so fast and my hands get so sweaty when I'm around Ace? If love is grand, why am I so confused?

Yours, in utter romantic turmoil,
Peggy

CHAPTER TWENTY-THREE

"YOU'RE MAD AT ME," Seth said. He'd joined her on the patio a little while ago and tried to act normal, tried to flirt, tried to turn on the usual charm. But Meg was having none of it and it was making him feel shitty.

"Not mad," she said quietly, sitting at the same café table where they'd shared meals before. He'd come back thinking they'd have dinner together, only to find that she'd eaten without him. Not that he necessarily *deserved* dinner with her—but he still wanted it. Not the dinner so much as the company—her. Her mood worried him, making him feel lost in the only place he'd ever really started feeling happy since he was ten years old.

"What then?" he asked.

"Just confused. About a lot of things."

"Me, too, I guess," he confessed. "What are *your* things?"

"The fact that I don't know why you won't tell your grandfather who you are, for one."

Damn—she was going to press him on that? Why couldn't she get the obvious? Did he have to keep saying it over and over? "I'm ashamed, Meg. Ashamed for him to know what I turned into. Maybe I don't want to burden him with that. Or myself. I mean, I'm changing, but…maybe I'd rather let him think his grandson is out there doing better for himself than I am. Can you understand that?"

She stayed quiet for a minute and he wondered if now *he* seemed like the angry one. And maybe he was. Not at her. At himself. At his dad. And yes, at his grandparents for not being in his life when he'd needed them.

"Yeah," she finally said, softly. "Yeah, okay, I guess I can."

"It's probably hard for you to relate, darlin'——when you've never done anything to be ashamed of."

She caught him off guard, however, by replying, "No, I relate because…maybe I'm ashamed of myself right now."

He blinked back his surprise. "For what?" What on earth could someone as good and pure as Meg Sloan have to be ashamed of?

She swallowed visibly, lowered her eyes. "Sleeping with you."

He didn't get it. "Huh? I thought you and Zack were…"

"We are. Uncommitted. Free agents. But somehow it still feels like a secret I'm keeping from him, something I'm doing wrong."

The words lowered an anchor onto his chest. "Don't do that to yourself, darlin'. You're not doing anything wrong, I promise."

"Maybe. I've just never been a sleep-around kind of woman, and I guess I'm not sure how it looks on me."

"It looks fine on you, darlin'. And if it's any consolation, you don't have to think of it as sleeping around, because…like I told you, I don't have plans to go anywhere. And I know you have a history with Zack, but…

what's between me and you—it's not nothing, Meg. It matters. To me anyway."

Her eyes widened slightly. "To me, too."

And damn, that was good to hear. It lifted that anchor right back up. The truth was, he'd spent the afternoon thinking about a lot of things, and one of them was Meg. And that there was something *right* here, between them—right enough that the risk of running into his grandfather hadn't kept him away.

But she moved instantly on from that to, "There's more I'm confused about, though."

"Tell me."

"I keep wondering what other secrets you have."

He let her words hang in the air. Not because he was choosing his reply carefully, figuring the best way to charm or con—he simply didn't know what to say. He *was* keeping something else from her, and he didn't want to lie. But hell—he couldn't tell her the truth, either.

He was saved when the back door opened.

Though…not really saved at all because his grandfather walked out, wearing a smile Seth had missed, and completely unaware of the tension he'd just sliced through with his arrival. "Pretty night," he said to them both.

"Did you have a nice day, Mr. McNaughton?" Meg asked.

"Surely I did. Wasn't certain these old legs would carry me around the island on a bicycle, but I made the circle twice! Then had a scrumptious meal of biscuits and gravy at the Skipper's Wheel, and followed it up with some delectable rocky road fudge from Molly's."

Of course, while Seth had known coming back tonight might bring him into his grandpa's path, it had seemed so quiet upon his return that he'd thought maybe fate would work *with* him rather than against him. But fate never had much been on his side.

"Molly's daughter has actually taken over the shop now," Meg informed his grandpa.

"Is that right?" his granddad said. "Well, it was mighty delicious fudge, I can assure you of that. Thinking I'll try a different flavor every day I'm here."

Meg laughed in her good-hearted way. "That sounds like a plan I can get behind. Though I have to avoid the fudge myself—living here is dangerous in that way."

"I'll have to keep biking around the island to make sure my waistline stands a chance of breaking even." His grandpa stopped, chuckled. "But the last few years it's been winning."

The two exchanged a little more small talk, allowing Seth to quietly stand back and take it in. It bordered on surreal to be with his granddad, on the very same patio, after all these years. It made him *miss* those years— even more than he already did. It made him wish for a different kind of life. If only that phone call hadn't come that last day on the island the year he was ten. Nothing had gone right for him after that…until coming back here two weeks ago. It was easy to understand why Meg had stayed—Summer Island did have a way of making you not want to leave.

"Guess it's time for me to turn in," his grandpa said after some conversation about the many varieties of lilacs currently coloring the island and talk that Meg might have a cookout for the guests early next week. "But I thank you for the hospitality—it's always nice to come back here."

It was as if he'd just read Seth's mind. And relief spilled through Seth as he turned to go—until he stopped, looked back. And planted his gaze squarely on Seth. "Young man, you mind if I ask where you're from?"

The answer was easy—the usual. "No particular place—I move around a lot. Mostly down south. Spent some time in Mississippi."

"What brings you this far north?"

That one was a little harder. "Needed a change of scenery. Cooler weather for the hot summer months."

Now the old man nodded, accepting the answer. And said, "I imagine the heat down there can be oppressive."

Seth almost smiled. Oppressive. Splendiferous. Still using those five-dollar words. But instead he just said, "Yeah, it can. Goodnight."

Of course, as his grandpa disappeared through the door that led into the kitchen, Seth remembered he'd been damn glad for the interruption—because he still had no better answer for Meg's question than when she'd first asked it.

He met her gaze, not foolish enough to think she wouldn't come right back to it now that they were alone. And he hoped she could see—somehow—beyond this moment, beyond his past, beyond his lack of answers. *You want so damn bad to be this better guy, want her to know that about you, and yet how good a guy are you if you still have that ring?* It was in the cabin now, safely hidden in a place he wouldn't forget this time.

Maybe you just want *to be a better man but you're really not. Maybe you're not worthy of her at all. Maybe you should tell her she'd be better off with Zack, no matter what the guy's issues are. Maybe letting her think anything else is just selfish. If you can't be honest with her, now, this woman you're so drawn to, who will you ever be honest with?*

"Do you remember what I asked you right before we were interrupted?"

"Yep."

"And are you going to answer me?"

And damn but if it didn't feel like the heavens were parting to allow in a ray of sun—despite the fact that darkness had just fallen on Summer Island—when the inn's back door opened once more.

He looked up expecting this time to perhaps see elderly Mr. Carmichael. One more savior. But instead it was his grandfather again.

And this time he walked straight toward Seth, his eyes wide, intense—and when he reached him, he held up the bottle of lilac water Seth and Meg had made together.

He pointed at the label. That very specific label Seth had created to honor an old memory. *Eau de Lilac.* With the outline and the swirl.

"Seth?" the older man said. "Seth, do you not know me, son? Because *I* know *you.* I thought it from the first, but I wasn't sure. Now I am, though. Because of this." He pointed at the small bottle again.

Making that damn label had been reckless. Sloppy. And now he'd given himself away.

"Seth, I'm your granddad."

CHAPTER TWENTY-FOUR

SETH STOOD SPEECHLESS before his grandfather.

And so the older man went on. "You *are* Seth Darden, right?"

Seth gave a small, solemn nod. No need to keep lying.

"Seth Darden." His grandpa repeated the name as if wanting to make sure. But his eyes searched Seth's face in a new way now—perhaps seeking recognition, or possibly just taking him in as a grown man. After all, Seth had had a little time to adjust to this new, older version of his grandfather—but only in this moment did his grandpa know for certain this was him.

The two men stood staring at each other—frozen in time, it felt like to Seth. Time that was going backward, racing back to some of the last days they'd been together, neither knowing they'd soon never see each other again. Or not, as it turned out, until now.

When Seth said nothing more—because damn, any charm or skills of manipulation he'd ever possessed had fled him—Meg volunteered, sounding almost as on edge as he felt, "I should leave you two alone."

But the declaration made him grab her wrist as she moved to go past him toward the door. He wasn't ready to be alone with his grandpa yet. And though he said no actual words, the gesture halted her in place.

And his grandfather went on, apparently not minding her presence. "Son, I don't know where to begin. I'm wondering where on earth you've been, where your daddy took you off to all these years. And how you ended up back here again. Right now, in front of me this way." The old man stopped, shook his head, now balding and gray compared to when Seth had been a kid. He appeared truly thunderstruck, so much so that...even in the new silence resting between them, Seth began to understand. His grandpa hadn't left his life willingly.

"Mississippi, but we moved a lot, like I said," Seth answered him.

His grandfather appeared tired. "We tried to find you but didn't have the first idea where to look. Your daddy's family was no help at all—didn't seem to know, either."

Seth found that perfectly believable since he'd never seen or heard from that side of his family again either—but they hadn't been close, so he hadn't noticed the loss as much.

"So you looked?" Seth asked. He hadn't planned the words, but they'd tumbled out. Out of a part of him that was much younger, some last little hint of a ten-year-old boy wondering what the hell had just happened to his life.

His grandpa's eyes widened upon grasping what Seth had thought all these years. "Good Lord, son— of course." But it came with another sigh. "We didn't have many resources, though—just the telephone and your daddy's last known address, along with a few other places we found out he was known to go. The internet was brand new back then—and even now, I wouldn't call myself an aficionado of the thing."

Aficionado. Seth smiled to himself, even if a bit somberly now.

"Not sure much would show up there anyway," he informed his grandfather quietly. He and his dad hadn't given their real names most places. And though they'd both always kept a legal driver's license, they'd also possessed a variety of fake ones. Ron Darden had known how to lie low and fly under the radar, even in a world bursting with technology.

"And the authorities were even less help," his granddad said. "Not being your parents, we didn't have any legal rights to you. They said it was within Ron's rights to take you wherever he pleased, and that you were probably just fine. I think some laws have changed since then, but without knowing what state you were in, that never helped us out much."

"We loved you," he went on, "and we thought we should have a hand in raising you—but the law didn't see it that way at the time."

He stopped again, clearly sinking a little deeper into the moment, the reality. His next words came lower, slower, like maybe he was afraid to ask. "How have you been, son?"

It was a damn hard question to answer. And Seth's first instinct was to fall back on old habits. Grin and say fine. Keep it short. Choose his words with care. Act as if he had everything under control.

But there was something about hearing his grandfather call him son. He always had, as far back as Seth could remember. It was a term of endearment that had always rung true, and hearing it leave his grandpa's mouth now filled him with...trust. Maybe a child's trust. Maybe a foolish trust. His father had made him believe *all* trust was foolish—except between the two of *them*, because they were a team. And Seth *had* trusted his dad—because he'd had no one else. For twenty years, he'd had no one else.

But trust, like charm, could be a habit—anything could—and his grandpa was making him feel…safe. Maybe safe like this island and Meg's grandmother had once made *her* feel. So he let himself do something he'd not done much of until recently—he spoke from the heart.

"I…didn't know Dad left without telling you. As I got older, I wondered—but I was never sure. I thought maybe you'd just figured it was easier not having me around after Mom died."

He regretted the words immediately, though, when a wounded expression flashed across his granddad's face. "How could we ever stop caring for you, son? We always loved you—*always*—and after your mom was gone, well…it felt in a way like both of you had died. Your sweet grandma never really got over the loss—of either of you." His eyes looked glassy now. "I only wish she could see me standing here with you, wish she could see what a fine young man you grew into." He stopped, lowered his gaze, bit his lip. "She passed on three years ago this August."

Seth's mind was a blur of thoughts racing past so fast he could scarcely grab on to them.

Being without me doubled their loss? He'd never even imagined such a thing—it was like looking at the world through an entirely new lens.

And it made certain pains feel fresh, raw. It made him hurt for his grandma in a way he never had. It also made him hurt for his grandpa for being without her, as it was clear *that* pain still felt fresh, too—even after three years. His grandpa's eyes dripped with loneliness when he spoke of her death.

But his granddad had him pegged all wrong—he wasn't a fine man, not a fine man at all.

And he didn't know how to explain that to him.

Same as you did to Meg. Though it felt even harder with his grandpa, just as he'd known it would. He didn't want to let the man down, and after all this time, and all this loss, the reality of who he was would be a disappointment.

"I'm sorry." The words came past a lump in his throat.

"You didn't do anything wrong, Seth," his grandpa said, shaking his head, confused by the words.

"I'm not...who you think. I'm not...who I want to be."

The older man blinked, looked a little worried now. "What do you mean?"

Shit. He'd started all wrong, haphazardly, leaving him nowhere to go but straight into the ugliness. Yeah, his skills disappeared a little more thoroughly every damn day. And maybe on some level that was actually good. *It means you're stuck being real with people because it's all you've got left.* But it wasn't a place he was comfortable in or knew anything about. It made him the proverbial bull in a china shop, ramming and slamming his way around facts and confessions most people would probably handle with more finesse.

You've got nothing to lose now, though. Well, nothing you knew you had until five minutes ago anyway. "Dad...didn't raise me right, Granddad."

This time when his grandpa sighed, it came with a

certain knowing, a lack of surprise. Only whatever he was thinking probably didn't hold a candle to how bad things really were.

"This is…this is hard, because… I wish I'd grown up into the kind of man you could be proud of—and I'm about as far from that as possible."

His grandfather's expression turned solemn then, and reverent, and maybe even tolerant—as he said, "Son, I would never judge you for your upbringing—that's something none of us has any say over. Family is about unconditional love. Now why don't you and me sit down someplace together and just talk, catch up—you tell me about your life and I'll tell you about mine. How's that sound?"

It sounds better than I thought it could.
And…safer than I thought it could.

THE NIGHT WAS TEMPERATE, warm for June by island standards, and though Seth had wanted her to stay, Meg knew the time had come to give them some privacy, and that he'd be okay with that now. She stood up and said, "I'm going to head inside and leave you two out here to talk."

"All right, darlin'," Seth answered quietly. Their eyes met as she crossed the patio, and she saw so much in his, so much more than she even could have conceived of when they'd first met. His sexy charm still lingered there, beneath the surface, too much a part of him to disappear completely—but she was proud of him for facing this monumental moment with honesty and dignity. She still wasn't sure how she felt about his past, if she believed someone with that background could ever be fully trustworthy—even if that was unfair and judgmental. But on the other hand, she found herself trying to put herself in his shoes, understand what it felt like to have been drawn into that life without having any say in it, to regret it, to have left it, but to know it still brands you.

Normally, she would have cleaned up in the kitchen—especially now that there were guests on the premises. But she didn't want to accidentally overhear any more of such a private conversation, so she simply turned out the kitchen light and walked to the parlor, where she found Mr. Carmichael watching TV.

Glad for the distraction, she inquired about his day, pointed out the laminated channel guide she kept on the coffee table this time of year, and said goodnight. Normally during tourist season, she loaned her guests keys if they intended to be out late at the Pink Pelican or elsewhere, but since everyone was accounted for and it had been a long day, she locked the door and headed to the privacy of her room, a place that became a sanctuary for her in summer.

Miss Kitty followed, likely a bit jarred by the added comings and goings today—the first few days of the season were always like that, but then she adjusted and reverted to being her normal one-more-knick-knack self.

Meg showered and put on summer pajamas—her robe handy for any necessary departures from the room now that the house was officially an inn again—then gave herself a mini-pedicure since sandal season had finally arrived. After that, she curled up in bed with Gran's red leather diary. And she had just opened it to the page she'd last bookmarked—when a small knock came on the door.

"Yes?"

It opened and Seth peeked inside. "Hi, darlin'."

"Come in," she told him, instantly sensing the new calm that hung about him. "It went well?"

He nodded, sitting down on the edge of the bed. More like a visitor than a man who had shared it with her, but she appreciated him honoring her more recent emotions. "Better than in my wildest dreams," he said quietly.

Her heart filled, and despite herself she wanted to hug him—but made do with, "That's wonderful. I'm so happy for you."

"We're gonna spend some time together while he's here, and then maybe at some point I'll drive down to Pennsylvania and visit, stay with him awhile."

Why was that last part jarring? She prayed her reaction didn't show on her face. Because of course the two men would want to reconnect in a deeper, longer lasting way. And it was wonderful that Seth suddenly had a place that might feel like home to him. And that Mr. McNaughton would have his long-lost grandson back in his life on a regular basis. It made perfect sense for both of them.

Even if an hour ago he'd been a man without a home who'd assured her he wasn't going anywhere anytime soon.

"When…do you think you'll leave?" She feared it had come out sounding too whispery.

He shrugged. "No specific plan. End of summer maybe. Or when the work dries up here."

She nodded, tried to look natural, like this affected her not at all.

"Meg darlin', you look tense."

Crap. "Do I?" She tried again to relax. And failed.

He tilted his head, gave her a long look. "If this is about me telling you I wasn't going anyplace anytime soon, I won't if…if you decide you want me here. I guess it just didn't seem to me like things were leaning that way. But if I'm wrong about that, Meg, all you gotta do is let me know."

She swallowed, taken aback that they were suddenly in such a serious place again. Taken aback that he was telling her he'd choose her over his grandfather. "You're saying…you feel that much for me? That you'd stay here with me instead of going to your grandpa's?"

His nod was short but sure. "That's exactly what I'm sayin'." But then he pushed to his feet. "I'm not trying to rush you, though. You take your time and think things through. End of summer is still a while away—it's just getting started."

She found herself smiling gently up at him. For making this so easy on her. For making his intentions known, something she hadn't had from a man in a long time. She liked the returned sense of calm and confidence the reunion with his grandpa had brought. It suited him.

"Okay," she said quietly.

He pointed vaguely in a westerly direction. "I'm gonna head back to the cabin now, but I'll be back in the morning. Gonna spend the day with Granddad if you don't have any work for me to do."

"Nothing that can't wait," she assured him. And when he started toward the bedroom door, she said, "Seth?"

He looked back.

"Would you like to stay here—in one of the rooms—while he's here? Just to be closer, more convenient?"

But he shook his handsome head. "No need, darlin'—I'm good where I'm at." Then he gave her a classic Seth wink. "Sharing your bed's better, but if I'm not doing that, I kinda grew to like the walk."

Even now, the mention of their sex filled her cheeks with fresh heat. Part old-fashioned embarrassment, part wanting more of it right now but knowing it was best not to indulge that whim.

"Um, by the way, I was thinking of taking Granddad to that watering hole up the street tomorrow night—the Pink something?"

"Pelican," she said.

"Any chance you might wanna come along? Make it sort of a party? Suzanne, too, if you think she'd want to. If that's not too weird. I, uh, don't exactly have a wide circle of friends here—but guess I'm just thinking I'd like to celebrate a little."

How could she turn that down? Even if it might look more like a date than it actually would be. But given she'd be there with one of her longtime inn guests as well would make it seem less so. And maybe she was finally tired of worrying what her island community thought of her and her relationships. So she said, "Sure. And I'll invite Suzanne tomorrow."

"Goodnight, Meg," he said, something in the warmth of his voice nearly curling her toes even now.

"Goodnight."

She decided not to read, after all, setting the diary aside on the bedside table. And it was only after she'd brushed her teeth, turned out the lights, and climbed back beneath the covers that she realized... Seth had never answered her question. About secrets. And if he still had any from her.

CHAPTER TWENTY-FIVE

MEG SAT ACROSS a table at the Pink Pelican from Seth and his grandpa, Suzanne beside her. The old wooden floor was uneven—had been since she'd been old enough to come in—and the food was only so-so, but the vibe was laid-back and easy, the music pleasant, and the decor fun. It was hard for pink pelicans—painted on the walls and the bathroom doors and behind the bar, which sported pink stools—not to be fun. The stage, never meant for more than one person, was a small platform behind the semi-circular bar, and currently held Trevor Bateman and his well-worn guitar, a microphone standing in front of his chair.

The Eastmans had arrived today, and the inn felt truly alive now, the throes of summer here in a way that always made Meg happy, because it had always made her grandma happy before her. And the doors to the Pink Pelican were wide-open tonight, admitting a warm breeze, along with back windows that overlooked the water—another sign that summer had really come to the island.

She wore a turquoise sundress that twirled when she spun, and had danced numerous times with both Seth and Mr. McNaughton to the likes of "Brown-Eyed Girl" and "Bad Moon on the Rise." The Pelican didn't have a proper dance floor, but that had never stopped it from happening in the wide area between the bar and the tables. Suzanne danced, too—Mr. McNaughton attempted to show the ladies some swing dancing moves while a few other patrons filled in the space around them.

"Since when do you swing dance?" Seth asked his grandfather.

"Since your grandma and me took some lessons for a while."

Seth looked surprised. "No offense, but never thought of you as the dancing type."

"Me neither," he confessed. "But your grandma saw a sign for it somewhere, and turns out sometimes you *can* teach an old dog new tricks."

Meg had never thought of *herself* as much of a dancer, either, but she'd had a few cocktails—tonight imbibing the bar's signature drink, aptly called a Pink Pelican, a mix of vodka, cranberry juice, and a few other ingredients she never remembered after she'd had a couple.

The crowd was mostly tourists dotted with a few locals like herself, and as far as she could tell, no one was particularly gawking at her being out with another man besides Zack. And the Pink Pelicans she'd consumed made it so she didn't care much anyway.

At one point, Mr. McNaughton made a toast. "To my handsome grandson, and to reunions!"

"Hear, hear!" Suzanne agreed. She'd been as bowled over as anyone when Meg had told her the story of Seth's grandfather being her longtime guest at the inn and that a childhood memory had brought Seth to Summer Island. "It's so amazing you two found each other again."

"And to Meg," Mr. McNaughton added, surprising her.

"Me? What did *I* do?" she asked with a smile.

"Well," the gray-haired man said, "one summer after your sweet grandmother passed, you told me you'd never intended to run the inn, and that you'd concocted a whole different life for yourself somewhere else." Meg and Seth exchanged looks—but when Mr. McNaughton placed his hand gently over hers on the table, she returned her gaze to his. "If the inn hadn't stayed open, well…neither I nor Seth would have had it to come back to. Oh, sure, maybe I'd have found another inn and kept coming to the island—and maybe Seth would have still been here this summer. But maybe not. Who knows? Who can say? All I know is that I'm tremendously grateful for the Summerbrook Inn. More than I can say."

"Me, too," Seth added. "Me, too."

"I'm very grateful for it, as well," Meg said softly, "in many ways. And I couldn't be happier that you and Seth have reconnected." As they all sipped their drinks, she recalled that past conversation with Mr. McNaughton, in which she was pretty sure she hadn't given him any details—about leukemia or desertion. But it served as a reminder that the world—God, fate—worked in mysterious ways. And made her glad she'd stayed, glad she'd kept the inn open. Maybe the inn had more meaning and purpose for more people than she even knew.

At moments through the evening, her eyes met with Seth's across the table in a way that felt like they were touching just from looking at each other. Because of what Mr. McNaughton had said? Because it made her feel unwittingly close to Seth, like it or not? Or was it just more of the intoxicating chemistry between them, amplified by music and drink and the ease of a fun summer night? No matter the reasons though, there it was, pulling at her, almost clawing at her from the inside— that magnetic connection that still seemed as dangerous as it was euphoric. In one way, finding out Mr. McNaughton was Seth's grandpa had been a soothing balm to her—he and his late wife were wonderful people. And yet, Seth had lived a life far apart from theirs, and putting real trust in him continued to feel risky.

At moments, her knees mingled with Seth's to send a skittering sensation up her thighs. She'd thought sitting across from him—which she'd deftly orchestrated— would provide a sort of distance between them, but she'd miscalculated.

Trevor was gifted at engaging the crowd, and he'd indulged in a few adult beverages himself—to the point of flubbing some song lyrics, in a way that was more funny and endearing than off-putting. When he began playing the unmistakable chords that began "Peaceful Easy Feeling," but then totally blanked on the first line, Meg spontaneously shouted it from her seat. The crowd laughed, Seth laughed, and Trevor thanked her with a lighthearted, "After a few thousand times, you'd think I'd remember, right?"

Meg felt obnoxious for a second—it wasn't like her to be the loudest person in a room, let alone a crowded bar—but also carefree. The night was beginning to wane—enough that most in the crowd, including her, were content to sit and listen quietly or sing along, letting the tune lull them.

When the song ended and Trevor took a break, Suzanne said across the table to her, "I'm seeing a new side of you here and I like it."

"Don't get used to it," Meg said. "I don't know what got into me. Except these." She pointed to the nearly empty glass in front of her.

"Think they've got into me, too," Mr. McNaughton said. "And this has been an eminently convivial gathering, but I think it's time for this fella to get his old bones back to the inn."

"You and those big words of yours," Seth said on a laugh—just as Suzanne added, "It's time for this younger gal to get home, too."

"Yes, I'm ready to turn in myself," Meg chimed in. But Mr. McNaughton cut her off. "Now I didn't intend to break up the party. Don't go leaving on my account—stay out, have fun."

Meg was pleased when Seth agreed with the rest of them. "Naw, it's late. It's been a real nice evening, but probably best we call it a night while we can all still walk home and not have to be carried there."

They all laughed along, and soon were heading out the door, saying goodnight to Suzanne. Both men had chivalrously offered to escort her home, but she pointed up Port Street and said, "My cottage is right up that hill so I'm good." And no one insisted further because among the simple joys of living on Summer Island was being safe to walk here at night—the way it should be everywhere.

A sweet breeze that carried the scents of lilac and magnolias wafted over the trio as they made their way up Harbor Street, Meg strolling between the two men. She leaned on Seth lightly at moments, not intentionally but the drinks had her slightly unsteady. Though leaning on him was nice—almost too nice—and something about the night felt too much like the one when she'd met Zack. The problem with a one-bar town: Not enough places to make new, different memories.

And yet despite that one drawback—this felt easy, pleasant, right.

Mr. McNaughton made conversation as they walked—about "that nice Trent fella" at the bicycle shop, about fried egg sandwiches at the Skipper's Wheel, about maybe doing a little fishing tomorrow if Seth was interested. And he was.

Then Mr. McNaughton said, "Forgive me if I'm off base here, but I can't help thinking it seems like…there's something between the two of you—like romance."

Same as earlier, she and Seth exchanged looks. A week ago this would have been less complex. A little, anyway. Finally, as they turned onto the front walk of the inn, she replied, "There is. Or there was. It's just…"

"Complicated?" Mr. McNaughton asked. "Isn't that what they say nowadays?"

She laughed softly. "Yes."

"Well, I won't pry then. But I'll just interject that I don't think my grandson could find a nicer woman than you." And as they made their way up the stone walk, he added, "I'll say goodnight now and thank you both for a splendiferous evening." And with that, he pulled the door shut behind him, leaving them out on the front porch on a perfect summer night.

Seth smiled at her. "He loves five-dollar words like that. *Splendiferous*."

"I've noticed that from time to time." She smiled back. But was pretty sure neither of them were thinking much about big words. And she knew it for sure when Seth kissed her.

Kissing him back wasn't a choice or a decision—just the only viable response he evoked from her at this point. It was like that piece of cake you intended to say no to but couldn't when it was right in front of you and someone put a fork in your hand. Kissing was easier than not kissing—and infinitely more fulfilling. Especially with sweet night air swirling around them, filled with every lovely scent of June on Summer Island.

They kissed and his hands were on her face, and then her hips, and then rising higher, nearing her breasts—until he stopped the kissing, leaned his forehead against hers, and whispered, "Should I come in or go home?"

Ah. Cake. Fork. Charmers gonna charm, whether or not they were even trying.

She held her breath. Let a million thoughts race through her head.

A night like this with Seth could erase the disappointment that came with the memories of that first night with Zack.

Or it could create even more.

And that shouldn't even matter. One is not a replacement for the other. They're two very different men, two entirely different relationships.

The scattered emotions made the answer clear, though, even if it came with a wistful sigh. "You should go home."

Forehead still against hers, he pulled in his breath. Then stepped back, away from her. Though he held her hands in his now. "Another reason it's better for me to stay at the cabin than here if I'm not in your bed—makes it easier. Otherwise, fear I might just slip into your room in the night. Catch you unawares. Start kissing you and hope you let me keep on."

Now it was she who sucked in her breath. At that vision. The temptation. Charmers gonna charm and seducers gonna seduce, and Seth was a natural at both. So he was right—if she really thought that was a bad idea, the cabin was the best place for him. Though she said, "Thank you. I mean, for not doing that."

He shifted his weight from one foot to the other. "Can I tell you the truth about something?"

"Please." Because she needed more of that—*infinitely* more of that—from him. To help her know who he really was, and if she could really believe in him.

He swallowed, looked a little ashamed. "My whole life, I just went after what I wanted—with women, with anything. But with you, darlin', I don't want anything you're not ready to give me. 'Cause that's the only way it's worth having."

And with that, he leaned in to kiss her forehead, then descended the porch steps and front walk, soon disappearing into the darkness.

SETH HADN'T GONE fishing since the last time he'd been on this island as a kid. Before that, it had been a common activity he'd learned from and shared with his grandpa, but as he climbed into a rented wooden fishing boat, handing off two reels and a tackle box to the older man, it felt as foreign as if he'd never done it before. But then, a lot of stuff was feeling pretty new and foreign to him these days.

The sky was bright and the sun warm. Meg had insisted they take sunscreen, which she'd thrust in his hand and he'd almost left behind anyway thinking it was unnecessary this far north. But as the little green boat puttered away from the Summer Island harbor into the slightly deeper waters where more fish could be found, he realized she knew what she was talking about.

He started out trying to fake his way through the general skills of fishing—hoping it would all just suddenly come back to him—but it wasn't long before his granddad said, "You haven't been fishing in a while, have you?"

Seth raised his gaze and confessed, "Not since the last time I was here with you. Possible I'm not quite remembering how."

"Nothing that can't be relearned," his grandpa said, and it again brought back a long-forgotten feeling of safety. His grandfather had always been patient, forgiving, and kind. It was almost jarring because he'd forgotten that—how easy it was to be with the man—until just now. Oh, he supposed he'd been feeling it these last couple days already, but this was more concrete—his grandpa didn't care that Seth had forgotten how, he didn't even care that he hadn't been up front about it—he was just patiently ready to move on from that.

ONCE THEIR LINES were in the water, they talked and caught up some more. Though Seth didn't add much, except maybe about places he'd been that his grandpa hadn't—towns in the South that he'd particularly liked or had some interesting memory about. Mostly it was his grandpa telling him things about life after he'd gone, about his grandparents missing him, about how they'd grown even closer amid their shared losses, about his grandma's death after a stroke.

"I'm sorry you had to go through that alone," Seth

said. That was the main thing he could feel in that moment—how hard it must have been without anyone to lean on.

"Wasn't easy," his granddad confessed. "But this…" He stopped, looked over at Seth, the sun shining down on them from a clear blue sky. "This helps. Finding you. This helps a lot, son."

A lump rose in Seth's throat. He wasn't the world's most sentimental guy—his life had made that sort of thing a liability early on—so he kept his reply short and sweet. "It helps me, too."

"So about you and Meg," his grandpa said a few minutes later. Seth had just caught a trout that Granddad said he might cook up for dinner on the grill if Meg didn't mind. But now they were back to sitting, their lines in the water, surrounded by nothing but quiet. "I said last night I wouldn't pry, but now that it's just me and you, gotta admit I'm curious."

"It's like she said—complicated. She's got another guy in her life—but he's not around all the time. He's not around right now, for instance. And…she's not sure she can trust me."

His grandpa looked over at him. "Because of your past."

Seth nodded.

"Can she?"

He took his time answering. Again no longer with the intention of choosing his words carefully, but because it just took some time to think through the truth of it. And he wasn't proud of the answer he gave, but at least it was honest. "I want to be a good man. But I'm afraid my dad took a lot of that out of me. There are things I don't think I can tell her."

"Suppose you just…did. Tell her. Whatever it is you think you can't. See how she takes it. That's the only way to ever know."

Seth nodded. He understood all that—but all this truthfulness business was so new to him. And it wasn't easy to keep admitting he *wasn't* as good a man as he wanted to be. He probably wasn't even as good as most. And Meg deserved better.

"She's the only woman I've ever really cared about," he confided. "And I'm afraid of hurting her. I'm afraid that's who I am—a guy who hurts people in the end. I know you're supposed to put other people first sometimes, take care of them. But I never learned how to do that—not sure I know how."

His grandpa peered over at him as the boat wobbled on the waves of the ferry that had passed in the distance a minute earlier. "I love you, son, and there's nothing I wouldn't forgive you for. But it's true you were taught some bad lessons from your dad. And Meg's a good woman." He stopped, sighed. "I guess what I'm saying is…if you think you can do right by her, I'm in full support of that. But if you don't, that's another story."

The silence hung heavy between them until his granddad looked to his fishing line and the bobber floating nearby to say, "Think I got a bite. With any luck we'll have more than one measly fish on the grill tonight."

CHAPTER TWENTY-SIX

IN THE DAYS that followed their night at the Pink Pelican, Meg went about enjoying the June days at the inn.

Seth and Mr. McNaughton had gone fishing one day and brought home a catch that they'd cooked up on the grill together, sharing the dinner with Meg on the patio. The day after, a young married couple, the Merritts, had checked in. There were towels to launder and bathrooms to tidy each day—and during her downtime, a cat to feed, bike rides to take, and time in the garden as the lilacs began to fade.

It still saddened her in a way, that fading, but Seth was right about not fully enjoying something if you're worried about how long it will last or when it will end. There'd been a lot going on, and she'd soaked up the lilacs' beauty and scent as best she could, and now was the time for that to pass. She would have their lilac water to remember it by until next year.

Today Seth and his grandpa were hiking the interior of the island. She'd given them a map and circled some points of interest: The stone remains of an old church, an early cemetery on the island, the lighthouses, and the same meadow she had taken Seth to before—which should be bursting with wildflowers of every color by now if her calculations were correct.

She was happy they were getting to spend these days

together. And despite her kisses with Seth after the Pink Pelican excursion, she was glad—in a practical way—to only be interacting with him in a more distant fashion. It was almost as if he were a guest, coming and going with Mr. McNaughton, seeing her only for an hour here, twenty minutes there.

When he asked if there was any pressing work she needed him to do, she assured him again that it could wait. And when he stole a moment alone with her to ask how she was doing, she assured him she was fine, and she truly was. Her heart ached a little, in that confusing way that had become the norm lately, but inn life in June—quiet time in the garden and house, busier times with guests, and the hustle and bustle of bike traffic and walkers going past in both directions from morning until night—was enough to distract her from any big looming decisions.

She'd heard from Zack, too—intermittent texts, and a phone call she'd chosen not to answer, mainly because she'd been busy cleaning up the kitchen and making a fresh pitcher of pink lemonade.

But today, having finished her innkeeper's chores, she'd just seated herself amid the remaining lilacs, their scent no less potent for their fading beauty, with a glass of iced tea and her grandmother's diary. And when the phone rang and she glanced down to see his picture, she experienced that old feeling: A charge of hope and desire and a longing to hear his voice.

Is it just because you want a man? Any man? One isn't around so the other will do?

But no. You simply want the right *man.*

With that in mind, she put the phone to her ear, saying, "Hey there." With a smile in her voice. Easier when she was actually happy to hear from him.

"Hey there yourself, Maggie May." He could hear the smile, too—she could tell. There was more comfort, relief, in his greeting than in other recent calls. "How are things?"

"Good. Guests are coming and going, the weather is beautiful, flowers are blooming—that sort of thing."

"You sound…happy."

Was that unusual? Maybe lately. With him anyway. Or maybe just in general—she wasn't sure. But she was happy today. "Content," she said. "Just…remembering I actually like it here, on the island, which I guess I sometimes forget." She added a short laugh.

"It suits you, the island," he mused—and she could feel that the idea was new to him. It was new to her, too. But perhaps true. "At least this time of year. When I'm not there, that's how I picture you—surrounded by flowers and trees and your cat and your books. I picture the flowers blooming and the trees being green, even in winter. It's how I see you. In summer all year long."

For some reason, the words stole her breath. Zack was seldom that poetic. Or doting. "I…like that."

"I like it, too."

Who *was* this masked man?

"How's the fishing?"

"Still good. Best early season catch I can remember in a while. Maybe the whitefish are finally making a comeback."

"I hope so—that would be great." *Except…it keeps you away longer.* An idea that tugged at her heart in an old, familiar way.

But maybe I should stop caring.

Those big decisions—they did loom.

When he asked after Dahlia, Meg had to admit she hadn't seen her in a few days—but sometimes that happened when the busyness of summer came, so it wasn't unusual. She was surprised and even a little touched when he then even asked about Suzanne, because he knew her friend wasn't his biggest fan and was nice enough to inquire anyway.

The silence that followed the natural end of typical conversation lingered only a moment before he said, "I do miss you, Meg." And she could hear the heart in his voice, same as he'd heard the smile in hers. This wasn't said to convince her—it was said because…he actually missed her. She wasn't sure why, she wasn't sure when this missing had started, but she knew it was real.

"I miss you, too." And in that moment anyway, she did. She missed the ease of their togetherness. She missed his face, his grin. She missed the broadness of his shoulders, the strength in his embrace. She missed the times between them that were about nothing but him wanting to be there.

"I'll be home to you soon, Maggie May—promise."

Her heart caught in her throat. *Promise*. Would he keep it? Was it too late? To start keeping promises?

She answered softly. "'K."

"See you then."

After hanging up, she set down the phone and opened the pages of her grandmother's diary. It was tempting to linger over the call—the sincerity she'd felt and the emotions it had drawn from her—but maybe she didn't want to examine it too thoroughly. She'd spent so much time analyzing her relationship with Zack. And right now she felt all too warmly toward him—but perhaps she was afraid to trust that. It was easier to just dip back into her grandma's world in 1957—let *that* drama again take her away from her own.

July 15, 1957

Dear Diary,
It's been a strange summer. Warmer than usual— downright hot, in fact. The windows are open all the time, but it never gets cool enough, even at night.

And that's not the only strange thing. Over and over again, Ace has come to my window.

At first, it was worrisome—I was so afraid Mother and Father would hear. But they never seem to and that's made it...too easy. I shouldn't enjoy talking with him, but—God forgive me—I do. I used to send him away after only a few minutes, but the time grew longer and longer. He talks to me about so many things. Trouble at home, but he loves his mother and sister. They don't understand him, and I've pointed out it's because he acts like a hoodlum, and he just smiles and says, "It's just who I am, Peggy Sue."

Despite myself, diary, I think about him too often during the day, and I hope for him to show up at my window at night. Now, when I hear him tapping there, my heart beats so fast I worry it'll jump out of my chest. He always kisses me before he leaves, and I try not to like it. But I do.

That doesn't change how I feel for J.T., though. I still love him so much, diary!

His mother cooked the best dinner at their house after his graduation ceremony last month. I wore the yellow dress again. I feel pretty in it, and J.T. likes it on me.

It's not long before he'll start his classes at Michigan State. I'm so proud of him! No one I know has ever gone to college. I'm going to travel with him and his parents to help him move into his dormitory in Lansing next month, and we're planning visits during his first year until after I graduate next June. Then we'll get married next summer and I'll move to Lansing, too! We haven't told our parents that part yet, though.

Of course, I know how terrible this sounds. My heart is beating double time for Ace in one breath, and I'm ready to walk down the aisle with J.T. in the next.

It's crazy that I even talk to Ace, let alone let him kiss me. J.T. is perfect for me, and I can't wait to visit him at school, and then move away. It's what we've both always wanted, what we've waited for. Ace keeps saying what a cool place the island is, even without hot rods, but I think he's just trying to talk me out of leaving.

At the end of summer Ace will go back to the mainland, though, and none of this will even matter. Part of me can't bear to think about that, but I know it'll be for the best. For all of us. I'll be a better girlfriend then, I promise. This is just...a

flirtation. It will go away and I'll become J.T.'s
loving wife, the way it's meant to be.
    If love is grand, why am I so miserable about it?
        Yours, dreading summer's end because
            I'll miss them both like crazy,
                            Peggy

MEG HAD A love/hate relationship with fish. Silly as it seemed, she almost resented them. Fish were what took Zack away from her, after all.

And yet, when Seth and Mr. McNaughton had shown up with some a few nights ago, she'd enjoyed the trout dinner they'd prepared. And they'd shown up with even more for tonight's cookout for the inn's guests, which now shared her large gas grill with burgers and boneless chicken breasts.

"I'll grab the plates from inside," Seth told her as he passed by. The colorful outdoor set of twenty, purchased for just such occasions, and which Seth had seen during the kitchen renovation.

"Thanks," she said, thinking that he somehow seemed…less mysterious since his reunion with his grandpa.

Mr. McNaughton was leaving tomorrow, so for Seth, tonight was a going away party. She still thought it would make sense for Seth to leave *with* him—and it was tempting to ask more about that decision, but it wouldn't serve the purpose of keeping things between the two of them a little distant. She wasn't sure how that would go once his grandpa was gone, either. Nor did she know when the "soon" was that Zack would arrive home and how things would be then. She kept waiting for things to get clearer, but she doubted the bottom of

Lake Michigan could be any murkier than her love life at the moment.

Even as she socialized with her guests on the patio the Merritts were from Chicago, which provided a common point of interest—her mind stayed on her grandma and that last diary entry. She kept expecting clarity there, too—with each new entry, each turn of the old, yellowed pages—but young Peggy seemed as conflicted as Meg right now.

"It'll always be the Sears Tower to me," Mr. Eastman was saying—he'd just joined the conversation. But seemed the Merritts were young enough that the name change wasn't a point of contention for them.

"My mom still misses Marshall Fields, though," the youthful Mrs. Merritt added. "Says since it became Macy's it just isn't the same."

Meg made an appropriate reply, about having loved Marshall Fields when she lived there, too—but it forced her to realize how little meaning such things held for her now. If she moved back to Chicago, or to any city, would where she shopped or the name of a building or the latest craft beer matter to her the way such things seemed to matter to other people? Maybe her life had become more like her grandmother's than she'd even realized—for better or worse.

It was unsettling in a way to know her grandma had technically cheated on Grandpa John while they were engaged. Talking wasn't cheating, but kissing was. And even without the kissing, her grandma's teenage words dripped with animal attraction to her James Dean wannabe. Though she certainly sympathized, understanding the powerful spell passion could cast over you when you least expected it. Funny—every generation seemed to think only *they* experienced true passion and temptation, that older people never had. And maybe it left her feeling even more connected to her grandmother to know they'd suffered the same confusion over love, which indeed was only grand some of the time.

When Seth returned with the plates, she excused herself from the Chicago discussion to resume assisting with food. Mr. McNaughton manned the grill well, though, making her work light—and Seth helped her organize a buffet table with bread, condiments, plates, utensils, and side dishes without her asking.

"Are you sad?" she heard herself inquire. "About him going?"

He nodded. "Little bit. But it's okay. I know where he is now, and likewise. And we'll keep in touch."

Again she wondered why he wasn't leaving with his grandpa, despite what he'd told her that night in her bedroom. He'd been missing this man for most of his life—and what he shared with *her* was brand new. But maybe it was a scary question. Because maybe he really *was* wild about her, ready to have something concrete with her. Or maybe not. And either answer seemed distressing.

"Just think," she said, "if he hadn't found that bottle of lilac water."

He cast her a sideways glance from where he stood removing the twist tie from a bag of hamburger buns. It came with half a grin. "You trying to say I told you so, darlin'?"

She smiled. "Something like that, I guess. Since I was right, after all."

He laughed at her smugness. "Guess you were, guess you were."

"And just so you know…"

"Yeah?"

She wasn't sure why she was telling him this, but… "I don't think I could have kept the secret the whole time he was here. Because I knew it was in your best interest. And his, too. I hope that doesn't make you mad at me, but sometimes we just have to do what we think is right. Not sure I could have lived with myself otherwise."

Seth gave the woman in front of him a long look. She was especially pretty tonight—wearing a long summer dress with a little sweater over it, open in front to show just a hint of cleavage, her hair pulled back into a ponytail tied with a pink scarf. "You're pretty when you wear feminine stuff like this." Then he caught himself. "I mean—trust me, darlin', you're pretty all the time. But just especially like this."

She gave her head a sizing-up tilt. "Is that your way of saying you're not mad at me?"

"Of course I'm not mad at you. The part about you being pretty was just…what I was noticing right now, that's all."

Their gazes met and held, and for a minute it felt like they were the only two people on the patio. He wished it were that way. Oh, he loved having his granddad here, and the rest of these people were nice enough—but he missed how things had been between the two of them there for a few short, sweet, hot days when it had been just him and her in this great big house. And he wished like hell he could get that back.

"Gonna let the burgers go a few minutes longer," Granddad was suddenly next to them saying, with a full platter between his hands, "but the fish and chicken are done and ready for eating!"

It was a good night of plentiful food and music that played from a speaker Meg had brought outside. After dinner, the adults threw horseshoes in pits at the rear of the property along the trickling stream while the Eastman kids played badminton without a net in the wide space between the lilac grove and rose garden. Meg said she counted it as a win that not once did a birdie end up stuck in a tree. Later she served up old-fashioned Neapolitan ice cream in small chilled silver cups, announcing the cups had belonged to her grandmother and that it had been tradition to serve the triple-flavored ice cream at such events from the time the Summerbrook Inn had opened.

After dark, fireflies began sprinkling the grounds with blips of light and crickets chirped in the trees. The children drank pink lemonade, and the adults wine, Meg trilling her pretty laugh to announce, "And this, by the way, is *my* tradition, not my grandma's."

Everyone joined the laughter and Mrs. Eastman lifted her wineglass to say, "I'll drink to that tradition!"

A few minutes later, Seth watched his grandpa twirling Isabel Merritt around the patio to "Mustang Sally." It started a trend—Meg dancing with Mr. Eastman, and others joining in. Seth found himself pulling the Eastmans' daughter out into the fray by both hands without much thought, because it was easy to be part of this, and because the wine was potent.

This place was changing him. Or his grandpa was. Or Meg was. He only knew that before coming here, he never would have pulled a little girl onto a dance floor without some kind of ulterior motive like building fake trust to steal something from someone connected to her. But this...this was just dancing. He held his arm up, the girl's hand in his, motioning her to spin beneath it, hearing her laughter, seeing her smile. He envied her childhood for just a few seconds. But it wasn't envy of *hers* so much as just missing his—the good parts.

Yet the thing to do—the only thing to do—was move forward, since no one could go back. And as one song blended into another on the patio, as more wine was consumed and dance partners changed—he made sure he ended up hand in hand with Meg.

"It was nice of you to dance with Ashley," she said as they came together. With her, he danced closer, though, one hand curving around her waist, the other folding over her outstretched one. Their torsos brushed lightly.

He leaned in to speak low. "She's sweet. But you're my favorite partner, darlin'."

She lowered her gaze, bit her lip. Trying to hide the response he knew she wanted to give.

Because she still wasn't sure of him. Because she had good reason not to be.

But damn, he wanted to change that. He wanted to change that almost more than he wanted to breathe.

And like it or not, he knew what he had to do to be the man he desired to be. He knew beyond doubt.

The problem being—doing it would probably achieve the exact opposite of making Meg believe in him. It would probably make her throw him right out of her life.

CHAPTER TWENTY-SEVEN

SETH STOOD ON the dock, watching the ferry leave, taking his grandfather back to the mainland. Granddad stood on the rear deck, holding up his hand in a last wave. Seth waved back as his grandpa got smaller, smaller, too small to see, the ferry's wake pushing the boat farther into the distance past the striped lighthouse and toward the Mackinac Bridge, just a tiny silhouette on the horizon.

It had rained this morning, a steady drizzle on his walk into town, but now the clouds were parting, the sun spilling out from behind them to reveal a blue sky.

God knew he didn't want to tell Meg what he'd done. But nothing else could ever make things right. And even if it meant losing her—losing more than he already had—it was the only answer he could come to. It was what his grandfather had advised him. It would make him proud of his grandson. And that seemed a good measuring stick to live by.

Leaving the dock, he patted his pocket to make sure what he'd put in it earlier was still there. He turned left onto Harbor Street, taking in the coffee shop and neighboring yarn shop, the flower shop and Dahlia's Café, the Skipper's Wheel and the bicycle livery. Flowers dripped from window boxes, and picket fences lined tidy lawns. He passed pastel-colored bikes and pedestrians, as well as a large gray tomcat he'd come to know from the islanders as Mrs. Farley's cat, even though he'd never met Mrs. Farley.

Suzanne stood outside Petal Pushers watering cottage green window boxes of verbena and periwinkle, smiling and waving as he walked by. He returned the wave but kept up a brisk stride rather than going to say hello—he was suddenly a man on a mission. He had to do this now, clear his conscience now. It couldn't wait another day; it couldn't wait another hour or even another minute.

Damn, the last few weeks really *had* changed him. His conscience had always been a thing easily quieted, shoved to the background—and he'd been good at justifying his own actions to himself as his father had taught him. But suddenly, all that was different.

He stepped into the inn—the front door being like that of a hotel in summer, with a buzzer just inside to ring for service or check-in. Ringing it would be the easiest way to find Meg, but the least personal. And what he was about to do was personal as hell.

He walked through the common areas of the house room by room—Miss Kitty lay curled up in the nook's easy chair, breakfast dishes littered the kitchen counter, and the library stood quiet and untouched. The TV in the parlor wasn't on, but a Scrabble game had been left spread across the coffee table, likely sometime yesterday. Where was Meg?

Not in the laundry room, not on the stairs, not in her bedroom when he was so bold as to ease the door open a few inches to peek inside.

You could just leave it here. Leave it here like some otherworldly miracle without explanation.

Tempting as hell. But not the right thing to do.

Returning downstairs, he exited the back door to find the patio empty, as well as the lilac grove.

But the vague, almost imperceptible sound of garden tools led him through the lilac bushes into an open area of the yard, past clumps of daisies just starting to come up, and into the rose garden. Meg held a pair of pruners, kneeling next to a yellow rosebush. She smiled up at him. "The lilacs are gone, but the roses are blooming."

He'd barely visited this far region of the vast grounds—and when he had, the bushes had only looked thorny and thinly leaved. Now roses of yellow, pink, and white bloomed around a sitting area sporting old-fashioned metal chairs that he thought dated from the fifties.

She saw him eyeing them. "The maintenance on these is rough, but they've been here my whole life so I paint and rustproof them every few years and only leave them out during tourist season."

"I couldn't find you," he said. It sounded dumb to him as a response. But not being able to locate her had thrown him for some reason. He hadn't liked it. Even re-alizing she could have just stepped out to run an errand or see a friend, he felt better to know she was here. And the idea of her leaving this place for good felt as wrong to him as…well, as his whole existence up to now.

"While the roses are blooming," she replied, "this will pretty much be my go-to spot. I don't love them as much as the lilacs, but they last longer and do the trick." She grinned.

And he wanted to grin back. His usual grin. It wouldn't come, though. A first.

She noticed. "Is something wrong?"

How the hell to answer. He had no idea.

"I know you just saw your grandpa off. Is that it?" She tilted her head, narrowed her gaze, trying to understand.

But there was no way she was going to understand what he'd come to tell her. Which maybe made telling her the craziest thing he'd ever done. And still something that didn't feel like a choice or a decision—just what had to be done to make the world a little more right.

His grandpa had said if he couldn't do right by Meg he should move on, and he was taking that seriously. He'd played with people's lives for so many years, uncaringly, so much that it was in his blood, a natural behavior for him—but now was the time to change that, quit playing. And there was only one way to do it.

"Seth?"

She looked downright concerned now—he'd taken too long to answer and was standing in front of her like some sort of zombie. *So start. Somewhere.*

"I have some things to tell you, Meg."

Her face changed. She heard the gravity in his voice. "This sounds serious." She'd been on her knees, pruning, but now lowered herself to sit in the grass.

So he did, too. And shit, he'd given this no thought— where to begin, how to say it. One more piece of evidence that he didn't operate the way he used to. He'd even forgotten how. For better or worse.

"When I was last here, with my grandparents, as a kid, I did something wrong. I took something."

Her gaze narrowed with concern and her voice sounded cautious. "What did you take?"

He couldn't quite look her in her eye now—so he focused on a pocket, a breast pocket of the shirt she wore open over a tank. The shirt was blue, the pocket outlined with darker blue stitching and held closed with a small pearlescent button. It was old-fashioned but pretty, like Meg.

He didn't answer her question—because he couldn't yet; because it was all too hard. "My dad, he…wanted me to take things. He made me feel like it was the only way to make him proud of me. He'd already started teaching me how to do that—steal things, hide things."

He stole a quick glance at her face—she looked sullen, rightfully so. The pocket was easier to look at, so he shifted back down.

"When I came on that trip, he told me to bring him something back, something valuable. And… I just didn't quite understand the wrongness of it yet, Meg. I don't mean to make excuses—or maybe I do. But the honest truth is—I didn't understand what I was doing, or how it could hurt someone."

"What did you take?" she asked again.

Swallowing past the boulder that seemed to fill his throat, he dug down into the front pocket of his blue jeans and extracted the diamond ring. He held it out in his palm, not knowing if she'd recognize it or be aware that it had gone missing. "It was your grandma's wedding ring."

She gasped slightly. Reached out to touch it, but then drew her hand back as if it might burn her.

He squeezed his eyes shut tight for a second, then willed himself to go on. This wasn't even the hard part yet. So far, it was the confession of a little boy. But it was about to become the much more heinous confession of a grown man.

"I hid it in a book," he told her. "A copy of *The Wiz-*

ard of Oz my grandparents had given me. And I hid the book behind a baseboard. I guess maybe it was one of those spots your grandma knew about when she was young. And then a call came." He stopped, caught his breath. "We had to leave. Right away. Throw everything into our bags fast and catch the next ferry. It was when my mom had her accident. She was in the hospital for a day before she died—we got there just in time to say goodbye. I mean…she wasn't awake, I don't know if she knew we were there, but we got to say goodbye."

The breath Meg took was audible—drawing it in, letting it back out. Sounded shaky. "I'm still so sorry that happened to you, Seth. That's awful. Especially for a little boy."

He pressed on. She wouldn't feel sorry for him in a few minutes. "I didn't take the ring with me—forgot all about it until my dad asked me later if I'd brought him anything."

"Bastard," she whispered.

Yeah. He was a bastard. Seth had always known it—it was just harder to see it in someone whose only saving grace was that he loved you. And who, right about that time, had become Seth's only lasting human connection in the world.

His heart beat hard now, remembering. And knowing what came next. That the bastard had trained him too well.

Talk faster. Get through this. Get it all out. "It's why I came back here, Meg. To see if it was still here, after all this time. To see if my memory of taking it was true. And it was. Took me a while, but I found it."

Another gasp from her. And a soft murmur. "Those times I found you looking around…"

Just keep going. "I came to find it—and take it with me. Sell it. Use it to get a new start. I thought it made sense. That if it was still where I left it, if it had been missing all this time, me taking it for good wouldn't matter—it wouldn't hurt anyone any more than it already had back when I took it the first time." He stopped, let out a breath. Found the courage to raise his eyes back to hers again. "So who's the bastard now?"

Meg sat before him, breathless. Dumbfounded. She knew the story of the ring—how it had gone missing one summer when she was a teenager. Her family had arrived soon after, in fact, and they'd searched everywhere for it. Never in secret hiding places in walls, but in obvious spots it could have fallen—behind furniture, between couch cushions, in all the house's known nooks and cracks and crannies. "All these years," she whispered, "it's been in a wall?"

He nodded. "Where I left it as a kid. I'm so sorry." He was still holding it out to her, and now gestured with it again. "Take it, darlin'. It's yours now."

She still just looked at it, though. It was like…seeing a ghost in a way. "But…why? If you came here to take it, why on earth are you giving it to me?"

"Because… I can't. I thought I could, but I can't."

She let out a breath. "This makes you a pretty terrible crook."

"Good. I don't want to be that anymore."

But she hadn't meant to absolve him—and in fact, now it was running through her mind how long he'd lied to her about this, even if just by omission, and how close she'd felt to him in moments when he'd been keeping this ring, this secret, from her. It answered so many questions—but not in good ways. "No wonder," she said, more to herself than to him.

"No wonder what?" he asked, looking appropriately wary.

"No wonder I never could quite trust in you completely. No wonder I felt some kind of secret still between us."

"This is the last of them, though," he told her. "I know you have no reason to believe that, but it's true."

Meg reached out, took the ring from his palm, the ring she hadn't seen in over twenty years. "I'm sad my grandma died without it," she said, "but I'm glad it's back."

Sitting across from her in a patch of thick green grass, Seth shut his eyes a second, then reopened them on her. "Can you forgive me, darlin'?"

It was a good question.

He'd come clean. But after a reprehensible choice. He'd been so dishonest when they were so close. And yet he was being honest now.

Maybe it was the act of a sincerely repentant man who was truly changed.

Or maybe the act of a man who would sin again because it was in his nature.

Can someone really change that much? Can someone really break away from their upbringing? She had no idea. Was he the man who'd spun little Ashley Eastman around on the patio last night, the man who'd done an honest day's work for an honest day's pay since he'd arrived here? Or was he the thief who'd snuck around her house to steal her grandmother's ring a second time while he bedded her in the process?

"The part that stings the worst," she said softly, "is

that you kept this from me even when we were having sex, when I was trusting you, feeling connected to you, close to you."

He lowered his eyes. "I hate that I did that, Meg. I wish I could go back. But I can only go forward. And… I understand if you don't want anything more to do with me. I just…" He stopped, shut his eyes again, shook his head. Then reopened them. "I feel like there's something good between us, darlin'. Something real, something solid. I'd hate for us to lose out on that because I made one last mistake—no matter how big."

She took that in, let it settle in her heart. *Something good between us, something solid.* He was a charmer—she'd known that about him from the start. But she'd gotten lost somewhere along the way and didn't know how to find that line where the charm became the truth—or not.

She stared down at the ring in her hand. It had never lost its sparkle hidden away all that time—even now the sun shone down through tall tree limbs to make it shimmer in the light.

"I need some time to think."

He nodded. Sat there for a moment more, but then pushed to his feet. She did the same, not in the mood to let any man tower over her.

"I'll head back to the cabin. Be there if you want me—if you want to talk, if you want me to do some work around here, anything. Anything you want at all."

She was out of words, so just briefly met his gaze one last time before walking away, pruners still in one hand, her grandmother's long-lost wedding ring closed in the other.

The summer of 1957 had nothing on this one.

Part 4

"There is no place like home."

—L. Frank Baum,
The Wonderful Wizard of Oz

CHAPTER TWENTY-EIGHT

THE SKIPPER'S WHEEL RESTAURANT was four times deep as it was wide—with a total width from one side to the other of about twelve feet. It was mostly a long counter with a griddle behind it, but a handful of tables had been crammed in every imaginable spot down the side. It served breakfast all day—and only breakfast—its walls whitewashed and hung with fishing nets, black-and-white pictures of old boats and seafarers, and of course a few ship's wheels.

The place was always packed, making it a less than ideal setting for an intimate conversation, but that was where Meg and Suzanne ended up after Meg texted her: Calling an emergency lunch! Can you go?

Let me hustle a couple of customers out of here and I'll lock up and meet you in ten at the Skipper's Wheel.

Suzanne already had a table in a rear corner beneath a polished wooden eight-pronged captain's wheel when Meg squeezed her way past the counter stools and bustling waitresses to take a seat.

"What's the emergency?" Suzanne asked, wide-eyed.

Meg held up the ring, which was far too big for her but on her finger just the same—because she wasn't sure quite what else to do with it.

Suzanne's jaw dropped at the sight of the diamond. "Where did it come from?"

"Seth."

Suzanne raised her gaze from the ring to Meg, appearing flummoxed. "He proposed?"

Meg gasped softly. "God, no. It was my grandmother's." And then she explained the whole twenty-plus-year story.

"That's a pretty good emergency," Suzanne replied when she was done.

"So what do I do?"

Suzanne scrunched up her face, clearly stumped for an answer. Finally she settled on, "Follow your heart?"

Meg let out a long sigh—just as a waitress named Jolene who she'd known forever came skidding up to their table to say, "What can I get you two today?"

When they'd placed their orders and Jolene departed, Suzanne said, "The fact that he came clean means he's not trying to play you—I think. And frankly, I'd be more skeptical about that if you had a trust fund or something, but you don't, so seems like if he was trying to get something from you, he'd have just taken the ring and never let you be the wiser."

"I agree with all that," Meg said. "I guess I just don't know…how to know if there are any *other* secrets. Or that there won't be more. And for something that was supposed to be a fun, casual fling, this has all gotten pretty heavy. If it's just a fun, casual fling, why wouldn't I go ahead and throw him out of my life right this minute?"

Having just unrolled silverware from a white paper napkin, Suzanne pointed her fork at Meg. "That is indeed the question. And I think the answer is—it's not casual anymore. And maybe it never was."

"I know. But I don't know *what* it is. And to complicate matters, Zack could be home any day now. So that I can have *two* men I don't know where I stand with. One I can't trust, and one who keeps leaving me. Only…"

"What?" Suzanne prodded.

Meg sighed, almost hesitant to say it, believe it. "Zack has seemed different lately. Like something's changed. He keeps saying he misses me."

"He misses knowing he can be complacent because he's the only man in your life. Seth still has him jealous."

"And you think if Seth weren't here, he'd go back to being the same old Zack?"

"Only time can tell. Or not— maybe you want to head in a new direction. Maybe you want to try trusting Seth and see where this goes."

"Is that your official advice?"

"No way. I have no idea if you can trust the guy. I like him, but liking someone doesn't make them honorable." She shook her head. "To be honest, I'm not sure *what* you should do, Meg, about any of it."

That quickly, the food came, Jolene rushing up to plop down two plates filled with eggs, sausage, and biscuits. Service at the Skipper's Wheel was always fast, but especially during tourist season—because the menu was small, the griddle was always full, and they wanted to get you in and out so the next customer could take your place.

"All I can say," Suzanne told her, "is that I bet my no-dating lifestyle is looking pretty attractive and peaceful right about now."

Meg tilted her head. "I do like peaceful," she agreed.

As they dug into their food, Suzanne added, "By the way, we can't keep avoiding Dahlia's—it's summer and I miss the waterside lunches." It was true Meg hadn't been in to the café since before the picnic table painting party—she hated that she felt awkward now with her older friend, but she did.

"At least the food is good here," she replied.

"Yes, but we eat here all winter. Summer is Dahlia time. And this place doesn't invite you to linger. We sometimes like to linger."

Just then Meg looked up to see a tall, handsome man enter the small, crowded restaurant. "Well, apparently it's good enough for Beck Grainger."

"One more strike against him," Suzanne groused.

Meg rolled her eyes. "Oh brother. Can you please do me a favor and just get real about him."

Across from her, Suzanne blew out a heavy sigh and looked a little sad. "You're right, you're right. In a way, I mean."

"Which way?"

"I know he's been perfectly nice to me and I've been perfectly horrible to him." She took a deep breath and let it back out. "And like it or not, given that he keeps turning up like a bad penny, I should probably do something to fix that."

Meg sat up a little straighter, lowering her chin. "How shockingly mature of you. What did you have in mind?"

"Give me a few minutes to think about it," she said, and they continued their meal as Beck took an empty seat at the end of the counter nearest to them. Meg almost harbored a little hope that Suzanne was going to relent and decide to give the guy a chance—but at the same time she knew that probably wasn't the case. She'd seldom met anyone so stubborn.

When Jolene brought their bills, handwritten on an old-fashioned order pad and placed facedown on the table, Suzanne scooped them both up. "You've had a cruddy day so far—lunch is on me."

They rose to leave, Suzanne leading—when she suddenly pulled up short, paused, and took a step backward, placing her directly behind Beck Grainger's stool. She looked back at Meg—a courage-gathering look—then tapped his shoulder.

He turned his head—then blinked, appearing understandably taken aback that she would instigate conversation with him.

"Um," Suzanne began, and inside Meg cringed, silently willing her not to somehow crack up and be as mean to him as she usually was. It was bad enough as a response, but would be beyond horrific if she was the one starting it. "I…just wanted to tell you…that I'm not actually rude or crazy—usually."

"Okay," he said quietly, his expression a bit wary.

She pressed awkwardly on. "I'm just a widow not really ready for male attention." She stopped, winced. "If that's what you were giving me. If not, now I'm doubly embarrassed."

He looked more comfortable at this point. "No," he said assuringly, "it's what I was giving you."

She pursed her lips, clearly a little embarrassed anyway. "I'm sorry, for how I've been, and that I can't reciprocate. It's not you, it's me. For real."

He sighed, pursed his lips, acceptant if a bit disappointed. A prince of a man in Meg's opinion. "I'm sorry about the reciprocation part."

"If I ever snap out of it, I'll let you know," Suzanne rattled on. "And until then, I'll try not to treat you like a pariah."

He offered a small smile. "It would be nice to be in the same room with you without feeling like you hate me."

"I don't. I promise."

And then she walked on, toward the cash register, quick as that—conversation over. Meg gave Beck a short, awkward smile and then followed her friend. "Well done," she whispered as they squeezed past the rest of the stools.

Even if she didn't love the way it had ended, she respected Suzanne for making peace with him. Yes, she did like peace. And the very thought reminded her—that was what had brought her to Summer Island. And what had kept her on Summer Island.

She wanted it back.

THE NEXT DAY Mr. Carmichael checked out, along with the Eastmans, and the Merritts left the day after that. A group of friends, three women in their forties, checked in. As did an older couple who'd stayed at the inn once before—the Hinkles.

A family of five named the Waltermans were due this evening, but for now, the Summerbrook Inn lay quiet, its guests all out and about, giving Meg a taste of that peace she'd been yearning for, even if it didn't stretch all the way to her heart.

She'd just done some washing of linens, freshening up towels in all the guestrooms and putting fresh sheets

on the beds to be occupied by the Walterman family—
and also changed the sheets on her own bed.

As she finished, she caught sight of the bottle of
lilac water she'd made with Seth sitting on her dresser.
She picked it up and spritzed a bit into the air, over her
bed. Ahhh—he was right, it was potent. She breathed
it in, let it fill her senses. It brought memories of her
time with him—before things had gotten so heavy and
worrisome, when it had been only about the clawing
magnetism of chemistry and flirting and touching and
connecting.

But as quickly as all that came, she tried to push it
aside. It was those things that had gotten her into this
confusing mess—and right now she just wanted to enjoy
the simple scent of lilacs in her room, and maybe revisit
her grandmother's sixteenth summer.

With that thought in mind, she made her way downstairs, poured herself a glass of freshly made pink lemonade, and fetched the diary from the bookshelves in
the nook. She exited the back door and walked across
the yard to the rose garden, settling in one of the metal
chairs.

July 25, 1957

Dear Diary,
J.T. wants to go all the way before he leaves for
college. He tried to get me to the other night. We'd
picnicked with his family up in the meadow, but
they'd all gone home. It started getting dark and
the moon came out in a big clear sky, and the
weather was so lovely that when he started kiss-
ing me and laying me back on the picnic blanket,

*it was easy to let him. When he tried to go further,
though, I pulled away and told him we couldn't,
that it wouldn't be right. He asked me what difference it made since we're getting married anyway.
And he says it will make college life without me
more bearable if we do it before he goes.*

*Part of me thinks it would be nice to send him
off with that memory. But I also think it might be
better to wait until our wedding night, make it
special that way.*

What should I do, diary?

Yours, tempted but confused,
Peggy

Meg stopped without turning the page. If her grandmother were here right now, if she knew Meg had found
her diary, would she want her to be reading this? Maybe
that was why people *kept* diaries—a place to write
down things they didn't want to share with other people, thoughts and feelings that were too private to tell
anyone else.

The diary didn't talk a lot about close friends, particularly after the early pages. It seemed her social life
had become largely about J.T.—if you didn't count the
ever-aggressive Ace—and so maybe young Peggy had
ended up with no one to confide in the way Meg could
with Suzanne. And maybe in the fifties the idea of having sex with your boyfriend was so forbidden that some
girls wouldn't tell their friends anyway—Meg didn't
know. And she wasn't sure she was meant to read about
her grandparents' first sexual encounter.

But the pages of the diary were like an unfolding
mystery in a way. For one thing, she knew her grandpar-

ents didn't actually marry until her grandma was twenty
and her grandpa twenty-one, so now she was curious
why it ultimately didn't happen sooner, as the diary implied it would. And she supposed she also wanted to
reach the part where her grandma seemed truly happy
with only Grandpa John, and less tempted by other
boys. Even knowing it ended up that way, she yearned to
see it on the page. She wanted the mysteries cleared up.

And despite the surprises wrapped in that worn red
leather cover, reading it still helped her feel that strong
bond with her grandmother—she still missed her all
these years later, and right now especially, the sense of
connection was a balm to her soul.

So she turned the page.

August 4, 1957

Dear Diary,
The most awful thing happened. I went all the
way. But not with J.T. With Ace!

It happened last night. J.T. was sick with a sum-
mer cold, and I was bored, and it was a pretty
night out, so I wandered up to the Five and Dime.
I shouldn't have, I know. But once I was there,
nothing seemed so terrible about just drinking a
black cow and talking to a boy on a quiet sum-
mer night.

When the shop closed, Ace wanted to walk
me home. It was dark out, the streets empty, so I
agreed, hoping no one would see. Only when we
got to my house, he wanted to keep walking. Onto
the island road, where it's so much more deso-
late—and then up into the meadow near the old

stone church. I kept saying no, but I kept going. I can't explain it, but... I couldn't not go.

And that's how it was when he began to kiss me, too. I never thought of stopping, not once. I never thought of getting caught or being seen. I never thought of all the reasons it was wrong. Because it didn't feel wrong, not at all. He sets something in me on fire.

And diary, it was perfect! I worried it would hurt, but it didn't. I worried it would be scary, but it wasn't. The air was warm and soft all around us, and I could smell something sweet—flowers I couldn't see in the dark, I suppose. Ace knew just what to do, and he didn't make me feel awkward or embarrassed at all. It was like being in a dream.

Until afterward, when I realized what I'd done. How could I have betrayed J.T. this way? What kind of a girl am I?

I ran away from him afterward—ran all the way home in the dark. Ace chased after me for a while, calling to me that it was all right. But how can it ever be all right?

What am I going to do now, diary? How can I keep this from the boy I love? Yet of course I have to. I'll have to take it to the grave.

And I have to find a new place to hide this diary, too! I've been keeping it in a dresser drawer, but will need a better spot now that I've confessed in ink!

Poor J.T. He's so excited about leaving for college, so excited for me to go down to Lansing with him. He has no idea what a despicable girl I am!

And I can never see Ace again! I'm not sure
how I'm going to keep from it—but I have to.
Yours, ever so shamefully,
Peggy

Meg just sat staring at the ink signature, stunned.
Oh Gran.
Gran, Gran, Gran.
Her heart broke for her sweet grandma. It was so
strange to be getting to know her as a young girl, and
even stranger to see how her wise and whimsical grandmother had once judged herself so harshly for her hu-
manness, her feelings of desire. She longed to somehow
go back in time and tell her that giving in to passion
didn't make her a bad person.

On the other hand, though, it stung to learn that Gran
had betrayed Grandpa that way. Even if Meg hadn't
been too crazy about him pressuring Gran before she
was ready.

Meg let out a sigh. Had Gran ever told him? Had he
ever found out? Worse, had things continued with Ace?
Or did she follow through on not seeing him again?
She forgave her grandmother's youthful indiscretion
instantly, but it hadn't been the right thing to do, so
at the same time it made her hurt for her grandfather,
whether or not he'd ever known.

She'd never dreamed her grandparents' relationship
had started out on such rocky ground. When she'd
opened this diary, she'd expected it to be the fun mus-
ings of a teenage girl who loved Elvis and *American
Bandstand*—she'd had no idea the things she would
learn about her grandma's past.

Maybe this just proved that no one's life was as simple as it might look from a distance.

She was trying to gather the courage to turn to the next page—when voices caught her ear and she glanced up through the flowers and summer foliage to see a family strolling up the inn's front walk. The Waltermans had arrived early.

And maybe it was just as well. She wasn't sure she could take any more surprises from Gran today.

Closing the book, she picked up her empty glass and crossed the yard toward the back door, ready to go inside, empty her hands, and head to the entryway to greet her guests. She'd just stepped onto the stone patio when something shiny on the ground caught her eye.

Another penny.

She gasped softly, surprised.

And yet maybe not as surprised as before. Since this was starting to feel almost commonplace.

Transferring the diary into the opposite arm, she bent to pick it up.

And like when she'd found the last one, something made her check the year. 2004.

The year her grandmother had died.

THE FOLLOWING MORNING came early, as she'd offered to make her guests pancakes. Sometimes such an event was planned, other times more spontaneous—and on this occasion it had simply spilled from her lips when Mr. Walterman had asked about a good place for breakfast and she'd found herself explaining how crowded the Skipper's Wheel and Dahlia's got this time of year.

Part of her wanted to kick herself—it meant getting up with the birds, and certainly made the inn no more money. But on the other hand, any distraction was good right now—and it was also the kind of thing her grandmother used to do. The innkeeper didn't fall far from the tree.

Climbing out of bed as dawn began to break outside her eastern facing bedroom window, she dressed quickly, then grabbed up a brush and ran it through her hair. Standing at her dresser, her eyes fell to the penny she'd stumbled upon last night. The fact that it was minted the year Gran died surely meant nothing, same as the other penny bearing the year of Aunt Julia's passing meant nothing. Coincidences.

About loss.

About losing women Meg had loved—strong, beautiful women who'd lived and died on this island.

You're reading too much into this. The very nature of a coincidence was that it made random things seem connected when they were not. They were just pennies, for goodness' sake—hardly rare objects.

She wasn't sure what had become of the others—stuck in pockets somewhere probably and hadn't yet worked their way out in the washer or dryer—but meaningless or not, she felt compelled to hold on to this one. Just in case somehow it wasn't. Meaningless.

Next to it lay her grandma's diamond ring. It wasn't practical innkeeper wear, but she still found herself slipping it on at times, wishing it fit any one of her fingers better than it did. Perhaps she should have it sized. Or maybe it was odd to wear someone else's wedding ring, even as a keepsake—she wasn't sure. Though it also seemed sad to just stick it in a jewelry box and let it be forgotten again after having been hidden so long.

For this moment, however, the jewelry box was

where she decided to put it. She'd never had a problem with inn guests coming into her room—it was clearly marked and usually locked during the day—but she couldn't help thinking that apparently her grandmother had once found it safe to leave lying around, too, and look what had happened.

Soon she would call her mother and tell her about the ring—but she wasn't sure how to explain where it had come from, so until she figured that part out, she'd keep it here in her room, her secret now instead of Seth's.

Her heart pinched thinking of him. True to her request, he'd stayed away. Though Suzanne had seen him at Koester's Market. They'd exchanged hellos, he'd asked her to tell Meg hi, and she'd promised she would. Meg took a deep breath, let it back out. Started toward the stairs. There were pancakes to make.

Before heading to the kitchen, though, she remembered she hadn't checked the mail yesterday. And sometimes, during the busy season, she found it nice to step outside if she was up early and just soak in the stillness before Harbor Street filled with bicycles and walkers and the occasional horse-drawn carriage.

Heading down the front walk, she lifted her gaze to see a misty fog rising from the water in the distance, already dissipating with the sunrise, the sky caught between orange and pink. And through the haze she caught sight of a fishing trawler, its white wheelhouse gleaming beneath the first rays of sunlight—the *Emily Ann* was headed into port.

CHAPTER TWENTY-NINE

MEG INSTINCTIVELY CROSSED her arms over herself, pulling her loose shirt tight around her in the morning air even though she wasn't exactly cold. Zack was home. A familiar elation spread through her veins—a habit, an almost Pavlovian response. But it wasn't the same as it used to be. She felt as lost inside as she had when he'd left.

She drew in a deep, cool breath of sweet Summer Island air. Blew it back out. Went inside to make pancakes.

Mixing up the batter felt mechanical in a way, as did setting out the plates and heating the griddle. He stayed on her mind. Yes, she was lost in so many ways, but her gut reaction was that of her man coming home, of things being a little bit closer to right in the world. Whether or not that was actually true.

Before pouring batter on the griddle, she made the rounds, quietly knocking on doors, gently telling her guests breakfast would be ready soon.

Fifteen minutes later, the kitchen and sunroom bustled with people eating buttermilk pancakes, some plain, others sporting blueberries or chocolate chips. It was a happy gathering—she could tell the breakfast was appreciated and enjoyed, and she liked that familiar feeling of guests who were excited to be here on her little island on their relaxing summer getaway.

She'd just poured hot maple syrup over her own plate when she heard the front door open. A few seconds later, Zack's rugged figure filled the kitchen doorway. "Morning," he said to the guests at large, not appearing surprised to see them. It was summer, after all. Then his gaze fell on her, warm and possessive. "Hey there, Maggie May. I'm home."

Her heart blossomed in that old, familiar way. And yet it felt a bit new, too. She'd been through a lot since he'd departed, some good and some bad, and to have him suddenly back in her kitchen was an instant source of comfort, like a bed to a weary traveler. She met his gaze, gave him a soft smile. "You're just in time for breakfast."

He returned it. "So I see. Smells great."

"Grab a plate."

"Sure there's enough?"

She nodded. "Of course. You know I always make too much."

He chuckled softly. "That I do." And as he came to where she stood, eating on her feet at the counter due to lack of seating, to take a plate from the stack there, he leaned near her in a way that felt like touching and spoke low in her ear. "It's good to be home, honey."

ZACK LOOKED BACK from the bicycle he rode, toward Meg, rolling along behind him. He wasn't much of a bicycler—but when she'd asked him to go biking today after they'd cleaned up the breakfast dishes together, he'd gotten himself over to Trent Fordham's livery and rented one.

Meg's was carnation pink, sporting a cream-colored silk rose on the handlebars, and she looked good on it—pretty, sporty. She'd packed a lunch for them which now rode in the wire basket above her front wheel. "Looking good, Maggie May," he called to her.

"I've been trying to make a point of riding more."

"Good habit to get into—and you look pretty with the wind in your hair."

"It feels good, too. Freeing or something, I guess."

"Maybe the way I feel on the water," he said—but instantly regretted the comparison when a little of the light faded from her eyes.

"Maybe."

"I should see about buying a bike of my own so I can ride with you," he said—and it was the right way to turn things around. Her eyes sparkled again.

"That would be nice. But I thought you didn't like bicycling."

"Times change," he said simply, then refocused on the thin tree-lined road in front of him, growing busy with other bikers now that it was late morning.

Something had indeed changed in him, undeniably. He'd been realizing that more and more the last couple weeks, but it had hit him square in the face when he'd walked in and seen Meg in the kitchen. He'd never before felt quite that same…hell, what would you call it? Some kind of completeness? Or just a warmth—like when you came in out of the cold and felt that immediate relief, like you could relax again.

Meg had always been a good cook, but he'd sworn to her as they'd stood eating together that her pancakes had never tasted better.

"Why, Mr. Sheppard, you flatter me."

Damn, he loved when Meg was flirty. It wasn't every day—she wasn't a naturally flirty woman. But when she was, it made him want her all the more. And it reminded him how good things were between them in bed. In bed, Meg *loved* to flirt. In bed, Meg let go of her usual self. And he hoped to get her there very soon.

He knew they probably had some talking to do. Things had been tense when he'd left. But they seemed better now. God knew *he* was better now—just clearer on how he wanted things to be with her. He wanted more. More like what he knew *she'd* always wanted.

There were plenty of places to picnic along the solitary road that circled the island—the trick in summer was finding one that wasn't already taken. The pebbly shoreline beyond the thick, tall trees was dotted with parked bikes, their riders wading in the cold Lake Michigan water or sunning on large rocks or sitting on blankets.

They'd ridden leisurely for half an hour—Zack realizing he actually did enjoy the ride more than he'd ever let himself before—when he spotted the perfect place. A hidden strip of pebbles-and-sand beach behind a line of thick oaks, the little stretch flanked by boulders that ensured privacy. He slowed his bike and pointed. "Good?"

A glance over at the woman on the pink bicycle to his right found her nodding and braking, as well. "Yeah."

The sky was more clouds than blue, but still a nice day on Summer Island. Ripples of water lapped gently at the shore, the Great Lakes being sizable enough bodies of water to possess a tide. They'd always taken care of him, these wide, expansive lakes—they'd provided a refuge in his youth that had lasted, become a habit, a safe place. But being on their shoreline, on the very edge of the water, was the next best thing for him—and even better when Meg sat down next to him on the thin blanket they'd just spread there.

They ate—sandwiches, some grapes, and pretzels dipped into a jar of peanut butter she'd brought along—then shared a piece of chocolate fudge from Molly's. They talked—about business at the inn, Miss Kitty's summer adjustment period to having guests, the fact that he needed to stop in and let Dahlia know he was home since he'd gone straight to Meg's from the *Emily Ann*. She offered to help him with his laundry later while he cleaned out the boat. He thanked her. Kissed her. The kiss filled him up with being glad he'd come home sooner than he normally would have.

Then she turned to him, looking into his eyes—trying to look deep, he could tell. Trying to see beyond their simple conversation. "Can I ask you something?"

His chest tightened slightly. He'd known the more serious stuff would come, knew it had to. "Sure."

"I've never wanted to pry, but on the other hand, maybe I should have asked this long ago, when we first met. Who's Emily Ann?"

The question caught him off guard. He'd never told her? But then, probably not—because the answer was both simple and complex. "She was my baby sister."

Meg's eyes widened, her jaw gone slack. It had never before occurred to him, but... "All this time, you thought I'd named my boat after another woman."

She bit her lip, looked sheepish. "Yes." It came in a whisper.

He gave her a soft smile. "Naw, Maggie May—that's not really my style."

She blinked, tilted her head. "You're right. I guess I should have known that. You just never mentioned..." She stopped, giving him a chance to say more, but he didn't. Not much else to say on the subject. But she found something anyway. "So...you said *was*?"

A slight nod. He refocused on the water, the horizon, the tiny shape of the East Bend Lighthouse off the shoals a half mile down the curving shore. His chest tightened further.

Of course, she was waiting for more than a nod. And damn him to hell for still being so uncomfortable talking about this. But he'd just never had to. And it seemed a little late to start. He didn't like dredging up past sorrows. So he kept it simple. "She died."

He heard Meg's sigh next to him, a wisp of air expelled. "I'm sorry, Zack. How old was she? And how did it happen?"

He shut his eyes. *Aw, Maggie May, don't. Don't make me go there.* "She was just a baby. Not quite two years old. I was eight, a pretty little kid myself at the time."

"So...you don't remember exactly, I guess?"

"Yeah." *Thank you. For assuming that.* He actually remembered all too well, but refused to revisit it in his head. Dark times were best left in the past.

"I've always felt," she began, "that there are things you've never told me, things from when you were young."

He still kept his focus on the water. The ferry from St. Ignace to neighboring Mackinac Island created a tiny silhouette crossing the horizon. "Suppose that's true."

"All I really know about your youth is that you ran

away to work on a fishing boat at sixteen. And this now—that you once had a baby sister."

Taking a deep breath, he turned to meet her gaze. "I want to be what you want me to be, Meg—I want more with you now. But I'm not good at talking about stuff I'd rather forget—that's all."

Next to him, she stayed quiet a moment. And he felt like he'd yelled, even though he hadn't. When she spoke again, it came out cautiously. "I guess I find it…therapeutic at times. To talk about hard things I've come through."

"I know you do. And I've always been glad to listen. I'll always listen, Meg, if you need to talk. But we're not all put together the same way. You get something from talking about it. But me, my stuff… I'd rather not think about it, so I don't. I wish…"

"You wish what?"

"That you could accept that. Just let me be me."

"Is…that why? Why you always leave? Why we're not, you know, in an official relationship?"

"No," he told her. "And I didn't mean to make it sound that way. It's just…something I'm asking of you. I'm…really trying, honey—really trying to repair things between us. And that's the only thing I'm asking for—that you accept that about me."

Damn. It had been such a nice outing, such a nice day. Now a cord of tension stretched taut between them. Yes, there was bad shit in his past, a ton of it. But he didn't see why the hell she pushed him to talk about it when he didn't want to. If he told her everything, it would take a damn long time, and would be damn painful. What the hell was the point of *that*?

"The thing is," she said, "I just feel like… I don't

know you. Like how can I really know you if I don't know the things you've been through. It's not that I'm trying to put you through anything unpleasant, it's just…how people connect, Zack. People who care about each other anyway."

This drew his gaze sharply. "Maggie May, I love you. I don't say it enough, but I do. And like I said, I want more. I want us to have what you just said, a real relationship. I'm yours and you're mine, whether we're together or apart. Something that lasts, something that matters. You're already that to me. You're the place I come home to, the thing I hold dear.

"I never even *wanted* anybody or anything to hold dear, Meg—but you've become that to me, like it or not. And if…if you need more, need to know about what happened when I was a kid…here it is."

Spit this out. Not the details, just the highlights. Don't feel it or remember it—just say the words and be done with it to give Meg what she needs. "My mom was violent. She beat the hell out of me when I was a kid. I eventually started fighting back, and by the time I was sixteen, I was afraid I might kill her—and I'd had more than enough of that life anyway. That's why I took to the water, Meg. Nobody's screaming there, nobody's hitting. That's what it gives me, what's it's always given me, why I'm a fisherman. That's all I can tell you and I hope it's enough."

He went quiet, not sure if it would be.

But then she leaned over, warmly kissed his cheek. Slipped her hand into his.

He guessed it was enough.

CHAPTER THIRTY

I'M YOURS AND you're mine. The words had stayed in her head all afternoon, through laundry, other chores, and checking in a new guest—and all evening, through dinner with Zack at Dahlia's and as they parted ways for him to get settled back into the apartment. They were what she'd always wanted from him and now, finally, she had it. That and the story of his past.

It was hard to believe Emily Ann was his sister. Oh, the torturous stories she'd spun in her head over some fictional woman whom he'd loved so deeply he'd named his most treasured possession for her. The truth actually made so much more sense. Her fault, actually, for never asking. She supposed if you didn't ask for what you wanted in this world, you could only blame yourself for not having it.

And so now she knew—Emily Ann was his sister who'd died as a baby. And his mother had been horribly abusive and driven him to run away. These were the things Dahlia knew but had asked her to be patient about. These were the things she'd waited to hear for five long, emotionally tumultuous years. And she could have easily enough guessed at the abuse, but it was different hearing it, knowing for certain, and feeling how deeply it still affected him no matter what he said.

She stood in the laundry room at the inn, long since

done with Zack's clothes but now folding her own—a load of underwear and pajamas.

To Meg, something you couldn't talk about was something that still ruled you, controlled you. To talk about it was to face it, overcome it, make it so that it no longer owned you. That was why she'd always talked about her leukemia—it had been hard for a while, but got easier every time. Even now. It was how she conquered it—over and over again.

And now Zack had opened himself up to her. She'd felt the effort it took to reopen an old wound.

So was it crazy to still feel he was holding back, not telling her everything? Was it crazy to remain not wholly satisfied? He was trying, finally, to give her everything she wanted from him. So why did she still feel like he wasn't—like he was only scratching the surface, telling her the bare minimum, and as if there was so much more lurking underneath?

I'm yours and you're mine.

That should be the part that matters here, though. Commitment. Love. She was home to him. What more was a woman supposed to want from a man?

It was nearly dark when she finished. All the guests were in for the evening, so she made herself a cup of chamomile tea and took it to her bedroom. A light breeze wafted through open windows, making her appreciate summer once more. But it had been a full day and she was tired, emotionally and physically, and ready to turn in. She changed into summer pajamas, and had just turned back the covers and spritzed a mist of lilac water over the bed—when a light knock came on her door.

"Just me, Maggie May." Zack. He opened the door a few inches to peek inside.

They hadn't talked about sleeping arrangements, and she'd thought he, too, might be so tired that he'd just fall into bed at home after hauling some more things from the *Emily Ann* following dinner.

"Hey." She smiled. Pleased to see him again so soon, despite herself. Pleased to truly *feel* like she was home to him, tired or not.

"Glad I caught you before you went to bed." Then he smiled, winked. "Thought you might want a bed partner."

She tilted her head, felt playful. "Maybe."

The response led him to circle the bed toward her, ease his arms comfortably around her waist. It was so warm there, in his strong embrace. She peeked up at him from beneath shaded lids. "The things you said today, Zack—thank you. For all of it."

He gave a nod. But answered more fully with a kiss. And kissing him was so easy. He was home to her, too.

Which led her to ask something that had been on her mind along with all the rest of it. "Do you plan on... being here more? Being home more?"

His brow knit, gaze dropping slightly. "During fishing season? Meg, you know I have to make a living."

"I know," she said, trying to sound understanding. "But plenty of fishermen come back to port each night. Couldn't you cast your nets closer to home? Or even close enough to come home, say, every *other* night?"

He loosened his arms around her. They fell away. "Honey... I fish where I fish. I know those waters. I have relationships built up along the Huron shores with buyers."

Part of her thought maybe she should just shut up because she was ruining this—this easy closeness, the joy of having that back, having *him* back. Zack had offered her a commitment today, the one thing she'd always wanted from him, the thing she'd been sure would be enough to make her happy.

And yet—hadn't she just told herself to ask for what she wanted or she'd never get it? "You…couldn't build new relationships? Closer to Summer Island?" She even managed a playful smile. "We eat fish around here, too."

Zack didn't return the smile, though—instead just sighed.

And she couldn't help thinking, despite all the things he was saying—about commitment and being hers—that maybe he was only willing to make concessions to a certain point. And that maybe, even if not on purpose, he was doing only the bare minimum he thought it would take to keep her, for "her to be his and him to be hers." She wanted to see this from his side—she truly did—and yet…

"It's like a moat to you in a way, isn't it?" she pondered aloud.

"What?"

"The water. The boat is like your castle and the lake is a moat, your place to be safe and keep everything else away."

He let out a short laugh at the analogy. "Pretty sad excuse for a castle, but…sure, I guess you could look at it that way."

Once upon a time, the water surrounding this island had been her moat, too, the inn her place of safety and escape, so it made perfect sense to her. But now she didn't *need* the moat, she didn't need the escape—

and whether or not she stayed here had become about something else besides safety. And she wanted Zack to quit needing the moat, too. "There's no one screaming here, Zack. There's no one hitting. There's nothing to run away from here."

His answer came low, barely audible. "I know that."

Her chest felt as if it were being stretched, as if she were somehow being ripped apart. She felt like a shrew in a way, and yet…commitment or not, would she ever really be happy with a man who spent more time gone than at her side? No matter how much she might love him? "Then why…?"

He blew out a heavy sigh. "It's just my life, Meg, and how I live it, how I've *always* lived it." He met her gaze again, even lifted his palms to her face. "I'm trying, Maggie May—I really am."

"I know," she whispered.

He dropped his hands and they stood there together, close but not touching. Familiar desire floated in the air. And so did a familiar hurt.

"Smells like lilacs," he said a long moment later. Perhaps to fill the void, perhaps because he realized, even having been on the water awhile, that their season had passed. She wondered vaguely if he ever missed that, the blooming of the lilacs. He was never here for it and she wasn't even sure they'd ever discussed it, which suddenly struck her as odd.

She pointed toward the small spray bottle she'd lowered to her bedside table when he'd come in. "Lilac water."

He looked, perhaps noticed the hand-printed label. "Where'd it come from?"

She drew in her breath. Thought of lying, but what

was the point? "Seth helped me make it when they were in bloom."

She sensed Zack tensing slightly. "He still around?"

"Yes and no. Still on the island, but he hasn't done any work for me in a while." She looked at his chest as she spoke.

She could feel his eyes on her then. And hated that it was suddenly hard to look up into them. "Is there something between you and him, Meg?"

In that instant, it grew difficult to breathe. How had the conversation turned this way? Maybe she *should* have fibbed about the lilac water, but...if they were talking about commitment here, shouldn't she be able to tell him the truth? "There wasn't before, when you left," she explained. "And then there was. But then I sent him away, because I was confused."

"About?"

"Both of you."

"And now?"

She drew in a deep breath, let it back out. "Still confused."

This was more than she'd intended to say, of course. And despite everything, it surprised the hell out of her when Zack slipped one bent finger beneath her chin to lift it slightly, to bring their gazes together. "Meg, you know that guy isn't right for you. It's always been you and me, Maggie May, and that's how things are supposed to be. I know you feel that, too. I know it."

When his mouth came down on hers, this time it was a deeper, more possessive kiss that reached inside her and grabbed hold of her soul. It was the way every woman longed to be kissed whether she knew it or not, a kiss of intent and seduction.

Her palms rose to his chest. He was warm to touch. And she had missed that, touching him. She kissed him back, let his kisses own her. And when his hands gripped her bottom and he pulled her to him, the sensation spread all through her. "Let's get in bed, Maggie May," he said on a low rasp.

Yes. Yes, let's get in bed.

She almost whispered that—but something stopped her.

The fact that she wasn't sure it was enough, what he was giving her.

There had been moments today when she'd thought it was—and stretches of time in between when she'd been floating on a little cloud of happiness just to be with him, just to hear his professions of love—content to keep floating and see where the cloud landed since it had seemed to be traveling in the right direction.

But now, even as her body ached to connect with his, ached to just keep on floating, and hoping, she heard herself say, "I can't."

He stiffened in her embrace. "Why not?"

"I love you, Zack—you know that. You've always known it, I'm sure. But… I guess I need time to think."

He slowly released her from his arms, stepped back, closed his eyes, and let out a sigh. He appeared crestfallen—he clearly hadn't expected this. That anything had really happened with Seth. That he might not be able to win her back with promises of commitment.

"I do love you," she heard herself whisper, unplanned, somehow trying to comfort him. Maybe she shouldn't care after all the times he'd hurt her —but that was who she was.

"I know, Maggie May," he said sadly. "And I love

you, too." He looked up then. "So you take your time and do your thinking. But I know I can make you happy." He lifted one hand, pushed a wayward strand of hair from her face. "I know I can."

With that, he lowered a kiss to her cheek and left the room.

THE FOLLOWING MORNING led Meg to Petal Pushers to update Suzanne on the latest developments in her suddenly-turned-soap-opera life. Each move she made, though, felt a little surreal, like just going through the motions—because she wasn't sure she'd done the right thing last night by sending Zack away.

But after a few minutes of free therapy from her friend, she went through some more motions—errands to the market, hardware store, and drugstore. As she walked up Harbor Street, she absently found herself wondering where the Five and Dime had been located and wishing Summer Island still had an old-fashioned soda fountain.

As bicycles whizzed past, along with foot traffic and a horse-drawn carriage, she felt content to lose herself in the busyness of high season on the island. Someone was playing a guitar in Lakeview Park along the waterfront near the marina, and colorful kites dipped and swirled above the treetops.

"Meg darlin'."

She drew her gaze back to street level to find Seth standing in front of her. Despite the temperate seventy-two-degree day, a wave of heat ran the length of her body. "Seth."

"I saw you from across the street," he said. Now that it was warmer out, he'd changed his blue jeans for khaki cargo shorts. "Is it…okay if I say hello? I've missed you."

"Yes," she said. "Of course." *I've missed you, too.* She didn't say that part, but seeing him brought the unexpected sensation of…a similar comfort, familiarity, as when Zack had shown up in her kitchen yesterday morning. And if she hadn't been toting plastic shopping bags in each hand, she might have given him a hug.

"How…have you been?" It came out awkwardly. How did you greet a man you'd banished from your life until you decided if you wanted him there or not?

"Good, good," he said but the answer didn't quite make it to his eyes or his voice. He sounded more convincing, though, as he added, "I've been doing some work for the Fishers—a little painting, a little gardening."

Despite herself, her spine stiffened slightly. Did she actually feel possessive about his labor? "That's… great."

"Just to pass the time, make a little money," he said, as if he owed her an apology.

"Of course." She nodded.

"I heard Zack's back."

She blinked. Tried to mask any reaction, good or bad. "Yeah."

He shifted his weight from one work boot to the other. "Sorry, darlin'—I didn't mean to make things awkward."

"I know," she said. "It's a weird situation." Then, partly to move past the awkwardness but also because it suddenly seemed convenient, she asked, "How do you feel about mowing?"

"Mowing?"

"The guy who usually does the inn's grounds is vacationing this week. There's a riding mower and a Weed Eater in the shed."

Did his eyes actually light up at being invited to do some work for her? He was trying to play it cool, but she was pretty sure they had. "I'd be happy to, darlin'."

"Though...this doesn't mean anything."

He nodded. "Okay. Only..."

"What?"

He gave his sexy head a tilt and looked more like his usual, easygoing self as he told her, "Well, my grandpa said my best hope with you was to just tell you everything, every truth I thought might scare you away. Knowing it might do just that. Because it was the only way to try to make things right. So that's what I did, and no matter how things turn out, Meg, guess I have no regrets." With that, he reached out to gently squeeze her hand and added, "I'll be by tomorrow to mow if that's good."

She nodded. "Perfect."

Tomorrow really *was* perfect, because it would be the rarest of June days at the Summerbrook Inn—only two guestrooms were occupied at the moment, and both would be vacated by this evening with no one new checking in until late tomorrow. It would be a good day for linens and cleaning, and a good day for mowing. Mowing had to happen whether there were guests or not, but an empty house made it an ideal time.

That afternoon, she checked the gas in both the mower and the Weed Eater, and made sure the gas can was full. She started a load of sheets taken from recently vacated rooms, then carried Gran's diary to her cozy chair in the nook, the window behind it raised to let in the fresh air. For some reason, she didn't want to read outside—maybe she was worried Zack would see her and come by, or Dahlia or anyone else, and she didn't want to squander her current solitude.

Though the thought made her wonder what Zack was doing today. And if he was sorry he'd come home only to have her send him away. Two men she'd sent away now. Two men she didn't know what to do about.

As Miss Kitty sauntered into the nook and bounded silently up next to her in the chair, she reached out a hand to scratch behind the cat's ears. "Let's see what's happening in 1957 today, shall we?" she said absently in the kitty's direction. Then she opened the book to where she'd last placed the ribbon.

September 10, 1957

Dear Diary,
So much has happened.

Things I thought were going to change forever aren't going to change at all.

And things I thought would stay the same for-ever have changed completely.

I'm so very tired, and I feel much older than I did only a couple of weeks ago. But wiser, too.

It all started when Mother got sick the week before the trip to take J.T. to Lansing. At first she only felt a little weak and wobbly, but then she started having chills, and in no time at all she was running a high fever. And then Father came down with it, too. That left me to care for them, and to hope I didn't get sick as well.

Next thing you know, diary, a lot of other people on the island fell ill, too. And Dr. Zentmeyer says it's the Asian Flu! It came from China and has been spreading all across the globe! I got vaccinated as soon as the doctor could get the medicine, and he gave Mother and Father antibiotics. Someone must have brought it over from the mainland—it could have been anyone who's been there recently, as there are outbreaks in St. Simon and Mackinaw City, too.

Needless to say, I asked J.T. to postpone going. For at least a week, in hopes Mother and Father would improve and that maybe some of this horrible epidemic would begin to blow over. He'd planned to arrive well before his classes started, so postponing made all the sense in the world. If he had any sense. But he refused, diary! And not only that, he got angry with me for not going with him and his parents as scheduled and even broke up with me!

It was hard to believe he expected me to leave Mother and Father like that! Their fevers were both so high, and at times Father had trouble breathing. Dr. Zentmeyer said it was very serious and that people sometimes died. I've never been so afraid, and I did my best to take care of them, but sometimes it was hard to know if I was doing the right thing. Every time the doctor left, he gave me so many instructions that it was hard to keep track, especially as exhausted and worried as I was.

I couldn't believe J.T. jilted me that way, diary. And at first, I thought it was God's way of punish-

*ing me for what happened with Ace, that maybe
I deserved it. But Mother and Father certainly
didn't, so I decided that was a silly way to think.*

*Then things got even worse, though. Father's
flu progressed into pneumonia. By that time, I
was at the end of my rope. And that was when I
ran into Ace one day at the Five and Dime when
I was walking home from the drugstore. I told
him everything. And later that day a knock came
on our door—and there was Ace standing on the
other side.*

*He said, "I'm here to lend a hand, Peggy Sue."
And in one way it was strange, because he's only
met my parents when they've been in the Five and
Dime, and they had no idea Ace and I knew each
other at all. But at the same time, I was so over
the moon to see him that I just threw my arms
around his neck.*

*I found out his uncle had wanted him to go
home rather than risk catching the flu here, but
instead he got the vaccine. And he said he'd
stayed because of me, that this had made him realize how much he didn't want to say goodbye at
the end of summer. He said, "Afraid I've fallen for
you, Peggy Sue. I'll stay as long as you want me
to. If you wanted me to stay here forever, I would."*

*Things got even stranger then, diary, when...
slowly, everything began to make an odd sort of
sense and all the crazy pieces of the whole summer began falling into place. Ace was so kind
to my parents, and they were so grateful for his
help that he was in like Flynn. Mother's condition improved rapidly after that, and though it*

was touch and go for a few more days with Father, he soon turned a corner and started getting better, too. And through all of it, Ace stayed by my side. Sometimes he slept in one of the spare rooms—but at other times, he would sleep in my bed, just holding me and trying to make sure I got enough rest.

We talked a lot while my parents were getting well. He told me he was serious about staying here. I asked him what about his hot rod. He said no hot rod could compare to me.

And maybe it sounds odd from a girl who's spent her whole life wanting to get as far away from this little island as possible, but it would be hard to leave after this. Because who will take care of my parents when they're sick? When they're old? What if another epidemic comes? What if the commies drop the big one? I can't leave them here alone, diary—I realize that now.

Ace is different than he first seemed. Oh sure, he still wears that jacket and ducktail, and he still talks in his hip, cool ways—but he stayed with me when I needed him, and he's willing to stay with me forever. What more could I ask for?

It's funny how your whole life can change in a heartbeat. How even all your dreams can change, too. All I ever wanted was to leave. But I'm suddenly seeing the island in a new way. Everyone and everything I love is here. The skies are blue. The nights are peaceful. And even if the winters are long, maybe they won't seem that way with the right person to keep me warm.

It all seemed so complicated for a while. But

then it became easy. You pick the one who stays when you need them. It's that simple. You pick the one who stays. You love the one who stays.

Yours, seeing clearly now,
Peggy

P.S. Ace's real name is John. That's how he introduced himself to my parents, so they wouldn't think he was bad news. After all this time, it's hard to get used to calling him that, but I'm trying.

CHAPTER THIRTY-ONE

WHOA. MEG STARED at the page in disbelief. So many questions answered, so many mysteries solved. J.T. wasn't her grandpa at all! Instead, the sweet, quiet man she remembered planting lilac bushes and bouncing her on his knee had once been a James Dean wannabe named Ace who stole kisses from another guy's girl.

Now her grandmother's fascination with Ace made perfect sense. And now Meg understood with clarity what had kept Gran on this island and why she'd always been happy here. She understood how the sometimes frivolous-seeming teenage Peggy had transformed into the wise, happy woman Meg had always revered.

She knew well how tragedy could transform your heart and your life with no warning. And so it turned out she hadn't been the first woman in her family to find the solace of Summer Island too sweet to give up after something difficult reminded her what a tough place the world can be.

Looking again at the girlish flourish of Peggy's signature, she realized it was the last. When she turned the page, she discovered the rest of them lay empty. A short gasp left her.

This was goodbye. There was no more of her grandmother to find. And only now did she realize just how deeply reconnected this diary had made her feel with her grandma these last weeks. *Maybe that's why you stretched it out, made it last. You wanted to keep that connection, keep consuming her words and her thoughts and her life.* Yet this was the end.

Gran had always been fond of saying nothing lasted forever, though, and that it was one of life's hardest lessons—but that once you accepted it, change came easier. Meg was so thankful for Seth finding this, giving her this sacred link, this personal glimpse into her grandmother's girlhood.

As she pressed the open book to her chest with a wistful sigh, some of Gran's last words played again in her mind. *You pick the one who stays. You love the one who stays.* Was it that simple?

THAT NIGHT IT RAINED, so Meg went around closing the inn's many windows, then fell into bed early, the diary still foremost in her thoughts.

She'd had no idea her grandma had dealt with such serious illness at such a young age. Sort of like *she* had. Different, of course, but…such things did have the power to reroute one's life.

And it was hard to believe J.T. had dumped Peggy, but then, it had been hard to believe Drew had left her in *her* time of need, too.

In a weird way, it made her feel less alone.

Sometimes people did what was right for them, not what was right for you—sometimes people let you down.

But then, sometimes they didn't. Sometimes they… stayed. As her grandfather had.

She fell asleep thinking about all that, and feeling pleased not to have set the alarm clock—a luxury she had all winter but seldom in summer. And she awoke the next morning to the return of the sun, and the sound of the lawn mower. Seth had come.

She didn't rush to get up, though—she took her time. She took a warm shower, dressed, walked down and made herself a bowl of cereal and some toast. She ate leisurely, in the sunroom, and when he passed close by it on the riding mower, they exchanged a smile and a wave. She continued watching him as he wove a path around shrubberies and trees and flower beds, looking intent on his work, needing a shave, and maybe a haircut.

How strange that he'd become a significant part of her life. One day a guy who saved her from dropping a shutter, the next a man she cared for on a deep level. Deep enough that she'd been afraid to feel it too much or examine it too completely. Maybe she still was.

After breakfast, she went back upstairs to make her bed, and then prepared a couple of the upstairs rooms for the next guests, all the recent revelations still swirling in her mind. If her great-grandparents hadn't caught the Asian flu in 1957, her grandmother might have indeed left with J.T. There wouldn't be a Summerbrook Inn, there would be no family connection to Summer Island, she wouldn't have come here after leukemia, she wouldn't have taken over the business. In fact, she wouldn't have the same grandfather, and that meant she wouldn't even be the same person. Heady stuff.

After cleaning, she took Seth a bottle of water to make sure he stayed hydrated while he worked.

"Thank you, darlin'—that's just what the doctor ordered."

And there was that charmer grin of his, trying to do

its usual bit on her. She felt it, almost physically, trying to wedge its way into her heart—and she glanced away, toward the shed, still not quite ready for that. "The yard is looking good. Do you know where the trimmer is?"

"Yep, sure do."

She gave him a sincere but perfunctory smile. *Let's be pleasant but keep this about work.* "Great. I'm headed back in, but help yourself to anything else you want from the fridge."

Once inside, she straightened the parlor and polished the banister in the foyer. She used the quiet time—even with the mower going, it *felt* quiet knowing the house was empty—to clean some of the public spaces, a task which sometimes got more challenging during tourist season.

Then she made her way back up to her bedroom. The diary rested on her bedside table, its presence for some reason reminding her this had been her grandmother's room, and the one she'd shared with Grandpa John before his death.

Walking to the dresser, she opened her jewelry box and drew out the wedding ring. Somehow the ring meant even more than it had yesterday. It had come from Ace, not J.T. He'd wanted her to have something special, something valuable, to symbolize their love. And though Meg had never given a whit about expensive jewelry—at least not in the post-Drew phase of her life—she liked the sentiment, the *love* she felt behind the giving of this ring.

But…maybe she was getting too caught up in the past. Using it as a crutch—a distraction from having to face her own future. Maybe it was time to put Gran's diary and ring away and figure out how she wanted to answer the questions in her own life.

When a knock came on the frame of her open door, she turned to see Seth, sweaty but handsome as ever. She'd realized lately that she almost actually liked sweaty men. It meant they worked hard, which she guessed she found attractive. Drew had never sweated that she remembered. But Grandpa John had always come in smelling of earth and water and perspiration, and other masculine things she couldn't name.

"Done?" she asked.

He nodded. "Edged the front walk, too, since it needed it. Everything's put away."

"Thank you. And you'll bill me?"

He grinned. After her original request that he come up with a billing system, he'd gone to the Summer Island Library and used a computer to make an invoice. "Yes ma'am, I sure will." Then he gestured to the ring between her fingers. "Trying that on for size?"

She cast a soft smile. "No, it's still too big. I finished my grandma's diary last night and I guess that just made me want to pull it out for a minute. Seems a shame to keep it tucked away in a jewelry box—but unless I decide to take it to the mainland and get it cut down to something closer to a size 5, I don't really have any better plan for it right now."

"Maybe you'll think of one," he suggested with a wink. Charmers gonna charm. "But in the meantime, I've got something else to give you."

Her eyebrows rose in surprise.

Then he motioned vaguely over his shoulder. "On the front porch."

After returning the ring to the jewelry box and closing the lid, she followed him down the stairs. When they exited onto the porch, three small lilac bushes stood before her—to her astonishment, just now starting to bloom.

She raised her gaze to the man next to her. "Where on earth did you find blooming lilacs this late in the season?"

"They're called Himalayan lilacs. They bloom later than other varieties."

She couldn't have been more taken aback. "Where did you get them? And how did you know about them—since *I* don't even know about them?"

He shrugged like it was nothing. "Just started asking around about lilacs, and did an internet search at the library. I asked Suzanne if she could get some in as a surprise."

At this, her jaw dropped. "Suzanne knew about these and never told me?"

"Suzanne didn't know you were so crazy about lilacs."

She scrunched her nose. "Really?" She'd never mentioned it? Funny, the things you think you share with people but maybe you don't.

"Anyway, they came in yesterday. She says these are actually blooming a little early, since they've been in a greenhouse. Usually they bloom in July. And so I thought you might like to add 'em to your grandpa's lilac garden to stretch out the season a little. Since lilac water's nice, but can't compare to the real thing."

Meg bit her lip, deeply touched. That he would go to that much trouble for her. That he understood why they were the perfect gift for her. A gift no one else had ever given her, or probably ever would have. And now they'd change her garden forever.

Overcome, she bent and cupped one purple bloom in her palm to inhale the sweet perfume. "Mmm." Then she stood upright and looked into Seth's eyes. "This is amazing. I love them. And I'll get to keep on loving them for a long time to come."

"You're an easy woman to make happy, Meg."

A slight laugh escaped her. "I'm not sure everyone would agree." Zack always made her feel…hard to please. Sometimes her sister and other people made her feel that way, too. Maybe it was all just about circumstance. Or maybe it was about someone taking the time to *try* to make her happy. She smiled again, utterly delighted by the new lilacs.

And Seth said, "You'd think I'd just given you…a diamond ring."

This laugh came louder. "Well, my grandma always said that sometimes the little things in life are the big things in life. And I guess I agree with her. A lilac bush might seem small, but it brings me so much joy."

"My point exactly, darlin'. You find a lotta joy in everyday things. And you *put* a lotta joy in every day. It's hard not to notice that. Makes you nice to be around." Then he shifted his weight from one grass-stained workboot to the other. "What you said before, about getting to enjoy them for a long time to come—does that mean you've officially decided not to sell the inn?"

She tilted her head. Had she? Somewhere along the way? "I'm not sure, but I guess it seems…well, like leaving might be harder than I thought." She didn't want to talk about that, though—she wasn't quite ready to sort out all the factors involved in that decision. Tomorrow she'd start sorting. But right now, a soft breeze blew past on a perfect blue-sky day, the scent of the lake and roses—and lilacs—filling the air. Right now, she just wanted to enjoy the simplicity of an easy Summer Island afternoon, the same as she might have when she was younger.

She dropped her gaze back to the lilacs. "I think I'll plant these right now."

"Want help?"

Their eyes met. Connected. Ah, that chemistry— it was always there, a magnet, a fire that endlessly burned. She hadn't seen the offer coming but should have. "Okay," she said even as she thought better of it.

Together, they picked spots for the new bushes. She spaced them out in different areas of the yard since the lilac grove was already full and towering—here on the island, lilac bushes often grew into trees so they needed room. One would go near the parlor window so the perfume would waft in and the blooms be visible from inside. Another near the nook window for the same reason. The last in a landscaped area that had lost a young crabapple tree last winter.

Seth dug near the parlor window as Meg watched. Then together they worked to loosen the root-ball from its plastic pot, and Seth held the bush as Meg gently pulled the container away. They lifted and lowered the plant into the ground together, then both knelt and used their bare hands to further loosen the roots and then push the rich, newly dug dirt in around it. Their hands touched in the cool, dark soil.

At the first little touch, she raised her gaze to find him studying her face. But she dropped her eyes again, kept moving and adjusting the dirt, smoothing it out, getting it just right.

They repeated the process twice more.

Sometimes there was small talk—"That seems deep enough."

"Can you hand me the shovel, darlin'?"—and sometimes there was silence. But through it all existed that same, gnawing awareness of his body near hers, his face near hers, their dirty hands mingling in the moist island soil. Her heart beat too hard as they worked.

When they were done, together they carried the plastic bins to the garbage can near the shed and put the tools away, then rinsed their hands in cold water from the garden hose. Meg knew it would make more sense to invite him inside, to a sink, with soap, but *that* she thought better of before suggesting.

She walked him back around the house, conscious of birds singing and bicycles whirring past on another busy, beautiful summer day, but at the same time feeling as if the two of them were wrapped in a cocoon there. She hadn't thought at all about anyone seeing them planting together—Dahlia, Zack, anyone.

And as they reached the front walk, she finally addressed the elephant in the yard. "Thank you, Seth. This was…nice. And I love the lilacs. But… I think it's only fair to tell you that I still don't know what I want."

He looked unsurprised, maybe a little sad, yet gave her a short nod. "I understand. I know I'm not the kinda guy you ever saw yourself with. Maybe that won't change. But… I could be happy here, with you, if you decided that's what you wanted. Think maybe I could be happy with you *anywhere*, darlin'. So you just let me know if anything changes."

She bit her lip, her skin rippling from his words, as she softly said, "Okay."

And when she least expected it, he kissed her—hard, potent, in a way that reached the tips of her toes—before turning and striding down the front walk. It reminded her of Ace in the diary. A stolen kiss. But not really stolen when it leaves your heart reeling.

THE EXPECTED GUESTS arrived right on schedule—a dad with two kids under ten, and a retired couple, the Farbers, who had stayed with her a few times before.

Over lemonade on the patio that evening, Meg found herself telling the Farbers about her grandmother and the pride she'd taken in the inn, and how she tried to live up to that. She'd been very aware of that aspiration in the first years after Gran's death, but maybe it had faded, all becoming routine over time. The diary and the wedding ring had somehow brought it back. She gave Mr. and Mrs. Farber a tour of the freshly tended grounds, telling them how her grandfather had planted the vast majority of the flowering shrubs and trees and carved out most of the flower beds.

She lay down to sleep that night thinking of "Grandpa Ace" and how much he'd enjoy knowing there was a late-blooming variety of lilac. It really *was* the little things.

You pick the one who stays. You love the one who stays.

That still lingered in her mind as well, and it was with a fresh sense of peace that she resolved to begin figuring out tomorrow, once and for all, how that sentiment was going to apply in her own life.

CHAPTER THIRTY-TWO

As Meg stepped out of the house and started down the walk, a thick, dark blanket of billowy gray stretched across the sky, promising rain. The hour was early, the streets still.

She lamented the dreary sky for her newly arrived guests—it wasn't the "first day of vacation" anyone wanted. And she'd always resented rainy days in summer on a more personal level, too—the summer here was short, so she held tight to every single day of sunny warmth.

But as she walked toward Zack's apartment, it hit her how silly that was, to resent something as arbitrary and without intent as the weather. Trying to hold on to summer was like trying to hold on to lilacs—like Seth had said, maybe it kept her from fully enjoying it if she was busy dreading its departure.

When had she become this person who held on to things so tightly—even the blooming season of a flowering bush—trying to make them last, stay, knowing full well she couldn't? Maybe it had come with leukemia, and various kinds of loss. Maybe it was about security, wanting dependable things in her life. Even if it seemed unreasonable to demand that of the weather.

Today seemed like a good day to stop being that person, once and for all. It was time to just enjoy the

beautiful things in her world when they were here and…
well, maybe just make her own beauty somehow when
they weren't. Perhaps she'd take up a hobby, a craft of
some sort. For a long time, her craft had been the inn—
keeping it pristine to honor her grandma's memory. It
was a good enough hobby—it gave her satisfaction. But
maybe it was time to add something strictly her own.

She'd worry about that another day, though.

She was about to walk up the steps to the rooms
above the café when Dahlia stepped out the restaurant's
front door. "He's not up there, honey."

Meg looked over. "He left?" Again? Now? Without
even telling her at all?

But Dahlia shook her head. "Oh—no. He's just at the
marina, giving the boat a good cleaning. Headed that
way about an hour ago."

"Oh." Her heart—which had leaped to her throat—
settled calmly back in her chest. "Good. I need to talk
to him. Thanks."

With that, she proceeded up Harbor Street to the
docks where the ferry came and went several times
each day in summer, and where fishing and pleasure
boats shared space.

She saw Zack before he saw her. Though he didn't
appear to be cleaning. Instead he sat on the *EmIly Ann*,
stretched out on a built-in bench, his head leaned back
as if to soak up the sun—if only it had been shining
today. And while she didn't begrudge anyone spending their time as they saw fit, she had to wonder why
he would choose a wooden bench on a boat where he
was often sequestered for weeks on end when he could
sit anywhere else on the island right now.

"Good morning," she greeted him.

He flinched, eyes opening.

"Sorry—I didn't mean to sneak up on you."

He smiled, but looked tired. "No worries. It's good to see your face, Maggie May."

"Yours, too." And it was. This face she knew. This face she was so familiar with touching, kissing. This face that was like coming home, even in this moment when the whole idea of home was changing, reshaping itself—in some ways staying the same and in others transforming into something new. The new part was that home was only home if you felt safe there. Zack could only be home to her if he gave her that. "Can we talk?"

He sat up straighter, his back stiffening. "Sure. Yeah." Did he sound cautious, worried? Or maybe he just wasn't quite yet fully alert from the rest he'd been taking. *Don't make assumptions. Give him a chance to be the man who can make you happy.*

As she stepped onto the boat, he stood to come give her his hand, but she was already on board when he reached her.

They both sat down on the bench and she said, "I've been thinking a lot about us, and about how we can both be happy."

"That's good," he said. "That's great."

But no. He was mis-hearing her. He didn't realize it wasn't a done deal.

"I don't ever want to make you unhappy, Zack, but I don't want to make myself that way, either. So I'm going to ask you for what I need to be happy. And what I need is...for you to stay. Find a way to be a day fisherman, like I suggested. And more than that, I need you to do it without being miserable about it—because you want to, because living here with me sounds good to you, and would make you happy, too."

The words hung in the flat, gray morning air, the silence that followed them broken only by the distant call of a scabird. *Say yes. Say it would make you happy, too. Say it's what you want. Me. Forever. That nothing else matters. Just once, let me feel that cherished.*

"Meg," he finally began, "I *do* want to make you happy, but… I told you, I can't give up my work that way. I can't give up my whole way of life. I wouldn't even know how to. It's a part of me."

A short, perfunctory nod from her. "Okay," she said. "That's fine."

He lowered his chin, squinted slightly. Seeking the clarity she'd just gotten. "And by fine you mean…"

"I mean I understand if that won't make you happy. But it leads us to an impasse."

He blinked uncertainly. "What do you mean, an impasse?"

"It isn't enough anymore."

Again, his spine went ramrod straight—with surprise, she guessed. "What are you saying, Maggie May?"

She swallowed back the lump in her throat and pushed words past it. "That part-time love isn't enough for me."

He let out a sigh, looked confused, maybe a little disbelieving. "Just because I'm gone a lot doesn't mean the love is part-time. The love is there all the time, Meg. You know that—surely you know that. I mean, I'm always there for the big things. And I always will be." Aunt Julia, he meant. And yes, yes, that was so truly important, and relevant—but still…not enough.

She bit her lip. She knew this would be hard, but she needed to explain herself to him, had to make him understand as best she could. "Being there through bad times is important, Zack, but…what about being there when I want someone to have dinner with, or take a walk with on a summer night? What about having someone to share life with? Really *share* it. Every day. All the ups and all the downs and everything in between."

She stopped, shook her head. "I'd spend all the time you're away knowing you only want to be with me part-time, and you'd spend that time knowing you're not making me happy—just like now. It doesn't seem like a winning proposition for either one of us. And I don't want to go on like this anymore."

And even as she said the words, it was hard to believe she was really letting him go, this man for whom she felt such passion, and compassion—but she'd given him one last opportunity today to show her things could change. And now that she knew they couldn't, any future with him seemed fraught with heartache—and she deserved a chance at better.

She'd been looking past Zack the whole time she'd spoken, focused on a piece of fishing net draped over the side of the boat. And when she gathered the courage to meet his gaze now, he appeared…lost. "Are…are you serious, Maggie May? You'd really…end us? Because… I don't know how…"

He trailed off—but she felt the words he couldn't say. He wasn't sure how he'd…*be* without her, *live* without her, *get by* without her—something along these lines. Dahlia had implied that losing Meg would crush him— that somehow she was saving him, that without her he was a broken man. And she'd never really believed it, but regardless which was true, it was time to quit feeling like she'd never come first with him. Even if it felt, in a strange way, like abandoning him. Maybe every breakup on the planet was a sort of abandonment—a necessary evil to moving on.

She swallowed. "I'm not the one ending us really. You could fix this and you aren't. And that's…okay." No, it actually *wasn't* okay—it was closer to heartbreaking and gut-wrenching—but it was better than him making a promise he couldn't keep. "You need the water more than you need me—that's all."

He stayed quiet. It was as if he'd heard the truth in the words but just wouldn't admit it.

Yet then he found his voice, enough to protest. "Meg, please don't do this. It doesn't make any sense. If I haven't said I love you enough, I'm sorry. If I haven't ever told you this, I'll tell you right now—honey, you're like…my family. The only place I really want to come home to after I've been away, you know?"

She tried to take a deep breath. Part of her had thought maybe he'd just let it be, let it happen, that pride would make him act like it was no big deal—the same way he'd always treated his departures from her. But now, instead, he was making it harder—for both of them.

"You're like my family, too," she whispered sadly, her heart breaking. Because how did you cut someone like that out of your life? How did you say goodbye to a man you love like he's part of you? Even if he's deeply flawed. Even when you've given him the road map to making you happy and he won't follow it. Her eyes began to burn. "But it's the fact that I'm always waiting for you to come home that's the problem." A hot tear rolled down her cheek. "And you don't want to fix that." She shook her head. "And, truly, I wouldn't want you to if it wasn't your choice. We both just have to accept that we want different things. I want steadiness and dependability, and you...want to be someplace else." She stood up, tears wetting both cheeks now, and held out her arms. "*This boat* is your home. I don't know why, and I probably never will, but it's the truth. You're happier here than anywhere else, including with me. I'll always love you, Zack, but...okay, I guess you're right—I *am* ending us. It has to be that way, once and for all. I love you."

And with that, she stepped off the boat and walked away. Put one foot in front of the other as she moved up the dock, watching the sun-bleached planks pass beneath her. Her heart was in pieces, but it was over.

And as she made a left turn back onto Harbor Street, now beginning to teem with bike and foot traffic even on this grayest of days, she remembered something her grandma used to say. *When you try to make something grow and it doesn't, you might as well quit watering it.*

ZACK SAT FROZEN on the boat for a few long minutes, his heart pounding so damn hard it hurt. He tried to imagine going after her, telling her he'd do things her way. He tried to imagine this life she kept wanting with him—this life full of dinner at home every night and a good woman to sleep next to and love and be there for.

But he didn't go—instead he just sat there.

Sat there waiting to give her time to get back to the inn.

And then he strode briskly back to his apartment and

methodically packed a duffel bag, the same he always used, with everything he took for a few weeks—or more—on the water. He changed into working clothes and locked the door on his way out.

He'd nearly made it past the café when his aunt came running out. "Zack! Are you leaving?"

He glanced over to find her wide-eyed—but he kept his voice low, trying to dial back the drama and just get to where he was going. "Looks that way, doesn't it?"

Her expression was one you give to a man you think is making a huge mistake. "Meg was looking for you a little while ago. Did she find you?"

He nodded. "Yep."

"And now you're leaving?"

"Yep."

"Maybe this once, Zack, you should stay."

He took a deep breath, let it back out. Spent a second appreciating her love, and then another wanting her to mind her own damn business. "Nah, it's time for me to go. I'll see you later, Dahlia."

She reached out, grabbed the hand that held the duffel, and squeezed it tight. Despite himself, his heart beat harder than it should.

"Don't worry," he told her. "I'm fine." The words came out rough, raspy, and he wasn't sure they were true—but he'd be fine soon enough.

When she let go, he turned and strode back to the *Emily Ann*. He focused on stashing his bag in the wheelhouse, then untethering the boat. He'd need to get gas—maybe at Mackinac rather than here. Hell, maybe he'd grab a few provisions there, too—since he'd taken off without eating or thinking about food, and he'd be on the water all day and overnight at the very least until he could get some nets set and bring in at least a small catch.

He went through all the motions of pushing off from Summer Island same as any other time—the same except for his heart still pumping too hard, the same except for not quite understanding what the hell had just happened with Meg.

He had thought…things would be okay. He'd thought he loved her enough, and that she loved him enough, for things to just go back to the way they'd been—but better.

Maybe…she'd change her mind. Maybe the next time he came home they'd work things out. Maybe.

But all he knew was that as the boat got farther from shore, and as Summer Island grew smaller and smaller in the distance, he began to breathe easier, as always when he took to the water. He began to feel safe again, as always when he took to the water. Maybe she was right—he needed the water more than he needed her. Even if he hated himself for it.

MEG HAD STRODE boldly back to the inn, head held high, tears at bay because she refused to let any more fall. She'd cried too much over Zack in the years he'd been in her life, and as hard as it had been to let him go, she knew it was the right thing to do. And besides, she had an inn to run. Despite the weather, all her guests had been up and out early, headed for bike rentals and day hikes, so she suspected the house lay empty—but she couldn't be sure.

She somehow felt stronger walking in the door just knowing she'd no longer have to wait, or to wonder when he would come home. When someone invited her someplace, she'd no longer wonder whether or not Zack would be with her; and she wouldn't have to try to explain his absence away like it was nothing.

A part of her would be missing now and it would take a while to get over that—she'd meant it when she'd said she'd always love him. But at the same time, she felt… free in a way. Free of the worry. Free of the neglect. Free of feeling less-than and second-best to a ratty old fishing boat. His wounds were no longer hers to suffer for.

And as she stepped into the parlor and glanced out the window to catch sight of the Himalayan lilac she and Seth had planted yesterday…she suddenly knew what she wanted.

I trust him now.

That trust was tenuous, as new and fragile as that freshly planted shrub, and it would need to strengthen over time—but she was ready to take that chance. It would be…perhaps the first real chance she'd taken since she'd come to Summer Island to recover from leukemia.

And she didn't want to wait.

She headed for the stairs, ready to change out of flip-flops and into tennis shoes so she could bike around the island to Seth's cabin.

Only when she whisked into her bedroom through the open door, her eyes were drawn to a sheet of paper on her pillow. She walked around the bed, picked it up.

Wanted to let you know I'm leaving the island, darlin'. Have some things to take care of. But I'll see you soon.
Seth

That was all. Just those few, short, mysterious words. Just when she'd thought there were no more mysteries. Her heart dropped as she let out a heavy breath.

Wow, Meg. Way to go. How do you lose two men in one day? One hour, in fact. It seemed almost a miracle to her that she hadn't passed Seth leaving or seen him boarding the ferry. Timing was everything in life.

He said he'd see her soon, but that seemed unlikely. A nicer way of saying so long—nothing more and nothing less.

She stood there for a moment, too stunned to move. A certain familiar numbness set in. Drew had left her a note, too. *I'm sorry, but I just can't do this.* An invisible hand squeezed her heart tight as her throat thickened with impending tears.

But before they leaked free, her mind raced—and she found herself turning to the dresser, and the jewelry box. She lifted the lid and looked inside.

The ring was gone.

CHAPTER THIRTY-THREE

SHE STOOD STARING at the empty space in the jewelry box. Unlike the last time the ring had disappeared, she didn't bother looking anyplace else for it, wondering if she'd moved it and forgotten. He'd seen her put it there. She'd trusted him enough not to keep that a secret. *Foolish.* Apparently he changed his mind and decided the money was more important than being with her. And more important than being the good man he claimed to want to be.

She'd known making a change like that would have to be hard. Like a tiger trying to change his stripes. She realized she had been gullible to even think he could, to even believe he wanted to. And she supposed anyone who heard this story would think the whole thing had somehow been a con to begin with and that she'd fallen for it—hook, line, and sinker.

But she didn't believe that. He'd told her things he'd never had to if none of it was real. She knew in her heart that he'd tried to be that better man—and failed.

A glance out the window brought the departing ferry into sight, en route to St. Simon, leaving every hour on the hour this time of year, yet seldom so full that anyone had to wait. Sorry she could almost feel him getting farther away from her, bit by bit, second by second, same as every time she'd ever watched the *Emily Ann* float away.

Maybe he'd go to his grandpa's. Maybe she should call Mr. McNaughton, tell him what happened. Maybe somehow it would get her grandmother's ring back.

But no. It seemed more likely that Seth would sell it long before reaching Pennsylvania. Maybe a returned shame or embarrassment would keep him from contacting his grandfather right now anyway. And even as special as the ring was to her—it had been lost a long time and maybe it would be easier to just pretend it had never been found than to try to chase it, and him.

Hell, if she wanted to chase after it, she could call the police in St. Simon and have them meet the ferry when it arrived—it was a half hour trip to the mainland. She could call the ferry runners, too. Or she could get a ride there—she knew at least a dozen people on the island with boats who would do that for her in a heartbeat. There were a lot of ways she could try to get her ring back. But if the money was that important to Seth that he'd steal it a second time, from a woman whose happiness he claimed to care about, then she'd just let him have it.

She picked the note back up off the bed, crumpled it in her hand, tossed it in the trash.

Two heartbreaks in one day was admittedly tough to take, so she crawled under the covers, knowing she had most of the day before new guests were due to arrive, and that she deserved—for a little while—to curl up in a ball and mourn. Losses of all kind. And one more abandonment.

But even as she finally let herself dissolve into tears, the covers pulled over her head, she knew she'd be stronger than she'd been when she'd first met Seth. And not because what doesn't kill you makes you stronger— but because somewhere along the way, somehow, she'd changed. Maybe it was herself she'd been watering, more successfully than Zack.

The outcome? She'd gone through this whole relationship with Seth without actually worrying much about when it would end or what would happen. Now it was over, but it had been better for the not worrying—she'd soaked him up, just like the scent of lilacs, while she could.

THE WILD HONEYSUCKLE at the edge of the brook was fading along with June. But the enormous tulip tree that dipped over the water from the far bank suddenly bloomed with large yellow flowers rimmed in hazy sunset orange, reminding her that things were always changing—dying, blooming, season after season. This too would pass.

She looked up from where she walked along the gurgling stream when the inn's back door opened.

"Good morning, Mr. Keller," she called, her cheerful innkeeper's smile in place. Time marched on and her guests deserved her hospitality. And it lifted her up a little to give it.

The older man—slight, balding, and wearing wire-rimmed glasses—laughed. "Closer to noon, actually. Afraid I overslept."

She smiled. "Sometimes that's what vacation is for."

Another chuckle from her guest. "Helped myself to some coffee—and thought I'd explore these grounds a bit while the wife primps for the day. Think we're going to see about getting a tour of the island from that horse-and-wagon fella."

Meg nodded. "You'll enjoy it—Anson gives a lovely tour. And the sun is back out today."

"That it is, that it is." Mr. Keller and his wife had been among yesterday's late day arrivals, and the gray billows in the sky had persisted even then. Today they'd dissipated, leaving behind the friendlier, white fluffy ones that Meg considered part of a perfect day.

"If it's almost noon, then I'm off to a lunch date. But if you or your wife need anything, just leave me a note in the foyer."

And with that, she made her way around the house and up Harbor Street to the café, where she was meeting Suzanne and Dahlia for lunch. She could have taken a few days to lick her wounds, but life was short, and it was time to get things back to normal around here—as much as possible anyway.

So she'd texted them both and made the plan. And even if an unavoidable sadness pressed on her chest as she walked up the lakeside street, she looked forward to seeing her friends.

Both women waited for her at a table on the deck overlooking the water when she arrived. White masts and rigging towered in the near distance at the marina as gentle waves lapped at the pilings below. Neither woman knew the recent developments in her life, but the air felt weighted with the knowledge that something had changed. Lots of things, it turned out.

"Thanks for getting together on such short notice," she said, sitting down, taking a sip from the iced tea already there for her. "A good lunch with good friends is exactly what I need today."

When Dahlia spoke, it came out sounding cautious. "I guess you know Zack left yesterday. In something of a hurry, too."

Meg pursed her lips, sighed. "Did he? No, I didn't know. But we…broke up. For good."

Across from her, Dahlia seemed to wilt in her chair. "I was afraid of that."

"I…asked him to stay. To really stay. To build a clientele closer to the island so that he could come home at night, so that we could have a real life together. But he couldn't do that, and I couldn't go on the way things were." She reached across the table to squeeze her older friend's hand where it rested next to her glass. "I hope you understand. I didn't want to abandon him—but I didn't like *feeling* abandoned every time he left, either." She shook her head. "He and I just want two different kinds of life, that's all."

Dahlia let out a heavy sigh of her own. She wore a large purple flower in her silvery hair today and the petals ruffled in the breeze. "I do understand. I do." She looked Meg in the eye. "I shouldn't have butted in to your relationship—I regret that I let things get tense between you and I. My love for the boy got the best of me. And I wish things were different, that you two could have worked things out—but I understand."

The words heartened Meg. "Then you're not mad at me? I hated feeling like you were."

Dahlia shook her head. "Of course not. Zack will always be my nephew, and you'll always be my friend. There's room enough in my heart for the both of you."

Then Meg glanced over at Suzanne. "Seth is gone, too, by the way."

Suzanne gasped. "Say it ain't so. I loved him. For you, I mean."

"I know. And I thought...well, I thought something good was happening there. But I was wrong. And *all* of this happened yesterday in the space of about an hour—hence my needing a ladies lunch."

"An hour," Suzanne repeated. "Hell, you don't need a lunch—you need a stiff drink."

Meg laughed. "Yeah, maybe that, too."

"We should go out tonight. All three of us. What do you say?" Suzanne glanced back and forth between them. "Drinks and dancing at the Pink Pelican?"

"I don't know how much dancing I'm good for," Dahlia said, "but sure—I'll give it a whirl. Been a while since I tied one on."

And while the Pink Pelican might actually be a little more excitement than Meg was really up for at the moment—a girls' night in with movies and ice cream might have sounded better—she didn't want to dampen her friends' enthusiasm. And she'd never seen Dahlia tie one on. And maybe any diversion from her woes would help them pass faster. "Okay—I'm in, too."

"If I were you," Suzanne said, "I would throw all caution to the wind tonight and get rip-roaring drunk."

"Sure, okay," Meg replied, at this point thinking, *why not*? "As long as I'm still able to clean bathrooms and make beds tomorrow."

Suzanne smiled. "Tell you what—if you aren't, just call me and *I'll* come clean."

"Me, too," Dahlia said. "Assuming I'm not hungover myself."

IT WAS A FUN NIGHT. Dahlia danced to Trevor's version of "Wild Night Is Calling." They all drank sex-on-the-beaches and Meg got a little weepy when he sang "Fire Lake"—for no particular reason other than it struck her as somber in a way she'd never noticed before. When he asked someone to yell out a request, Meg obliged with, "'Peaceful Easy Feeling'! And let me know if you need me to feed you the lyrics this time!"

After the friendly laughter died down and the song began, Suzanne said, "Sometimes you surprise me."

"It's the liquor."

But her friend laughed. "No. I mean, I would have thought that song might remind you of the last time we were here, with Seth, and maybe make you sad."

"It does," Meg said, then explained. "Hair of the dog." After Trevor got past the first verse, and Meg got past some of those memories of that sweet, care-free night, she added, "Now I can enjoy the song again without it having anything to do with him."

No one got too tipsy to walk home, even if there was giggling along the way, and hugs when they all parted. Suzanne asked Meg quietly, "Are you okay?" It wasn't about intoxication—it was about love, and loss.

She answered just as quietly. "Yeah. Or I will be anyway."

More hugs, and as they all headed off to their respective homes, Meg felt thankful to be a part of a strong trio of independent women.

Of course, once she was in the door, up the stairs, and in her room—away from the eyes of any guests who might be up late—she wept. It was still so new. Zack was out of her life—by reluctant choice. And Seth was out of her life—not by her choice at all.

You're better off without him, though, if this is who he really is. She knew that. And it really wasn't much different than the situation with Zack—turned out he just wasn't the man she wanted him to be.

I love him. She'd known that deep down. And now she knew it without doubt. *I love him and, like Zack, maybe I always will.* And there would be more mourning to do. But life would go on, even if it felt a little empty and much less rich for not having him in it.

THE NEXT DAY started out blessedly quiet—no check-ins or checkouts, the house empty early as all her guests spilled out the front door for biking or hiking or fishing or Harbor Street shopping. The worst thing that happened was discovering that Miss Kitty had apparently gotten into a tussle with the phone on Meg's desk, as well as a cup of pens—likely last night while she'd been out. Occasionally such little messes occurred— her generally calm cat sometimes liked to explore. And upon finding the landline and its answering machine base on the floor, the short cord yanked from the wall, and pens and pencils strewn about, Meg reassembled the desk, gently scolding the kitty with, "You'd better hope I didn't miss anyone wanting to make a reservation, young lady."

She continued using the quiet time to tidy the office, kitchen, and common areas. When she passed through the nook, a feather duster in hand, it startled Miss Kitty from where she sat perched on a high shelf. The cat screeched and leaped to the easy chair, knocking a book to the floor with a thud in the process, then darted from the room.

"For heaven's sake," Meg breathed, pressing a palm to her chest—Miss Kitty was having a rough day or two. Kind of like she was. So rather than be annoyed, she only sympathized and resolved to give the cat some extra treats later.

Upon bending to pick up the book, she found it was her grandmother's Bible. Black, soft cover—Gran had once told her she'd received it upon her baptism at the age of fourteen. And it had been sitting untouched on this shelf for…well, Meg didn't know how long. Or actually, she did. It must have been among the stacks of books she and Seth had moved when he'd painted in here, most of which had belonged to her grandmother, and which she kept more out of sentimentality than anything else.

Like in Gran's diary, a red ribbon served as a bookmark, and the Bible fell open in Meg's palm to where it lay: Matthew, Chapter 28. The page also held an old pale yellow Post-it note, which had been pressed carefully beneath the words: *I am with you always, even until the end of the world*. An arrow was drawn in ink on the sticky note, pointing to the words to make sure they weren't missed. And on the Post-it in her grandmother's handwriting, especially recognizable now, having just finished the diary:

Look in the garden, under the loose bricks!

CHAPTER THIRTY-FOUR

SHE CAUGHT HER BREATH, remembering ever so vaguely a long-ago day when her grandma had instructed her to "climb up to the high shelf and get down my old Bible, Meg." She tried to call up the details. It had been summer, hotter than usual, and she had the sense that perhaps she had been in a foul mood. It was the family's usual lengthy summer vacation on the island, and Gran had spoken the words in her playful way—a way that told Meg a treasure hunt was afoot.

Meg had been…how old? A teenager perhaps. An age at which the magic of Gran's treasure hunts had lost their verve for her, seeming silly and childish. She'd meant to do it, check the shelf—she was sure of it— but something had kept her from it. What? *Remember. Remember.*

Ah. Had it been Lila? A scream from outside. Yes. If she was remembering right, that had been the summer Lila fell from a tree she'd been forbidden to climb and broke her arm. They'd all ended up on the first ferry to the ER in St. Simon.

Of course, Seth had pointed out to her that memory was sometimes a tricky thing—so maybe she was wrong. Maybe not checking the shelf and Lila's broken arm had come at two entirely different times and she was conveniently shoving them together to justify never having found this note, something that seemed precious to her just now. But that didn't matter—what mattered was the note itself.

Look in the garden, under the loose bricks! She knew the ones, the exact ones. She'd even stopped Seth from repairing them this summer, thank goodness.

Of course, whatever Gran might have placed there over twenty years ago was surely gone now. Surely.

Except…what if it wasn't? Because where on earth would it have gone?

Even if she could find a mere remnant of something that had rotted into the earth over the years, it would be worth looking.

As she lowered the Bible to the nook's wide windowsill and made her way out the back door, her heart beat the same as it had on childhood treasure hunts with Gran. But for a different reason this time. Those treasure hunts as a little girl had held anticipation and mystery—but this, now, went beyond that. It was the same as finding the diary—one more piece of Gran to connect with, one last gift from her.

She entered the lilac grove, absently pleased that the large bushes would hide her search from passersby on the street. This felt private, personal.

She knelt in the grass next to the brick pathway, eased her fingertips between two bricks long missing their grout, and lifted one up. Underneath, dirt.

She raised the one beside it then. To find…more dirt. She sighed.

For a moment this had seemed so magical—but maybe it wasn't. Maybe whatever Gran put here had long been lost to the elements and she'd never know what silly, wonderful little trinkets Gran had wanted to give her.

However, after setting both bricks aside, she pulled up a third. Just in case.

And caught sight of something—solid, maybe metal. She reached down to touch it. Dirt came off on her fingers, and what hid beneath the soil was silver in tone—but also covered in a thick layer of earth.

She removed a fourth brick and realized the item was cylindrical. She chipped off more dirt with her fingernails, digging to reach it. She encountered an earthworm wriggling past, and a few gray pill bugs. Then after a moment, she touched something smooth—glass.

A jar. It was a Mason jar.

A little more digging, a little more prying, and enough earth fell away that she could grasp the dirty jar between her hands, extracting it from the ground.

She fought to loosen the lid, and was about to give up and go in search of tools to help—when it finally twisted in her now-sore hands.

Removing the lid was opening a time capsule. She held her breath as she peeked inside and began drawing the treasures out one by one.

A package of the grape bubblegum she'd liked at the time, but hadn't thought about since high school until just now.

A few brightly colored pencil erasers—hot pink and lime green. She'd once gone through a neon phase, as most kids did, and Gran had remembered.

And a roll of pennies.

A roll. Of pennies.

Curved around the hand-wrapped penny roll was a sheet of paper, folded twice, fragile at the creases. She opened it with care to read yet a few more words in her grandmother's hand:

Just some baubles to cheer you up. A broken heart is a broken heart, no matter how young or old you are. I know it hurts, but I promise they mend with time. Two things I want you to remember: The right boy won't hurt you—he'll make you feel as special as you are. And you're never alone—I love you and I'll always be here for you, whether we're together or far apart.

A soft gasp left her as she finished the letter. So much became clear all at once.

She remembered now—she'd just broken up with her first real boyfriend at the time. Blake Milner had dumped her on the last day of school for the new girl, who had been enviably pretty and worn a bikini to the Junior Class Car Wash the week before.

He'd been her first love—but this letter, which had somehow escaped her finding it *then* felt even more like it was meant to be read *now*. It felt as if Gran was with her *now*.

And as crazy as it might sound if she ever told anyone, she knew without doubt that those pennies, those mysterious pennies, really *had* been pennies from heaven—Gran somehow trying to let her know she wasn't ever really alone, ever really abandoned.

Gripping the letter in one hand, the roll of pennies in the other, Meg sat in the grass amid the faded lilacs as tears of joy and love streamed down her cheeks. Somehow fate or God or her grandmother had known she needed this letter today more than she'd needed it back when it was written. She would treasure it always. And she would never ever let herself feel alone again.

Distant laughter, the call of a bird, a squeaky bicycle—despite the noises of a tourist season day on the island, a peaceful solitude closed around her. And she realized how much she'd *always* felt her grandmother's presence in the house, in the garden—everywhere on the island really. It had always been there—she'd just let heartache and confusion keep her from it for a while.

And she no longer had any intention of leaving this place. What better existence did she think she'd find somewhere else? Why did she think she'd be happier on the mainland? Her life was here, in this community, in this inn. Her heart was here, too, just as her grandma's had been. She never would have made this her home otherwise.

She felt like Dorothy when she realized that whatever lay beyond the rainbow wasn't actually what she needed at all. She already *had* what she needed.

After reading the last diary entry, she'd thought that either Zack or Seth would be the one who stayed—but turned out the one staying…was her.

JUNE BECAME JULY. She attended the Fourth of July Kite Fly on the wide lawn of the Algonquian Hotel on the easternmost tip of the island with Suzanne and Dahlia, where she watched dozens of colorful kites dip and swirl and arc across a field of blue overhead. Cooper Cross flew a kite shaped like a jellyfish and Meg even took the strings herself for a few minutes with his instruction. Later the party moved to Lakeview Park, where she judged a pie contest, and later sat on a blanket watching fireworks. There were moments of remembering such events with Zack—but just as quickly remembering the events he *hadn't* made it home for. And there were also moments of thinking it would have been nice to share it all with Seth—but then reminding herself that he'd chosen not to be here, too.

More guests came and went at the inn. One morning she offered another pancake breakfast—and she soon held another cookout, wore a skirt, played horseshoes. The Himalayan lilacs blossomed more fully, making her emotions bittersweet. True to her plan, she rode her bike more, going out for morning jaunts around the island that reminded her why she loved it here.

Every day, she looked for things to be grateful for, and always found plenty. Miss Kitty. Messages from Gran to cherish. Roses that bloomed all summer. The idyllic South Point Lighthouse that graced her view every time she left the inn. The rustle of leaves from a breeze. The path of a butterfly across the yard. A call from her Mom to say she and Dad were coming up for a week next month. Blue skies. Soft summer nights that blinked with fireflies and were good for taking walks.

She bought an old bicycle from Trent Fordham and painted it pale green, then hung flowerpots from each side and made a planter from the front basket, as well. Parking it in a flower bed behind the house visible from the patio, she decided she'd found her new hobby: Adding to the gardens her grandpa had started in her own crafty way.

She had lunches and dinners with Suzanne and Dahlia. She stopped into the Pink Pelican one night by herself for a drink, realizing she didn't need a companion for such an outing in her own little community. "Meg!" Trevor called through the microphone when she walked in. "That's Meg, everybody," he said to the tourists in the crowd. "She runs the Summerbrook Inn and likes it when I sing 'Peaceful Easy Feeling,' which I think I'll do right now. This is for you, Meg."

Life went on. And when she thought of the loves she'd lost, it came with a wistfulness but also a sense of peace. She'd been bold enough to go after things she'd wanted. She'd taken chances. She'd been lucky enough to know what it was to love. And she'd had some amazing sex in the bargain. Maybe she would again. Maybe not. But either way, she had no regrets because she'd stayed true to her heart every step of the way.

It was the last day of July when she rested in the rose garden, enjoying their color along with the last gasps of the Himalayan lilacs in the distance. She sat in one of the antique metal chairs that had likely been here since Gran's girlhood, drinking a glass of pink lemonade and sketching out crafting plans for a few old wooden milk crates she'd just bought at a flea market in St. Simon. Catching a glimpse through some foliage of someone coming up the walk, she set her pencil and pad aside to go greet them.

And she'd just pushed to her feet when Seth appeared beyond the roses. "Hello, darlin'."

CHAPTER THIRTY-FIVE

IF MEG HAD been holding her glass of lemonade, she'd have dropped it. It was as if a ghost had just walked into her yard. The ghost of a man she'd loved and had just started forgetting the feel of, the scent of, the sight of.

She finally found words. "You're back."

He grinned. "Of course I'm back. Told you I would be."

She blinked nervously, then tried to stop by widening her eyes, letting out a sigh. "Well, not exactly. You said you'd…see me soon or something. But I thought that meant…never."

Now the handsome man in front of her narrowed his gaze, let out a sigh. "I'm so sorry, Meg darlin'—everything happened fast. I stopped to say goodbye and you weren't here, so I scribbled that note quick without thinking much about it. And then I called the next evening, but—"

She blinked once more, despite herself. "You called the inn?"

Now *his* eyes widened. "You didn't get my message? On the machine? Right after I left?"

She shook her head. But then remembered…the answering machine. Miss Kitty's clumsy day. Maybe she'd missed more than someone calling for a reservation. "It's possible," she said, still too stunned to think straight, "that Miss Kitty erased it."

He tilted his head, slight but ever-charming grin back in place. "And here I thought she and I were friends."

"I suspect it was more a slip of the paw than anything malicious."

He nodded, and said, "Well, darlin'…guess what matters is—I'm back now. If you want me to be, that is."

She could barely process this—and had no idea what it meant that he was suddenly here, standing before her. She only knew that she didn't want with him what she'd had with Zack. She wouldn't live that way again. "I… *did* want you to be. On the morning you left, I was ready to tell you that. But then you were gone."

"Aw, Meg." His face fell. "Darlin', I didn't know. Especially when you didn't call me back. I didn't want to keep calling if maybe…you were glad to have me out of your life. I had no idea the cat was scheming against me." Another quick grin, but it faded as fast as it came. "I didn't know if you really felt anything for me or not. I thought there'd always be Zack. Truth is, I didn't know if my leaving would matter all that much."

She swallowed. "Well, it did. And Zack's out of the picture for good now." She shifted her weight from one foot to the other and hated that her vulnerability was showing just when she'd thought she'd gotten her life completely under control. "Where did you go? Where have you been all this time?"

"Pennsylvania. With Granddad."

"Oh." It came in a whisper. For some reason, she hadn't expected that answer.

"I called him one day from the old pay phone in the Huron Hotel and he asked me to come. Said he hadn't been feeling right and was getting some tests done, and he sounded kinda scared. So I went—and like I said, didn't really think it would matter much if I wasn't around."

She blinked again. "Tests? Is he all right?"

"He is now. Turned out he had pneumonia. Doctors said it can come on slow in older folks. He'd had bronchitis back in the spring and they suspect the meds just didn't get the whole infection and it took a while to start wearing him down. Truth is, I hadn't planned to be away anywhere near this long, but he was in the hospital, and after he got home I still wanted to stay and make sure he was okay, you know?"

She nodded. "Of course." Her mind flashed on the diary—on the fact that pneumonia had been enough to threaten her great-grandfather's life. "Pneumonia is serious business."

"Yeah, I found that out. But he's good now. And while I was there…well, I did a lot of thinking, and a lot of talking to him about things."

"What things?" she asked.

"Hard as I was trying, Meg, I wasn't sure I was good enough for you. Wasn't sure I was the man you deserve. But Granddad believes I'm becoming that man more every day. Enough that he said I should quit wasting time and get my posterior back up here and let you know it." He grinned softly. "Posterior. You know him and his big words."

But then he resumed looking more serious again.

"So here goes. I love you, darlin'." Stopping, he shook his head. "Can't say I've ever loved a woman before—it's all new to me. And I just want to do things right. I want to be a better man, and I want to live the best life I can because…well, you inspire me to, I guess. And if you'd consent to let me, I'd like to stay here, be here for you—in the way I wish my mom and grandparents could have been there for me."

Then he dug down in his pocket and pulled out a small gray velvet box. He opened it to show her the ring inside—her grandmother's ring. "I took this with me to have it sized. A five, right? Like I said, I had no intention of being gone so long—thought I'd have it back here in a week. In fact, that's why I called—when I figured out I'd be gone longer, thought you might notice it missing. All this time, I assumed you'd heard the message and knew." He stopped, shook his head. "Damn, I'm sorry for whatever you must have been thinking about me since then. Guess I *should've* called again—but like I said, I thought maybe you were working things out with Zack and didn't want me in the picture."

He blew out a breath, then took a look around the big yard before bringing his blue eyes back to her face. "Now that I know that's not the case, though… I guess I have this idea that maybe someday, Meg, I'll get you to marry me. And we'll live in this house and run this inn together and I'll make you happy. I know it's too soon for that. I know I've got a lot of proving myself to do. But someday I want this to be your wedding ring, darlin'. And for now, I want to give it to you as…a promise, I guess. To be there for you. To do my best. And to—"

"To stay?" she finished for him.

"Yeah. To stay."

She pulled in her breath. That was all she'd ever really wanted—a man whose love for her would make him stay. And she was no longer naive enough to believe this would be simple—but it felt real to her. Real enough to trust again, real enough to try again. "That promise sounds good to me, Seth."

"Like I said," he told her with a grin, "you're an easy woman to please." And with that, he took the ring from the open box and slid it onto her finger. A perfect fit now. Then he leaned in to lower a soft, sweet kiss to her cheek. Charmers gonna charm. And he was charming her all over again.

She'd been through a lot in her life—she'd been through a lot the past few months, for that matter—but nothing could have surprised her as much as Seth's return. And that, despite the darker path his own life had taken, she believed with her whole heart that he *was* a good man.

Men came and went in a woman's life, but not nearly as many came *back*. And this one had returned with a long-lost ring and a promise. A promise to stay.

* * * * *

ACKNOWLEDGMENTS

WRITING THE SUMMER ISLAND books has been a true journey for me in many ways. And as we seldom complete long journeys in life without the support of others, I want to thank those who took the time to help me make these books richer.

Thank you to Lindsey Faber and Renee Norris for early feedback on parts and pieces of the manuscripts. Your responses and input, as always, were invaluable to my process.

Thanks to the Mackinac Island Tourism Bureau and the Mackinaw City Chamber of Commerce for answering various questions about wintertime on a Great Lakes island.

Much gratitude to Dr Yasmeen Daher and Dr. Syed K. Mehdi for suggestions and help on some injury-related issues in the final book. My apologies for any missteps in the writing, with hopes that I represented the variables and possibilities in a true and realistic manner.

It would be impossible for me to acknowledge every website or article I drew some small bit of insight from along the way, but among noteworthy online sources are: Main Line Gardening, Diane Vautier and Care24.

Thanks to Lisa Koester for taking my messy map

of Summer Island and turning it into an adorable work of art.

Sincere appreciation to my longtime agent, Christina Hogrebe, for championing the first book, and for supportively and patiently sticking by me through a long illness that sidelined me for a while during the writing of it. And to everyone at the Jane Rotrosen Agency for many years of wonderful representation.

And finally, thank you to my incredible editor, Brittany Lavery, for such an uplifting publishing experience: for insightful and detailed editorial input and for helping me make these books the best they can be. And to the whole team at HQN Books for giving Summer Island an amazing home.

*After escaping her abusive ex, Cassie Zetticci is
thankful for a job and a safe place to stay at the
Gallant Lake Resort. Nick West makes her nervous
with his restless energy, but when he starts teaching her
self-defense, Cassie begins to see a future that involves
roots and community. But can Nick let go of his own
difficult past to give Cassie the freedom she needs?*

Read on for a sneak preview of
A Man You Can Trust,
*the first book—and Harlequin Special Edition debut!—
in Jo McNally's new miniseries, Gallant Lake Stories.*

"Why are you armed with pepper spray? Did something
happen to you?"

She didn't look up.

"Yes. Something happened."

"Here?"

She shook her head, her body trembling so badly
she didn't trust her voice. The only sound was Nick's
wheezing breath. He finally cleared his throat.

"Okay. Something happened." His voice was gravelly
from the pepper spray, but it was calmer than it had been
a few minutes ago. "And you wanted to protect yourself.
That's smart. But you need to do it right. I'll teach you."

Her head snapped up. He was doing his best to look at her, even though his left eye was still closed.

"What are you talking about?"

"I'll teach you self-defense, Cassie. The kind that actually works."

"Are you talking karate or something? I thought the pepper spray…"

"It's a tool, but you need more than that. If some guy's amped up on drugs, he'll just be temporarily blinded and really ticked off." He picked up the pepper spray canister from the grass at her side. "This stuff will spray up to ten feet away. You never should have let me get so close before using it."

"I didn't know that."

"Exactly." He grimaced and swore again. "I need to get home and dunk my face in a bowl full of ice water." He stood and reached a hand down to help her up. She hesitated, then took it.

Don't miss
A Man You Can Trust *by Jo McNally,*
available September 2019 wherever
Harlequin® *Special Edition books and ebooks are sold.*

www.Harlequin.com